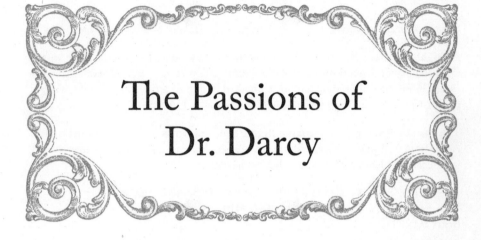

The Passions of Dr. Darcy

Sharon Lathan

sourcebooks
landmark

Published by Sourcebooks Landmark, an imprint of Sourcebooks, Inc.
P.O. Box 4410, Naperville, Illinois 60567-4410
(630) 961-3900
Fax: (630) 961-2168
www.sourcebooks.com

Library of Congress Cataloguing-in-Publication Data is on file with the publisher.

Printed and bound in the United States of America.
BG 10 9 8 7 6 5 4 3 2 1

The Darcy Saga
BY SHARON LATHAN

Dedicated to my husband,

Steve Lathan.

Through twenty-six years

of better and worse, he has been my comfort and strength

second only to my Lord Jesus, who is my Rock.

Contents

A Message from Sharon

SOMEWHERE IN THE MIDDLE of writing what became my first novel in the Darcy Saga, I decided Mr. Fitzwilliam Darcy was going to have an uncle. My vision was a man who had been away from England for decades, traveling the world doing… something. I wanted him to be brilliant but eccentric, ebullient, and irreverent. In short, the opposite of Mr. Darcy! I named him George and, after a tiny bit of research, made him a physician in India with the British East India Company. Partially this decision was based on my knowledge of medicine and how that profession would work into the greater story line. Primarily the decision was because India was far away and sounded exotic! The truth was, Dr. George Darcy was a misty character who was meant to breeze in, ruffle Fitzwilliam a bit, add some fun and humor, and then breeze back to far away India. All through *Loving Mr. Darcy* that was the plan. He didn't need a back story or serious purpose. He was an expendable character! I no longer recall exactly when I decided I loved George too much to let him go. Probably around the time he delivered Elizabeth Darcy's son in *My Dearest Mr. Darcy*. I stubbornly clung to the plan, even as George was revealing more of his life on the pages I typed. I swear the pushy fellow took over the keyboard! I was learning about him without forethought. He decided long before I did that he was not expendable, that his life was far more exciting than I imagined, and that England was now his home. Furthermore, George knew before I did that his future wasn't that of a simple country physician happily dwelling with family. Oh no! He had lots more life in him!

That is the inspiration of this novel. Dr. George Darcy was birthed in my brain as a passionate man with an incredible story to tell even if I did not realize it. The drops of his past that he shared while I was writing were the tip of the iceberg. I passed those hints to readers, but it wasn't until delving deeply into George's history that everything took shape. In the year plus spent researching and writing this novel, I learned far more than my previous cursory studies for an expendable character required. Setting George Darcy entirely in India from 1789 to 1817 proved vastly different from providing the brief glances of his experiences as I had done before. Because of this, I discovered that a few of the casual references to George's past that are strewn throughout the Darcy Saga novels did not always coincide with his adventures and timeline in this book. Every step of the way, I plotted his life as close to what I had established as possible, and 95 percent of it worked out. There are some exceptions, however, and I hope my readers will understand why and forgive me. For instance, in *Loving Mr. Darcy*, Fitzwilliam tells Elizabeth that George visited after his father James died and then again four years later. While this sounded reasonable at the time, I later learned that the average sea voyage from India to England was five months. This calculates to nearly a year on a ship! Add in the time visiting, and I realized George would need a very good reason to undertake that journey. As revealed in this novel, he had every reason *not* to make that trip. Another issue was calculating the precise passage of months and years to correlate with historical events happening in India that I wanted George to be a participant in. Plotting his intricate lifetime to mesh with history, other characters, and the future I created for him subtly altered what I had originally delineated. The differences are slight and nothing that affects the whole. I only mention it to assure that these are not errors from neglect but due to fine-tuning Dr. Darcy's life course while writing his story.

Another item to note is that the George Darcy I originally introduced and fell in love with—and that those of you who have read the Saga know well—is a man of fifty years who has already experienced the story I am now revealing. My challenge was imagining George Darcy at twenty-two! Who was he then? How did the events of his life mold him into the mature man we love? This, of course, was one of the incredible joys in writing this novel! A person at one point in life is not identical to who he is a decade, two decades, or three decades later. Therefore, anticipate that you are meeting a new George Darcy with attributes similar to the man from my Saga but also possessing traits that will surprise you. My hope is that you will enjoy acquainting yourself with the younger George, your love growing stronger as you travel with him through his evolution.

Lastly, the final three chapters of this novel cover the years after George's return to England in June of 1817. I do not rehash what I have already written within the pages of the Darcy Saga, so to fully enjoy George's interactions with the Darcys or to understand the references, those novels will need to be read; instead, I remain in George's point of view to fill in the blanks, share his thoughts on what occurred, and to recount new events not hinted at previously. And of course, the end is not really the end, because George lives on for many years. Hopefully, I will write more of his life at a later date. If I do, you can be sure it will be fabulous, because if there is one incontrovertible fact of Dr. George Darcy at any age, it is that he is never boring!

Thank you for joining George and me on this journey.

Sincerely,

Sharon Lathan

Cast of Characters

Dr. George Darcy: born January 12, 1767; second son of James and Emily Darcy; siblings Mary, James, Alexander, Estella, and Philip; earned doctorate of medicine from Cambridge University and licentiate from Royal College of Physicians in London at twenty-two years of age; contracted with the British East India Company as a physician in 1789

In India

Dr. Kshitij Ullas: Indian physician, friend, and mentor

Jharna Dhamdhere Ullas: Indian wife of Dr. Ullas; daughter of the Sardar of Thana; cousin to the Maratha Peshwa

Nimesh Ullas: oldest son of Kshitij and Jharna Ullas; born 1787; wife *Ziana*

Sasi Ullas: second son of Kshitij and Jharna Ullas; born 1790; wife *Daya*

Dr. Searc McIntyre: Scottish physician in Bombay with British East India Company; wife *Lileas*, daughters *Kenna* and *Lorna*

Dr. White: Physician General of Medical Services on Bombay Island

Commander Doyle: Commanding Officer of Bombay Headquarters for the British East India Company

Lord and Lady Burgley: Bombay residents

Reed Dawson: ensign, later Lieutenant, at Bombay Headquarters

Miss Sarah Chambers: daughter of the *Viscount and Viscountess Powis*; resident of Mazagaon on Bombay Island

Thakore Sahib Pandey Dhamdhere: Sardar of Thana; Jharna's father

Duke of Larent: English aristocrat

Lady Ruby Thomason: daughter of the Earl of Yardley

Anoop: Indian manservant to Dr. Darcy

Vani Ullas Nirmal: Dr. Ullas's daughter from first marriage

Dr. Trenowyth: Physician General of Medical Service on Bombay Island, successor to Dr. White; later Surgeon-General of the Bombay Medical Services for the Bombay Presidency

Gita Dhamdhere: Jharna's aunt

Dr. Raul Penaflor Aleman de Vigo: Spanish physician in Calcutta and later Bombay

In England

James Darcy the Elder: Master of Pemberley in Derbyshire and Darcy House in London; George's father

James Darcy II: heir to Pemberley; George's older brother

Lady Anne Fitzwilliam Darcy: James's wife, children *Alexandria* (deceased), *Fitzwilliam*, and *Georgiana*

Henry Vernor: Pemberley neighbor and close friend to the Darcy family; wife *Mary*, children *Gerald* and *Bertha*; residence Sanburl Hall in Derbyshire

Sir Louis and Lady Catherine de Bourgh: family to Darcys (Lady Catherine and Lady Anne are sisters); daughter *Anne*; residence Rosings Park in Kent

Earl and Countess of Matlock: parents of *Catherine*, *Anne*, and *Malcolm*; surname Fitzwilliam; residence Rivallain in Matlock

Mary Darcy Oeggl: George's eldest sister, husband *Baron Oeggl*; home Austria

Estella Darcy Montrose: George's older sister, husband *Xavier Montrose*; home Exeter, Devon

Alexander Darcy: George's twin brother; died in 1779 at twelve years of age

Fitzwilliam Darcy: son of James and Lady Anne Darcy; George's nephew; "William" to his family; heir to and later Master of Pemberley and Darcy House

Elizabeth Bennet Darcy: wife of Fitzwilliam Darcy

Georgiana Darcy: daughter of James and Lady Anne Darcy; George's niece and namesake

Mrs. Amanda Annesley: companion to Georgiana Darcy

Earl and Countess of Matlock: Malcolm Fitzwilliam and wife Madeline; parents of *Jonathan, Annabella,* and *Richard*

Richard Fitzwilliam, Colonel: Fitzwilliam Darcy's cousin and closest friend

Charles Bingley: friend of Fitzwilliam Darcy; wife *Jane Bennet*

Mrs. Sutherland: Pemberley housekeeper until 1791, then *Mrs. Reynolds*

Mr. Wickham: Steward of Pemberley Estate until 1811, then *Mr. Keith*

Mr. Taylor: Pemberley butler

Mr. Higgs: Pemberley gamekeeper until 1800, then *Mr. Burr*

HISTORICAL FIGURES

Shivaji Maharaj: also Shivaji Bhosle, or Chhatrapati (sovereign) Shivaji; February 19, 1630–April 1, 1680; founded the Maratha Empire, an independent nation in India free of Mughal rule; a brilliant military leader, exemplary warrior, morally upright, believer in civil and women's rights, devout Hindu but advocate of religious freedom, capable administrator, and abolisher of the Indian feudal system, Shivaji is considered one of the greatest Indian leaders of all time

Sawai Madhavrao Peshwa: ruler of the Maratha Empire 1774–1795; death by suicide without an heir

Baji Rao II Peshwa: ruler of Maratha Empire from 1796–1818

Tipu Sultan: the Tiger of Mysore

Jonathan Duncan: Governor of Bombay Presidency from December 1795–August 1811

Arthur Wellesley: Commander of East India Company army from 1798–1804; later Duke of Wellington

Richard Wellesley, Earl of Mornington, Marquess of Wellesley: Governor-General of India from 1798–1805; elder brother of Arthur Wellesley

Earl of Minto: Governor-General of India from 1807–1813

Earl of Moira, Marquess of Hastings: Governor-General of India 1813–1823

Dr. John Shoolbred: Superintendent and Surgeon of Calcutta Native Hospital

Elizabeth Darcy opened the well-oiled door slowly, hesitating outside as her eyes scanned the room not stepped foot in for over a month. Tears welled as her gaze lingered over the odd but familiar objects, sadness mounting as she noted how many of the once-shiny instruments and immaculate tabletops were now covered with a thin layer of dust.

"No need to lurk without, dearest. Please come in."

"I thought you might wish for more time alone," she replied as she swung the door wider and crossed the threshold. "I am overcome with a renewed rush of grief so can only imagine the state of your emotions."

Fitzwilliam Darcy sat on a worn leather wingback chair. On the floor in front of his knees was a massive old trunk. It was scraped, patched in places with glued pieces of cloth and leather, dented on the right side, rusted along the edges of the metal bracings, and missing the strap to lift the lid. Yet despite the evidence of hard use and age, the trunk was structurally intact. Darcy's hands were spread on the top beside a brass plate etched with the words *George Darcy, Physician.*

"This trunk was a gift to him from my parents and grandfather," Darcy whispered.

Lizzy knew this, of course, George having told them the story of when it was gifted to him. She also knew that her husband simply needed to talk and was not seeking a conversation. She sat on the ottoman that had been shoved aside when the trunk was dragged over, folded her hands into her lap, and waited.

"I haven't been in here since..." He swallowed and blinked several times before continuing. "I felt it was time, but now I am not so sure." He ran his fingers over the plate bearing the name of his beloved uncle, fighting the tears not because he was embarrassed to shed them in front of his wife—goodness knows he had done so often enough over the long years of their marriage, especially recently—but because he wanted to control himself so he could attend to the task at hand. Inhaling raggedly, he resumed, "She said that George no longer kept his medical supplies in his trunk, which makes sense, as he had the cupboards here in his hospital and the smaller traveling cases. Apparently he kept his personal memoirs in here instead. I had no idea he wrote in a journal."

Darcy looked up at his wife, a hint of a smile on his face. "I am not sure why I am surprised. It is something we Darcys do. Me, my father, and grandfather. My mother did as well, although not diligently. Alexander does, and a smattering of other Darcys from the past. The glass cases in the library are proof of the habit. Yet somehow I doubt any of our dry narratives of estate management, antics of our children, or London social events will compare with his adventures. She told me it was George's wish for me to read them and then display them with the others in the library."

He reached into his waistcoat pocket, removed a key, and unlocked the lid, which pushed open with the faintest of squeaks. Lizzy scooted closer and leaned in just as Darcy did, both gazing into the trunk with jaws dropping.

The trunk was filled with bound books in dozens of varying sizes and types of covers. Not an inch of space wasted, the books neatly stacked into piles with dimension the qualifier rather than chronology. A journal dating 1803 sat on top of one from 1782 and beside one from 1838. There were easily seventy separate books, a few thick, spanning the bulk of one man's life.

"No wonder the damn thing was so heavy. I nearly dislocated my arms dragging it the four feet to this chair. Reading all of these will take a year!"

"Then I suggest we get started. Any ideas?"

"She said that the first was on the top. This one here, I am guessing." Darcy picked up one that was fraying at the binding and opened it gingerly. "1779."

"Has she read them all?"

"I believe so, or most of them at least. She is his wife, after all, and they shared everything. I am not sure about his children, but if not, they will want to. And for certain these will require, and deserve, a case specifically made to house them."

He turned to the first page, silent for a minute as they studied the childish but familiar cursive of a man they loved deeply and would achingly miss forever. The raw pain of their loss made the first words scrawled by a then twelve-year-old George Darcy especially poignant.

Dear Alex,

Father insisted I start keeping a journal. He said it will help ease my grief if I air out my feelings. I have stared at this stupid book for a month now. I think the blasted thing is mocking me. Then he asked me if I had written in it yet and you know how it is when Father looks at you in that certain way of his that makes you feel guilty even if you haven't done anything wrong, although usually I have, so it is even worse. That look. So I said no and he just nodded, and for a second I thought that would be the end of it, but then he said, "Write in the book, George." So here I am. Writing to you as if you were alive and I were talking to you, which I do all the time anyway. Does that make me crazy? Maybe. I don't care though. So I'll do what Father bids, since the consequences of another lashing don't make my rear end all that happy. Here goes...

TEN YEARS AGO, ALEX died. On this day. At this precise moment.

James Darcy glanced at the ticking clock to be certain, and then looked at his brother sitting across from him. As he suspected, George was *not* looking at the clock. George didn't need to. The month, day, hour, and minute when Alex drew his final breath were embedded into every cell of his twin's body.

As fanciful as it sounded, James often wondered if that last exhale had crossed the tiny space between George's blotched face and the ashen one of Alex, mingled with the air as George gasped with each sob, drawn into his lungs to then be distributed and implanted into each cell. Is that why, year after year, George knew the exact second he had lost his other half? Or was it merely another aspect of the strange connection Alex and George Darcy had shared in life?

James did not know. What he did know was that before the minute ticked away, George would say, "This is the moment Alex died."

Every year he said it. On this day. At this precise moment.

Even when James or others in the family took him away or tried to distract with a frivolous activity, he said it. Two years ago, they decided to give up trying to make him forget. That was the year they had traveled to Brighton, dragging George away from his university studies to frolic in the surf. Frolic he had, until

April 17, when somberness overtook the perpetually gay twenty-year-old. He said nothing and tried to carry on for the sake of the family until 2:34 in the afternoon, when he had abruptly dropped the bucket of sand, walked toward the water's edge until the waves lapped over his feet, and stared out at the roiling sea for the full minute before turning back to his sympathetic siblings and father.

"This is the moment Alex died."

They had offered what consolation they could, and in a short time the worst of the grief had passed. Their Brighton holiday recommenced and had proved to be a nice memory overall. Yet they had discussed the topic away from George's hearing and agreed there was no point in pretending.

That was why James sat with his younger brother in a sunny parlor at Pemberley, glasses of wine in their hands, and remained silent until the familiar words were spoken. Ten long years but this was the last year, for an unknown time to come, when George would be with family on this day. James had no doubt that even if lost in an Indian jungle or trekking across the barren Thar Desert, George would know it was April 17 and 2:34 in the afternoon.

So he steeled himself for the words even while feigning nonchalance between sidelong glances and sips of his wine.

George sat with his thin body slumped in the chair, long limbs stretched onto the ottoman in front and bony elbows resting on the padded chair arms. The negligent pose was familiar to James, as was his brother's choice of clothing. Today he wore an exquisitely tailored suit of brown woolen broadcloth with a green waistcoat—quite conservative and sedate until one noted the wide ribbon of bright yellow and green tartan used to tie his wavy brown hair into a pigtail, that same fabric draped about his neck and knotted into a puffy bulge at his throat. Pinned to his lapel was a Celtic cross of polished gold with inlaid emeralds. Why the Scottish motif in April was anyone's guess and James did not ask. It was George's flamboyant way and barely registered upon James's mind.

No, being surprised was not an emotion James expected on this day. But then, George Darcy was a man who frequently shocked people.

"Do you think Alex would be proud of me?"

Yes, James was surprised. And it showed.

"I have been thinking on the topic lately," George explained, his intense blue eyes steady on James's startled face. "Actually I have pondered the subject for ages. The irony does not escape me and that is what I wrestle with."

"What irony?"

"That it was Alex's death that prompted me to become a doctor. If he lived, I would not be sitting here with my formal education behind me, a licensure I treasure, skills already superior to most in England, ready to embark on an expedition to single-handedly rid the East of disease."

James smiled. George's flippant arrogance never failed to amuse him. "That I don't believe for a second." Then he laughed at the indignant expression that flickered over his brother's face and clarified, "Not the superior skills part or that you will undoubtedly succeed in eradicating disease from the earth. Rather that the idea of you not becoming a doctor under any circumstance is ludicrous. Your fate was sealed at birth, my brother."

"Yet it was never a thought until that quack allowed my brother to die," George flared. "Happiest day of my life when old Wilson had his worthless carcass thrown in jail for botching Lady Messerman's delivery and murdering a perfect infant. Don't even think of frowning at me, James! Call it whatever you like. It was murder in my book, and not his first by a stretch."

"Then it will please you to hear that he has been barred from practicing medicine."

"He should have been escorted to the gallows, if you ask me. What is to stop him from relocating to another unsuspecting community? Someday, mark my words, Brother, there will be standards of medicine to prevent hacks like Wilson from treating patients, and I use the word 'treating' loosely."

"I pray you are correct, Dr. Darcy." James took a sip of his wine and then leaned forward. "Listen, I will never argue about Wilson. He has a long list of tragedies behind him and we both know it pained Father to call upon him when Alex was injured. If Dr. Meager had not been away to London... Well, you were there," he stated unnecessarily as the cloud of renewed grief marred George's handsome face. "The point is, even when Dr. Meager returned, he concurred that there was nothing that could have been done for Alex. And your studies"—he ignored George's wince—"have proven the truth of that."

"Yet, I read a study not too long ago about theories of evacuating accumulated blood or pus from the thorax to relieve the pressure on the lungs.

Both de Chauliac and Boerhaave describe insertion of a tube to drain the fluid. Someday such treatment modalities shall be the norm."

"Yes, and someday men will fly."

"Perhaps someday they will!"

"Did you not hear the sarcasm in my voice?" James teased, happy to revert to the safety of their brotherly banter to ease the tension. "Even if men someday fly"—he rolled his eyes—"that won't help you at the present, now will it? You still have to take a boat to India, like it or not."

George shuddered, grief and irritation momentarily replaced by a grimace and sickly green cast washing over his cheeks.

James bent to pour more wine into George's glass and chuckled. "Future marvels of medicine or physics do not change the present, dear Brother. No one, with the possible exception of arrogant you, would have remotely considered sticking a tube into Alex's chest. Now, to answer your initial question, yes, Alex would be proud of you. Very much so."

"You state that with confidence."

James sat back with a grin. "Ha! Confidence is your failing, not mine. However, in this case, I am indeed. Who was it that treated the endless parade of injured animals Alex and Estella brought into the manor? Damned bleeding hearts. The orangery resembled a veterinary hospital!"

"Until the fallow deer got loose and destroyed Mother's orchids. Father tanned our hides over that one."

"And then sent you all packing to the gamekeeper compound, driving Mr. Higgs crazy." They paused to smile in recollection of childish antics. "It was always within you, George. Alex had the softer heart and never passed by a wounded creature no matter how small. But he brought them to you, knowing you could cure them. And you always did."

"I couldn't let him down," George mumbled.

"But you cured them," James emphasized, his serious eyes holding his brother's gaze. "Your need to submerge your grief and emptiness after Alex's death simply prompted you to do the inevitable sooner than you would have, George. Maybe you wouldn't have been thirteen when you started tagging along with Dr. Meager or fifteen when you apprenticed with Lambton's apothecary, what was his name?"

"Mr. Jones."

"Right, Jones. Saint he was to tolerate your million questions an hour. Mr. Higgs also."

"Thanks to my insatiable curiosity, Pemberley now boasts a medical section covering two wide cases," George interrupted indignantly, "and Mr. Jones and Mr. Higgs were thrilled to have me around, especially since I did not mind doing the dirty work."

"You *thrived* on the dirty work," James again emphasized. "There is a difference. You were unrelenting—*are* unrelenting. Your ambition may have started as a way to forget, it may have been fed by a driving need to prevent others from suffering such a loss, that catalyst setting you on the path so young, but I know there is more to it. So do you, Brother."

George did not respond immediately. Instead, he returned James's hard stare, his mind flipping through the truths shared with James over the years. Vividly he remembered the day early in his clinical education in London, when after a grueling twelve hours at the hospital, he returned to the closet-sized space that served as his sleeping quarters and began stripping his blood-soaked clothes. Instead of moaning in agony and exhaustion, he had realized he was smiling. He had glanced into the mirror, noted the blood- and dirt-streaked gray skin and red-rimmed eyes incongruous with the smile, and had his first true epiphany.

He had forgotten Alex.

Not literally, of course, as Alex inhabited a portion of his soul and forever would. But he recognized that his insatiable thirst for knowledge in the healing arts had became more than a desire to cure for the sake of curing. It grew to encompass the joy of discovering new techniques and the satisfaction of solving a diagnostic riddle. Passion for medicine consumed his waking hours and filled his sleeping minutes, often taking the place of sleep or food if a complicated case presented itself. He studied diligently to advance his skills and willingly did anything for the goal of becoming a masterful physician.

All of it was as easy as breathing.

"What was it your instructors at Cambridge said?" James prompted. "That you had a 'gift' and were 'naturally born to be a physician' with an innate comprehension of the human body and disease that was 'magical' is what you told me."

George nodded, his expression neither proud nor humble. "Those that weren't jealous or afraid of me, that is. Do you know how many times I have deftly diagnosed a patient's illness after the briefest of examinations, James?"

"As you did Gerald Vernor."

George waved his hand dismissively. "Any fool could tell he had the croup, except for Wilson probably."

"Perhaps. But only someone special could be one of the youngest men to obtain a doctorate of medicine at Cambridge University and also be admitted for licentiate by the Royal College of Physicians. Don't forget that!"

"I haven't," George murmured blandly, "but you know it means nothing to me, James, except as a means to an end. Whether a blessing bestowed from Heaven above or the result of determined effort, I've done it all because of Alex."

"Hogwash! If Alex had lived, you might have been a few years older than two and twenty before you got your degree and maybe, just maybe," he held up his hand to halt George's rebuttal, "you wouldn't be so hasty to leave England and the memories that haunt you here at Pemberley, but I think you would have done that too. Look, I know this is a tough day for you. It always will be, I reckon. But really, this humbleness and self-doubt is beginning to worry me. Are you sure the strain has not addled your brains? Or does the anticipation of a sea voyage so unnerve you that your spirit is cracking? Say it isn't so!"

George laughed and shook his head. "No. The brains are superior, as always. Not so sure about the spirit cracking, or at least splintering a sliver. Maybe I'll ride a horse all the way to Bombay instead. You think one could swim the Channel?"

Before James could frame a witty reply, they were interrupted by the door opening. In an instant, both men stood to their feet to greet the man who entered, bowing respectfully. It was an automatic reaction that not even George Darcy, who was known for ignoring manners of propriety more often than not, would have dreamed of neglecting.

The elder James Darcy, Master of Pemberley in Derbyshire and Darcy House in London, was imposing in every way imaginable. Physically he stood well over six feet, with a broad chest that could conceivably contend with that of a gorilla. At seventy years of age, his hair was iron gray and his face creased with lines, yet he walked with the confidence and vigor of a man half his years. Power and authority surrounded him as an unmistakable aura, and if one doubted their initial impression, the first sentence spoken in his resonant rumble or focused look from his penetrating gaze clarified the matter. His eyes were a unique color that transformed from indigo to a greenish tint that did not exist on any charts to a brown resembling dark roasted coffee, yet it was the intensity of his stare that unnerved.

Women were drawn as if he were a magnet, yet since the death of Emily Darcy nearly five years ago, not a single one of the ladies who vied for the attention of the robust man with extreme wealth and prestige had gotten anywhere. Mr. Darcy ignored them and went about the business of managing Pemberley with the same drive and intelligence that had served him as master for over four decades.

He was a man no one trifled with, whether they revered him or feared him or hated him. He was Darcy or Mr. Darcy or sir, even to his children and his wife. Only his sister, Beryl, the widowed Countess of Essenton who was soon to be the Marchioness of Warrow, called him otherwise. To her, he was Jamie, and his children had never been brave enough to ask if this was a childish endearment or meant to annoy him. Knowing their Aunt Beryl, probably the latter.

"George, I apologize for being late. Of all the days for my horse to throw a shoe. The ride from Vernor's ended up a limping walk. How are you, my boy?"

"Well enough, sir. James is doing an admirable job of keeping me entertained."

Mr. Darcy nodded and paused to pat his son on the shoulder. George did not expect to be enfolded into a warm embrace—that sort of demonstrativeness a rare occurrence even when they were children—but he sensed his father's concern and recognized the grief buried within his stern eyes. Losing a son had branded the father's soul as well.

"As I suspected he would." Mr. Darcy looked at his oldest son and heir, lips lifting in a minuscule smile. "Nevertheless, I am sorry for being detained and could benefit from some of that wine, if you do not mind, James?"

"What news from Sanburl Hall?" James asked while pouring.

"The usual business for the most part. Young Master Gerald is recovering from the croup, as I have already reported to Anne. The boys shall be playing together in no time."

"That is good news indeed. George's medicine helped?"

"Well of course it did!" George responded before Mr. Darcy could. "Crushed ma huang and lobelia added to the heated mist in a tent over the boy are far more effective than cold mist alone. Or mercury, which has too many negative effects. Fortunately, it was a moderate case and a tracheotomy was not necessary. As you said, Father, he and William will be terrorizing the nursery ere the month is over."

"I said they would be playing together," Mr. Darcy corrected, while James choked on his wine over the thought of his friend's baby having a hole drilled into his neck. "Fitzwilliam is a behaved boy, and Miss Reese will not allow the nursery to be disorderly."

"That is because she is a Hun, lacking anything remotely soft and feminine. Why you let Lady Catherine recommend a nurse is beyond my comprehension. I shudder to imagine who she hired to care for her daughter."

"Anne is beginning to think as you, George," James interjected. "Miss Reese does her job, though, so we cannot complain at that."

"A few more hours with young Gerald and that imp Richard Fitzwilliam will break Miss Reese's iron rod. William is a gentle, mannerly boy as you say, Father, but terror follows in the wake of those other two!"

Mr. Darcy grunted. "Praise to God Master Gerald will be with us to raise some terror, no small thanks to you, Son."

George's brow lifted at the compliment and proud paternal smile, even as a warm glow spread across his chest. It had taken years for Mr. Darcy to approve of his chosen profession and it remained infrequent that he verbally acknowledged his skill and accomplishment. "Thank you, sir," he replied simply.

"I know I do not say it often enough, George, but I am proud of you. I recognize your talent and passion. These are traits I admire and respect, as I possess them myself. James does too, I am pleased to proclaim. I know you have your heart set on leaving England, but I do pray you reconsider. Think of the good you could do here, with your people, as you did with Vernor's boy!"

Never had his father expressed his emotions toward George's leaving so vehemently and the borderline pleading was affecting him more than he would have imagined. Yet George would not hurt his father, the one person he respected above all others, by telling him that while Pemberley was the only place he truly felt at home, it was also the cause of his deepest agony. The memories of sweet-tempered Alex, who had been so much more than merely a brother, remained alive and vivid, as if his ghost stalked the halls, filling the rooms with the high-pitched laughter George remembered as one of the few attributes that differentiated the identical twins.

He needed to forget Alex, at least to a degree, and while pursuing his studies or up to his elbows in blood, he did forget. The downside of this, as evidenced by his question to James, was guilt and doubt, neither emotion one George struggled with too often. It was damned annoying! Hearing James's words of encouragement helped more than he wanted to admit. Hearing his father practically beg him to stay home after praising his accomplishments incited an irritating stinging sensation in his eyes that he flatly refused to succumb to.

So instead, he reverted to standard George-ism. He lifted his brows, feigned shock, and responded, with dismay pitched with stage-worthy precision, "What? Stay here and scandalize the good citizens of Derbyshire when I actually touch a patient? Can you imagine what old man Matlock would do if he found out I performed surgeries?" George gasped and shuddered dramatically. "Best I make a hasty retreat before you are disbarred from the Gentleman's Guild of Obscenely Wealthy and Worthless Landowners, Father."

James chuckled, and George flashed a cocky grin his direction.

"I own the clubhouse, so they can't ban me." The unsmiling Mr. Darcy responded in a bland tone so convincing that only one who knew him well would distinguish the teasing hint. "As for his lordship, I doubt he would protest too loudly or his daughter might bar him from visiting with his grandson—"

"And that would be a tragedy why?" James interjected. "That possibility is the best reason I have heard yet for you to stick around, George. Maybe while you are at it, you can rob a grave or something, so Catherine will refuse to ever visit Pemberley. I would owe you for that."

"Alas, no matter how obnoxious Lady Catherine finds me, she keeps coming back. Family and all. I fear you are on your own with that one, James. No, as highly enjoyable as it is to irritate Catherine and Lord Matlock, and as much as I adore stirring up controversy and causing trouble, I don't relish being clapped in chains or fined half my inheritance by reneging on my East India contract."

"Indeed, the Guild might not take an arrest as lightly as performing surgery." Mr. Darcy frowned and scratched his chin as if George's fictitious Guild were a real problem. "Then I suppose there is no way around it. This dilemma means we are forced to move forward with plans for your farewell party—"

"A party? For me?"

Mr. Darcy smiled at his son's enthusiastic interruption, delight illuminating George's eyes and erasing the final vestiges of grief. "We planned it as a surprise but decided that it might be difficult to deceive you when carriages begin unloading on the drive. We have arranged an extravaganza, or I should say Anne and Mrs. Sutherland have. It isn't every day a son of mine completes his studies with stupendous honors and then sets sail for a foreign land."

"What Father is not telling you," James added before emotion again assaulted his brother, "is that my wife has invited half the shire and practically everyone we have ever spoken to. *Everyone.*"

"Lady Catherine is coming?" George groaned at James's wicked grin and nod. "Fabulous. And since she recently delivered a baby, I can't in good conscience needle her too much. Please tell me Sir Louis is coming? Give me that measure of hope?"

"He is, and I already have Mr. Higgs tracking where the best of the coveys are nesting and the deer grazing. We shall keep you occupied, Brother, so that your need to annoy Catherine won't overcome your reason. Cheer up! Malcolm is rounding up the blokes, so it promises to be rousing fun."

The "rousing fun" comment earned a frown from Mr. Darcy, but his sons pretended not to notice. They were still naming the expected guests when the parlor door opened and all three men rose to greet the woman who entered.

"Am I allowed to enter the male sanctuary?"

"Of course, my dear," James began, but George's booming voice drowned his brother's softer tenor.

"We are in the parlor, so you are safe and welcome, Anne. If we were in the billiard room, you would be forbidden unless capable of smoking an entire cigar without vomiting and hitting the spittoon at ten paces."

"Alas, George, I cannot manage more than half a cigar and five paces is my spitting maximum, so it is fortunate you are in the parlor instead. Fitzwilliam awoke from his nap asking for his uncle. I do believe he somehow knows you are to leave us."

Lady Anne Darcy approached the standing trio, her sweet smile not hiding the sadness in her eyes. George bent, kissed her on the cheek, and took the sleepy-faced toddler into his arms. He hugged the boy against his heart, the young heir to Pemberley estate contentedly nestling over the broad expanse with thumb in mouth.

"I was telling George of our little surprise. I do think he was about to cry." James's tease lightened the air and George sat back into the chair with a grunt.

"The tears were only at the news that Catherine is coming. Really, Anne, I thought you liked me?"

"You know as well as I do that your farewell would not be complete without the opportunity to annoy my sister one last time. I truly had your best interests at heart. You can thank me later."

"You do have a point." George's grin was faintly evil. "Shall I thank you by elaborating on the dreadful consequences of cousins marrying, tossing in a wealth of medical jargon that she won't understand just to prove the point?"

"Be kind to Lady Catherine, George," Mr. Darcy said. "I shan't disagree too vehemently that she possesses traits that are… annoying at times, but she is a mother now and traveling a considerable distance to wish you farewell."

"Very well, Father. I shall resist my natural tendencies. Maybe motherhood has positively affected Catherine as I have seen with other women. Strange how babies, especially one's own, have a way of twisting themselves into the hearts of those close to them." He kissed William's dark brown hair, the toddler pausing in his rapt inspection of his uncle's colorful cravat and shiny lapel pin to glance upward and smile.

"In addition to bringing our son to visit his uncle, I also have a message for you, Mr. Darcy." Anne flashed a secretive glance toward George before turning her attention to her father-in-law. "The particular item you ordered has arrived and is in your study awaiting your inspection."

Mr. Darcy nodded once, rose, and left the room without a single word.

"Now that was odd!" George looked over at his brother and Anne who were wearing innocent expressions. His eyes narrowed. "What do you have up your sleeves?"

"Nothing at all. Now," James hastened on before George could counter, "your departure coincides with the annual Pemberley Summer Festival for the tenants and staff. It will be a grand going away in your honor."

"There will be a ball," Anne added, "and every lady in the vicinity will be there for you to dance with."

"My wife has it in her head that you are traveling to the farthest reaches of the earth, where civilization, dancing, and beautiful women do not exist."

Anne elbowed her husband in the ribs. "I am not that uneducated! Nevertheless, you will be five months on a ship with little in the way of luxury or entertainment, then in a compound primarily inhabited by soldiers, and knowing you, dear George, probably spending far more time in a hospital ward than enjoying whatever pleasant diversions there might be."

"Some of what you say is true. But rest assured that when it comes to beautiful women, I shall always keep my eyes open." He grinned. "I hear that the women of India are exceedingly attractive. Maybe I shall bring home a stunning Hindu wife and a passel of copper-skinned children when next I visit!"

James burst out laughing. "Oh my lord! Can you imagine Lord Matlock's face if you did that, George? I am not even sure how our lover-of-humanity father would take that!"

"He would promptly head to the chapel and pray for their heathen souls—after he lectured me for several hours. No, on second thought, I'll pass on the idea. I don't wish to go looking for a reason for Father to lecture me."

"Have I missed a chance to lecture you, George?"

Instantly, James and George rose to their feet, but George changed the direction of his response upon noting the two footmen trailing behind his father. They carried a trunk between them, the wood covered with tanned deer-skin held in place with gleaming brass tacks. Scalloped brass strips and layers of dyed deerskin adorned the edges of the lid and base, the same design worked into the wide handles on each side that the footmen grasped. As they placed the heavy trunk onto the floor where Mr. Darcy indicated, George absently handed Fitzwilliam to his mother and drew near, noting then the sturdy iron lock and brass plate above, upon which was etched *George Darcy, Physician.*

George was speechless—a state that had occurred less than five times in the total of his life—so he could only shake his head in awe while running his palm over the supple deerskin and cool metal.

"The trunk you have is adequate, I suppose," Mr. Darcy explained, "but not big enough to carry your personal belongings and the tools of your trade."

"Sir, I cannot… This is incredible! I truly do not know what to say! I am without… words."

"Brilliant. Never thought that would happen." James nudged his brother with his foot. "Go ahead and open it. Perhaps that will wrest all thought from your tiny brain and earn us an hour or two of blessed silence."

"What? You mean there is something inside?" George looked at his smiling father, too shocked to jump on James for the playful insult.

"Indeed," Mr. Darcy replied, reaching into his pocket and tossing the key, which George caught deftly. "If a son of mine is to practice medicine, then by God, he is going to do it with the best instruments available and ingredients necessary."

George knelt before the trunk, surgeon's hands steady despite his inward trembling excitement, and slid the large key smoothly into the lock. The click was audible, the latch swung up, and the lid lifted noiselessly on well-oiled hinges, as the three onlookers gathered closer to see inside. George fell back onto his heels, hands clutching the trunk's rim for stability, and looked up at his father in stunned amazement. "Are these what I think they are?"

"If you think they are nicely bundled and boxed medical instruments and apothecary supplies then you would be correct," Mr. Darcy answered. "Just do not tell me what they are for. I have no desire to imagine the uses of amputation kits and bleeding knives, let alone the leech jar, which, by the way, is from Staffordshire, where I was told the finest are made."

"The physician's saddle bag and apothecary case are from me and Anne." James stooped to pull a foot-sized square box from inside and settle it onto the corner edge of the trunk. It was of leather-accented wood—horsehide rather than deerskin—and secured with iron rivets and a keyed latch. George came out of his stupor to open the box while James held it stable. The front panel fell flat when the lid was lifted to reveal several detachable trays across the top, one with an assortment of tiny metal devices for measuring, cutting, administering, and grabbing. The trays hid three rows of empty, stoppered glass bottles underneath, each nestled into velvet padded pockets, and six drawers across the bottom with sections in varying sizes in each one. "We decided you could fill them with whatever herbs or concoctions you prefer for drugs. I am sure that will make the Lambton apothecary happy."

"Or we can send to London for anything Mr. Haughe does not have in stock," Anne added. "We want you to have the freshest ingredients."

"Right. Because you are heading to an uncivilized place that will certainly not have dancing or herbs." James kissed his wife's cheek to offset the tease. Anne took it in stride as she had since she was sixteen and first fell in love with James Darcy, entering a relationship with him and his brother George and sister Estella who were a trio of jokers.

"What do you think of Uncle George's trunk, William?" she asked instead.

"Pretty," was the boy's official proclamation, everyone laughing.

"Not sure I would go for 'pretty,' but it is astounding." George stood and turned first to James and Anne on his left to thank them with a hug and kiss. Then he turned to his father on the right. "Sir, words are inadequate. I am overwhelmed and can promise you, swearing upon my soul, that I will always strive to do my utmost and make you proud."

Mr. Darcy nodded solemnly. "I know you will, Son. The East India Company is lucky to have you, and the ship you sail on from Portsmouth will have the best surgeon aboard."

Then he did something so rare that James audibly sucked in his breath and George finally gave in to the stinging tears. He opened his arms and gathered George into a tight embrace, kissed his forehead, and said, "I have complete faith and confidence, George. You are a Darcy and can do nothing but."

George's Memoirs
November 22, 1789

They say we will be in Bombay inside a week, Alex. I do pray the sailors know what they are talking about. I swear I have lost ten pounds since this interminable journey began and you know I can't afford to lose weight. Even when we were young, I was mostly skin and bones, another way people could distinguish between us, and sadly that has not improved with age. Of course, it might help if I didn't skip meals as often as I tend to while at study or enmeshed in a medical dilemma. Yet, at this point, that isn't the problem as much as bouts of boredom, bland food, and a stomach that continues to embarrass me on a regular basis. At times I am not sure which is the larger culprit, although my frightening happiness when the bout of dysentery broke out requiring my medical services might point to the first being the winner. In truth, the voyage has been swifter than what I expected—four days past five months since I embarked at Portsmouth. There are many aspects to being on the ship that have been interesting, almost pleasant at times, and although I can't say I shall miss any of it precisely, I won't dread making a return journey when the time comes. The sea has its own beauty, especially at night. I can understand why some men take to the life with joy. Not that I haven't enthusiastically leapt onto the shore the two times we halted, but sailing has long moments of leisure and quiet speculation. I may not have such opportunities once in Bombay.

The sailors themselves I shall miss. The way they rush about and climb the riggings like monkeys is astounding to me. The one time I gathered my nerve—on a dare—and climbed halfway up the mizzenmast was enough for me. They are excellent gents. A goodly number of them have proven to be more agreeable than the passengers. Too bad I shall encounter the respectable English citizens sailing with me more often than the lowly seamen once this journey is over. They shall sail away, taking their ribald humor, crusty rusticity, and rousing songs with them. I, alas, will be forced to dress properly and behave as a gentleman.

Devinder and Vinod got in another argument today during our lessons. Those two old men act like a bickering married couple. I do think if I added up the hours, I would discover that they debated a word's origin or meaning or spelling more often than they actually taught me anything. Thank the Maker one of them was often busy at a ship's chore when the other sat down to teach me Hindi. Luckily, my ear for languages proved true and with a dozen Indian crewmen speaking in their native tongue, I at least have a foundational understanding that I can build on.

The heat and intense humidity has lessened the closer we near land. Lord Burgley has dwelt in India for some two decades and assures me the four or so months ahead are the most temperate in Bombay. Warmer than England in November to be sure, and it will be odd to celebrate Christmas while wiping sweat from my brow, but hopefully not too uncomfortable for a suit and cravat. Do you think a single loincloth and muslin tunic would be acceptable? No, probably not. Ah well, I am a Darcy and shall survive.

I am anxious to make shore and begin my new life, Alex. Despite the hazards and illness, the journey has been a marvelous adventure. If nothing else, I learned that ginger brewed with mint works the best for seasickness. Should I bottle the concoction and sell it as Dr. Darcy's Elixir of Health and Healing? I could make a fortune! Well, another fortune, that is. Father's endowment for my living requirements was more than sufficient to meet my needs for a decade, not that I had any luck convincing him of my humble demands. He was appalled by the EIC stipend, interpreting it as an insult even though I assured him it was comparable to what I would make in England. Maybe I'll invest the money, save it for my future progeny and all that. This is the opinion of Mr. Henderson. You know how dull I find talk of financial matters, Alex, yet I do confess to being moderately intrigued by Henderson's facts and may heed his advice. You never know the winds of the future.

Speaking of winds, the breeze tonight was refreshing. I enjoyed a round of cards with Henderson, Ashley, and Patel. I did not win, but no matter. The interlude was pleasant and the wine Lord Ashley pulled from his stock was exceptional. The common room grew crowded with the gents determined to celebrate their last night aboard. A handful of brave ladies joined in, most notably Captain Connelly's wife and Lady Burgley. The latter opened a carved box brimming with fine East India cigars. She graciously passed them out before lighting one herself. I do believe Mrs. Connelly nearly swooned at the sight. Thankfully that did not happen, sparing any of us from being crushed or suffering a hernia if she fell our direction. I know I was not the only man who rapidly side skipped! Annoying woman, but her husband is a gem and I am pleased to be working in his division.

Dr. White is another matter. Pompous, insufferable hack! What addle-brained logic connects bleeding and restricting fluids as a treatment for dysentery? How some men manage to acquire a medical degree is beyond my comprehension. He has not *taken the fact that I am the ship's conscripted surgeon very well. Pointing it out on a frequent basis has not helped him to love me, I know. Holding my tongue is a gift I possess, but I tend to lose control when dealing with fools and incompetent doctors. I foresee rough waters ahead, Alex. God help me. Ah well, I never expected this profession to be easy! At least my life will not be boring.*

CHAPTER TWO

Bombay Island

FEBRUARY 1790

"D R. DARCY!"

George gritted his teeth and forced himself to remain silent until the young man nicknamed "Reed" due to his lanky physique had finished panting after his sprint from the commander's office on the far side of the compound.

"Commander Doyle wants you in his office now! He said to tell you it was of the utmost importance and haste was essential! 'Fetch Darcy,' he said to me. 'Tell him to leave his ridiculous test tubes and scribbled papers immediately.' So here I am to fetch you!"

"Well done, Reed. Your efficiency and ability to follow orders, and recall verbal insults precisely, is commendable."

Reed's face blanched. "I meant no disrespect, Dr. Darcy!"

George smiled and patted the young man on the shoulder, feeling paternal even though Reed was only two years younger. "I know you didn't, Ensign Dawson," George reverted to the stricken Reed's formal name, turning back to the table he had been bent over before the interruption. "Allow me a moment to separate these elements first—"

"But, sir! I have taken so long first going to your bungalow, then the hospital, searching to find an orderly who knew you were not there but here, and—"

"Why did you visit those other places when the opinion was that I would be here, with my ridiculous test tubes?"

"Yes, I suppose… Well…" Reed stuttered to a halt and fumbled with the wrinkled paper he held in his hand. The names of the men he was sent to fetch were now blurred, but the paper served as a reminder of his mission. "With all due respect, Dr. Darcy, Commander Doyle said—"

"I am sure the dire emergency of Lady Burgley's cough or Miss Marsh's headache will not escalate to a severe crisis in the next fifteen minutes. These three ingredients, on the other hand, will lead to an explosion intense enough to destroy this table and cause a fire if left untended. My 'ridiculous' test tubes are, in this instance, more frightening than Commander Doyle's ire."

Reed frowned, clearly dubious, but arguing with Dr. Darcy was as pointless as arguing with a tree. He shifted foot to foot as the physician secured a lid on one bottle and then covered a brown-liquid-filled wooden bowl with an oiled cloth. Using careful, confident movements, Dr. Darcy organized the strange items spread across the table, fascinating Reed into forgetting his errand.

"What are you doing with all this stuff, anyway?"

"Filling the empty spaces of my time and keeping my brain active are the main purposes," George responded with a trace of irritation. Then he shrugged, the gesture a minuscule lift of his left shoulder so as not to shake the bowl in his right hand. "Truth is, I have a fascination for chemistry. I have read everything written by Fordyce and Cullen, attended Saunders's lectures and studied in his laboratory at Guy's Hospital—his facility is impressive and no comparison to my ramshackle attempt—and became good friends with George Pearson at St. George's. His lectures on organic chemistry were enlightening, let me tell you." He glanced over his shoulder to note the serious expression on Reed's face. "Have you suddenly developed an interest in chemistry, Ensign? Or are you merely curious?"

"Curious. We always wonder what you are doing in here."

"We? And what do 'we' say I am doing?"

Reed shrugged, his gaze intent on the bizarre apparatus connected with tubes and the piles of papers jammed with mathematical equations. "Fiddling with herbs and oils and"—he waved his hand over the table—"whatever an apothecary uses to make medicines."

George grunted. "Perfect. Years of medical training and I am merely an apothecary. That's the extent of it? Nothing more nefarious bandied about?"

"Of course not!"

"Pity. I was hoping for something exciting. Maybe rumors of experimenting with live animals or formulating hallucinogens for spiritual rites." George turned to a nearby chair and retrieved his jacket.

Reed gaped at the older man as if he had sprouted a second nose. "You are a very strange man, Dr. Darcy, and I don't understand you at all."

"Well, that's something at least!" George clapped Reed on the shoulder and leaned closer. "Life is too short to be bored or boring, Reed. A gentleman with a scandalous past or naughty reputation is far more interesting to the ladies, trust me. Now, lead me to Commander Doyle before he has a seizure. After three uneventful months, I am anxious for a real medical emergency but would rather it not involve our fearless leader."

George followed Reed from the room and pulled the canvas drape that served as a door down from the roof, that the extent of security to his precious instruments. The odds of thievery or mischief were slim, most inhabitants of the military compound on Bombay Island either uninterested or afraid of the makeshift "laboratory." The label was one used jokingly by the medical staff, including Dr. Darcy, since it was no more than a bamboo and thatch hut among a cluster of similar huts located behind the hospital. In the three weeks since he took over the space and set up his equipment, he had accomplished more than the six weeks prior.

They walked through the sparsely populated waiting area of the hospital building and exited the double doors on the west end. George waved to the lieutenant stationed at the desk, the officer saluting in return. Once outside, they traversed the lush garden that fronted the entrance to the two-story medical facility, crossed an open expanse of gritty sand, and stepped onto the wooden walkway that ran the length of the barracks. The covered path was a longer route to Commander Doyle's office, but navigating around the dozens of obstacles and hundreds of people crowding the massive courtyard of the British East India compound would take far longer.

Their pace was brisk and the long-legged physician easily kept up while also managing to observe the bustle of activity that was becoming familiar but remained fascinating. Five months on the ship had prepared George to some degree, primarily in learning the language and listening to the stories from others who dwelt in India. Yet the exotic environment had struck him forcibly the second his feet stepped onto the dock. Everything from the aromas to the garments, from the animals to the music was vastly different than England. George loved every last speck of it and his only annoyance thus far was that he had yet to travel beyond the large island of Bombay other than for one outing to Mazagaon, the island nearest to Bombay.

Newly connected by the Hornby Vellard—the causeway an engineering feat destined to lead the way in the planned transformation for the seven islands to be combined into one—Mazagaon was already established as the prime suburb and fashionable place to live. Wealthy families wishing to escape the rough, crowded fort and busy populous of Bombay settled on the rocky but beautiful coastline of the small island, building luxurious houses amid the mango trees.

George's visit to Mazagaon had been part of a major excursion to harvest the unique mangos that fruited twice yearly, but he also managed to explore the landscape, pick an assortment of interesting plants for later study of medicinal properties, and enjoy the untouched stretches of beach.

As delightful as the adventure had been, George chafed at the restraints when he knew there was so much more to India than Bombay and Mazagaon. However, with thousands of souls, British and Indian, dwelling on the crescent-shaped landmass that was Bombay Island, and within the rustic headquarters of the British East India Company, there was a plethora of intriguing sights for the curious man who hungered to absorb his new country.

At the far end of the barracks, they jaunted over another patch of land shaded by tall java plum and golden shower trees and bordered by thick oleander hedges. George and Reed kept to the straight path with single-minded purpose and did not realize until attaining the next sheltered porch that they had company walking with them.

"Dr. McIntyre, how are you this fine day?" George greeted the physician.

"I was feeling verra fine until interrupted by Ensign Dawson with summons to see Doyle."

"That's where you're going too? Interesting. Might be something to this 'emergency' after all, although his asking for the two of us is more trouble-some than heartening. Who else did you fetch for the commander, Reed?" George looked at the messenger, but Reed's reply was a mumbled "no one" and his flaming red face was averted. George glanced back at McIntyre, noted the unbuttoned waistcoat and shirt that was actively being tucked into the Scotsman's kilt, and chuckled under his breath. "So, you went first to the bungalows looking for me and Dr. McIntyre," he went on in a vague tone as if sorting through a tough puzzle. "You roused him before searching in the hospital and then the laboratory for me. We tarried for a good fifteen minutes and are still ahead. Whatever were you doing, Dr. McIntyre?" He ended with false innocence and wide eyes directed toward the ruddy-skinned physician.

"Something far more enjoyable than playing with sterile glass bottles and drugs, I can assure ye. Damned if Doyle or the young pup here was gonna take precedence." McIntyre winked at George and then nudged the scarlet messenger. "Jesus, Reed, we need to find a woman so ye won't nearly stroke every time someone mentions tupping. Now tell us what is going on that we needed to drop our activities."

"Sir, I was simply told to fetch you both as quickly as possible." Reed shot a quick glare at them. "A task you both made very difficult!" George and McIntyre's brows rose at his uncharacteristic boldness, but he went on before they could reply, "All I know is that a group arrived this morning from Surat, and then a bit ago, I saw a couple of Indian couriers pass through the east gate." He paused to wait until a loud troop of soldiers on horses cleared the avenue separating the administrative buildings from the southern portion of the complex, resuming as they continued their brisk stride. "Oh, and Commander Doyle was talking to Dr. White when I left."

McIntyre groaned. "That canna be good."

"Probably not," George agreed, "although I haven't done anything to annoy him lately."

"Lately? As in, what, the past few hours?"

"He's not exactly your bosom buddy either, you know."

"Me he just ignores because I am a Scot. He hates ye with a personal vengeance. Canna imagine why, since ye are so charming and likable."

Dr. Searc McIntyre and his wife Lileas had arrived in Bombay about a month after George, and the two men had taken an instant liking to each other. They discovered a shared enjoyment for pursuits such as dancing, billiards, and outdoor games of sport. McIntyre was a good fifteen years older and married, which set him apart in some respects, but he was an excellent physician, his skills earning George's instant respect and Dr. White's instant dislike.

George's negative relationship with the Physician General of Medical Services on Bombay Island began on the ship and hadn't improved once on land. White wasted no time in exerting his authority, George forbidden to enter the wards where the sickest patients were treated or go anywhere near the surgical rooms. Instead, he was assigned to care for certain English citizens whose ailments ran the range of gouty feet and nervous swooning with the occasional fever or skin rash tossed in. It was boring as hell but did provide direct exposure to the luminaries who were in charge of everything that happened in Bombay.

Still, it irritated him to have traveled halfway around the world to end up treating minor illnesses and enhancing his chemistry skills. His patience was at a breaking point, and as they climbed the stairs leading to Commander Doyle's office on the third floor of the administration building, George realized he was praying fervently for an outside intervention before he exploded.

Reed led them into the busy anteroom, the clerk indicating they needed to wait for the commander to finish with another meeting. McIntyre released a rude expletive, but there wasn't much choice but to comply. Whispered speculation as to the nature of the emergency that did not seem to be an all-fired emergency after all passed between the two doctors until George abruptly halted at the appearance of a group of people farther down the lengthy passageway.

"Reed, who are they?" George lifted his chin their direction.

"General Kendall and His Grace, the Duke of Larent—"

"Of a cert Darcy knows who the duke is," McIntyre interrupted. "How often have ye been told ye resemble his most exalted eminence, the Duke of Cold Arrogance, Darcy?"

But George was not looking at the tall man with the dark handsomeness set into a mold of features startlingly similar to his own.

"No, I mean the others standing with General Kendall," he clarified for Reed. "I have never seen them before."

"They are Viscount and Viscountess Powis. They live in Mazagaon but have been away for a few months. Sailed through the southern islands, I think it was."

"The young lady is their daughter, I assume?"

"Miss Sarah Chambers, yes."

Reed's voice was oddly tight but George did not notice. Lord Powis was talking to General Kendall, the Duke of Larent, and two additional English gentlemen vaguely familiar to George as prominent aristocrats living in Bombay for the fortunes to be acquired as well as the tropical climate. However, his thoughts were not on politics or business affairs. Sarah Chambers drove everything from his mind. His eyes were focused on the tawny-haired beauty standing in serene splendor to the left of her father, the fluttering in his chest making breathing difficult, but a pleasant sensation nevertheless.

"Don't get any bright ideas, Dr. Darcy. She isn't friendly at all. An ice princess some call her. Aloof. I have never seen her talk to anyone or even give the time of day."

Ensign Dawson's bitter tone was lost on George, but not the individual words. Yet, as he gazed upon her averted face, studying the tension in the corner of her eye and firm set to her jaw, he knew Reed's report of the lady's character wasn't true. Just as he could often diagnose a disease through subtle signs or some other indefinable talent he possessed, George was absolutely certain that Sarah Chambers was not icy at heart.

Seconds later, the group walked out of view, Sarah trailing behind her parents and never glancing George's direction. Seconds after, the inner door opened and the clerk called to the two doctors.

Dr. White leaned against Commander Doyle's desk, his fat arms crossed over a round belly covered with grease-stained fabric. His tiny eyes followed the two men as they crossed to Doyle's desk, the glint of malice discernible. George did his best to maintain a neutral cast to his face and ignored the Physician General. Instead, he bowed respectfully toward Commander Doyle, as did Dr. McIntyre, even though the commander was bent over a large map spread across the surface of his desk and not looking at either man.

"Ye sent for us, Commander?" McIntyre asked after two minutes passed without Doyle acknowledging their presence.

The gray-haired man held his palm up in the universal gesture of silence and turned instead to a soldier standing nearby. "Lieutenant, inform your captain of the troubles in Khandesh. Have him begin preparations for deployment, then report to me as soon as possible." The lieutenant saluted smartly, pivoted on his heels, and exited the room after which Commander Doyle straightened and directed his attention to the two physicians.

"About two hours ago a messenger arrived from Poona," he began without preamble. "Actually from Assaye, a small village in Poona not too far from Lonauli. A pestilence of some kind is infecting the citizens on a grand scale, which in and of itself would probably not concern us. However, the Maratha Peshwa has family in the area and with the request bearing his seal, and written in the hand of Dr. Ullas, I cannot ignore it. Dr. White tells me you are his finest physicians"—he nodded toward the smirking but silent White—"so I am commissioning the two of you for this task. Gather whatever essentials you need. You will be leaving within the hour."

Commander Doyle bent back over the desk, it clear to McIntyre and George that discussion was not expected or desired. They shared a brief, nonverbal exchange and headed toward the door. Neither paid Dr. White any heed nor were they aware that before crossing the threshold and reaching the passageway he left his casual pose on Doyle's desk to follow them.

"Finest physicians' my arse," McIntyre whispered as soon as the door clicked. "More likely he hopes 'tis the plague and we'll succumb to it."

"At this point, it *could* be the plague and I would not care. As long as I can leave this island and have an opportunity to put my skills to use, it suits me just fine," George countered. "And on the off chance it is a serious infection, it is a blessing he is sending us. Those poor people don't know how lucky they are that we are coming to help instead of the alternative."

"And what 'alternative' is that, Darcy?"

Dr. White's growled question startled the men, and they halted midstride to turn about. White's fat face was flushed, his eyes belligerent and hard, and his fleshy hands balled into fists at his waist. George's desire to burst out laughing choked his throat. Did the old dog really intend to brawl with a man thirty years his junior in the corridor of a building filled with soldiers and one brawny Scotsman? It was too ridiculous to fathom, but on the off chance fisticuffs were on White's agenda, George stifled the laughter choking his throat with a cough.

"The alternative of no additional assistance for this Dr. Ullas with the potential of the infection becoming an epidemic or a worsening sequelae for those afflicted—"

"Spare me the fancy dance and technical terms, Dr. Darcy. I know perfectly well you meant the alternative of my medical skills versus yours. Oh yes. Dr. Darcy, the brilliant young physician with the prestigious education—"

"Thank you, Dr. White."

"It was not meant as a compliment!" He stepped closer, his face now a rather alarming shade of purple. "I know you think you are better than me, Darcy, but having a rich father who can buy your way through Cambridge and the Royal Academy in record time does not make you a better doctor!"

"Perhaps that is how you made it through medical school, and it does answer the mystery of how you ever obtained a license or the title of Physician General. Yet believe it or not, I earned my degree the old-fashioned way: by being an apt pupil and having true skill. Now, if you will excuse me, I have to organize my instruments and medicines. You know, those necessary implements that real physicians use."

George bowed and turned away, long-legged steps echoing across the wooden walls as he headed for the far stairwell. Dr. McIntyre fell into his colleague's wake, leaving the sputtering and fuming Dr. White where he stood in the middle of the hall. It was at the door, George's hand on the knob and twisting, when White shouted his final volley.

"Mark my words, Darcy. One of these days, your arrogance and blunt tongue will bring you grief. I sincerely hope to be there when it happens and, better yet, to cause it."

George did not respond or break his stride. They stepped onto the outside landing and unhesitatingly descended the stairs to the first floor landing. Only then did George slow his pace. He inhaled deeply of the fresh, clean air smelling of camphire flowers and the sea, the sunlight and cool breeze drying the perspiration off his brow and calming his anger.

"Yer self-control surprised me, Darcy. I expected ye to clobber him. I would have if he insulted me like that."

George shrugged, the gesture at odds with the thunderous expression on his face. "Only because I do not want to miss our departure. Besides, he is a bellicose fool and not worth the time or effort. Certainly not worth the risk of damaging my hands on his ugly face." He shrugged again, this time convincingly, and stopped walking. "Truth is, McIntyre, men like White anger me because of their incompetence and how that affects those who are infirm and foolishly relying on them. At times I have wanted to physically beat some quack for maltreatment, but I never have. What would that accomplish? I would get clapped in chains and they would go on hurting innocent people. The problem is bigger than individuals such as White." He shook his head, and they resumed their course along the wide veranda leading toward the front of the building. "Ultimately, I am not sure if my skills will change anything, even as excellent as they are, but I intend to do everything in my power. Losing my temper is counterproductive, no matter how good it might feel to bash Dr. White's teeth loose or knock him onto his fat, useless ass—"

The double S morphed into a sound resembling a hissing snake as they rounded the corner to be drawn to a halt in words and momentum.

Standing not two feet away from George was Miss Chambers. She was leaning against the flat railing at the corner of the veranda, one hand wrapped around a curved post and the other toying with a diamond pendant hanging from the velvet ribbon encircling her slender throat. She was staring straight into his eyes, a small smile dancing on her lips, and instantly George knew that she had not only heard his diatribe, but also agreed with his vision of Dr. White sprawled onto his backside.

Later Dr. McIntyre would compliment George on his lack of embarrassment and swift recovery. In all honesty, George was not one to easily embarrass, and rapid reflexes—mental and physical—were a gift he possessed. Therefore, he did not flush, nor did he bow as would be proper, the latter sure to break the eye contact he had craved from the moment he had noticed her in the hallway above. Instead, he flashed her a cocky grin and winked, the combination widening her smile and adding a shine to her eyes. *Beautiful eyes a grayish-green with flecks of amber around the iris.*

"My lady," he drawled, "I do apologize for the crude language and ungentlemanly references. I am a physician honor bound to heal, not inflict, so I assure you the scenario was pure fantasy."

"I believe your oath never to harm another binds you only in regard to one who is already a patient, so none shall convict you if your fantasy is acted upon." She spoke softly, almost as if talking were a foreign occupation, but blurted the sentence with conviction.

George's left brow rose. "My, and I thought I disliked the man! It seems you and I have something in common, my lady. I am intrigued."

Sarah's cheeks flamed, her smile faded, and she stepped back a pace while diverting her eyes. Unconsciously, George leaned closer, the widened gap between their bodies unwelcome.

"What I should say," he whispered, "is that I am fascinated. I was intrigued when I saw you outside Commander Doyle's office before."

She kept her head bowed but stole a glance at his face. It wasn't much, George able to catch the minutest hint of emotion from the corner of her gray eyes, but it verified what he had sensed in the corridor above. With no wish to frighten her, George straightened and pulled away. McIntyre chose that moment to subtly clear his throat. George had momentarily forgotten they were on a tight time schedule. He did not remove his eyes from Miss Chambers, but nodded for McIntyre's benefit.

"Perhaps we shall encounter each other at upcoming social events. If my good fortune continues, we may discover other opinions we have in common. I shall pray for the opportunity, my lady. By the way, my name is Dr. George Darcy. This uncharacteristically silent gentlemen is a colleague, Dr. McIntyre." George paused and indicated the Scotsman, McIntyre tipping his hat toward Miss Chambers, who acknowledged with the faintest of nods. "May I be so bold as to request the honor of your name?"

He watched the rosiness on her cheeks increase. She swallowed, her lips parting a second later as if to speak. George did not move; time suspended as he waited for her response. Another swallow and quick glance upward into his warm eyes and relaxed grin was followed by a barely audible, "Sarah. Sarah Chambers."

"Sarah Chambers," he repeated, speaking gently and caressing each syllable. Slowly, she lifted her gaze to again engage his eyes. "It is a pleasure. I can imagine nothing more delightful than passing the afternoon in your company, Sarah Chambers, but alas we are ordered to leave within the hour so I must hasten away. I shall return and will seek you out. After all, I must unveil the mystery of a woman with such exceptional judgment in character." He was thrilled when she chuckled and nodded her head.

Finally he bowed deeply, wished her a good day, and turned away, McIntyre falling into step. George did not look back until off the terrace and several yards across the open courtyard. The distance was not too great for him to see the serious cast to her face and to note the bewildered expression in the eyes that followed him. He flashed another wide grin and waved his hand, expecting her to flush anew and turn away. To his surprise, her lips curved in a tentative smile and her hand lifted to return his wave.

In the hours and days that followed, George had scant time to dwell on the impact of his encounter with Sarah Chambers. The excitement of new sights and people every step of the way occupied the bulk of his attention.

The boat trip across the narrow eastern inlet of the Arabian Sea was short enough not to elicit George's tendency toward seasickness, thank goodness. The trek across the rugged Konkan coastline and the western spur of the Western Ghats, where Poona was located on the fringe of the Deccan Plateau, was rough in places but beautiful. The deeper into the interior of India they traveled, even if no more than sixty miles from the sea, added to George's sense of liberation. At every turn, there was something fascinating and new to avidly examine, even if merely a strange bird or unknown bush, and he felt a pang of regret when they arrived at Assaye.

Unlike the tiny villages consisting of thatched mud huts erected in erratic clusters near streams that they had passed on their journey from Bombay, Assaye was a thriving town.

Or rather, it had been a thriving town. For all the appearances of a town that boasted a rich community of several thousand souls, it might have been inhabited by ghosts.

The wide streets, many paved with river stones, were laid in a grid formation. The buildings were primarily of wood or stone, a few constructed with bricks formed from the hard clay in the riverbeds, and although far from being grand or architecturally stylish, they were well built and spacious. For the most part, the native trees and shrubs were allowed to grow in their natural state with the walkways, roads, and houses built to accommodate their presence. However, to George's surprise, there were a number of designed and tended gardens attached to the larger houses as well as a park in the town square.

George dismounted along with the others, but his eyes were not on the two-story brick building their escort was already entering. Instead, he scanned the area that was devoid of people except for a handful of brave merchants with their carts spaced far apart, the dozen shoppers walking singly and in wide circles around each other. Even when conducting the important business of haggling over the items for sale, the seller and customer stood five feet apart, yelling back and forth to be heard.

"'Tis serious."

George nodded, McIntyre's muttered sentence not needing a reply.

The silence was deafening. Even the horses seemed to sense the strangeness and stood still with only an occasional swish of a tail. It wasn't but ten minutes before Captain Connelly returned, his face grave as he approached the physicians.

"I didn't receive a great deal of information. The administrator, a Mr. Phineas, looked healthy but tired and harried. He said it would be best to hunt down Dr. Ullas, who is in the hospital, that being the long building we glimpsed three streets back."

It was a short jaunt to the narrower street running alongside a small park with an eroded stone statue of an unknown holy man. The hospital was a one-story building with square, unglazed windows cut into the clay walls at regular intervals. Three smaller doors and a double entrance door interrupted the symmetry of the windows. Crossing the threshold, George and McIntyre were confronted with a familiar but impressive tableau. Nearly a hundred occupied beds lined the walls and filled the spaces in the middle. At least three-dozen medical personnel dressed in clean robes moved from crisp linen-draped bed to bed with a purpose. The murmur of voices, moans of the sick, and clank of equipment drifted to their ears, yet the overall scene was calm and orderly. The smell of putrid flesh, blood, and diseased bodily fluids hung on the air but was overshadowed by floral scents and soap. One could close their eyes and almost imagine they were in nothing more than a busy office.

Neither George nor McIntyre closed their eyes. Rather, they were alert, trained diagnostic scrutiny assessing the men and women lying in the beds as they walked toward an adjacent room where an attendant indicated Dr. Ullas was working with other patients.

"I see a number with respiratory symptoms," George whispered to his colleague, "yet others seem to be suffering abdominal discomfort. Very odd."

"Those three are clearly photophobic and stiff in the neck, indicative of a meningitis, while others have faint jaundice or rashes. I've ne'er seen such a mixture of symptoms."

"Is it possible there is more than one disease entity happening here?"

McIntyre shook his head at George's question, not knowing the answer. They had reached the room where Dr. Ullas supposedly was and discovered the chaos not seen in the larger ward of the hospital.

This room was a third the size of the previous, and there were no more than twenty patients George guessed after a rapid visual survey. However, these patients were undeniably extremely ill. Several were gasping for air, their wasted chests heaving with each breath. Most of them were jaundiced, the yellow tinge of their skin ranging from golden to pumpkin orange to the deeper bronze indicative of end-stage liver failure. Three were tied to the metal bed frames, an action George disliked but saw was clearly necessary when seconds later one of the restrained men suddenly awoke. His eyes were clouded, drops of blood pooled at the corners, and he yanked against the straps securing his limbs while he screeched a torrent of Hindi. George's understanding of the language was far from fluent, but he knew enough to interpret the man's raving as not coming from a sound mind.

Two Hindu women dashed to his bedside, their dulcet voices and gentle hands attempting to calm, but the majority of the room's staff paid the delirious man no heed. They were gathered around the bed of a woman suffering a seizure. Three men were holding on to her jerking limbs, preventing her from rolling off the narrow cot. A *sadhu*, with his face painted brilliant orange and red and his hair tied into coiled knots, stood at the foot of the bed, his chants in Hindi a rhythmic undercurrent to the woman's strangled cries and the commanding orders that came from the man kneeling by the woman's head.

Darcy and McIntyre watched in fascination as the kneeling man rubbed a strange, mud-colored ointment over the thrashing woman's forehead and bared chest. Then he pressed his fingertips deeply into her wrists and upper lip, his soothing voice almost a singsong chant similar to the holy man, but as the Englishmen drew closer, they realized he was talking to the woman at the same time as instructing his assistants where to apply pressure to her feet and inner knees. Seconds later the woman's seizure stopped and her eyes fluttered open, briefly connecting with the kneeling man before closing as she fell into a relieved sleep. For several minutes more the kneeling man continued to give hushed instructions and administer a series of prods with his thumb into places on her body. After a last check of her pulse, he rose, stepped away from the bed, and turned toward Darcy and McIntyre.

George sucked in his breath. Never had he beheld a man who oozed utter exhaustion while also piercing him with eyes one hundred percent alert and hard. Short, moderately fleshy, plain of face, and with thinning hair, Dr. Kshitij Ullas was unremarkable in every way—except for his eyes. Though a common brown, the depth of intelligence, compassion, and awareness discernible within was powerful. Later, George would wonder if what he felt in those moments was a true epiphany or merely hindsight making more of an initial meeting than there truly was, but he vividly recalled that his instant reaction was one of awe and that this was a man, a doctor, he would walk over hot coals to spend time with.

"Who are you two?" Dr. Ullas growled in English, brushing by them and walking to the next bed where he leaned to peel back one eyelid of the sleeping man lying there. "Why are you in my hospital and doing nothing?"

"I am Dr. McIntyre and this is Dr. Darcy. We arrived just now but are here to assist as per yer summons."

"I can use the help." The hint of relief in his voice was genuine, but the look cast over George was dubious. "Aren't you too young to be a doctor? Last thing I need now is a novice who doesn't know the difference between a pustule and a vesicle. Where are you from? Who sent you?"

"Bombay. Commander Doyle—"

"Bombay?" Dr. Ullas interrupted, staring at them angrily. "I told that imbecile not to send a dispatch to Bombay. I suppose White picked you, yes?"

"Yes, but—"

This time McIntyre was halted by the string of Hindi bursting from Dr. Ullas's lips. After a heartbeat of shocked silence, George began to chuckle. McIntyre looked at him as if he were insane, but Dr. Ullas ended his tirade, his eyes narrowing as he looked at George.

"You understand Hindi?"

"Enough to know we share a similar opinion of Dr. White. Trust me, Dr. Ullas, we are nothing like that hack. He chose us for this mission of mercy to get us out from under his feet and in hopes we would succumb to this illness and spare him the job of strangling us."

Dr. Ullas grunted, his expression not placated despite George's assurances. "Further proof how stupid the man is. If he had read the missive I sent—specifying it *not* go to Bombay so I would *not* be burdened with one of his incompetents or on the off chance he came himself—he would have noticed I said the disease is not contagious. It is undoubtedly a contaminant that is affecting so many, but none are acquiring it from contact with each other. Not that I can ascertain, that is."

"If you threw those big words at him, I am sure he skimmed over them."

"Perhaps." He speared Darcy and then McIntyre with his intense gaze before responding with another grunt. "Well, you are here now, and if you are doctors, as you claim to be, you will know your way around a hospital. Go to it." He waved his hand in a dismissive gesture and moved to the next patient without another word.

Lesser physicians might have floundered at the abrupt order. Darcy and McIntyre were not lesser physicians, so they grabbed on to the first person they found and, after a brief orientation to their surroundings, set to work. George was at a significant advantage over McIntyre in that his understanding of Hindi was good. Unfortunately, within minutes he discovered a glaring omission in his education. A natural ear for languages had helped him learn the foreign tongue, adding it to his repertoire of French, Latin, Italian, German, and a smattering of other tongues. What he had not diligently studied was how to read or write Hindi. The odd script was unlike English or any of the Romance-based languages and aside from a rudimentary familiarity with the alphabet and a handful of words, he was lost.

"Probably should have spent time reading the copy of Gilchrist's *A Grammar, of the Hindoostanee Language* that Lord Burgley gave me rather than with my chemistry experiments," he mumbled, eyes scanning the sheet with neat lines of what he presumed were Dr. Ullas's notes on the patient in the bed he stood by. The patient, an old man with a rash covering his chest and an intermittent dry cough, was smiling and nodding encouragingly. George was not sure whether to be bolstered by the man's faith or crushed by the possibility of not being able to live up to the grandfatherly gentleman's expectation. Luckily, the hospital personnel were sympathetic. One young woman voluntarily served as George's guide. She spoke not a single word of English and her Hindi was of a different dialect than what George had learned, but between pantomime and common verbiage, he discovered that her name was Ajastha and managed to fumble through.

Dr. Ullas spoke to them rarely. For the most part, this was not out of rudeness but rather due to the workload. Four more patients arrived before one in the morning, when George was finally able to collapse in exhausted sleep. On the positive side, five had been judged well enough to return home, and no one had died. All through the afternoon, evening, and late night, the staff bustled from bed to bed. George and McIntyre joined two other English doctors who had arrived from Gujarat three days prior, two Portuguese physicians from Goa who had also responded to the plea for help, and three *vaidya*. The latter were especially intriguing to George, the practitioners of Ayurvedic medicine, a uniquely Indian creation with philosophies and practices foreign to Western medicine and, until now, a system he had only read about. His curiosity was piqued, the giddy delight at being able to learn new techniques and discuss theories of medical treatment buried for the present but looming heavy on his mind nevertheless.

For four days the process continued with scant variation. Two patients died and there were new arrivals each day, yet the gradual trend was one of improvement. None of the physicians had ever seen a disease like this nor could any of them recall reading or hearing of a virulent contagion with the broad spectrum of symptoms seen here.

Except for Dr. Ullas.

"I have encountered what I believe is the same disease twice. The first was some fifteen years ago when I was in Burma. We saw a similar outbreak, and I was one of those who became ill, although fortunately only with the milder symptoms."

It was evening and the first opportunity George and McIntyre had to sit with Dr. Ullas and carry on a conversation lasting more than five minutes. A lull in the constant drama inside the hospital allowed the doctors and staff to gather on the shaded terrace and dine on a hot meal. The food was fresh and nourishing, and they were eating it off plates rather than with their bare hands while on the run. Listening to Dr. Ullas's soft voice was mesmerizing and the intelligent discourse pleasant.

"I was traveling from one village to another when the group of us were forced to take refuge due to a sudden monsoon. The Burmese who sheltered us lived in a small commune not large enough to qualify as a village. We were required to sleep in the barns and saw that several of the animals were sick, mostly the dogs, but we found five dead rats as well. We did not concern ourselves with this, animals not of much interest to doctors, but when we began growing ill and realized that some of the family members were ill, the coincidence was curious." He paused to take a large bite of spiced chicken wrapped in flat bread. "No one grew terribly ill nor close to death, so we were able to move on within a week. Yet the jaundice, abdominal pains, high fever, rash, and strange mixture of symptoms were notable and I did write of it in my personal journal."

An interruption from one of the Hindu women serving as nursing assistants gave the men a chance to refill their plates while Dr. Ullas gave her instructions. Then he resumed his narrative precisely where he left off.

"It was an odd incident and minor in comparison, so when I encountered the disease a few years ago in Kashmir, my anamnesis wasn't immediate. Even when I did recall the farm in Burma, many of the finer details were hazy, and since my older journals were at my house in Thana, I could not compare. Yet I did remember the curiosity of the animals."

"Were there sick animals in Kashmir as well?"

"Not obviously, Dr. Darcy, at least not at first." Dr. Ullas focused his gaze on George. "In truth, the possible connection to animals did not occur to me at all until I overheard one of the patients mention that he worked with the pigs used in the toilets and needed to return to the sty because other workers were ill. The comment piqued my interest, and as I questioned further, the discovery was that a large portion of those who were infected were either workers at the toilets or lived in the vicinity and used the facilities. Upon investigation, a number of the pigs were reported sickly."

"Forgive me, Dr. Ullas," the Portuguese physician broke in, "but there is a big difference between dogs and pigs."

"They are both animals," George answered before Dr. Ullas could reply. "And history has shown that there are many cases of transmission from animals to humans."

"Yes, of course, but the differences here are glaring. And there are no commonalities or sick animals reported, are there?"

"Not that I have heard of, Dr. Simas. Yet. The epidemic was severe before I arrived with my team and I have been preoccupied keeping people alive. However, I immediately recognized the similarities and have asked locals to investigate. No report has reached me yet."

It would take another three days before word reached the hospital that a group of hunters from a village over ten miles away had stumbled upon a herd of wild boar huddled around a watering hole that were in various stages of disease. The muddy water was reeking and stagnant with a dead carcass damming the stream of fresh water feeding the pond and thus slowing the exiting rivulet to a trickle. That trickle led directly into the larger river where the citizens of the northeasterly areas of Assaye drew their water. A rapid scan of the patient information revealed that the majority resided in that part of town.

"I have never seen a water sample teeming with this amount of particles. There are easily a dozen distinct shapes, all moving as if fighting for space." George did not remove his eyes from the microscope's ocular lens as he turned the knob to enhance the magnification. "Increasing makes it worse. Fascinating."

"And frightening. This microscope is nearly ten years old. I imagine advancements have been made. Describe to me the one that resembles coiled strings."

George dutifully complied with Dr. Ullas's request while the older doctor drew the shape on the page of his journal. After another examination of that slide and then three more prepared with droplets of the dirty water sample taken from the suspected source of the contaminant, Dr. Ullas added more detail to his etchings before straightening and turning his attention to George.

"There are five unique shapes of organisms, or *seminaria* as Fracastoro named them, that I have never seen before. No possible way to determine which one may have been the source of this infection, if the causative agent at all, but it is intriguing."

"You add the disclaimer, Dr. Ullas, yet I can tell you believe these invisible organisms cause disease."

"I do. Some infections, that is. The term 'disease' is general and encompasses a vast array of causes, perhaps a mere handful the result of these creatures. I have drawings of organisms viewed from the samples I examined in Kashmir, and I will compare out of curiosity once I am home. There will be similarities, even as you see here."

George watched as Dr. Ullas flipped back through pages of his book until reaching a series of pages with oddly shaped drawings, at which point he gestured for George to lean closer. Some of the drawings were spherical while others resembled clusters or connected rods and spirals. None were exactly the same, but there were congruous attributes.

"I have never seen most of these," George said, "not in any of the books at the Royal Society. Van Leeuwenhoek's writings are comprehensive, more than any in the field, yet I am sure he never encountered some of these."

"Proves his theory that God's design is wondrous." Dr. Ullas laughed at the surprise on George's face. "Yes, I know of Van Leeuwenhoek and have read his papers, those I can obtain copies of. You English are stingy. Our religious views of creation and divinity differ, but I agree that these organisms are not generated spontaneously. Nor do I believe they are bad or good, but simply a part of our world."

"Is this a deep interest of yours, Dr. Ullas? I could acquire letters and texts on the subject for you."

Dr. Ullas shook his head. "It is not a prime area of interest, Dr. Darcy, although I appreciate the offer." He shut the book and tucked it into the pocket of his flowing robe. "Divining the entity that causes a disease is important, and perhaps someday there shall be names for all of these organisms, and scientists shall know their functions. When they do, I hope to hear of it. But I personally do not care to stare into a microscope all day long. My old back cannot handle that."

"My young back likes it no better. I have a fascination for chemistry and have a laboratory in Bombay. Primarily it is to relieve my boredom, and I do enjoy it to a degree, but after too long, I want to throw the tubes against a wall." George smiled sourly and the edge of bitterness was audible.

"It is a matter of only so much time in one's life, I suppose. I treat illness and search for modalities to aid in the course of healing. After thirty years, I have accepted that this is a worthy endeavor to absorb my mind."

George removed the dirty slides and wiped the microscope with a soft cloth. "Let others perform the research. Like you I prefer to be at the bedside with the patient. Of course, discerning the causes of all disease would make our job much easier." George winked as he handed the microscope to Dr. Ullas, who laughed as he took the instrument and began carefully wrapping it with a thick wool cloth.

"Indeed. Although there would still be injuries from accidents, so somehow I doubt physicians shall ever be useless."

Dr. Ullas slipped the fragile bundle into a sturdy box, concentrating on the task of securing it for safe travel, as George leaned against the table and crossed his arms over his chest.

"I envy you, Dr. Ullas. You have traveled widely and amassed a wealth of knowledge. In my short time here, I have seen how you apply skills that are amazing yet foreign to me. It must give you great happiness to have accomplished what you have."

The Indian doctor turned his gaze to George, his brown eyes intense but unreadable. He said nothing for a full minute and George began to squirm under the scrutiny. Finally the silence was broken with a question.

"What would you say is your greatest fault, Dr. Darcy?"

George's left brow rose at the unexpected query, and he hesitated half a second before answering truthfully, "Arrogance."

But Dr. Ullas shook his head, his eyes locked on George's face. "No. That is not your fault. Arrogance in your case is earned and a strength. Annoying to some, I am sure, but a strength. You are skilled, Dr. Darcy. More than you realize, I think, which having been told this, will increase your arrogance." He did not smile, the words not meant as a jest. "No, your fault is impatience. And unbelief, I think."

When George did not respond, Dr. Ullas again broke the silence with a question. "Are you a religious man, Dr. Darcy?"

"I was raised in the Church and my father is extremely devout—"

"No," Dr. Ullas interrupted with a dismissive wave of his hand. "You English are all raised in the Church. Usually it means nothing to you."

He stepped closer, his eyes intimate in an odd way that was both disturbing and exhilarating.

"Your reasons for coming to India are your own, Dr. Darcy, and I am not invalidating them. Call it fate, God—yours or mine—or some other happenstance. It makes no difference to me. Just believe that you are meant to be here and that it may not be for the reasons you think brought you here. Believe that you are on the path of your destiny, including meeting me. Believe that fully, open your soul to the truth, and then you shall learn patience. Only then will you discover what happiness is."

❦

George was in no rush to leave the company of Dr. Ullas, but once settled back into the compound, he began his quest to discover everything about Sarah Chambers. He started by seeking out Reed.

Ensign Dawson's father was a field marshal and rarely at the compound because his duties sent him all over the western portions of India, but Reed had been born in Bombay and his post as a courier for Commander Doyle meant he was the best resource. It took George over a week before he had enough free time to go on a serious hunt for the busy ensign, and then it took him two hours to ascertain that Reed was on a mission to the far side of the island. In the end, George planted himself at the main gate, right next to a merchant selling carpets and another selling herbs for cooking. Before Reed rode through the crowds entering and leaving the military compound, George learned several dozen new Hindi phrases and purchased two small rugs and a basket of herbs that he knew to have medicinal qualities, so it wasn't a total waste of his time.

Finally sitting at a table with ale in each of their hands, George broached the subject. "I need you to tell me everything you know about Miss Sarah Chambers."

Reed blinked in surprise and then narrowed his eyes. "Why?"

George shrugged and leaned back, suddenly feeling that he needed to act nonchalant. "Professional curiosity," he answered semitruthfully. "I am a skilled diagnostician, Reed, and I sensed something about the lady that intrigued me. From a medical standpoint."

"What! Are you saying she is ill?"

"No, no. Nothing like that, so don't panic."

"Then what do you mean?"

"Remember how you referred to her as an ice princess who speaks to no one?"

"I have never called her that," Reed countered hastily. "Others have, but I do not like the term."

"But you did say she never speaks to anyone and appears aloof and unkind. I don't think that is it at all. I think she is merely shy."

"And you figured this out from one glance down a long corridor?"

George chuckled at Reed's condescending tone. He was used to people mocking him or using sarcasm when he gave a quick diagnosis. "As it happens the 'one glance' in the corridor led to a hunch. It was when I spoke to her after leaving Doyle's office that I knew I was correct."

"You spoke with her? When? Did she talk to you?"

"She did, haltingly. It was long enough to see all the signs of one who is stricken with a case of paralyzing shyness."

"I don't know, Dr. Darcy. That sounds odd to me."

This time, his bitter tone was not lost on George. "Most people who are moderately shy learn to overcome their timidity, Reed. A person who suffers from severe phobic shyness cannot control their reaction. I am sure Miss Chambers never meant to be rude to you."

"She talked to *you* though, didn't she?"

"Only because I surprised her and have an innate talent for soothing people. That comes with being an excellent physician, which brings me back to the point. I think I can help Miss Chambers to conquer some of her fear. Or at least I want to try."

Reed was staring at him with suspicious eyes. George smoothed his features into as innocent an expression as possible, but it was still hard to maintain the look when Reed asked the next question.

"So your interest in Miss Chambers is entirely professional? You don't want more? You don't think of her in *that* way?"

"I am far too busy to think of any woman in *that* way, Reed. At least not seriously." And it wasn't until he spoke the words that a few weeks ago would have been one hundred percent true that he realized they were a lie. Dimly, he heard his father launching into a lecture on the sin of lying, but before the guilt set in, Reed's voice drowned that of his father, the ensign buying the fib and seeing a personal advantage.

"All right then. I am not sure I swallow the 'shy' bit, but if you think there is a way to make it easier to talk to the lady, I am all for that. The Powis estate is in Mazagaon on the north face just past the…"

❧

"Ye look like a cat who has eaten a whole family of mice so no need to ask if ye were successful."

George took the tray of instruments and strips of cloth from the orderly and waited until the man had walked away before responding to Dr. McIntyre. "Even better than I anticipated. Is Dr. White around?"

"Nay. What would he be doing here? Helping me stitch Mr. Morgan? Dinna be ridiculous."

"Just wanted to be sure. How much laudanum did you give him?" George jerked his chin at the man snoring on the narrow cot.

"None. He was brought to me this way, or almost this way, I should say. He did rally when I cleaned the wound. Hooper gave him a swallow of *tharra* to top off his buzz and out he went. Makes my job a lot easier. 'Course I wouldn't be doing this at all if he weren't a stinking drunk."

"How did he get that gash? It is quite ragged."

"Apparently, he thought it was a fine idea to cozy up to a Brahma. Not sure if he thought 'twas a fuzzy kitten or if he was feeling invincible. Hand me those scissors, will ye? Thanks. So when did ye finally find Reed?"

"Yesterday I hunted him down and we had a nice long chat."

"So why are ye here? Why aren't ye engagin' the fair damsel?"

"I planned to ride out to the Powis estate on Mazagaon this morning."

"Bold move, Dr. Darcy. At this rate 'twill be married by the end of the month."

"I seriously doubt it. Want me to hold him before you do that?"

"He has enough liquor inside him, I wager, so won't feel me pouring it over the wound this time. Just grab those towels over there to sop up the blood and *tharra*. Pathetic waste of good Indian moonshine, but its the strongest around."

"I don't know how you can drink this stuff. One sip sets my stomach on fire."

"I'm a Scotsman, remember? So what stopped ye from riding to Mazagaon?"

"Initially it was a medical call that I wanted to strangle White for, but as it turned out, fate was on my side. Let me get some fresh bandages." George crossed to a wall cabinet where white linens were stacked in neat piles, selected three large, folded cloths and one roll of narrow stripped cloth, and resumed the topic while holding up the patient's lacerated arm for Dr. McIntyre to dress. "Lady Burgley requested my presence immediately—the woman is a valetudinarian but her persistent cough is troubling—so naturally I went. Besides, I do like Lady Burgley. She amuses me with her stories and brash character. Like always, she calls for tea and we end up chatting for a good hour or more after I examine her and deliver a fresh bottle of elixir for her 'ailments.' I have to tell you, McIntyre, the cook she has makes these cookies out of persimmons that are surely sinful."

"The fairy folk passed me by on the blessing to be indispensable to the grand people of Bombay. Ye have that honor, my friend."

"I brought a half-dozen back for you, so don't pout. And I owe my good luck to Dr. White, as ironic as that is. I always suspected that his shuffling me away from the hospital would eventually work to my advantage and now it has."

Finished with tending Mr. Morgan's wound, the two doctors washed their hands and retreated to a small courtyard outside the rear entrance. George retrieved his travel bag and McIntyre grabbed two mugs and a pot of steeped coffee off the stove on their way out, the story of George's good fortune recounted as they went, and finished just as McIntyre took a bite of cookie.

"Saint's preserve us, ye weren't exaggerating. These are delicious!" A number of nonverbal expressions of delight ensued before the Scotsman was able to talk. "So," he said between chews, "an excursion tomorrow to Malabar Hill and the temples with dinner after at Lord Montstuart's, and ye are invited. Well played, Darcy."

George laughed. "I wish I could claim some sort of clever manipulation, but nepotism is closer to the truth. As it happens, Lord Montstuart and my father went to school together as boys and at university. Lady Burgley mentioned that a Dr. Darcy was caring for her, he asks if there is a connection, and viola! I have an invitation to a social outing with the crème de la crème in Bombay, including Lord and Lady Powis and their beautiful daughter, Miss Chambers."

"There is that satisfied cat look again. Not that I can blame ye. Miss Chambers is a bonny lass."

"She is, although my interest is primarily professional. Well it is! Quit laughing! I said 'primarily' so admit to an interest not so… clinical. But truthfully, McIntyre, have you even known anyone with serious shyness? No? I have. A colleague of mine at Cambridge had a sister who was so terrified of people that she became a recluse. I felt so sorry for my friend and his family, but mostly for the poor young lady who, in my opinion, suffered a malady no different than any other except for being one of the mind or spirit rather than the flesh."

"Miss Chambers did talk to ye, so her shyness canna be that paralyzing."

"Yes, but Baynes's sister's condition worsened over time." George leaned back in his chair and sighed. "Oddities like this fascinate me, not that illnesses of the mind are of particular interest to me in general. I shan't deny that Miss Chambers's beauty does increase the interest, but maybe I'll learn something too. You never know."

"If nothing else, ye will get to rub elbows with the Bombay elite. Maybe the Duke of Larent will be there and ye can discover if he is a long lost uncle or something."

"He doesn't look *that* much like me. Besides, I think getting Miss Chambers to hold a conversation with me would be easier than that man, if I wanted to, which I don't. And now that we have divined the truth of my motives with the lady, I have more news to divulge."

McIntyre's brows rose questioningly at George's smug grin.

"You have been invited as well. Apparently our fame has spread. To quote Lady Burgley, 'We have heard of your and Dr. McIntyre's recent journey to Poona and success in curing those poor people.' There was more, but that was the tenor. I was blushing!"

"I doubt that," McIntyre snorted, "but the rest does no surprise me. I have noticed an increased respect and notoriety, and Dr. White is obviously irritated with us. At first I thought it was just because we came back alive, but he has been even nastier lately."

"Nastier but strangely less restricting. He is as condescending as ever, but more careful how he insults and who is within earshot. I came back determined to ignore his limitations and to put up a fight when he ordered me out of the critical wing and surgery, but other than murderous glares, he has done nothing. Somewhat disappointing, actually. I was beginning to relish the vision of knocking him on his ass. I thought it might be a perfect conversation starter with Miss Chambers. Why does she hate him so?"

"No idea. As for our newfound popularity, we have Dr. Ullas to thank, although why an Indian physician from Thana is even known here is curious."

George shrugged then stood. "The cookies are yours to enjoy. I will see you tomorrow at ten o'clock sharp by the west gate. I have secured a carriage for the three of us."

"Three of us?"

"Oh, I forgot! Mrs. McIntyre is invited too. Between my dashing good looks and superb charm, your exotic accent and manly knees"—he pointed at McIntyre's hairy legs exposed below the kilt—"and Mrs. McIntyre's motherly demeanor, we should have no trouble cracking Miss Chambers's shell."

Dr. McIntyre harrumphed and bit into another cookie as Dr. Darcy pivoted about and walked away. Then he chuckled under his breath at the sight of his young friend's jaunty gait and spirited whistling. "Professional interest," he muttered with a shake of his head. "I should take bets on it."

George's Memoirs
April 17, 1790

Alex, I can't believe it has been a year since I sat in the parlor at Pemberley, drinking wine with James and discussing my departure. I should be used to life passing swiftly and my months replete with activity. Never could I sit for more than an hour without feeling as if I were going to jump out of my skin. Do you know how often I pray that God will give me the gift of laziness, even if only for a short interval? Maybe when I am gray-haired and my decrepit bones no longer allow me to be otherwise. Of course, you know the truth is that I relish staying busy and I probably forever will. My delight these past few weeks proves that God has answered my other prayers, those being the ones I delivered in frustration in the early weeks after my arrival in India. Perhaps the lesson to learn is to watch what one prays for! So well has He delivered my desires that it has been two and twenty days since I last wrote in my personal journal.

I have much to report and shall recount the highlights for posterity's sake. Nevertheless, I am not ignorant as to why this day was chosen to hide in a quiet garden, stare at the undulating waves of the sea glimpsed through the swaying trees, and listen to the hum of bees whilst I write. Is that not poetic, Alex? Are you impressed? Of course you would be, after teasing me for the horrid attempt first. Somehow I doubt that part of our relationship would have changed. You the gentle soul, as James aptly stated it, yet also skilled at needling me! Ah, my brother. Will there ever be a time in my life when I shall no longer acutely miss you? Will this date ever arrive without my dwelling upon it in such a morose fashion?

Dr. Ullas's words have lingered in my mind. I muse on them and remember the expression in his eyes. This is a strange land, Alex. Exotic, beautiful, warm. Yet strange. I have yet to venture far afield, but what I have seen of the culture and people intrigues me. They are mystifying in so many ways, alien and unlike us. But they possess a harmony and balance with the world that I have never seen. Not all of them, naturally. Human nature is what it is, the result of sin, I suppose, as the preachers teach. Still, as I observe and converse with the natives, I feel a sense of peace.

I know I am explaining it poorly. No, I am not a poet, and you would be correct to tease me for trying. I shan't try to describe it then. All I can say is that Dr. Ullas struck a nerve with his talk of fate. All of my reasons for coming here, not the least of which was to escape the strong memories of you, and yet here I sit dwelling on my memories of you. I could be with Sarah. God knows I would rather be. Yet so sure was

I that my company would be less than pleasant today that I evaded her invitation. I miss you, Alex. I always will. Yet do I sit here because of my grief or because it has become a habit? If I admit to the latter, will you rejoice from your place in Heaven or be disappointed?

See how awful my scientific mind is at figuring out affairs of the heart? Frightening! Especially when I am wondering daily if I am falling in love with Sarah Chambers. Isn't a man supposed to know these things? Instead, I try to rationalize it! Pathetic.

Very well then. The rational facts. I started to write "cold, rational facts" but stopped myself because, although rational, there is nothing cold about how I feel for Sarah. What began as an interest that was partially professional is decidedly not so any longer. I suppose I should try my hand at poetry since that is how a lover is expected to describe his sentiments. Indeed, the glint of sunlight on her golden hair dazzles me. And her voice sends shivers up my spine. I should say "dulcet voice as an angel" or something similar, right? Her touch, even of a gloved hand, or nearness to my body stirs other reactions that I have no idea how to write in a poetic way. And although unlikely to be seen by eyes other than my own, I best not clinically clarify what those reactions are in indelible ink.

Yes, as you have probably deduced from these paragraphs, I finally cracked through Sarah's self-imposed barriers. Persistence paid off, as it were, with my charming personality aiding to some degree. I admit to being altogether too cocksure and encountered one of the few instances in my life where my humor and easy manner acted against me. Can you believe she thought me brash and frightening? Yes, you probably can and are undoubtedly screaming, "I told you so!" from heaven. Happy you will be then, dear Alex, to hear that I have learned that a quiet presence is more effective with a person who is highly reserved. I shall spare you the medical babble. These past three weeks or so, we have spent more time together in actual conversation. I have not seen an improvement in her affliction as it relates to other people, but at least she speaks to me with animation and greater ease.

Simply put, I delight in every moment we are together and wish it could be more. What keeps me away from her, ironically enough, is my profession. My second greatest joy these days, Alex, is how busy I am and how irritated Dr. White is! Oh, I am evil, indeed I am. Tried and convicted, and without shame. Dr. Ullas's fame and connection are greater reaching than I suspected. I gleaned hints as we traveled from Assaye to Thana, and by the size of his house alone, it was obvious he is wealthy.

One servant commented that Dr. Ullas's wife is somehow related to Madhavrao, the Maratha Peshwa. Whatever the truth, it has benefitted us and is worth the wrath of White. He glares and mutters nastily under his breath, but has yet to do more. I have no doubt he is biding his time. Then again, perhaps I am assuming where I should not. You must be proud of me, Alex, because I remain pleasant to the old windbag and avoid him for the most part. I know, shocking! My stunning reversal of the typical George is due to my happiness more than any radical transformation, I am sure, and I shall stop at that; otherwise, I will revert to bad poetry again, and neither of us wants to suffer through that.

S TUNNING ENSEMBLE. YER PATIENT was surely impressed, although I hope this isn't expected of the rest of us."

George finished washing his bloody hands before taking his coat from McIntyre's hand. "You can't pull off this color of red, my friend, so don't worry. Besides, my patient was unconscious." He adjusted his sleeves and slipped the coat over his broad shoulders. The jacket matched his breeches, both a hue somewhere between crimson and maroon with accents of shiny gold. The combination was a sharp contrast to his white stockings and shirt. "How do I look?"

"Like a man ready to woo a prospective father-in-law. Today is the planned day? Are ye nervous?"

George was looking into a mirror and fixing the limp neckcloth to a respectable poufy knot. "Today is the day, and I am a little nervous. I have never asked a father for his daughter's hand in marriage. I have been practicing the proper phrases. Usually my knack for articulation does not fail me, so I am hopeful."

"Practice is smart. However, I wasn't talking about the proposal part."

George turned from the mirror. "What do you mean?"

"I mean, what's the all-fired rush? Yer twenty-three, for God's sake! Why the hurry to get hitched?"

"I'll be twenty-four soon—"

"Not until January, and that is still too young in my book," McIntyre countered.

"You love being married! At least that is what you say, so why this sudden reversal?"

"I love being married *now*," the older doctor emphasized, "but I didn't get married until I was thirty-two. Think of all ye are going to miss."

"Nothing I am particularly interested in." George grabbed his medical bag and started walking toward the door.

McIntyre followed. "Look, Darcy, I mean no offense. Miss Chambers is a beautiful woman and I know ye care for her."

"I love her," George corrected. "There is a difference."

"How can ye be so sure?"

George whirled about. "I have never been so sure of anything in my life."

"In yer whole life of twenty-three years?" McIntyre met George's irritated glare. "And what I was asking is, how can ye be so sure that what ye are feeling is the kind of love to last a lifetime when never having felt love at all?"

"How do you know your love for Mrs. McIntyre is? How does any man know?"

"Honestly, I am not sure we can ever know. But falling in love or lust a few dozen times, ye gain a bit of perspective. Ye admit ye have done none of either—"

"I am not that inexperienced!" George interrupted indignantly. "I have felt my fair share of lust, believe me, and acted upon it when I could. All I ever said is that my life until now has been about the study and practice of medicine, with women far down on the list. I never felt the loss until I met Sarah." He inhaled deeply to calm his irritation and placed one hand on McIntyre's shoulder. "I know your questioning and advice is well meant, Searc. Furthermore, I suppose I would agree with you in regards to most men. For me it is different."

Dr. McIntyre's expression was dubious despite George's firm declaration. "I am short on time," he said with a glance at his pocket watch, "and already delayed after being grabbed to set that broken bone—a nasty compound injury that you need to keep an eye on for me, by the way. Over there in bed twenty." He lifted his chin toward the long row of hospital beds visible through the window they stood beside. "I know it will be hard to understand, but I never have been one to play the rogue. It just isn't in me. Maybe it is my upbringing. Years of moralizing lectures from my father drove us mad but sunk in. Maybe it's because I have been focused on medicine since I was young. Or maybe it is because of…"

George stopped suddenly, several heartbeats passing as he stared at the ground. Collecting himself with visible effort, he met McIntyre's gaze.

"I like the idea of having a wife and family, Searc. I see no reason to pass on the opportunity now on the off chance that there *might* be something else on down the line. I am not a gambler either. More of my father's influence," he finished with a grin that was almost up to his typical saucy style.

"Very well then." McIntyre reached out his hand. "I will wish ye good luck and I'll start preparing to dance a Scottish reel at yer wedding."

"Deal." George took the offered hand. "And thanks. I may need all the luck I can get. I hear fathers can be frightening."

"I know Lileas's was. I still shudder when I think of it. I'll keep one hospital bed open for ye just in case."

~❧~

George relinquished his horse to the waiting servant, uttered a quick word of thanks, and ascended the steps rapidly. The doors were open and the liveried footmen standing at attention on either side acknowledged his entry with a respectful nod. The servants of the grand house on Mazagaon belonging to the Viscount Powis recognized Dr. George Darcy as a frequent visitor to the mansion, which sat pristinely on the bluff overlooking the placid waters of the Arabian Sea.

Music drifted through the gaping portal, the massive foyer and visible chambers crowded with people in their finest attire. It was minutes after the stroke of noon, but the heat and humidity of late July in India meant that every hand fluttered a fan in a fast rhythm and every garment was constructed of the lightest materials possible while maintaining fashion.

George had not considered his attire with the temperature in mind. His goal was to please a particular lady.

As soon as he crossed the threshold and saw the ocean of guests invited to the Viscount and Viscountess Powis's garden party, he turned his gaze to the walls and shadowy corners in search of Miss Chambers. After walking through the rooms and deftly avoiding lengthy conversation with a dozen enthusiastic revelers, he spied her through the veranda doors. A broad rather silly smile burst forth, but without caring one whit, he quickened his stride and steered around a group of young ladies who hoped the dazzling smile from the handsome physician was for one of them. George acknowledged their attention with an incline of his head but did not pause.

Sarah was standing by a cluster of tall, potted bushes, half hidden behind the large leaves. Nearby, her mother sat on a divan with other ladies, their laughter ringing merrily and gestures animated as they talked.

George glimpsed a smile on Sarah's face and realized she was talking with someone she was comfortable with. Pride at her ease in conversation altered to jealousy when he recognized the young man leaning against the railing less than a foot from Sarah. With great effort, he calmly and properly paid his respects to Lady Powis and the other ladies before turning to greet Miss Chambers.

George wanted nothing more than to bask in the glory of her face and drown in the gorgeous gray-green eyes turned his way, but unwelcome reality was reasserted when the other man cleared his throat.

"Dr. Darcy. I see you have returned from your recent assignment. Welcome back to Bombay."

"I got in late yesterday afternoon," George explained, hoping Sarah understood that he had not wasted time coming to see her. "It is good to be back, thank you, Reed."

"Please, it is Lieutenant Dawson now, Dr. Darcy. Remember? I am leaving 'Reed' behind me. After all, I shall be a captain before the end of the year, if all goes well."

"Congratulations are in order then, Lieutenant." George inclined his head and turned back to Sarah. "It is a true delight to see you, Miss Chambers. You look well, although a bit flushed. I prescribe a cold drink and walk closer to the ocean in order to capitalize on the cooler breezes."

"That does sound lovely." Sarah eagerly accepted George's outstretched hand then turned to Lieutenant Dawson, "Thank you for amusing me, Lieutenant. Your kindness in sacrificing your time is appreciated."

"It was my pleasure, Miss Chambers, and not a sacrifice at all."

Sarah blushed at Dawson's heated gaze. George wanted to punch him. Instead, he gained permission from Lady Powis to escort her daughter and steered her away from the annoying lieutenant. Glasses of lemonade in their hands minutes later, George placidly strolled across the manicured lawn with Sarah's hand resting on his arm as they headed toward the cliff, Dawson forgotten.

Neither noticed the daggers he slung at George's back nor how he stomped away. There was a man who did notice, his smile triumphant and downright evil, and after casting his own hateful glance George's direction, he gulped the last half of his wine and headed in the direction taken by Dawson.

As they walked and sipped lemonade, George gaily filled the silence with idle chatter about his latest medical jaunt away from Bombay Island.

"I was impressed by the facilities in Diu. The Portuguese have a modernized structure with wide spaces and adequate equipment. As always, there were challenges to overcome and interesting cases to learn from, but of course I will not upset your delicate sensibilities with the unsavory details, my lady. It may please you to hear that the voyage across the Gulf of Chambay was pleasant enough. Nevertheless, it was fortuitous that I had some time to recuperate before today's party. And now, after gazing upon your beautiful face, my heart soars and I am whole."

Sarah giggled and looked up at his grinning face. Bolstered by the positive effect, and because it was true, George held her gaze and continued, "Your eyes sparkle brighter than the sun that has been dimmed behind the gray clouds of my distance from you."

"You are ridiculous, George Darcy. Promise me you will never attempt to write poetry? The Muses would be forced to embarrass you publicly for the sake of preserving integrity for all poets down through the ages."

"You wound me, madam! I practiced those pretty compliments for days!"

Sarah laughed harder and shook her head. "I have missed you, Dr. Darcy—"

"George," he amended. "Or 'sweetums' or 'honeydew' if you prefer."

"Honeydew indeed! George is adequate for the present, I think."

"I can accept that. For now." He caressed his thumb over the small, gloved hand resting on his arm and drew it to his lips for a lingering kiss to each knuckle. "I missed you as well, Sarah. More than I can say with bad poetry or plainly spoken sentences. You know how important my profession is to me and that I can easily lose myself while working. I shan't pretend that this summons wasn't as fulfilling as the others. However, I was exceedingly anxious to be back in Bombay. Much more so this time."

They had reached the copse of trees near the edge of the Powis estate. Several stone benches were set into the soft turf under the shade of the trees with a stunning view of the sea. George steered to a particular bench located in such a way that they had a measure of privacy yet were not entirely invisible. Once seated, George broached the topic most pressing upon his mind.

"The first bit of news I sought upon landing at the docks was whether Lord Powis had indeed returned to Bombay. I cannot tell you how thrilled I was to hear that he was back, Sarah. I might have danced a jig right then and there if not afraid my stomach would rebel. I have waited two months for his return so that I could ask for the honor of your hand in marriage, Sarah Chambers. If possible, I intend to speak with him today, unless you have changed your mind about me, that is."

The last was said in jest, George shooting a quick look around before leaning to plant a gentle kiss to her lips.

Sarah's breath hitched and her eyes fluttered closed, but she pulled away sooner than he wanted. "George, I haven't been completely honest with you. I haven't told you everything about our family and if my holding back changes your mind about me—"

"Sarah!" George interrupted sharply, and then bit his lip when she cringed. Cupping her cheek with his palm he turned her head until she was facing him. "Look at me," he commanded in a whisper, waiting until she obeyed. "I love you. Nothing you say will change that. I am sure I have not told you everything about my family either."

"You have told me of Alex. I know he is your dearest memory and deepest secret. I know you have shared him with no other and the honor shown me by telling of your twin is why I feel so wretched."

"I don't understand."

"I lost someone special to me as well." Her words were spoken so softly that George was not sure he had heard her correctly. Tears welled in her eyes and George swept one thumb across her cheek to catch the first to fall. The second tear he missed because she drew back and stood.

Sarah stared out at the waves, her voice hollow. "Six years ago, my sister died while giving birth. Neither survived. It was in every way a horrible time, George. Jane's husband remarried in four months to his mistress of many years and six months later they had a child. Everyone pretended not to be able to count as they hailed the new ducal heir. Father was devastated. Jane's marriage to a duke was a triumphant reflection on him. Her death without a surviving son he interpreted as a black mark. He packed our belongings and brought us here. Since then he refuses to speak of Jane in any way and we are forbidden to mention her."

"My God! I am so very sorry, Sarah. You were obviously close to Jane. Was she your twin?"

"No. We were dear to each other but not in the same way as Alex and you, I am sure. Yet I feel her loss keenly. Jane was beautiful, sparkling with verve and charm. She was witty and easy with everyone. She was all that I am not, and sometimes I envied her for it, but mostly I admired her and wished…"

"Wished what?"

"Wished that I could be like her. Jane was the only person alive who accepted me as I am. She never thought me a freak."

She murmured the last through trembling lips and George almost missed it, several seconds passing before the implication struck him and the anger welled. "Freak? Who dares to call you that?"

"No one now, at least not within my hearing. And I do not mind, really, since it is true."

"Sarah! It is not true! How often must I tell you that your shyness is not a fault of yours? There is nothing wrong with you!"

She smiled at him even while shaking her head. "I was only fifteen when we settled here, but I soon realized that my parents were evaluating the prospects for my marriage. I was utterly terrified at the idea. Every dinner party or casual introduction is designed as an evaluation of me as prospective bride. My… condition overpowers and I know Father's frustration is growing. After three years, I have learned to control myself enough not to fall apart publicly, but the control comes with a price. I know what is said of me."

"Sarah—"

"There is one other thing," she interrupted before he could reassure her. "I told you that I disliked Dr. White because he is unkempt and not doing enough to help my mother."

"Yes, and I can't argue on either count. I suspect your mother's heart condition might benefit from digitalis. The studies by William Withering are impressive, but also so new that I doubt White has ever heard of him. There are other treatments that might help her as well, but of course I can't be sure unless I were her physician and could examine her fully, and that is not going to happen with White around. It frustrates me as well, Sarah."

"You must try, George. Anything to remove Dr. White from my mother's presence!"

George cocked his head and frowned. "There is that passionate dislike again. What else do you know about Dr. White?"

"He was my sister's doctor," she whispered through a choked throat. "Mother had an attack while at the funeral, Dr. White swooping in and taking advantage of the situation. I know it was his fault Jane and her baby died. Dying in childbirth is not unusual, but his... incompetency and... uncaring attitude are enough proof for me. My parents do not agree. It was Father who arranged Dr. White's position here in Bombay."

"I wondered how he managed to become Physician General." With an effort, he willed his boiling blood to calm to a low simmer. Standing, he pulled her further into the shadows of the trees. He lifted her hands to his lips and planted a long kiss to each palm, after which he enfolded them between his hands and laid them against his chest.

"Thank you for sharing Jane with me, Sarah, and for giving me further insight into your life. My heart aches at what I know has been a painful period for you."

"Thank you, George. The greatest pain is how disappointing I have been to my parents. It never takes long for one of the many gentlemen introduced to realize I will never be an adequate wife."

"That is nonsense. I have no doubts you will be a most excellent wife."

George pitched his voice into a light tease and swept his gaze over her body, returning to her face and grinning in a suggestive manner that even she understood. Instantly, her cheeks flamed to brilliant red and she bowed her head, several deep inhales necessary before she could speak above a choked whisper. "I meant in that I cannot be a proper hostess or lady of the manor. I cannot carry a conversation for more than a minute!"

"You are conversing with me quite well, my lady."

She nodded, still unable to meet his eyes. "Yes. You are different, in every way. I can talk to you as I can few others. My sister Jane, my maid Hannah, our butler Mr. Chives, and Lieutenant Dawson."

"Yes, I noticed that you and the lieutenant were on friendly terms," George said in as even a tone as he could muster.

"He has been very kind and helpful while Father has been gone."

Sarah did not see the grimace that momentarily marred his face, her eyes focused on his hands that were clasping hers. With a free finger, she traced the silvery scar running across his left thumb. It was the result of a surgical scalpel slicing into him rather than a patient when a bungling fellow student shook during a procedure. He told her it was a constant reminder of incompetence and the result of not being confident.

"Lieutenant Dawson is a bit like me as well, shy I mean, if not as much so. I suppose it is natural to feel comfortable around those who share my problem. Those who are kindred souls, as you say." She raised her head, a perplexed cast to her face and brows knitted. "I have yet to understand why you suffer my deficiencies, you who are so assured and open with the world. In no time at all, you will grow vexed with a wife who cowers in the corner."

He reached up and stroked over her cheek. "I am confident that in no time you will grow vexed with a husband who brashly hogs the spotlight and will then shove me out of the way!" He flashed his most arrogant grin. "Whichever happens, I am content as long as you are waiting for me. We shall have a modest house of our own, perhaps in Byculla, you will want for nothing, and we shall be together, eventually with our children. What more can a man ask for in life? I have to tell you, Sarah Chambers, that if you meant to frighten me away you have failed."

He bent his head, his mouth zeroing in on the soft lips begging to be kissed. His touch was gentle, barely more than a brush of moistened lips tentatively savoring the sensation in anticipation for more, when a shout caused him to jerk away and hastily take a step to the side so he could see beyond the wide tree trunk they hid behind.

"Help! We need help! Has anyone seen Dr. White or Dr. Darcy? Dr. Darcy! Dr. White!"

In an instant, love and passion were forgotten, George dashing toward the frantic man as he shouted, "Here! I am here! What is it?"

The man swung about, relief mixed with blind panic. "The terrace. Hurry!"

"I left my medical bag with the servant at the door. Fetch it for me. Quickly!"

Brute force and George's baritone raised in command opened a gap through the press of bodies on the terrace and created space around the woman lying on the floor.

It was Sarah's mother, Lady Powis, her face pale and eyes filled with pain and fear as she gasped with each breath and clutched her left arm with a right hand stiffened into a claw. One of her lady friends knelt with Lady Powis's head resting on her lap and smoothed a wet cloth over her forehead.

"Stand back so she can breathe," George directed the press of spectators, "and get this off her." He grabbed the blanket that some well-intended person had thrown over her despite the oppressive heat and humidity and ripped it away. "A pillow, quick. That cushion there will do. Stay where you are, Mrs. Mason, and help me prop her up higher on your lap. Thank you. Slow your breathing, Lady Powis. Do you hear me? Inhale as deeply as you can. Yes, I know it hurts. Here, yes?" He held her eyes as he pushed the gauze fichu covering her left chest aside and lightly touched the skin over her heart. He paused to palpate the fluttering rhythm with his palm and then ran his fingertips up to her shoulder and down her arm until reaching the tight hand, kneading in a desperate attempt to ease the pain. He pried the gripping fingers away, soothing as he spoke, "Try to relax, my lady. Forgive me, but I need to listen to your heart."

Without waiting for consent, he bent and pressed his ear against her breast and closed his eyes to better concentrate on the faintly heard beats. Her heart was racing, the beats erratic, but he continued to auscultate for long minutes, his focus on ignoring the obvious for the subtle sounds hidden within and underneath. By the time he was satisfied with his diagnosis and lifted his head, Sarah had fought her way through the wall of witnesses and was kneeling at her mother's side. He spared only a rapid glance, his attention drawn to the black bag placed into his hands.

Mumbling his thanks, George opened the bag and withdrew two small, stoppered bottles. "I need a glass of water," he said to no one in particular, sending three people scrambling for a pitcher. "Lady Powis." He leaned forward inches from her face, holding her gaze and speaking with a unique melding of command and comfort. "Open your mouth and take the medicine I have here. It is bitter but will alleviate the pain in your chest. Trust me. It is crushed willow bark and hawthorn, the latter excellent for strengthening the heart and restoring a regular rhythm. There, that's good. Very brave of you, my lady. I know it tastes horrid. Have a sip of water to wash the bitterness away, just a swallow for now. Concentrate on slowing your breathing if you can. Your heart is starved for oxygen, which is causing the pain, and breathing as deeply as possible will help. Now chew a bit more for me. Excellent." He pressed two fingers against the hollow on her neck and smiled. "Your pulse is slower already and the pain is ebbing, isn't it? Yes, I can tell. That is most excellent. I know this is frightening, but the short duration of your episode is a good sign of—"

A series of abrupt exclamations and shuffling from the group watching the proceedings interrupted George's softly spoken encouragement. People hastily stepped aside to allow Lord Powis to storm through.

"Can she be moved?" Lord Powis asked.

George blinked in surprise, the question not what he expected to be asked first. "Yes. In fact I was about to suggest it. Lady Powis is swiftly recovering from her attack but rest in a quiet, hopefully cooler place is best."

Lord Powis nodded curtly, and with a snap of his fingers, several servants hastened to do his bidding. In no time at all, Lady Powis was lifted onto a cot and carried between two servants toward her bedchamber. George kept two fingertips on the pulse at her wrist and walked alongside until at the door, only letting go when Sarah grasped his arm.

"Stay with her, George. Promise me you will not let him bully you away."

George did not need to ask who she was referring to. "Do not worry, Sarah. I am not so easily bullied and am certainly not afraid of Dr. White. I will stay with her." He squeezed her hand and smiled to reassure. Hastily turning to enter the room before being shut out, on purpose or accidentally, George nearly ran into Lord Powis standing in the doorway.

His lordship held the door open, waiting for George to enter and clearly privy to the familiar exchange between the physician and his daughter, but his face was unreadable.

For thirty minutes, George attended to Lady Powis while her husband stood at the foot of the bed with arms crossed in front of his chest. His eyes trailed George's every move, but he said nothing. George ignored him. His purpose was centered on administering the proper dosage of dried digitalis leaves—a tricky bit of work due to the potential for toxicity—and a mild sedative.

Once Lady Powis was sleeping soundly, breathing normally and with a steady heartbeat, he rose from his perch on the side of her bed and approached

Lord Powis. Just as he parted his lips with the intent to whisper a full report, a tumult and an angry voice was heard in the corridor.

"How dare you stand in my way! I am Lady Powis's physician and demand that you let me pass!"

George's anger flared, and he rushed toward the door with Lord Powis a mere half step behind. The crash of something falling to the floor was followed by the reverberating bang of someone hitting the wall. George grabbed the knob and wrenched the door open. A servant was tumbling to the carpet, having bounced off the wall, leaving a crack in the paneling at about elbow height. A second unfortunate servant dashing to aid his comrade was caught in the downward momentum, both footmen tangled in a heap. Dr. White stood on unsteady feet with one hand as a vise on Sarah's upper arm and the other lifted with intent to strike.

"I'll teach you to defy me, you pathetic—"

Whatever slur he planned to toss was lost in a gush of air as George bodily slammed into the obese doctor, grabbing both wrists in the process and pinning him against the opposite wall.

"You ever lay one hand on her again, and I promise I will kill you!"

"You insufferable, arrogant guttersnipe. Lady Powis is my patient, and I should have been called to treat her!"

"You *were* called, but from the smell of you, I guess you were busy swimming in a beer keg. Thank God I got there before your drunken ass!"

White cursed and attempted futilely to shove George away. "Swine! You shall pay for your insolence. Now let go of me so I can see *my* patient!"

"She is no longer your patient, Dr. White. Lady Powis will henceforth be cared for by Dr. Darcy."

Lord Powis's blunt tone cut through the tension cleaner than a razor through butter. White pivoted his bulging eyes to his benefactor, as did George, both stunned at his lordship's calm composure. He stood by the now-closed door to his wife's bedchamber, face as impassive as it was the entire time George treated Lady Powis. As far as George could tell, Lord Powis had not glanced at Sarah, who had backed away and was leaning heavily against the corridor table.

"My lord! You cannot be serious! I have been treating Lady Powis for years, most efficiently—"

"Like hell you have," George interjected. "Her heart is weak, but nothing that cannot be treated with the proper medicine and change in diet. If you bothered to read the latest studies, you would know she needs exercise, digitalis, hawthorn, and a few other medicines she was not receiving, probably because you never heard of them. Did you ever condescend to listen to her heartbeat?"

Dr. White looked more horrified than he had a second before. "I would never violate a lady in such a way! Do you not see how infectious such behavior is, my lord? You cannot allow this!"

"What I cannot and will not allow is a brawl in my house. Nor will I allow Lady Powis to suffer needlessly. You are dismissed, Dr. White. I suggest you leave peacefully this instant before I lose my patience with you completely. The consequences of that would not be to your liking, I think."

The threat was obvious even to the half-inebriated Dr. White. Yet he remained pressed into the wall when George released him, his face set in shock.

"Dr. Darcy, come with me to my study. I wish to consult with you on my wife's medical needs. Sarah"—Lord Powis reached to pat his daughter's pale cheek—"go sit with your mother. And drink a glass of strong wine. I think you need it. Follow me, Dr. Darcy." And without another look at anyone, Lord Powis walked away.

George flashed a reassuring smile toward Sarah and made sure the servants were attending to the removal of the paralyzed White before hastening after Lord Powis.

At the end of the corridor, Lord Powis entered a moderate-sized room with two cushioned chairs and a long settee clustered in the middle. Off to the right was a large desk scattered with papers and books flanked with three filled bookcases. Lord Powis ignored all of this, heading directly toward the open window, where a view of the azure sea could be seen. He withdrew a handkerchief from his pocket and held it firmly over his mouth and nose as a series of raspy coughs burst forth.

George waited near the shut door, listening and observing Lord Powis. In those moments, the crisis with Lady Powis was shoved aside as tuned diagnostic skills cataloged the various signs and formed a tentative diagnosis he was not eager to prove true. At present, any speculations regarding Lord Powis's health could not be investigated, a reality Lord Powis made clear once he caught his breath and turned to look at George.

"Dr. Darcy, thank you for responding to the call for assistance when Lady Powis collapsed."

"I am a physician, my lord." George bowed his head respectfully. "It is my duty and my pleasure to use my skills where needed."

"Yes. I gathered as much. I am also sure you are aware that not all physicians possess the same sense of duty or pleasure?"

"Unfortunately I must agree with you, as much as it pains me to do so."

"Indeed. Now"—Lord Powis gestured to one of the chairs as he sat into the other—"explain to me what you think Lady Powis suffers from and how best to cure it."

"I can only base my opinion on what I have seen today, coupling that with subtle signs noted upon other occasions. I am aware of Lady Powis's history to a minor degree," George glossed over where he had obtained that information, "and would need to question her further in order to be one hundred percent sure of her condition and how best to treat it long term. Curing her condition is another matter entirely, and I can make no promises in that regard. That it is her heart which ails her is not a surprise to you, of course. Today she experienced angina pectoris, which simply means 'strangling tightness and pain in the chest' caused by insufficient oxygen delivered to the muscles of the heart."

For ten minutes, George explained the differences between angina and a severe heart seizure, discussed the causes and treatment modalities, and delved into some of the newer studies. Lord Powis asked some questions but mostly he listened intently without comment. When George ran out of information to share, Lord Powis rose from the chair and paced back to the window. He stared outside for several minutes, the handkerchief used for another short coughing spell, before he turned back to George, who had risen as well.

"Thank you for the lengthy explanation, Dr. Darcy. You have told me more in the past quarter hour than Dr. White ever has. I see that piece of information does not surprise you."

"No, it does not. I suppose there is no point pretending after our exchange in the hall. We dislike each other intensely, based in large part on his medical incompetency."

"So you say." Lord Powis held his palm up to halt George's imminent retort. "Hear me out, Dr. Darcy. The reasons for enlisting Dr. White as our physician are personal and I would prefer not to discuss them." He searched George's eyes for a hint of knowledge, but George shielded his thoughts and presented a calm stare in return. "Despite your claims to his utter incompetency, Dr. White has tended to Lady Powis's needs well enough these past several years. To be blunt, I have little faith in young men who think they know everything and disdain the wisdom that comes from age and experience. When I first heard the reports of your skills, I was skeptical at best. I find it difficult to imagine a man of your age with a medical degree at all, let alone the expertise to contend with a doctor of older years. Nevertheless, I am not above admitting I may be wrong. And when it comes to my wife, I am willing to take a chance."

He stepped closer to George. "If you will accept the assignment, Doctor, I am asking you to stay here for the time being and attend to Lady Powis. I greatly desire to see her health improve and am interested in discovering if you are as good as the rumors say. Will you do this for us?"

"I would consider it an honor to assume care of Lady Powis, your lordship, but my one condition is that I have exclusive authority, meaning that Dr. White is not allowed to interfere in any way or to see Lady Powis."

"Agreed." Lord Powis nodded once, although he held George's eyes with a penetrating, assessing stare that spoke volumes. "Never doubt that I will be watching you, however, and if I see the tiniest sign of failure, I will be calling Dr. White back. And I want constant reports. I will have a room prepared for you a few doors down from Lady Powis's suite. A man can be sent to retrieve anything you need from your bungalow in Bombay or the hospital."

"Thank you, my lord. I will make a list of items I require. If I may, I will include some medicines I know to ease a consumptive cough."

Lord Powis looked truly startled for the first time since rushing to his wife's side on the terrace. For a stunned minute, he gaped at George before smoothing his facial muscles into the icy expression George was growing familiar with. He nodded curtly but said nothing. Instead, he gestured toward the door in dismissal.

As George grasped the doorknob, Lord Powis confirmed his awareness of the one topic George had deemed inappropriate to broach under the circumstances. "My daughter's chambers are also on this wing, Dr. Darcy. On the other end of the hall from where I will house you. It will be obvious which door is hers because one of my servants will be guarding it at all times. I trust I am clear?"

The parting comment from Lord Powis delivered in a firm, matter-of-fact tone left George with no clue if the viscount was expressing fatherly caution to an ardent lover or issuing a warning that his daughter was off-limits completely. The uncertainty set George's nerves on edge. Ever the optimist, George decided to use the unique opportunity to present himself in the best possible light.

A fair portion of each day was spent tending to Lady Powis. Ever the physician above all, George devoted the bulk of his energies to testing the best medicine combinations, observing the outcomes, and ensuring her ladyship's regained health. She never mentioned Dr. White, and to George's relief, the hated man never appeared.

A steady stream of visitors flooded the mansion that week. Most came to see the viscount regarding the myriad business affairs to handle after his lordship's long absence. To George's annoyance one person who visited on a daily basis was Lieutenant Dawson. George wondered at Dawson's sudden attachment to Lord Powis rather than the Bombay Command, but when he questioned Dawson the response, "I am helping him with particular arrangements," was irritatingly unenlightening. At each visit Dawson made a point of engaging Sarah, a vexation that flared George's jealousy.

Lord Powis insisted on a report of Lady Powis's condition each morning, but he kept the conversation on topic and then brusquely dismissed George. It was frustrating but with scant else to do but accept the situation, George made the best of it.

Nearly a week passed before a surprise summons offered him the opportunity he sought.

"Dr. Darcy, thank you for coming so swiftly." Lord Powis gestured to the chair across from the desk where he sat. "I hope I did not disturb anything important?"

"I was playing backgammon with your delightful daughter, and I am saved the humiliation of another defeat."

"I had no idea Sarah was a backgammon master. Or is it that you are a dismal player?"

"The former, actually. Usually the dice are in my favor. I do have the upper hand at tennis, thankfully." George leaned forward. "If I may beg your pardon, Lord Powis, the mention of Miss Chambers is a perfect opening for me to ask a question of you that has been weighing upon my mind for some weeks now."

"I know what you wish to ask me, Dr. Darcy, and that is partly why I called for you. I am not averse to granting your wish in regards to my daughter; however, before you commit yourself, I need to share some information with you first. Will you indulge me? Thank you." Lord Powis looked down at the papers spread across his desk as if searching for a hint of where to begin. Finally seeming to gather his thoughts he started with a question of his own. "Your reports of Lady Powis's condition have been positive. Do you feel she is stable enough for travel?"

George leaned back into the chair and frowned. "That would depend on the type of travel, I suppose. Her heart is stronger and I have every hope that it will remain on a path of improvement with continued treatment and medical oversight. Overall, her health is excellent for a woman of her years. I know she loves to travel, based on her stories. Mental attitude can often be more important than physical, you see. Where are you planning on going?"

"What about me?" Lord Powis asked instead of answering. "Am I fit for travel?" George's brows rose in surprise at the viscount's oblique reference to his own health. Lord Powis's smile was faintly humorous. "I owe you an apology, Doctor."

"My lord?"

"At our first conversation, I said that I found it difficult to believe a man as young as you could be a good doctor. In general, I still think that with age comes wisdom; however, in the case of medical knowledge, I am changing my mind. It is a subject I know next to nothing of, and my ignorance shows through. We live in a changing world that is moving so fast." He glanced toward the window, his eyes distant for a few seconds before looking back at George. "I now see that this rapid change affects the art of healing in a profound way. What you have accomplished for my wife, and for my daughter, in such a short time is remarkable. It proves the truth of the rumors. You, Dr. Darcy, are an excellent physician."

"Thank you, my lord. I appreciate the compliment. You are correct that the advances in medical knowledge are changing daily. I am sure I have already missed much by being away from the university and London hospitals this past year. However, it isn't true that experience is not to be valued. I certainly hope that my skills ten or twenty years from now are vastly superior to what they are at this moment. Reading all the books or research papers in the world cannot take the place of learning by doing. I am on a journey of discovery, my lord.

Keeping my mind and eyes and ears open for new techniques, or old techniques if they work, and the chance to work with other healers is how I believe my skills will advance. Ultimately it must be a combination. Keeping abreast of the latest discoveries as well as seeking out treatments that are lost or lesser known, all the while not being afraid to delve in and get one's hands dirty, as it were, is the only way for a physician to excel."

"You are passionate. I admire and encourage this, but it does confuse me. A year ago, Dr. White diagnosed that I have consumption. He hesitated to give me that diagnosis, danced around it, in fact, and never seemed too sure of the label or how best to treat it. You, on the other hand, came to the same conclusion within minutes of talking to me and without laying a hand upon me." He cocked his head. "How did you do that?"

"It is a gift," George answered.

"Yes, I believe it is. So, what is your prognosis for me, Dr. Darcy? Am I fit to travel?"

George stared into Lord Powis's eyes, assessing, and then scanned over his face, examining each feature before moving on to the strong hands lying placidly atop a stack of papers on the desktop. "Your prognosis is that you will die from your disease if something else does not strike you first, but you already know that." Lord Powis nodded ever so faintly. "There is no cure yet, and there are various types of consumptive lung disorders, *phthisis* as Hippocrates called it, with varying symptoms and causes. I would need to examine you fully to ascertain the severity, but with proper care, I can assure with relative confidence that you will not be departing this earth for a while. I say travel while you can, my lord. Just be sure to keep a ready supply of medicine with you and seek help when you can. I would not suggest being far from proper medical care for long. Nor Lady Powis either, for that matter."

"I quite agree with you." Lord Powis held George's gaze thoughtfully before continuing. "There is a purpose to this apparently rambling conversation, Doctor. I decided some months ago to move my family back to England. Coming here has not been a mistake precisely, but perhaps we were hasty. Rather, I was hasty. Lady Powis was willing to do as I deemed necessary for us… under the circumstances."

George deciphered the unspoken query, and with a single nod let the viscount know that he was aware of the deceased Jane. The flash of emotion that crossed Lord Powis's face was brief and he quickly went on with his stunning revelation.

"Sarah was adverse to leaving England, although she never said much one way or the other. I assume it does not astonish you, Doctor, that my daughter is difficult to understand. You have managed to break through her barrier, and I appreciate that and pray you can help her to overcome her"—he waved his hand as he searched for the right word—"reticence completely. I have had no luck and confess to having largely given up. Whatever the case, we came and now I know it was not the best choice and it is time to go home. I have plans to leave in two weeks. I never anticipated the daughter who has resisted all attempts of mine at matchmaking with not one but two men asking for her hand in marriage. It complicates things."

George did not think he could be more shocked. Luckily, Lord Powis answered the unspoken questions for him. Unluckily, the answers were not to his liking.

"The fact is, both of you are worthy men who my daughter apparently holds affection for. I have rarely seen her at such ease with anyone else, especially not a man. It is remarkable. I know she is most drawn to you, Dr. Darcy, with a woman's passions driving her as they are not with Lieutenant Dawson. Yet he is more like her, their temperaments similar, so the connection is logical. My confusion is in what you have in common with her. How do you reconcile your passionate drive with her docile demeanor? To be frank, I can't understand it at all. Why Sarah?"

"Dawson? Dawson asked to marry Sarah?"

"Yes. Four days ago."

George felt as if his head was going to explode. It was inconceivable! Everyone knew George and Sarah were courting. And here that sneaky, conniving snake was going behind his back and attempting to steal the woman he loved, and who loved him! George was sick with anger.

"I see this news is unexpected, but from what I have been told, Lieutenant Dawson has been most attentive to Sarah for months now. He was eloquent in his sentiments toward her and, as I said, the match does make sense. What I need to hear from you, Dr. Darcy, are your sentiments regarding Sarah. Do you love her? Do you think you can make her happy? Tell me why I should give her to you over Dawson."

Lord Powis's words cut through the fog of conflicting emotions. George had not expected a competitor or the complication of her parents leaving India. Perhaps it was his towering arrogance biting him again. Suddenly, the picture of Sarah talking and laughing easily with Lieutenant Dawson as he had witnessed on a number of occasions did not appear so innocent. In a flash, he realized that what he said in the next breath was critical or his hopes for a future with Sarah at his side would be lost.

George scooted to the edge of his chair and straightened his back. Staring into Lord Powis's eyes and imbuing his voice with the full power of his resonant timbre, he made his plea.

"Lord Powis, I do love your daughter. Poetry is not my strong suit, so I shan't try to express my feelings in that way, but trust me when I say that all the pretty phrases in all the poetry ever written for lovers is a mere fragment of my love for Sarah. Moreover, I know she feels the same for me. She has made that clear in a host of ways. Nothing indecent or improper," he hastily added at the dark glower directed his way, "but I am sure you can appreciate that a woman's affection toward a man can be shown within the boundaries of propriety. We have talked of our life together, and she has consented to be my wife, pending your approval naturally. I assure you, upon my honor as a Darcy and with all that I am, I will strive to do whatever it takes to make Sarah happy."

"Including returning to England with us? I approve of you, Dr. Darcy. I truly do. I am not convinced that you and Sarah are ultimately compatible, but then I have also confessed my lack of comprehension when it comes to my daughter, so who am I to judge? As it happens, this relationship is of benefit to all of us. My daughter marries a man who she loves and who loves her, that a rarity in this world, and my wife and I have our own private physician."

"What? I don't... I can't..."

"Here it is. I will consent to your marriage to Sarah and you will return to England with us as her husband. As compensation for your lack of title or inheritance, you will be our physician. Naturally you can set up a modest gentleman's practice once we are settled in Nottinghamshire if you wish, as long as it does not interfere too greatly. Our estate is not too far from Pemberley so that is fortunate. The estate and title will pass to my nephew when I die, but I have already arranged for a substantial settlement for Lady Powis and Sarah so you shall want for nothing."

"My lord," George burst in, "please understand that this is impossible! I only arrived in India a year ago. Less, actually, and have a contract that binds me to the East India Company."

"That is of no concern. I have already spoken with Commander Doyle and sent a dispatch to the Governor of Bombay. An early dismissal can be arranged."

George could not believe his ears. It was too incredible to be real! He did not know whether to laugh at the ridiculousness of the situation, scream in frustration, or cry at the agonizing pain piercing through his insides. Return to England? Miles from Pemberley? Reduced to nothing more than a country physician shackled to one family? It was not possible. Not in any way.

"My contract is not the only issue. I cannot return to England, not now at least. I *need* to be here. I *want* to be here, in India. Do you not understand? You said yourself that I am a gifted physician with passion and skill. No offense intended, but I cannot be anyone's personal physician. It would be too stifling!"

"Precisely the point I was making, Doctor. I don't believe you would be happy unless pursuing your craft, and it would be a shame not to do so. However, I will not leave Sarah in India to be left alone while you travel about advancing your knowledge. That is not the life for her."

"It should be her choice, not yours," George countered hotly. Immediately he bit his lip at the cold cast to Lord Powis's face, but he did not look away.

"I disagree with you. It is my choice to make. I am her father. I have already lost one daughter and will not lose another. Not if I have an option and fortunately I do."

"You mean Dawson? Surely you cannot seriously consider his proposal?"

"I do consider it seriously. As I said, my utmost concern is my family's happiness. Sarah may not love Lieutenant Dawson as she thinks she does you, but that would change in time. He is willing to move with us and has a pronounced inheritance waiting for him, as it turns out. Nevertheless, I approve of you in a number of ways, including your skills as a physician that has proven miraculous for my wife and I. As I see it, we have something the other wants; therefore, an arrangement that is mutually beneficial is logical. I am offering the best solution for everyone. I am willing to give my only surviving child to a man I admire but have reservations about as it pertains to being a husband to her. I will consent as long as you bow to the conditions as proof of your devotion. That is the offer, Dr. Darcy. The choice is now yours."

George rose from the chair and walked away from the desk. If he sat looking into the viscount's coldly calculating eyes for one second more he would do or say something that he knew he would later regret. His insides churned and every muscle in his body was tense. How had this hour, anticipated as one to be remembered with rejoicing, turned into a horrific drama worthy of a Shakespearean tragedy? He could not comprehend it at all. Yet as his fists clenched with the yearning to hit something, or someone, his mind began to cool. He knew one thing for sure: He was not a man who could be bought or controlled.

George turned to Lord Powis, who still sat regally in the large chair behind the desk with his emotionless gaze locked onto George's face. George's mind clicked down the list of possible arguments one by one, discarding them all as futile against the stern man in front of him. In the end, he realized he had nothing to say at this juncture.

So after a slight incline of his head as a show of respect, George pivoted away and exited the room.

Walking in a stupor, George was halfway down the stairs before drawing up short and stopping. Automatically, his feet had been taking him back to the parlor where he had left Sarah and the unfinished backgammon board. A sliver of coherency knew that it was unwise to face her until he could think through the riot of emotions, so he turned left to make for the small herb garden outside the kitchen.

A murmur of voices did not impress upon his clouded mind, but a familiar laugh did. Before George could puzzle out why Sarah was now in the library rather than the parlor where he had last seen her, the feminine laugh was joined by a masculine chuckle and voice equally familiar but decidedly not as welcome. The friendly inflections and warm tones were louder than the individual words, piercing his heart as an ice pick would.

Blindly he made for the garden, Dawson and Sarah's laughter ringing in his ears after the door shut behind him. Staggering to the bench, George sat heavily and stared sightlessly at a rosemary bush while forcing his emotions aside so he could clinically examine the predicament he now found himself in.

As the minutes passed, his eyes focused—first upon the individual rosemary flowers and glossy stems, then upon the rough gravel covering the path under his feet. Lifting his eyes, he scanned over the garden, across to the thick hedge surrounding, and then to the glimpse of blue surf far beyond the branches of the shrouding trees. He inhaled, sucking in the humid air rich with exotic aromas. India had infused into his veins, and although still very much a man of English heritage with the beliefs and desires that had been crafted into his cells, George recognized the subtle changes.

"I love it here," he said aloud.

There was a hint of surprise in the tone, but for the most part he uttered it with firm conviction. No longer was it a matter of not wanting to return to England for all the reasons he had said; it was just as much about not wanting to leave India. There were so many places spoken of and read about in this vast country that he dreamed of visiting.

No, he could not leave India. Of that he was certain.

What about Sarah?

George winced at the answer. Then he bowed his head, burying his face into his palms, and gave in to the misery consuming him.

❧

The day before Sarah was scheduled to sail for England was also the day of her marriage to Lieutenant Dawson. That evening George sat at a corner table in Henry's, an English-style pub, with his back to the crowded room and his third tankard of dark ale between his palms. Hopefully, by nightfall, he would be thoroughly drunk and thus incapable of envisioning the newlyweds engaged in the act of consummating their marriage. Maybe before then he would find a willing female and do some consummating himself. Would that efficiently supplant his vivid imagination? Would physical pleasure and release ease the pain felt throughout his entire body? He knew it wouldn't any more than getting utterly foxed would.

Still, he drained the tankard in one long swallow and held his hand up in the universal gesture all pub attendants knew to be a request for another. George's head was spinning rather pleasantly but his thoughts remained too clear for his liking. He always had possessed a notable ability to withstand the effects of alcohol longer than most men. Not that he had ever tested the extreme limits more than a handful of times. George appreciated a fine wine or well-brewed ale or sharp whiskey, but his profession did not allow for unsteady hands or fuzzy brains.

He mentally ran through the list of alternative spirits with stronger potency, ignoring the sensible voice inside his head that told him this was pointless. He could not stop the pain. Maybe he could suspend it for a time, but it would come back with a vengeance tomorrow. Worse yet, George's overpowering guilt demanded that he accept the pain as his punishment.

Hell, maybe that's a good reason to get slobbering drunk and bed a whore, he thought, *so that I can add on the torment of morning-after illness and a case of the clap to my penitence.*

"I never thought I would see the day that the superior, perfect Dr. Darcy would be alone in a pub dipping in deep. Whatever could be the reason for such wallowing in an ale barrel?"

"Go away," George growled. He did not need to take his eyes off the half-empty tankard to know Dr. White was grinning with satisfaction. He had been wearing a smugly evil expression for the past week whenever George was unlucky enough to encounter him.

"Now, now. Is that any way to talk to your superior?" White emphasized the last word. He sat down at George's table and crossed his fat legs casually.

"I said, *go away*," George repeated in a deeper growl accented with a fierce glare. "You are not invited to sit at my table, White."

"It is a public place, Darcy, and filling up fast. Empty chairs are hard to find. Besides, can't comrades sit and drink together? I shall celebrate while you mourn, how's that?" White lifted the glass of port he held in his hand. "Here's to the new Mr. and Mrs. Dawson."

He swallowed a gulp without waiting for George to raise his mug. "It was a lovely wedding. The bride was radiant as one would expect and Dawson enraptured with his love."

"Please," George begged, closing his eyes and forgetting his hatred of White in the rush of acute agony. But Dr. White showed no mercy.

"Pity you were not invited, after all you have done for the family. But I suppose that would have been awkward under the circumstances. I was there despite our recent falling out," he added pleasantly. "How could I not be when I was instrumental in bringing the young lovers together?"

"Leave! I don't want to hear any more of your gloating and lies."

"Lies? I have said nothing that is an untruth."

"What are you talking about?"

"Ah! I thought you would never ask. It never once occurred to you to wonder how shy, docile Reed advanced so quickly? Did you ever wonder how he found the courage to engage Miss Chambers, to woo her right in front of you, and then ask for her hand in marriage before you? No, of course you didn't. You are too arrogant and cocksure. Dr. George Darcy who is smarter than everyone, smarter than me. Well, here is a lesson for you, boy," he sneered, leaning forward, all traces of false friendliness gone. "With age comes experience *and* connections. Maybe I am not as brilliant a doctor as you, but I am not an idiot. I know who to talk to and what to say. A nudge here and a nudge there will accomplish much. The right people given the right reminder of a diligent officer will take note earlier than they might have originally. A casual letter to a busy father will cause him to put in a word to those in authority for his son's career. Encouragement from a caring patron will do much to spark a fire under a lovesick man." He chuckled evilly. "Don't worry too much, Darcy. Dawson is innocent. He loves Miss Chambers and has for years. I just helped him to move boldly forward. He was thankful, and right about now, I am guessing his new wife is receiving the full thrust of his passionate adoration."

The insinuating turn of phrase was not lost on the stricken George. It was the final straw to what had been the second worse blow to his heart so far in his short life. He snapped. White did not see it coming. The punch that launched him backward out of the chair was followed by another and another. Later, George would remember little of the specifics. He only remembered a haze of blood red curtaining his eyes and the perverse satisfaction of hitting a man he hated beyond measure. Best of all was that while pummeling White, who rallied and retaliated with a number of impressive clouts of his own, George's internal pain was replaced by the physical.

At least for a time, he did not think of Sarah.

GEORGE'S MEMOIRS
JANUARY 17, 1791

We arrived in Daman today earlier than expected so naturally made straight for the hospital. After four months, I am no longer surprised that Dr. Ullas's preferred destination when entering a new town is whatever medical facility serves as a hospital rather than the quarters we are to stay in. Even when not sure where we will be housed, or if arriving late in the evening, when supper and a wash sound like heaven on earth, he insists on checking in. That is his quirk and I have to admit that there is some logic to it, Alex. It sets the stage for what to expect on the following day if nothing else.

So we made our introductions and ended up lending our services for a couple of hours. Personally, I was anxious to walk to the ocean and sit in the sand for a while. Something about warm sand, fresh sea breezes, and waves that is so soothing. As long as I am seeing them lapping and undulating from the safety of stationary ground, mind you! I have missed the sea during these months of traversing alongside the rivers of Surat and Khandesh. Strange how the sea can now call to me when we grew up miles from the ocean, isn't it, Alex?

That mystery aside, I felt the need for hours of solitude. I have had precious little of it lately, not that I am complaining, mind you. These months away from Bombay have been exhilarating. I am a new man! I have seen so much already and learned enormously from Dr. Ullas and the others. My God, he never fails to amaze me! Dare I pray that I shall someday be the miraculous doctor he is? Is that too much to hope for, Alex? I am over my surprise at how well versed he is in Western medical philosophy. I no longer raise my brows when he quotes Boerhaave, Ernst Stahl, Hunter, and a dozen others within the same breath. He does love a good debate. But then so do I, as I am sure you remember, my brother. I never could let an argument rest and know I frustrated you to no end, which, of course, was the point at the time, but now I regret driving you crazy. Still, those skills are aiding me now. Dr. Ullas and I can become heated, although I am sure he is aware just as I am that it is an act designed to increase our mutual mental acumen. Ha! Three days ago I found a copy of Erasmus Darwin's The Botanic Garden, *of which there has been such controversy, and reading it aloud led to a three-hour discussion on theories of biological transformationism, electrophysiology as espoused by Galvani and others, and the living anatomy* Naturphilosophie *of Haller. It was fabulous. He offers insights from all sides of an issue, almost to the point of making it difficult to pin down what he truly believes. Yet I am certain that for all his knowledge of Western ideas, he is a Hindu at the core. When he speaks of Ayurvedic medicine, I grow silent in awe. Yes, I grow silent. How shocking is that? He has lent me his copy of the* Caraka Samhita, *translated of course, since Sanskrit is beyond me, and little by little I am beginning to grasp the concepts and medical teachings. Modern science has moved ahead in many respects, but it is fascinating to see how much of these ancient remedies are still the standards of today. I am beginning to glean how lacking my education and how far my potential can lead me. When we are in Thana, Dr. Ullas has promised to give me a copy of the* Kama Sutra, Susruta Samhita, *and a few others, including the writings of Madhavakara. Dr. Ullas says that in order to understand Indian medicine of today, I need to understand where it came from and the philosophies involved. I agree. I also want to delve into the Islamic medical practices of* Yūnānī, *even if not as commonly seen here as they are in the north. Indeed, these are the tip of the iceberg, Alex. I now embrace the reality that my education shall never end, at least as long as my insatiable curiosity controls me.*

Getting back to today, I left all my reading material behind and sat on the sand within the shelter of a rock cluster and let my mind drift. We will soon be in Thana. Dr. Ullas has invited me to stay for as long as I wish before returning to Bombay. I will definitely tarry for the fiftieth birthday party of the Sardar, Thakore Sahib Pandey Dhamdhere, who I now know is Dr. Ullas's wife's father and a cousin of the Peshwa. I met him briefly in September before we left on this journey. Imposing man but there was a warm glint to his eyes. He is powerful, rich, and lives in a stunning palace, so I am anticipating a party to end all parties! How could I miss that? And, no, I am not simply avoiding being back in Bombay. Oddly I am anxious to go back. Does that revelation surprise you, Alex? Well it does me! That is what occupied my thoughts as I sat on the beach today. Let me see if I can place it into a few sentences.

I began to see a pattern that made me uncomfortable. First, I left England to escape memories of you. Then I left Bombay to escape memories of Sarah. Sure I was more or less forced to take a hiatus from my duties in Bombay, but I did not vigorously argue the point with Doyle either. It has bothered me that I might be a bit of a coward. You can imagine how this possibility would discredit my asserted confidence! I am far too arrogant to allow for any flaws to my character! Dr. Ullas maintains that fate plays a large part in our destinies. He never asked why I agreed to embark on this journey with him, but if he does know, I doubt he is crying over White's forced retirement from the EIC. He has expressed his desire to have me as a part of his team and offered me a permanent post. It is tempting to accept his offer, let me tell you! But I need to prove to myself that I am not a coward. I need to know for sure that when I join Dr. Ullas it is not because I am running away. We have spoken of these matters briefly and he has a maddening habit of growing very Hindu when we do! That is when he speaks of destinies and God's will and other Hindu beliefs I do not comprehend. Oddly, although our gods are different, his words echo what the Pemberley rector taught us. Without launching into a dissertation on religious tenets, the idea is that, though it may feel as if I was running away, it was all part of the grand design to give me what my heart desires, that being to travel India and learn. As wonderful as that sounds, I still need to prove myself worthy, I guess. Maybe I am simply not yet willing to admit that my relationship with Sarah was doomed from the outset. I don't relish feeling guilty or brokenhearted forever, and for the most part, I have let go of those negative emotions. Perhaps too easily, in fact, and that bothers me a bit too. Shouldn't I still be torn up over losing the woman I wanted to spend my life with? Dr. Ullas would say no. He would say to accept the reality and move on. Maybe in time I will learn to be as accepting, but for now I guess I am too English!

So my plan is to head back to Bombay after I recuperate from the Sardar's birthday. That promises to give me much to write about!

CHAPTER FOUR

Kalyan

FEBRUARY 1791

FOUR MONTHS AS TRAVELING companions had led to a growing familiarity between George and Dr. Ullas, but the older physician had remained somewhat aloof. Yet as soon as the wheels of their *tanga* touched the dirt of the open road after leaving Daman for Kalyan, where his family awaited, Dr. Ullas started talking with an easy openness George had not seen previously.

Kshitij Ullas had been born fifty years ago in a village far to the south in Mysore. He was the tenth child in a family that would eventually number thirteen children who lived to adulthood. Being people of strong faith, and a fair dose of superstition, their great fortune in regards to healthy prosperity was attributed to the school of Ayurvedic medicine located in the city of Mysore.

"The science of Ayurveda encompasses the eight components of medicine, which, in turn, arise from the need for balance and proper measure of the elements and energies every human body possesses." Dr. Ullas handed George a cloth square upon which was woven an intricate and colorful picture of the Ayurveda concept. "These humors and *doṣas* are unique to each person and closely linked to spirituality. The sacred Vedas enlighten us as to all aspects of living, including medicine. Practitioners of Ayurveda are often looked upon as holy men with their lives devoted to healing. We certainly saw them as such.

Miracle workers from the gods some said. Of course, they are fallible men, same as others, but those who embrace the art do possess a harmony and skill that is miraculous. Witnessing such a one is awe-inspiring. Witnessing dozens at a time is indescribable. Many young boys were captivated, including me and four of my brothers. Vish, Aatish, and Hakesh still live around Mysore and exclusively practice Ayurveda. Mihir and I were not as contented."

He chuckled and shook his head. "Mihir left as soon as he could, and I have not heard from him in over a decade. He was forever the adventurous one and has either been eaten by a tiger or is in an African jungle where the post does not deliver. I might have followed him, probably would have in fact, but instead I fell in love."

This time he dug deep into his traveling bag and withdrew an object bundled within layers of cloth. It was a medallion no larger than an English sovereign, the painting of the Indian woman worn and chipped in spots but clear enough to reveal a plain but pleasant face.

"Her name was Ira. We married when I was nineteen and she sixteen. In short order, we welcomed three daughters, and any dreams I had to journey away were ended. Mihir was long gone when Ira died giving birth to our son. Our families assumed care of the children, as is our custom, while I continued to serve as the village healer. In time, my wanderlust asserted itself."

Dr. Ullas took the portrait back from George and gazed at the faded image for a minute before resuming his narrative while rewrapping it.

Fate and world affairs played a large part, as Dr. Ullas stated it, with the outbreak of the First Mysore War in 1767 presenting the opening he secretly yearned for. Physicians were needed and he joined several others who heard the call, traveling to Madras and becoming army doctors. That decision set him on a path that would eventually lead him all over the east, as far north as Bengal, ofttimes serving the military during the frequent wars that cropped up, usually with the British. He also branched out as an itinerate physician, happy to apply his skill wherever necessary and in something other than patching up sword wounds.

"I once studied through my journals and concluded that the longest I dwelt in one place was six months, and that was because we were snowbound in Nepal."

"Did you ever go home? To Mysore?"

"Three times," Dr. Ullas answered. "The last was ten years past now. My daughters are grown and married. My son became an Ayurveda healer, much to my pride. My parents are gone and brothers old. Our lives have changed," he said with a hint of sadness.

It was while serving with the Maratha Confederacy in 1776 that Kshitij met Thakore Sahib Pandey Dhamdhere, who was then a commander and loyal to the legal Peshwa Sawai Madhavrao II. During the bitter war against the Bombay Presidency, when they chose to support the usurper and murderer Raghunathrao, Pandey was grievously wounded and nearly died. Dr. Ullas arrived in the nick of time to assume care, Pandey surviving his injuries and later leading a major offensive against the British at Sipri. It was a decisive victory that led to the 1782 Treaty of Salbai and the current peace between the two great nations.

"Pandey was most grateful and declared all sorts of promised payments. I thought little of them, having no desire for wealth or rank even if I had considered it necessary to be remunerated for doing what I am called to do. Among the promises was the choice of any of his daughters as wife." Dr. Ullas laughed heartily in remembrance. "Honestly, I paid no more attention to that one than all the others. Until, that is, while resting at his *griha* in Kalyan over a year later, he suddenly parades all sixteen of his unmarried daughters in front of me and tells me to take my pick!"

George joined him in the laughter. "What did you do?"

"Ah, you may be surprised, Dr. Darcy, as was I at the time, but I realized I liked the notion of being married again and establishing a home and family. I did insist on speaking with each daughter first, but the truth is that I was drawn to Jharna from the moment I met her eye. My wife is a marvel, as you shall discover."

"I look forward to making her acquaintance, Doctor, and consider it an honor. You have two sons, yes?"

"Nimesh and Sasi. I miss them. Now that I am a father and husband I do keep my absences as short as possible. Fortunately, my wife has her family close by and she understands the importance of my profession. This is the longest I have been away since Nimesh was born four years ago and I miss them sorely. I doubt my yearning to practice medicine in new and varied circumstances shall ever change, but I no longer feel suffocated at the idea of being stationary for a time either. Or perhaps it is merely advanced age creeping up on me," he finished with a laugh.

George laughed with him as he shook his head. Kshitij Ullas looked fifty with streaks of gray peppered all through his dark hair and fine lines creasing the planes of his face, but he did not act like a man of "advanced age." George's respect for Dr. Ullas had grown exponentially as he worked alongside him during their months abroad and the additional delight of conversing with him in the casual way of friendly comrades increased his respect. Kshitij spoke of his private life, his wife Jharna and sons, in the open manner of one who unquestionably trusts the listener. Without realizing it, George followed suit, talking of Pemberley and his family, sharing humorous stories from his youth and tales of his university days, and even mentioning Alex and Sarah.

Because of how naturally the conversation flowed, a mutual fondness was formed. Only later would George recognize this was the turning point in their relationship. Forever would there be an air of mentor and pupil with shades of father and son eventually added to their association, but henceforth, more than anything, they would be friends.

The residence of Sardar Pandey Dhamdhere sat on the banks of the Ulhas River approximately halfway between Thana and Kalyan. Dr. Ullas repeatedly used the term *griha* when talking about his father-in-law's home, the humble word for ordinary dwelling places utterly inappropriate for the palatial structure spread before George's eyes.

"This is a *mahal*!" George whistled. "Pemberley could fit in one corner of this place!"

"Technically it is a *haveli*, this one built some two hundred years ago by the Mughals. Chhatrapati Shivaji, our holy emperor and Maratha founder, awarded this *haveli* to an ancestor of Pandey for valorous service during the Battle of Kolhapur. It has remained in the Dhamdhere clan ever since. Someday you shall see a true *mahal*, such as the Naukhanda at Aurangzeb or Chandra and Mubarak palaces in Jaipur, and then appreciate the difference. Nevertheless, Pandey's *haveli* is vast. I lived here for four months and never encountered Pandey's daughter, who would later become my wife! Now you know why staying here for the duration is not a problem," Dr. Ullas said with a chuckle. "The architectural influence is Persian, but there are wings designed for English and other non-Indian visitors. Pandey is an excellent host and politician, so part of that is ensuring the supreme comfort of his guests."

Their *tanga* stopped in the bustling courtyard, joining a veritable army of conveyances and horses delivering guests and supplies for the epic celebration. Dozens of uniformed servants hastened to unload George's luggage, including the massive trunk that accompanied him on his travels, while Dr. Ullas delivered a string of instructions in Hindi. After a farewell bow and promise to meet him at the dining table in a few hours, Kshitij climbed back into the *tanga* to be taken to the private quarters on the far side of the sprawling building.

George swept his eyes over the white, glistening marble archways and pillars spanning the wide front façade of the *haveli*, many edged in gold or covered with vibrantly colored mosaic patterns. He followed a beckoning servant into the mansion, his thick boots adding their noise as they struck the veined marble tiles of the walkway before the six gleaming mahogany doors gaping open. He glanced around at the chaotic surge of people being efficiently handled by the Sardar's staff, the multitude of voices in several languages falling in waves before rising to be swallowed within the domed ceiling easily three stories above his head. Phenomenal architecture with acoustics he could not fathom dampened what should have been a deafening cacophony to a gentle hum, drowned under the soothing cascade of bubbling water that flowed over the gigantic fountain of glass and stone sitting in the center of the enormous foyer.

George was not an innocent. As a Darcy, he had entered many of the greatest houses and castles in England, including St. James's Palace in London for his formal presentation to King George III. It wasn't that this house was grander or more ornate than some he had seen. Rather it was the *foreignness* of it that rendered him as awestruck as a country boy. A thrill ran up his spine and he shivered with delight. Curiosity to explore his first true exposure to a place so utterly alien to anything in his birth land, as well as being beautiful beyond compare, created a burning itch within his bosom. Yet somehow he walked with controlled dignity behind the servants lugging his trunk up a broad staircase and then down a series of twisting corridors wide enough that five broad-shouldered men could walk in a row without their sleeves touching.

Along the way, he nodded at the people he passed, noting a few familiar British faces among the many he did not know. Finally reaching a quiet hallway far from the entrance, George was ushered into the chambers assigned to him for his stay. He released a low whistle and crossed to the arched windows and glass doors extending the entire length of the back wall. Each one was open, a gentle breeze causing the gauzy curtains to flutter, the private balcony without affording him the ready opportunity to gaze upon the stunning view of green lawn, verdant gardens, and cobalt river.

As tired as he was from his journey, George could not relax into the tub of warm water waiting in the bathing closet attached to his bedchamber until he had thoroughly inspected his quarters. The mixture of Persian architecture, Indian decor, and English furnishings should have clashed, but it oddly meshed into an exquisite atmosphere that was luxurious and comforting. The enormous four-poster bed was decidedly English, while the cushioned divans were right out of a painting of a harem. The oak sidebar laden with glass bottles filled with an assortment of spirits would have fit into any room at Pemberley, yet did not look out of place next to the writing desk that was clearly Indian.

"I think I could stay in here for the duration and be blessedly content," he muttered after a deep swallow of the best English brandy he had ever tasted.

Of course, that was not true. If nothing else, his stomach had a different idea, and George was a man who appreciated a fine meal.

It was no surprise to enter a dining area designed with low tables crowded with dishes of food to be shared freely by the diners who sat cross-legged on thick cushions carpeting the floor. What did surprise him was the immensity of the room and that nearly every space from wall to tapestry-covered wall was filled. An open expanse in the middle of the room was the only empty space, it surrounded on all sides with tables in varying sizes and heights.

Most of the tables were low to the floor with brightly colored cushions serving as seats, but a cluster along the left were higher and set in a proper English manner with tall-backed wooden chairs. Across the back wall, facing the arched and pillared entry, was a raised platform upon which a crimson and gold draped table fifty feet long was crammed with laughing men and women. In the precise center sat a man indisputably recognizable as Sardar Thakore Sahib Pandey Dhamdhere. That was partly due to the regal garments he wore, complete with a turban adorned with four rainbow-hued feathers, but it was primarily due to his presence. Even from a distance and concealed inside a loose fitting *sherwani*, George could discern the powerful warrior body that age had not appeared to diminish. Luckily, he did not look to be imminently planning to grab the *firangi*, *shamshir*, *pata*, or other dozen razor-sharp-bladed weapons mounted on the wall behind him. The only real danger he currently looked to be instigating was having his guests somnolent from so much food or overly stimulated from so much activity.

Properly adorned with a welcoming garland of orange and red flowers, a servant escorted a stunned George to the head table and the empty seat next to Dr. Ullas and two away from the Sardar.

"She will be along in due course," was Kshitij's cryptic reply when George asked about Mrs. Ullas, and with so much food and wine being passed before his eyes, it was an adequate enough answer to accept.

After an hour of ceaseless eating, Pandey stood to his feet and lifted his hands into the air.

"Honored guests, welcome to my humble home for this feast to mark the beginning of the celebration marking my fiftieth year of life. May your time dwelling here be replete with delights, entertainments, relaxation, fine foods, and wine that never ceases to flow!"

A hearty round of cheers and applause rent the air, the Sardar waiting patiently for silence. "Let tonight's entertainment begin!" He clapped twice, the staccato sound reverberating around the room but quickly lost in an abrupt swell of music. On the first beat, the side doors flew open and eight women dressed in a kaleidoscope of vibrant colors danced in. Their bare feet hardly touched the floor as they twirled with the rapid tempo, jewels and gold flashing as their limbs moved to the rhythm, their fingers clattering tiny cymbals while simultaneously fluttering gossamer fabric of silver around their bodies. They were fluid one moment, jerky the next, but forever in unison, purposeful, and timed to the exotic music and singing that came from the minstrels who had entered through another door at the same time. It was utterly mesmerizing.

"They are telling a story in the Sardar's honor," Kshitij whispered to George. He proceeded to explain in hushed tones the tale of a great battle being related through the chanting lyrics and swaying choreography of the dancers. Specifically, it was one of Pandey's battles when he was commander of the Peshwa's army, and as George listened to Kshitij's hushed commentary and those phrases he was able to interpret, the meaning became clearer. Even to an Englishman, it was rousing to the soul.

The dancers were slender and captivatingly beautiful. Dark eyes and flawless skin of milky chocolate dusted with glitter, they danced with the skilled grace of women born to do so. Although different in their features, they were sheer perfection of form from their painted, ringed toes to jewel-adorned, raven hair. Visually, it was a treat in a host of ways, most especially for the men who watched.

Then the song ended on a sudden, dramatic upbeat. The audience inhaled and stirred in preparation to express their appreciation, but before they could, new music burst forth. Only this time it was softer and slower. The dancers, who had splices of a second to rest, smoothly glided into the new tempo. Their lithe bodies undulated as if branches of a willow, their hands floating seductively near their skin as if in a caress, and their faces lit with expressions of deep emotion.

George knew this was a love song before Kshitij told him. He felt it to his bones and was deeply stirred by the romantic sensuality of the music and dancing.

Awed silence met the conclusion of the dance. The rapt assembly needed several moments to recover their wits and calm their pounding hearts before able to launch into well-deserved applause. The dancers bowed humbly, palms pressed together first toward the Sardar and then the honored guests. Only when all corners of the room had been bowed to did they again turn their attention to the Sardar, gracefully padding on tiny feet toward the head table. There they turned toward the room, Pandey having risen to stand at his place before sweeping his arms in a gesture encompassing all eight of the stunning female dancers.

"My honor to present to you my daughters!"

They bowed again, the crowd wildly clapping, as the Sardar's words fully registered to George. He looked at Dr. Ullas, whose eyes were fixed upon the dancer standing closest to them. She pivoted, pressed her slim hands together before her chest, and inclined her head in the standard gesture of respectful greeting known as *namaste* before meeting his proud gaze with sparkling eyes.

"Greetings, noble husband. I pray my dance was an honor to your name and pleasing in your sight. And if so, perhaps I have earned the pleasure of meeting your most fortunate companion. Dr. Darcy, I am Jharna, and I have heard so much about you."

"And I you, Mrs. Ullas." George returned the *namaste* greeting. "I hope that the reports of me have been as excellent as the high praise your husband has bestowed upon you."

"The praise has indeed been most high, although he would likely prefer I not reveal this." She glanced at Kshitij, a teasing glint in her dark eyes. "My husband has exacting standards, Dr. Darcy. He gives his endorsement grudgingly and would rather the subject of his scrutiny be terrified of pleasing him. Earning his respect is not an easy or pain-free task. That you have done so quickly is noteworthy and intriguing to me."

"Be cautious, dearest wife," Dr. Ullas interrupted, his smile warm as he feigned gruffness. "Dr. Darcy is entirely too conceited as it is. Best he remain in the dark and believe his skills paltry!"

George laughed. "Have no fear, Doctor. I am conceited, it is true, but I know I have much to learn. As delightful as it is to hear you have praised my efforts to Mrs. Ullas, I am certain you will find a way to humble me later, probably deserved for some error in judgment on my part."

George was not sure what he expected from Dr. Ullas's wife, but he was surprised on several counts. For one, he had not envisioned her youth. She was his age or perhaps a year or two younger. Why he had imagined her closer to Kshitij's age was a mystery, now that he thought about it. Women married young in India, much younger than English women in general, so it was logical that an unmarried daughter of the Sardar would have been in her late teens at the oldest. Secondly, Jharna was strikingly beautiful, her figure tall and remarkably svelte for a woman who had birthed two children in quick succession, and she possessed an air of nobility as befitted one who was of a royal lineage. She was a sharp contrast to Dr. Ullas, who, although not homely by any means, was extremely plain of face and short of stature.

The other surprise was the evident love they bore for each other. As Kshitij had spoken of Jharna during their travels, it became clear that he respected his wife and held great affection for his family, but as reserved as he tended to be, and with the typical hesitation all Indians seemed to have with revealing their private lives, George had not gotten a hint of more. The fact that Jharna had been given as payment by the Sardar did not shock George. After all, it was not unlike the English customs of the day. Daughters, especially of the wealthy and those who were titled, were more often seen as objects to be bartered to the highest bidder. George thought this somewhat depressing, but it was the way of it and had been for generations uncounted. Those who were fortunate found happiness or contentment within their marriages, and a few grew to truly love one another. Fewer still were blessed to make a match that was of deep, passionate love from the outset, such as his brother James and Lady Anne Fitzwilliam. Whether Jharna and Kshitij had fallen in love at first sight or gradually after their marriage George could not say. Whatever the case, the devotion between them was apparent, and it warmed George's heart even as it instilled a twinge of sadness for what might have been with he and Sarah.

"Dr. Darcy?" Jharna's voice invaded his musings, of which he was thankful. "My sisters approach, eager for an introduction. You are the mysterious stranger who has captivated my husband, thus increasing your allure in their eyes. Be warned," she added with a mischievous glance at the sisters who were now near enough to hear her, "as they shall monopolize your time and tempt you sorely if allowed!"

The girls tittered and blushed. Only one was brave enough to step forward and, with downcast eyes, inquired, "*Sahib* Darcy, would you like to learn the dance?"

"*Sahib* Darcy would love it!" George exclaimed, jumping up with enthusiasm and rushing to join the giggling females.

For an hour or more, George was surrounded by dozens of ravishingly beautiful Indian women who were laughingly attempting to show the more adventurous men how to perform a lively dance that was as far removed from anything he had ever learned at Almack's as the moon was from the earth. He could truthfully say he had never had so much fun in his life.

"What I am wondering is how the Sardar plans to exceed tonight when this is only the precursor to his birthday celebration!" George sank onto the comfortable cushions at his place beside Dr. Ullas with a sigh and reached for a nourishing drink.

Jharna laughed at George's remark. "Tonight is a simple feast, Doctor. My father is saving the best of his wine and amusements for when the Peshwa arrives in two days. His day of birth is on the eighteenth, and that is when the celebration shall truly commence. He may be a warrior at heart, but he knows well how to plan an epic party!"

The celebrating was respectable and in no way a wild orgy, yet as George swept his gaze over the room that to his eye was unequally jammed with gorgeous women, he experienced an overwhelming surge of sexual desire. The salacious sensations undoubtedly stemmed from not bedding a woman in a year.

George's self-control and moral scruples had earned him an enormous amount of taunting from his male friends over the years; nevertheless, he *had* left his virginity behind a decade ago and, until Sarah, hadn't suffered too greatly in the area of abstaining.

Well, he was definitely suffering now! He didn't exactly place it into blunt words, the decision a glimmer of a plan in the corner of his mind, but the basic idea was not only to embrace the joy of no responsibility and tremendous fun, but also to include a healthy dose of wild passion somehow. Once allowed to simmer, his amorousness only needed the proper fuel to leap to a roaring boil. How swiftly that happened was a bigger surprise than he expected.

An inexplicable tingling sensation flickered over his scalp and down his neck. Instinctively, he knew the direction to turn his gaze, sensing that someone was staring at him, and like a magnet, he was drawn. When he saw her, he gasped, his mouth opening and tongue immediately dry, though not for long, since the penetrating scrutiny soon had him drooling.

She is exquisite, beyond perfection.

Hair thick and black as a raven's wings, skin unblemished porcelain white, plump, red lips glistening, and features utterly flawless. No one outside of heaven should be so stunningly beautiful. Voluminous skirts left no doubt that her body was curvaceous and highly feminine, the low-cut bodice one breath away from spilling her lushly endowed breasts.

Her eyes were as dark as her hair, and they were indeed fixed directly on him in a challenging stare that spoke of intense interest in him and him alone. It screamed of attraction and desire with the unquestioning assurance that wanton passion and indescribable pleasure were not only attainable but the only option. Intelligence, playfulness, confidence, fearlessness, independence, covetousness, a hint of selfishness and danger, and much more all in one ebony-eyed enchantress.

George was smitten. *Hell, who am I kidding? I am enraptured! Who is she?* Then she opened her mouth and ran the tip of her tongue across her lower lip before smiling at him. *Bloody hell!* Combined with the libidinous thoughts previously planted in his brain, George felt such an extreme jolt of lust flash through his body that remaining in his seat for a few minutes was necessary before he could think about walking. As if she could read his mind, she arched one delicate brow and laughed. He could not hear her laughter, but he felt it deep inside his bones. There was no embarrassment, however, only a new rush of desire and blind hunger to share in her laughter, hear the musical tinkling in his ears, and then silence it with his mouth pressed to her lips.

She moved away at that moment, after a tiny wink and sensual smile, and was swiftly lost in the crowd. George panicked. There were hundreds of guests in the *haveli* and the place so vast that it was entirely possible he may never find her! He jumped up, peripherally aware of the startled looks from Kshitij and Jharna, but said nothing as he bolted like an arrow straight toward where the mystery woman had stood.

He didn't make it halfway there before being accosted by a group of men he knew from Bombay. It was his own fault, blast it all, his eyes focused on scanning the general area from where she had blatantly flirted with him so that he walked smack into the circle of laughing men.

"Darcy! I saw you sitting at the head table. What a coup! How did you manage that?"

"Greetings, Lord Burgley," George said, stifling the scream of frustration behind gritted teeth. "I have been traveling with Dr. Ullas, if you recall, and he is related to the Sardar by marriage."

"Ah yes, of course. Lady Burgley did tell me that."

"How is your wife? I hope Dr. McIntyre is taking good care of her?"

"Yes, yes! Quite well indeed! I am sure she will be happy when you return, however. When will you be back in Bombay?"

"I will be returning after the festivities here have ended. Commander Doyle was gracious enough to grant me a reprieve, but I am sure he will not remain patient forever."

George hoped Lord Burgley would say nothing about White or the Powis affair. His departure had happened rather swiftly after the severe reprimand Doyle had given him for attacking Dr. White. The hated older man had suffered nothing more than a busted lip and lots of contusions—thanks to three brawny pub guards pulling George off long before he was done inflicting his punishment—and Doyle had privately sympathized with George's reasons. Publicly he was obligated to make a show of discipline, not that being "banished" to travel with Dr. Ullas was remotely painful. George could care less what rumors had flown around the island, and he wanted to make this interruption brief. To forestall the conversation from sidetracking out of his control, George inclined his head to the man at Lord Burgley's right.

"Mr. Shapter, I trust the arm has healed well?"

"Thanks to you, indeed it has." The young man well known to be insanely reckless as well as clumsy addressed the cluster of men in general, bobbing his head George's direction. "I have broken this arm two times before and never regained full strength. Dr. Darcy set it clean, fashioned a constrictive splint with... what was it?"

"Strips of cloth soaked in a mixture of gypsum, lime powder, crushed seashells, and other ingredients," George replied automatically.

"Right." Mr. Shapter nodded. "Disgusting stuff but it worked wonders. The bone healed quicker than ever, and with the exercises he taught me, I was good as new in no time!"

"Just in time for you to probably break it again," piped in his friend Mr. Moir.

Several men laughed in agreement. George scanned the crowd, trying to be sly about it and not let his irritation show. He opened his mouth to voice an excuse to leave, but Mr. Moir spoke first.

"Darcy, have you met His Grace, the Duke of Larent?"

Unfortunately, yes. "I have," he said instead, forcing a pleasant smile on his lips. "It is always a pleasure, your Grace." He inclined his head. The Duke's reply was a short nod before he glanced away, boredom and disinterest oozing from his pores. Suppressing a grimace of distaste, George gave his attention to the man Moir introduced as the Earl of Yardley, newly arrived in India.

"Merely passing through, as it were," Lord Yardley said jovially. "My daughter begged me to take her on an adventure, and, well, I am a doting father who denies her nothing, so here we are! An adventure indeed it has been, and my Ruby has fallen in love with this country. I fear I may have difficulty dragging her home."

"I for one hope you never try, my lord," Mr. Shapter said. "The sun would refuse to shine and all of India would weep at the loss of the priceless jewel that is Lady Ruby."

With effort, George resisted rolling his eyes at such obsequious fawning. "Ruby—priceless jewel." It was nauseating! Yet no sooner had the opinion crossed his mind than he felt the same tingling sensation as generated by the mystery woman. His head jerked up, and after one heavy pound of his heart, he realized she was close behind him. He could feel the heat of her gaze burning the skin of his back right through the thickness of his clothing and started to turn around just as Lord Yardley spoke.

"Ah! And here she is! My priceless jewel! Dr. Darcy, I have the honor of introducing my daughter, Lady Ruby Thomason."

George had begun to think his response to her imagined. After all, he had been dwelling on sex, so perhaps he had fabricated her flirtatious expressions or only thought she was looking at him. Maybe it was the distance or a trick of the light that had created a vision of perfection. In close proximity, she may not be as stunning or have the same impact.

"Dr. Darcy. What a pleasure it is to make your acquaintance."

No, she is utterly breathtaking. Air was wrested from his lungs and most of his blood went straight to his groin, leaving his brain starved for oxygen so that coherent thought was impossible. The impact she had upon him was compounded a hundredfold up close. And she was *very* close. She spoke his name with a husky caress, gave the word *pleasure* a slight emphasis, and then smiled that same sensual, impish smile delivered before. He realized he had been wrong on one count: his imagination assuming her voice would be light and sweet and musical. Rather, it was rich and velvety smooth, smoky and warm, musical, yes, but as the deep chords played in a nuanced rubato.

Lady Ruby was pure sexuality encased in a living form. She knew her power full well and she relished it, enhanced it, and exploited it. George felt a tingling of danger radiating from her, but it excited him more. Before him stood a woman who he instinctively understood could never be tamed, yet therein was the challenge. George loved nothing more than a challenge! The raw, animal hunger to have her, to be the one who tapped into the fire that blazed from deep inside her, was undeniable and overwhelming. All men would feel the same—this George knew before he glanced to the men standing around him or noted how every male reacted to her—but she was looking at *him*, standing inches away from *him*, sending a silent message to *him*! The message was loud and clear.

George relaxed and flashed his most dashing smile. Lady Ruby Thomason may have been wreaking havoc on his senses and spinning his mind and body out of control, but he wasn't a green youth, unaware of his own charms. He was a Darcy—handsome, rich, brilliant, masculine, and confident. George knew the attributes he possessed, even if he rarely exploited them.

He bowed without losing eye contact. "My lady," he greeted with a reso-nant caress that was not lost on her, as noted by the slight widening of her eyes. "The *pleasure* is mutual, I am sure."

"I watched you dance earlier with the Indian ladies and was impressed at how quickly you learned the steps. You have a natural grace and rhythm that serves you well while dancing."

And other places also, he intimated with his eyes and a roguish smile.

"My daughter wanted to join in and was lamenting the standards that prevented it."

"It is unfair that women are denied the ability to express their desires and whimsies as gentlemen are," she retorted with an insinuating laugh.

"Perhaps, but no daughter of mine will be seen in a thin garment with skin bare while undulating for all to see," Lord Yardley countered. And of course, that planted the vision of Ruby doing precisely that firmly in every man's mind!

"More the pity. Do you see how tragic my life is, Dr. Darcy? I coerce my poor father into leaving our comfortable estate in England, begging him to show me the world in hopes of escaping the shackles that bind me, yet even in these exotic, romantic locales, I am surrounded by British mores." She sighed dramatically, all eyes on the rise of her chest as she did and undoubtedly praying the straining fabric of her décolletage would fail. She reached out and touched George lightly on his arm, her fingertips brushing his bare wrist before coming to rest on the edge of his sleeve. "You must be an adventurous man, Doctor, based on your performance on the dance floor. Do you not agree with me that rules stifle us and inhibit our creativity? Would life not be richer and more satisfying if allowed to live unencumbered?"

He nodded, keeping his arm still and rigidly clamping down on the wild rush of electricity instigated by her feathery touch. "I do agree, within reason, of course. Rules have their place and are necessary, but breaking them now and again is fun."

"Rules are what separate us from the animals, Lady Ruby." The Duke of Larent's cold voice cut through the playful banter. "Adhering to strict standards of propriety is our duty as the superior class. We act as rational man should and set an example for the lower classes who are unruly, largely due to allowing their baser instincts to govern them."

"Somehow I doubt adhering to 'standards of propriety' is a burden gentlemen of the ton suffer from, but thank you for your insight. Your Grace," she added after a rebellious pause.

She smiled sweetly at the duke, his only show of emotion a fleeting press of his lips before he glanced away—after a significant visual inspection of her breasts, George noted with a flair of jealousy. Apparently even the arrogant, icy Duke of Larent, thrice married and well over forty, was not immune to Lady Ruby's glamour. *Then again, is there a man with a pulse who would be?* George rather doubted it.

"Father, gentlemen, I apologize for interrupting. I only wished to say that I am weary and wish to return to my room. I did not want you to worry. I shall have a servant escort me."

"Nonsense!" Yardley exclaimed. "I am sure one of these fine gentlemen would be happy to assist you to our suite." He ignored pleas from Moir and Shapter. "Darcy, may I impose?"

"It is definitely not an imposition," George casually assured him. He was rather pleased to hear his voice sounded normal when his heart was pounding at the prospect of minutes alone with Ruby.

She took his offered arm, her hand firmly pressing into his forearm, and George steered her out of the hall. Neither said a word until away from the noise and then spoke of proper, safe topics while in the busier areas. George's fascination grew with each passing step. Ruby answered his polite questions about her travels with wit and humor. Before they had attained the second floor landing, he knew this was a woman whose personality and intellect were as formidable as the aura of seductive sensuality surrounding her. It was a lethal combination.

They were walking down a nearly deserted corridor, their pace consciously slowed as they left the crowds behind. Ruby continued to hold on to his arm with her warm body closer to his than strictly necessary or proper. Suddenly, she stopped and turned toward him, still holding his arm, and looked at him with an arched brow and an impishly sexy smile that made his blood boil.

"Have we exchanged pleasantries long enough, Doctor, so that we may now comfortably broach the topic that we are straining to ignore? You know I was shamelessly flirting with you from across the room, a well-orchestrated bit of coquettish maneuvering I might add, and I do hope it was not wasted."

"No, it was not wasted, my lady. A marvelous display of flirting it was, and

I commend you on your skill. Probably the best I have ever seen in all my years of women vying for my attentions. Bravo! And as always, when a lady flirts so outrageously with me, I must return the compliment."

George tilted his head and lifted one brow, his smile wide and cocky as he brought her hand to his lips. His eyes met hers from beneath thick brows, his gaze a mixture of smoldering intensity and playfulness. He brushed a gentle kiss across her knuckles while his thumb caressed her fingers, ending the brief contact with a saucy wink.

Ruby's rich, vibrant laugh echoed against the walls and sank under his skin. "Well done, Dr. Darcy. I see I have encountered a flirting competent. You are arrogant and audacious. I like that in a man. I predict that we shall get on famously." Then before he could reply, she resumed walking and carried on their previous conversation as if never interrupted.

She was incredible! No other word for it. Well, there were many words George could think of to describe Lady Ruby Thomason and all of them were positive. At the door to her room, down one short corridor and around the corner from his guest chambers, she thanked him for his escort, using phrases selected for innuendo, and bid him good night while somehow managing to press her breasts against his arm. As she closed the door, she watched him through the diminishing crack, her eyes bright and promising.

"I shall see you on the morrow," she whispered as the door shut. "*Pleasant dreams, Doctor.*"

For three days, George spent almost every waking moment with Lady Ruby on long walks, picnics, dining and dancing, horseback rides, cricket on the lawn, card games, and hours sitting on shaded chairs talking. Ruby drew men to her like a magnet and the guests were plentiful, so they were rarely alone, but when they had stolen minutes of solitude, she had shown her intense attraction to him in ways that were becoming increasingly bolder.

Tonight he escorted her to her chambers a little before eleven o'clock, the earliest she had retired for the past two days, but when he expressed concern for her health, Ruby laughed and tossed her head. "I am robust, dear friend. Put away your physician's cap and fret not. I merely thought a night of lying in bed sounded… gratifying and enticing."

Then she lifted on her toes and kissed his cheek. The gesture took him by surprise and he stood frozen as her lips caressed his skin and her breasts pressed against his chest. Mainly his paralysis was due to the tidal wave of lust that crashed within him, his muscles unable to function from lack of blood supply. She withdrew and slipped through the door, a final smoldering stare pointedly at his groin and suggestive smile rendering him unfit to go anywhere but directly to his room.

George stood at the railing of the balcony outside his bedchamber, staring at the stars and glistening water of the Ulhas River. His eminence Peshwa Sawai Madhavrao II had arrived that day, so the celebratory atmosphere had escalated. George could hear the music and hum of voices and knew silence would not completely blanket the *haveli* until close to dawn. Then the residence would be calm until noon, the guests emerging from their rooms to partake of the scheduled activities or stroll about the cultured gardens, wood-shrouded pathways, or sandy banks of the river. George was certain that the weeks he planned to stay would not be enough to cover the endless options. The prospect excited him and he was in no hurry to end the adventure and return to Bombay.

He ran a hand through his hair and lifted his face to catch the cooling breeze, hoping it would dry the sweat on his brow. Three days of amazing company and excruciating pain. Simply put, George had spent three days in a constant state of arousal, to some degree, and knew that if he did not do something about it soon, he might well burst into flames. What to do was the dilemma. Some men, those with lesser scruples, would think him mad. A woman who dripped wanton sensuality was seducing him and he hesitated. He could hear their laughter and, God help him, a large part of him joined right in. Was he mad? Yes, mad with lust and insane with a hunger never felt before. He had been feeling the yearnings before he set eyes on Ruby. However, it was one thing to seek out a willing servant or experienced woman with urges of her own. They were always easy to find, especially among the Indians, who did not hold with the same repressive sexual ideals as Westerners. Even while obsessed with Ruby, he had noted no less than a dozen women gazing at him with invitation. The maid who brought him his coffee and breakfast pastries each morning eyed him frankly, her demeanor conveying her interest as loudly as if she had stripped naked before him. He could walk out his door right now and within thirty minutes find a female ecstatic to welcome him into her bed.

"I merely thought a night of lying in bed sounded... gratifying and enticing."
There was the dilemma.

George did not want just anyone. His desire was firmly fixed on Ruby and the thought of being with anyone else was unappealing. Each night he dreamt of her, in vivid detail, waking so aroused that he was blinded by the agony of it. Taking care of matters alone provided momentary relief but made it worse, since he knew the pleasure with her would be a thousandfold greater.

So what is the problem? At times, like now, when he burned with need, he had difficulty answering that question. Then he remembered that he was a gentleman with morals drummed into him since he was born. As annoying as it often was, George valued the standards set by the Church and society. Lady Ruby Thomason was the daughter of a peer of the realm, presumably a virgin— although it was difficult to fathom considering her exaggerated sensuality—and while clever phrases and double entendres rolled off her tongue with ease, George could not ascertain if her invitations were serious.

Maintaining his resolve when he desired her as he had never desired anyone in his life was torturous enough. Compounding the issue was that he genuinely liked her. He knew he was not yet in love with her. George had never much believed in love happening swiftly. His brother and Anne were an exception, but even in their case, the love between them had grown stronger as they matured. George was not foolish enough to believe that passion was an adequate reason to marry someone or that love was certain to bloom from mutual passion, yet his attraction to her was not solely physical. He could imagine falling deeply in love with Ruby in time.

"Bloody romantic idiot," he muttered.

And of course it was true. Clinical man of science he might have been, but he was also a romantic and always had been. James would say he was searching for the mate God intended. Perhaps. James was far worse than he in the hopeful romantic department, lucky for Anne! George was more pragmatic. With that pragmatism came logic. Logic gave him the ability to examine himself rationally and he knew he was lonely on top of being overwhelmed with lust. He needed to separate the two, or he would be in trouble.

Take care of the most immediate issue with the pretty maid tomorrow, and then you will have a clear head while pursuing a relationship with Lady Ruby.

Feeling better having reached a solution, George walked back into the room, leaving the doors and windows open to admit the cooling air through the mesh screens. One by one, he doused the lamps. The room fell into shadow with faint moonlight bathing the bed, where it sat between two of the largest windows. His restless blood thrummed with unrelieved desire that would prevent easy sleep and bring on erotic dreams. Stripping off his shirt, he crawled under the thin linen sheet wearing only the loose Indian trousers called *paijamas* that were incredibly comfortable and unrestrictive, the latter especially beneficial considering the state he woke up in lately.

He was still plumping his pillows when the outer door opened, the faint squeak and beam of light from the passageway alerting him. Rapidly he twisted around, but the door had been hastily shut and only a vague shape was discernible near the door. Instantly, he knew it was Ruby. He could *feel* her. That fierce tingling sensation that thrillingly attacked the nerve endings of his skin whenever she looked at him flared abruptly, rendering him breathless and acutely aroused. A handful of palpitating heartbeats passed before she stepped away from the shadows, moonlight bathing her body and revealing her to George.

Ruby wore a long robe of thick fabric belted at her slim waist and that hugged every curve of her figure. A figure that even in the half light was perfection beyond what he had envisioned. Her hair was loose, falling in a wave of glimmering charcoal clear to her bottom. She was a goddess that no mortal man could refuse.

Coherent thought evaporated and words were pointless. Everything he had deliberated minutes before was irrelevant. If there were residual shreds of resistance—and George knew full well there weren't—they too went up in smoke when she spoke.

"I waited for you to come to me, George. When you didn't, I had to come to you. I have no choice. I want you too much."

And then she stepped to the edge of the bed and unbelted her robe, leisurely slipping it from her slender shoulders. George watched, mesmerized as she slid it incrementally down her body, unveiling the naked flesh underneath gradually. It was the maneuver of a skilled seductress, but her eyes were hesitant and cheeks rosy. She knew her power and delighted in it, that much was obvious, and she probably wasn't a total innocent, but the hint of bashfulness contradicted vast experience. Of course, all of this deduction was lost on

George until contemplated in retrospect. In the moment, he was not thinking of anything except how fervidly he wanted to touch her!

A second later, she was in his arms and he was rolling her under his body. Whether he had reached for her or she had launched herself into his embrace he never knew. It didn't matter. Their hunger was mutual. She wrapped her limbs around him, pulling and kneading greedily, and met his penetrating kiss with equal fervor.

George was drowning in sheer bliss. He poured his soul into the kiss, thrusting his tongue deeply into her mouth and drinking in her breath. He wanted to explore all of her, taste every inch of her skin, but it was impossible to pull away from her lips. Later he would take his time and delight in her, showing her that he was a masterful lover that could bring her pleasure in a multitude of ways. Later. Now was for animal lovemaking, Ruby wanting that as much as he did.

It was she who slipped her hands underneath the waistband of the *paijamas*, her hands gliding firmly over the bared skin of his buttocks as she pushed the garment down as far as possible. When the fabric refused to budge further, she shifted focus, caressing as she moved her hands between their bodies to yank at the tie holding the pants in place. George groaned as he lifted his pelvis as minimally as necessary to remove the impeding garment, aiding with one hand and somehow managing to kick the *paijamas* away. How he accomplished that when she took advantage of his nakedness and position to grasp on to him and stroke his entire length was a mystery.

He gasped and shuddered, control teetering on a sheer precipice. Ruby was as out of control as he.

"Hurry! Please, George!" she moaned against his mouth. She gripped him like a vise, her legs high over his hips as she propelled him into her.

There was wildness to their coming together. Both were frantic, starved, and demanding swift satisfaction. It defied logic, but George was not dwelling on logic. Sensation and instinct ruled. She was warm and wet and tight, surrounding him heavenly as he moved within her. Fancy love play was not needed. Simply the tempo of passionate kissing and hard loving was enough to spiral their ardor into realms higher than the clouds, leading to a shattering conclusion.

Afterward, George held her in his arms. He did not feel a twinge of guilt, oddly enough. Perhaps it was the haziness of a stunning release leaving him too satiated to care. Doubtful. Already he was stirring, still breathless and with heart racing yet growing hard and wanting her again. Maybe it was because she had not come to him a virgin—that had been notable even in his crazed state of mind—but he knew that if she had been, the only difference is that he would have rallied and taken her slower and with tenderness.

No. He felt no guilt because he knew it had been inevitable that she would be in his bed, be his lover, from the moment their eyes had met across the dining room. If there were consequences, it did not frighten him. Being with Ruby was right. He believed it with every cell in his body. He could not honestly utter *I love you* to her, nor did he expect her to say the words to him. But there was a connection between them that was enough for now. It made him blissfully happy.

They made love twice more before the dawn. Passion raged as before, but it was governed. George fulfilled the fantasies of his dreams, tasting her and touching her until she writhed and cried for him. They dozed in between, cuddled and entwined. Softly they talked but of general topics or of how they preferred to be loved, but nothing of the larger implications until saying good-bye at his door.

"Will I see you again?" he whispered against the sensitive skin by her ear. He did not mean in a few hours in the company of others in public.

"Yes," she breathed, knowing precisely what he meant. "I will return tonight, George. Tonight, the next, and the next, and any time in between if I can find a way to have you to myself." She cupped his face, kissing until his knees weakened and he was a hairbreadth away from whisking her back to his bed.

Then she slipped from his clutches and slithered out the door. George closed his eyes and leaned his head against the wood. Inhaling in huge gulps, he wondered how it was possible that his yearning for her could be more intense now than it had been yesterday morning.

❧

For three weeks, George was living in paradise on earth.

She had come to him the next night, and the next, and the next. Each time, they greeted each other at the door, George pacing until she appeared and rushing her inside, and instantly, they embraced and kissed. Always it was crazed with clothing dropped to the floor as they stumbled to the bed, fell in a heap of limbs, and rapidly merged as one. The third night she was later than usual, and George was frantic that something had occurred. Fear for her and insane lust combined, so that when she arrived after one in the morning, he pinned her against the door, grasped her legs, lifted her off the ground, and smoothly impaled her right there. Furiously they loved, Ruby as wild as he and refusing to accept his later apology.

"I like wild man George," she teased. "He excites me. And then you are mellowed and become gentle George. Both men bring me tremendous pleasure."

Truthfully, George liked both men too. Wild, wanton, out-of-control George was a new creation. Never, even when first experiencing sex as a youth, had he felt such depth of ardor. During his years at university, his focus had been tightly narrowed, not allowing for reckless abandon of any type. Perhaps it was time for him to relinquish his rigid discipline. George was honest enough to admit this was partially the impetus even while knowing it was not the primary reason.

It was Ruby.

During the day, they maintained a careful composure. Nothing changed other than a tendency to look for opportunities to steal kisses or clandestine caresses. Secluded pathways on the immense grounds and sheltered alcoves inside the enormous *haveli* were plentiful, and they discovered as many as possible. A linen closet at the end of the only corridor they had found that was not occupied by guests provided excellently for afternoon assignations. Three times. Once they were seated beside each other at dinner. George had taken to dining with the English guests at the high table, solely for the purpose of watching her and conversing when close enough to do so. On the night they dined side-by-side, the challenge was in how often they could touch under the linen-shrouded table, who was the boldest, and in how well they acted as if nothing was amiss. Ruby won the contest by not only calmly smiling when George lifted her skirt to her knee but by carrying on a flirtatious conversation with the gentlemen to her left while brazenly stroking George's groin.

Despite the fiery passion that ran unabated, they enjoyed all of their hours together. Day or night, George longed to be with her. His heart leapt each time he saw her face. He left his room after bathing and eating breakfast with a sensation of emptiness inside, though she had only been gone from his side for six hours or less, and felt whole when she was close.

For a week, they spoke of nothing related to their emotions or the future. George knew he was falling profoundly in love with her and was confident that she was with him. How could she not? What they shared was magical. He tried not to compare his feelings for Ruby with Sarah, but it was inevitable, and although he believed his love for Sarah genuine, it had never included such raw passion. Nor, as became clearer with each passing day, the depth of possessiveness and tenderness. Ruby was precious to him, a jewel he wanted to treasure forever. She held a part of his soul, just as the poets and Scriptures proclaim. It was no longer enough to bring her pleasure with his body alone. He wanted to touch the innermost part of her and give her pleasure in every way imaginable.

On their eighth night together, he made love to her with his mouth, fingers, hands—driving her to heights of rapture again and again until she was limp. Only then did he pull her into his embrace, her back against his chest as he entered her, moving slowly and caressing reverently, murmuring into her ear of his appreciation for her beauty and giving heart, expressing his love for her without saying the words, and waiting patiently until she again roused so that together they could obtain blissful release.

It was phenomenal, by far the most amazing time between them yet and exceeding any of George's previous relations by miles. He held her in his arms but was lost in a daze of satisfaction in mind and body so utterly that he did not immediately realize that her shivers and trembles were other than the aftermath of her climax.

"Ruby, love? Are you crying?"

She did not answer immediately. Then she shook her head before whispering, "It is nothing. I am a silly female at times." She removed his fingers from her cheeks and kissed the tips that were moist from her tears.

"A silly female that weeps from amazement at the astounding feats of her incredible lover," he teased, pausing to hear a laugh that did not come. "Or are they tears of another sort?"

"I am fine, truly. Merely tired and a bit overwhelmed. It has been an eventful week with scant sleep."

Her words made sense, but George heard the shakiness in her voice and felt the tenseness of her body. Furthermore, it troubled him that she had not countered his arrogant jest with a jab of her own. He kissed her shoulder and nestled his head into the soft bend of her neck, waiting to gather his thoughts and allow her to relax.

"I am sorry, love," he began in a tender tone. "I have been selfish in my desire for you. Too demanding and not considering your needs."

"My *needs* are to be with you, George, so please do not apologize. I know my mind and would stay away if I wanted or needed to. You demand nothing that I am not willing, happily willing, to give."

He smiled at the force in her voice, the slight irritation that conveyed her strength of character. "Yes, you are a woman who controls her destiny. I admire that about you. It is one of the many traits you possess that excites me so." He kissed her shoulder again. "Your self-assurance is a rarity for women in our world, sadly. Men are threatened by a woman who shows initiative and speaks her mind, more the pity. I think it is highly appealing."

He thought his praise would reassure and please her. He meant every word and wanted her to be confident of his respect before he revealed his hope to also be her protector and provider. She was brave and independent, that was without a doubt, but she was also a woman in a culture that men ruled. He wondered if she had momentarily forgotten that in her fierce drive to be in charge. He did not care how many other lovers she had taken before him—*well, maybe he cared a little*—but whether she ever returned the love he felt for her or not, his love birthed a concern for her well-being that could not be ignored. Seconds later, as he felt fresh shakes that she tried to suppress, he knew it was time to talk seriously about what was happening between them.

"Ruby, I want you to know that you can share your thoughts with me freely. Whatever force of nature initially brought us together, I now care for you deeply and will be here for you. I want to be here for you whether there are... consequences from our actions or not." He paused but she said nothing. In fact, she was still and slightly stiff in his arms. "Ruby? Talk to me, please."

"You owe me nothing, George, and there will be no 'consequences.'"

"I am not saying this because I think I owe you anything, and how can you be so sure of... the rest? We could have made a child, Ruby, and I will not turn my back on you or our baby! I would not—"

"There will not be a baby because I cannot have one." Her tone was flat, the sentence hanging in the air as a stunned George watched her leave his bed. She wrapped her body with the thin coverlet folded at the end of the bed and walked toward the window, her back to him. He was too shocked to speak, but she answered the questions racing through his dulled brain in a running narrative devoid of emotion, as if she were reading from a script about some other woman.

"When I was sixteen, I fancied myself in love. He was a viscount that my father was entertaining at our manor. Even then, I liked men and knew the powers of seduction I was blessed with—or cursed, depending on the point of view. But I was innocent and had little understanding of men's motives. I gave myself to him joyfully, numerous times, assured that he planned to marry me and was, so he told me, engaged in a discussion with my father about the dowry and so on. It was a lie, of course. He left, and afterward I discovered I was with child. I was terrified and hid it from my father. With the help of a servant, I sought the services of an abortionist. It worked, but I suffered complications, ones that I could not hide from my father. A surgeon saved my life but said I could never conceive."

"He could have been wrong—"

"No, he wasn't!" She glanced at him over her shoulder, pain etched onto her face along with bottomless sadness and traces of guilt. It tore at his heart. She looked away and hastily resumed her dry explanation. "You knew you were not my first, George. Nor are you my second." She shrugged. "I like men. I always have. Why play the part of the virtuous girl when I am a woman with strong desires who has no fear of the consequences, as you eloquently put it? Besides, no man will want a wife who cannot give him an heir."

"That is not true!" George burst out, sitting up in the bed.

"Isn't it?" She turned toward him, her countenance angry and bitter. "All men want from a woman is her body for pleasure and the babies she alone can create! Tell me that isn't so. They are not concerned about her heart."

"I am," he vehemently disagreed.

Her expression softened. "You are a dear man and may be an exception. But would you want me if the price was never having a child?"

The question stretched between them. She was gazing at him with such a mixture of emotions that he could not decipher them all. George was at a loss for words. Her revelation had rocked him to the core. Of course he wanted children! Admittedly, he hadn't given it a great deal of thought, but he knew it was a future he craved. He was a physician and aware that there were never guarantees that one's mate would not be barren or that he might not be capable of siring children for that matter. As far as he knew, none of his partners had conceived, although usually he was careful to prevent that. With Ruby, he had not once considered using protection. Had he somehow known she was unable to bear children? Or had he been reckless because he believed their relationship was special, the idea of her becoming pregnant not frightening him?

Before he could form a coherent reply, she visibly shook herself. Dropping the coverlet, she returned to the bed with a smile on her face that was almost normal. She sat next to him, sliding one silky leg over his thigh and cupping his face with her hands. "Let us not quarrel, love. I am happy with us as we are now. You are very dear to me, George. More than I ever thought possible or anticipated when I so outrageously flirted with you across the dining room. Can we not put these matters aside for now and simply enjoy each other?"

She did not wait for an answer. Covering his mouth with hers, she commenced a lazy exploration with nibbles and sweeps of her tongue. Pushing him backward onto the mattress, she lay partially draped over his body, one hand snaking down his chest and abdomen until between his legs, where she then teased him with leisurely caresses. His reaction was instantaneous, flames of sensation scorching all thought from his mind, including the amazement at how she could so swiftly arouse him with a touch after their stupendous interlude less than an hour ago. Deepening the kiss and increasing the pressure of her strokes flittered that out of his brain, George groaning and shivering with delight.

Minutes of intense kissing passed, Ruby finally leaving his mouth and traveling to plant wet kisses to his neck, down the firm planes of his chest and abdomen, dipping her tongue into his navel, and then with an arch glance at his drugged face, taking his hardness into her mouth.

"Oh God!" he cried, bucking and arching his spine, flashes of exquisite fire burning every nerve ending in his body. She had never done this to him before, few women had, and it was unbelievable ecstasy. He writhed and whimpered, alternating watching her and closing his eyes as the pleasure overwhelmed him. She knew precisely how to drive him to the brink of a violent eruption and then lighten her touch just enough to give him a slim chance to regain his breath before renewing her assault so that he spiraled higher. It was glorious! Intimate in a way that he had never imagined. To be completely within her power, unable to halt her—not that he wanted to—or control the situation in any way was liberating and acutely erotic. He now knew exactly how she felt when he did the same, dominating and teasing until she begged for the release he denied her, until he sensed she had soared as far into the heavens as possible.

"Ruby! Please! Come here!" He reached for her, needing her, but she ignored him. Instead, she licked, sucked, and stroked. Using every part of her mouth, hands, even her hair and face, to drive him insane.

"Let go, George," she commanded.

And he did. He could not hold back any longer. To say it was stupendous would have been a gross understatement. He was lost, utterly lost, his body convulsing with pleasure and heart bursting with love. Only the fact that he used all the air in his lungs to emit a guttural shout of ecstasy prevented him from shouting out *I love you!* The words were there, on the tip of the tongue that he was unable to command for the present, waiting to be uttered once he caught his breath, no matter that he was unsure whether she wanted to hear them or could return the sentiment.

But before he could inhale around the gasps, she moved. Quickly, she shifted, straddling his hips and impaling herself onto his manhood while yet hard. Giving him no time to soften, she rode him frantically, her eyes half-lidded and gazing at him. George's eyes widened. He knew that look! He had seen it often enough from Anne when looking at his brother James. Never in the throes of passion, of course, but it was the same shine of love as he had seen countless times, taunting them for being such lovesick fools to which James would laugh and nod his head while Anne blushed. Ruby stared at him that way now, only multiplied a hundredfold as she reached her peak, her hands pressed flat onto his chest and lower body rising and falling in a harsh, rapid rhythm, somehow keeping her eyes open through it all, so that he could *see* how great the joy she attained with him. It was almost enough to bring on another orgasm, but thanks to her skill at lovemaking, that was physically impossible. His heart twined with hers though, and he drew her into his embrace, squeezing with all his strength.

"I love you, Ruby," he whispered several minutes later, saying it a dozen times interspersed with tender kisses to her forehead. It was on the tenth, or maybe twentieth declaration that he realized she was asleep. He did not know if she had heard him, but it did not matter. He smiled, happier than he had ever been, and joined her in bliss-filled slumber.

"Stop tickling me and listen!"

"I can't resist. When you laugh, your breasts bounce deliciously. It is far too enticing and distracting, even with this riveting topic."

It had been three nights of incredible bliss since Ruby confessed her past to George, his love for her increasing. Tonight they were relaxing and playing on the large bed, having made love on the balcony under the bluish light of the moon. A tray of fruits and nuts sat on the mattress, the intended erotic play of feeding each other bites turning silly when pieces of banana accidentally matted in her long hair. Hence the instruction she was attempting to impart.

"I shall cover them up if you do not pay attention." Ruby crossed her arms over her chest and frowned sternly until George folded his hands behind his back and leaned against the propped pillows. "Much better. Now, what I was trying to demonstrate before you rudely interrupted is how important it is to hold the hair tight within your fingers as you twist the strands in the proper order, alternating each portion in the exact sequence; otherwise, you will have a loose braid that will not hold for any length of time."

"That would be unacceptable, of course."

"Indeed it would. And do not mock me!"

"Would I do that?"

His wide-eyed expression of innocence sent her into gales of laughter, George grinning at the spectacle of her breasts bouncing.

"You are incorrigible," she declared between giggles.

"I am, I truly am. I am also irresistible though, aren't I? Go ahead, admit it. You know I am."

"I admit nothing of the sort! You are conceited enough without me adding fuel to the fire." She pursed her lips and did her best to feign severity. "Do you want to learn how to braid hair or not?"

"I would rather kiss you and feed you more of these cherries, if you must know."

"You did ask," she accused.

"I have changed my mind. You did say I was incorrigible and I did not deny it. Come here and I shall show you just how incorrigible I can be. I can suck the banana from your hair, and if some lands on your breast, I shall attend to that as well." He broadened his grin and wiggled his brows.

"Absolutely not—oomph!"

He tackled her, tickling the sensitive area underneath her ribs as he tossed her onto the bed underneath him. Ruby shrieked and laughed until tears sprung in her eyes. George silenced her with his mouth, the kiss short but thorough.

"You are adorable when you try to be angry." He kissed the tip of her nose. "I love you, Lady Ruby." He kissed her cheek and on down her neck, waiting and hoping for her to repeat the words, but as always she remained silent. George told her he loved her several times a day, whispering it slyly when they were in public and crying it at the moment of culmination while making love. She had yet to say the words in return. It distressed him, especially when her eyes and touch conveyed the depth of her emotions. He knew she loved him! Somehow he had to make her realize that he wanted her now as well as forever and if that meant not having children, so be it.

He drew back, leaning on one elbow so he could look into her eyes. She was smiling up at him, love and happiness making her flawless features glow warmly, enhancing her beauty. For a moment George lost himself in contemplating her face, awe rendering him breathless. Slowly, he caressed her cheek with his knuckles, his voice tender but serious.

"You shared something personal with me, Ruby, and I know it was not easy nor an event you would reveal to anyone other than someone you trusted. I promise I will never betray your confidence in me. You know that, don't you?" She nodded. "Good. It is important to me that we have no secrets between us, at least nothing of deep significance. I am moved that you shared with me, but it also brought on a measure of guilt."

"George, there is no reason—" she began but he pressed his fingertips to her lips.

"Guilt because I too have a secret that I rarely share. I need to tell you about Alex."

For a half hour, she said nothing, listening in silence as George told her about his twin. By the time he had finished recounting select tales from their youth, Alex's death, and the subsequent years of feeling a yawning emptiness, Ruby was weeping soundlessly.

"Do not cry, love. I wanted to tell you about Alex not only because he is an important part of my life that I have no wish to keep hidden from you, but also because you need to know that the void within me that I have been unable to get rid of or fill with something else is smaller now. It started shrinking when I became a physician. Medicine is a passion for me and the joy of it pushes away a portion of the darkness. You illuminate the remaining shadows, Ruby. I love you." He leaned forward and kissed her, long and hard, expressing with his mouth the depth of meaning to his words.

Ruby wrapped her arms around him, clenching so that it almost hurt. She responded to the penetrating kiss with a desperate fervor, her body shaking and muffled whines catching in her throat. George broke the kiss, but she spoke first, her tone anguished and laced with sobs.

"Oh, George! Why do you have to be so wonderful? Why could I have not met you before? Life is so unfair!"

"No, life is fair. Do you not see?" He cupped her face, brushing away the moisture and kissing the tears off her thick lashes. "All we have been through already prepares us for what we have together. I admit that I have always imagined having children some day. But never have I wanted that without first being with a woman I can give my heart to. A woman who will complete my soul as even Alex never did. Nothing else matters Ruby. Nothing!"

She did not stop crying. Her eyes were squeezed shut and face turned into his large hand until half hidden from him. George was baffled at the degree of her despair. "I am not sure why you do not believe me, love. I assure you I mean every word. I love you and nothing on this earth will keep me from you. Tomorrow I will speak to your father—"

"No! You can't!"

"I won't tell him of what has passed between us, I promise. Unless he refuses me, that is." His countenance changed to deathly serious. It was a cast he knew she had never before seen on his face, her eyes widening and lips parting as she stared up at him. "Ruby Thomason, I *will* marry you. I know you are afraid, of me or of something else I am not sure. I will erase your fears, every last one, if you will only trust me. Never will I relent or let you go, do you understand? I love you, more than life, and know you love me too. Can you look into my eyes and say that you do not love me too?"

He held her gaze, his blue eyes dark with devotion and sincerity. Her eyes were melancholy and glassy with unshed tears but also serious with a hint of something he was not sure of. Before he could identify the myriad flickers within the shades of brown that exposed the emotions she was feeling, Ruby inhaled shakily and whispered the answer he was longing to hear.

SHARON LATHAN

"Yes, I love you, George."

George's heart leapt. It soared! He smiled brilliantly, kissed her soundly, and drew her body closer to his. "I knew it! You have no reason to be afraid, my dearest. I will talk to Lord Yardley and secure your hand—"

"Not yet, please, George. Promise me you will give me time," she interrupted, her voice urgent and pleading. "Just… be with me now, while we are here. Can you do that? Let us enjoy each other as we are before talking to my father. Everything will change then and I am not prepared to end… halt what we have. Do you understand?"

"Yes, I suppose." George frowned. She did have a point. Once the world knew of their courtship, they would be watched closer. Arrangements for a wedding took time and no longer would they enjoy such freedom. And, as much as he hated to admit it, after the horrible confrontation with Lord Powis, he was not anxious to speak to another prospective father-in-law.

"My father has been distracted with his own entertainments while here." She flushed, the implication obvious and considering that they were lying naked on his bed, it was humorous to see her blush at the idea of Lord Yardley engaged in like manner. "And he has also used the opportunity to conduct constant business. Every day he is with some rich Englishman or another."

"Yes, I have noticed that myself, with relief. He and Lords Aston and Milton, and the Duke of Larent, are quite chummy. Very well. We have a plan. What say we seal it?"

"What did you have in mind?" she purred, stroking over the muscles of his rear.

"Who is incorrigible now? In a minute, love. First, I have a gift for you."

He left the bed and walked to his trunk, kneeling as he opened the lid. A glance over his shoulder caused him to grin and raise one brow. "Are you examining my hindquarters, Lady Ruby?"

"That as well as every other fine attribute you possess, Dr. Darcy. Are you shocked?"

"Horrified. Now close your eyes and hold out your hand. Do it or you will not receive your gift."

He knelt on the bed beside her and placed the object onto her upturned palm. "You can open your eyes now. This locket was my mother's. It wasn't her favorite but I always loved it, hence my requesting it when she passed. Father

108

saw no reason not to grant my wish. I have no idea what I intended to do with it, other than to simply be a memento along with a few other items that remind me of her. Now I believe it was meant for me to give to someone special as an indication of my love."

Ruby was shaking her head, the hand not holding the pendant pressed against her trembling lips. "George, this is too special. I cannot accept it."

"You must. It is a gift and a gift should never be rejected. It would tear my heart asunder," he proclaimed dramatically. Then he laughed. "It is not a huge thing, love. I promise you, I will shower you with jewels and fine gowns galore once we are formally betrothed and then wed. This is a meager token. Do you like it?"

"I love it! Thank you. I will treasure it all of my days!"

She launched herself into his arms. George laughed and squeezed before gently pushing her away. "Before you sidetrack me with your irresistible self, I want to see it on. Here, lift your hair."

"If you had allowed me to finish braiding, it would be easier," she teased a few minutes later.

"If I have any say in the matter, you will never wear your hair any style but flowing freely when in our bedchamber. And it isn't the hair but this blasted tiny clasp! How do you women do this? Ah, there. Lovely," he sighed, his eyes roaming hungrily over her breasts with the locket lying in the valley between.

Ruby touched his cheek with her fingertips, drawing his attention to her shining eyes. "I love it and I love you."

Ah! The power of those three words! George pulled her back into his arms and there were no more words for a long while.

❧

Two hours after the dawn, Ruby sat on the edge of the bed carefully to avoid waking her sleeping lover. Most mornings they woke together and either made love again before she departed to her room or at least shared a handful of kisses. Today she decided to let him sleep.

He is so beautiful.

She extended one finger, held it near his skin without touching, and traced the features of his face. She loved his face! His high forehead with the unruly locks that fell into his eyes because he never tied his ponytail tightly enough.

The heavy brows a shade of chestnut and lighter than his hair but the same as the thick lashes framing his azure eyes. The mouth that was rarely not smiling with lips—the lower fuller than the upper—that were incredibly tender and velvety against her skin. His nose was perhaps a bit too large to be considered perfect, but it was straight and fit the sharp bone structure of his face.

She stopped at his chin and avoided looking at or thinking of his body. If she did, she would change her mind and wake him for sure. George joked about his thin physique, and it was true that he was not as muscular as men who spent hours fencing or boxing, but he was far from weak or unattractive. He was lean but strong, each muscle defined and hard. His thighs were well developed, a result, he said, of being raised on horses. This she could believe, not only because of his powerfully muscled legs but because she had ridden with him a number of times and he possessed the natural grace and skill of a man whose equestrian skills transcended the standard.

As for the other, more intimate parts of his body… Well, she was definitely satisfied with what was there!

"You are beautiful, George Darcy," she whispered, "and I do love you. More than you will ever know." She squeezed her eyes shut at the stab of pain. *How cruel life is. Why could I have not met him before? Everything would have been different.* She shook her head and inhaled. In the privacy of her room, she would cry as she had every morning for days now once realizing the depth of her love for him. When alone, she could give in to her despair, but not here, where he might waken and see the agony dwelling so close to the surface of her skin.

You are a coward, a voice inside her head accused.

Yes, I am, she silently agreed. It was horrid irony that he thought her strong and independent of will. Once she had thought that of herself as well, taken great pride in her dominant nature and control of her destiny. How tragically awry her planning had gone! Everything had spiraled out of her control and she lived in a state of chaotic emotion. Joy and bliss as she had never known one hour then plummeting depression the next. Maintaining her façade was becoming increasingly difficult. If she allowed a minute crack, all would be lost, and she could not bear to live with his hatred as her last memory. Best she live with the lies she had spun and the guilt that would torture her forever than to shatter his love for her with the truth.

Perhaps it will be easier if his heart is broken rather than betrayed.

She touched the pendant hanging between her breasts and so near her heart, absorbing his dear face as she removed it and opened the oval locket. Using the small pair of scissors from his desk, she lifted his hair from where it spread across the pillow, snipped a clump off the end, and secured the pieces in the locket's hollow. For a few moments more, she tenderly caressed his silky hair, running the strands through her fingers. She loved that he never wore a wig. His hair was thick and wavy, reached to just past his shoulder blades, and was the color of roasted coffee beans with amber highlights. The urge to press her face into the mass she knew would smell woodsy with a hint of lemon was overwhelming her. But the sun was higher in the sky and she needed to prepare for another day with him.

I must enjoy every minute we have left, my darling love. She kissed her fingertips, pressed them gently against his lips, and after slipping the pendant into her robe pocket, she left.

She hated the walk to her room. Not for fear of discovery. The corridors were always empty. It was the distance that each step created between them. "It was a mistake to tell him I love him," she murmured. Or was it? Her hand wrapped around the locket inside her pocket. She had not meant to confess her feelings, but the moment was too real, too raw. At least that was one truth she had told, meaning it with every ounce of her soul, and she prayed it would stay with him.

Closing the door behind her, Ruby drew the locket from her pocket and paused in the middle of the room to caress the silver. She fancied it felt warm, as if his hair was alive, possessing a particle of his essence that was captured inside the metal. She smiled, not sure whether to laugh at her whimsy or to cry. She had no opportunity to do either.

"Do you always return to your chambers at this hour? Does your lover exhaust you so that you sleep past the dawn, or is he keeping you up all through the night?"

Ruby gasped and whirled about, the locket clenched in her hand and rapidly hidden in her pocket. "What are you doing here? What if you were seen?"

"Don't be ridiculous. I can sneak about as stealthily as you, my dear. I have made sure of it, remember? Servants are easy to control and money buys blindness."

The man rose from the chair by the door and stalked to where she stood.

He wore a faint, humorless smile, and his eyes were coldly glinting as he examined her startled face. The first sign of emotion was seething lust when his gaze swept down her body. Next was a flare of his nostrils and pursed lips when he leaned in and inhaled.

"You smell like him. Like sex and a man's seed and sweat. Are you enjoying the lover I chose for you, *my heart*?"

The endearment was emphasized but lacking warmth. Ruby resisted closing her eyes in pain with tremendous effort. Instead, she presented a serene countenance, boldly held his gaze, and delivered a slow, seductive smile.

"He serves a purpose but cannot compare to you," she lied. "How could he?"

"Indeed. He could not." He stared intently at her for a full minute, Ruby never flinching, then he shrugged. "Honestly, I could care less if you enjoy yourself. In fact, I hope you have, since I read that makes it easier to conceive. Just remember who you belong to, Duchess. Never forget that you are *my* wife."

"Have no fear, Your Grace. It is never absent from my mind. *You* are never absent from my mind," she amended when he glowered at her.

"I am pleased to hear that."

The Duke of Larent stepped back a pace and lifted her chin, his thumb caressing her jaw. "So beautiful," he whispered. Suddenly his expression was as a starved wolf, complete with glowing eyes and tongue swiping over his lips. He bent and brushed his hard mouth over her neck.

Power radiated from him, burning her skin through the robe that might as well not be on her for all the good it did against his glacial magnetism. Ruby shivered. She had almost forgotten the piercing, all-consuming potency of him. The Duke of Larent, her husband, was dangerous and cold where George Darcy, her lover by assignment and now the man who possessed her heart, was warmth and light. She knew this and hated that a part of her responded to the man she had married with the same elemental greed that had struck her months ago.

"I tire of this game," he grumbled hoarsely. "I want you in my bed where you belong! It has been far too long."

"I doubt you are lonely," she snapped, and then clamped her lips together when he chuckled.

"Jealous are we? Good. It is flattering, but never forget that while I grant you leave to entertain the doctor, it is for one reason only. Once accomplished, you are never to stray."

"Does the same standard apply to you, husband?"

He laughed and did not reply, the answer as obvious as the question was redundant. Sitting down on the edge of the bed, the duke leaned back onto his elbows. Dressed in breeches and an open shirt, he was the epitome of virile masculinity. He was aroused, a fact unable to miss, adding to the image of prowess and capability. And in all ways but one he was.

When a mere fourteen, Lady Ruby Thomason had accepted her unique qualities of dynamic sensuality and extreme beauty. Furthermore, she had decided to use them to snare the best husband possible and never intended to settle for less than a marquess. She told her father in no uncertain terms what she wanted, and since a daughter served one purpose, even one dearly loved as his prized jewel Ruby, there was never any argument. Years passed and candidates were eliminated one by one until Ruby laid eyes on the Duke of Larent three months ago. Although more than twice her age and rumored to be cursed after two annulled marriages and a third wife deceased, a confident Ruby did not care. He was handsome, wealthy, powerful, and endowed with the identical inner sensuality as she. Fiercely, they were drawn to each other, attraction cementing the decision. That the duke had requirements did not bother her in the slightest. At least, it hadn't at the time.

"We have an arrangement," he reminded her, smoldering eyes raking her head to toe, "and I want to see it done, so we can be together as we should. What a fine Duchess of Larent you will be, Ruby!"

For a moment there was a hint of caring in his voice. *Strange how that never mattered to me before.* Love, affection, and kindness were not emotions she had expected from her life. Once upon a time, power, wealth, and status had been enough. Two weeks ago that had been enough. George had changed everything.

Wretchedness flowed through her body and she stifled a cry of anguish. Hopelessness momentarily clouded her sight. The charisma of the man before her was strong and the lure of the title "Duchess" as attractive as ever. Yet George had opened her eyes and heart to so much more. She thought she would die from the agony of loss that was beginning to consume her.

Then the duke spoke, giving her a glimmer of hope to grasp onto in the yawning darkness stretching years ahead of her.

"It may come as a surprise, but I hate this as much as you, Ruby. I hate that I can't sire a child. Do you have any idea how humiliating that is? One wife can be barren, perhaps two, but three is unlikely, and I know the rumors that are bandied about. I need an heir and you will give me one. Darcy," he spat the name, "resembles me, everyone says, so was the perfect choice. That does not mean I have to like it! No man should taste of your delights but me. No one should satisfy you but me!" His angry shout echoed and he sprang up from the bed. Clasping her upper arms in hands tense as a vise, he grated out, "All I need now is to hear that you are pregnant so we can depart this stifling place, marry publicly, and return to England. I will not keep this up any longer. Are you with child?"

"I... I do not know. It is too soon."

"If the man has not gotten you pregnant yet then he must be incapable as well."

"It is not an exact science and my cycles are not regular. We must be sure. This is too important to rush and goodness knows I do not want to take dozens of men until I conceive. Be patient."

I cannot say good-bye yet! Please, more time to make sure I carry his baby!

Ruby struggled to remain calm and not let the panic show. Despite the whole purpose of her seduction of George being to produce a child, she had always thought of it as for the duke. It was the bargain they had struck. She knew the Duke of Larent had lusted for her as all men did, but it was her willingness to agree to his conditions that sealed the deal. Never had she thought of the baby as something other than a necessary means to an end, an "it" that needed to be created. Suddenly her eyes were opened to the reality. She would forever possess a part of him! A part of the man she had inexplicably lost her heart to. The joy made her dizzy, giddy in fact, and she mustered all her theatrical skills to present a face of calculating indifference.

"Does he suspect anything? Did he believe the story of your inability to have children?"

"He did." She glanced away, remorse enveloping her and weakening her knees. She could not allow the duke to see the pain in her eyes. She knew he would punish her or, worse yet, George in some way. *That* she would never allow! "He is a physician but first he is a man, and men rarely care of the consequences, do they, Your Grace?"

He grunted. "How much longer can it possibly take? God knows you are with him enough. Oh yes," he sneered, "I am aware that you have been with him every night. I have seen you sneak away alone during the day to return with swollen lips and glazed eyes. I see how he stares at you constantly and how you pant after him like a bitch in heat while paying me, your husband, no heed. Are you falling in love with the whelp, Ruby?"

"You fool," she retorted icily. Shaking off his iron grip, Ruby stepped back and glared at him condescendingly. He was treading too close to the truth, a truth he must never know. "It would hardly be wise for me to pay attention to you when we do not want anyone to know of our marriage as yet, now would it? And your accusations are offensive. All men stare at me and I stare right back. Men want me to toy with them, just as you did, in hopes that they will be the fortunate one to win me. George Darcy is one of many who I gift with my attentions. You know it is true."

And that much was, just as it had always been. His awareness of her liaison may have given him an insight into subtle signs that were different from how she interacted normally with men, but Ruby had been very careful when in public to pay George no greater interest than the others who flocked around her.

The duke had not moved, and he was peering at her with deep intensity. "You did not answer my question. Are you falling in love with Dr. Darcy?"

"You chose him, remember? I could have seduced any man in this house, married or not, and none would reject my favors. I knew what the expectations were when you asked me to be your duchess. I did not question who I would have to bed or how many, for that matter. Thankfully you did not pick someone repugnant, but I would have done what was necessary to get what I want."

"To be a duchess."

"Yes." She nodded, not denying what they knew was a major factor. Then she smiled, lazily curling her lips upward and parting them just enough to run the tip of her tongue over the lower. The robe, she peeled from her shoulders, dropping it to her feet as she closed the gap between their bodies. Entwining her arms around his neck, Ruby lifted onto her tiptoes and licked his ear. Concluding her successful distraction from the topic she could not bear to discuss further, she whispered, "I wanted to be *your* duchess, my love. I wanted you."

Larent groaned and crushed her to him. Seconds later, he was ravishing her and the fact that she had never answered his question was forgotten.

George concluded he was unlucky in love. At four and twenty, he had fallen in love twice and lost both women.

Three weeks almost to the day after beginning his affair with Ruby, he and Dr. Ullas had been called away to tend to the injured in an explosion in Hallyacha Pada. When they arrived, it was to discover the report was in error, a development they thought odd and annoying. Only later, after returning to the Sardar's *haveli* and reading Ruby's short letter explaining how her father had arranged her engagement to the Duke of Larent against her wishes and their abrupt departure, had George wondered if Lord Yardley sent the message to get George out of the way. Had Ruby revealed their relationship when told she was being forced to marry the duke? George did not know. The letter said little, the bulk of it a reiteration of her love for him and pleading to forgive her. As if he could fault her for falling prey to the standard manipulations of the English elite, who treated daughters as property to be sold to the highest bidder! His fury was squarely on the shoulders of Lord Yardley and the Duke of Larent. Primarily, however, his anger was at himself for being a fool and not claiming Ruby as his own. The guilt of his cowardice and selfishness ate at him like a cancer, coupling with crippling grief so that he could barely move for days. Locking himself away did not last long, George not one to wallow in self-pity or avoid a decent meal. Nevertheless, it had been a rough period that he was yet to recover from.

"You told me not too long ago that I needed to learn patience. Do you remember that?"

Dr. Ullas nodded but remained silent and waited for his young friend to continue. They sat in the solarium at his house in Thana. George's distressed state of mind these past weeks had been obvious to the older man. Yet it was not in his nature to pry. When ready, if ready, George would share what had occurred during the celebration at Pandey's and Kshitij vowed to listen. It had taken a month, but finally George recounted the entire affair with Lady Ruby Thomason, who was now the Duchess of Larent, so the rumors went. George avoided the gossip as much as possible. He didn't need to hear it to know what had happened. He had Ruby's letter.

"It isn't that I doubted your words exactly. It is just that I never thought of myself as impatient. If asked, I would have said patience was one of my strong suits." George smiled sourly and took a drink of the cooled juice Jharna had brought the men. "I did think about what you said, Dr. Ullas, but I guess my impatience was revealed in that too because I did not dwell on it for long. Lately, I have thought on it and I realize you are one hundred percent correct. I was impatient to finish my education, pushing hard at every turn. I was impatient to leave England. I have been impatient with my duties in Bombay, as if I could only learn if constantly on the move. And I now see that I was impatient to be married. Ironic, isn't it?" George looked at Dr. Ullas's serene face. "I never particularly thought I was all that anxious to be married. If asked before, I would have stated with confidence that women and children weren't on my immediate agenda. That is such an English thing to do, and I have been striving not to be pigeonholed into following the proper English pathway!"

He shook his head and laughed.

"Are you saying you did not love your two ladies?"

"No," George said after a pause. "I loved them both. I still do. McIntyre warned me not to be hasty to get married. I suppose he saw the impatience in me too." George gulped from the juice to swallow past the lump of pain lodged in his throat. The empty spaces once inhabited by Sarah and Ruby had merged into a yawning chasm that grew deeper each day. At times, usually at night when alone in his bed, George felt as if the blackness was near to drowning him, and he wished he could throw himself into the chasm for the peace of oblivion. Then his good sense, and probably that blasted impatience he now knew to be a part of his nature, would reassert until he pulled out of pointless despair. Hours of quiet introspection were granting him clarity.

George stared into his half-empty glass and swirled the liquid gently. Minutes passed with the only sounds those of nature and the muted ring of the Ullas boys laughing from inside the house. When George spoke, his voice was sad but with an undertone of wisdom and maturity.

"Yes, Dr. Ullas, I loved them and the pain will stay with me for a while. Loss of a loved one is a reality I am all too familiar with, but I now realize I have never come to grips with it. With Alex, I mean. Falling in love with Sarah and then Ruby, as real as it was, happened in part because of a longing to replace what I lost so long ago. I have always tried to replace the gap left by Alex with something else. That has sparked my impatience. But I can't replace him. I can't ever fill that gap, nor do I want to any longer. It *belongs* to Alex and he deserves to live there. Maybe someday, if God wills it, I will find a woman and she will live in a new place inside of me, someplace yet to exist that is beside the one where Alex lives. I must learn to be patient and allow that to transpire naturally. It is funny, but I always thought that getting over Alex's death meant letting him go, purging his presence from my mind, as it were. As if I could not be whole and he could not be in heaven unless I said good-bye for good, which, of course, I could not do until someone else took his place and prevented the pain from overwhelming me. Now I understand that isn't how it needs to be at all. Nearly twelve years after the fact, I am finally dealing with Alex's death. Strangely, the compounding emotions of all this are not incapacitating me as much as I might have imagined! On occasion, I feel as if I am going to shatter from the weight of it all, but then I will experience an odd sort of liberation. I am not sure I comprehend it, but I am willing to give it time. And that is progress right there, isn't it?"

Dr. Ullas laughed at the grin George flashed. That he could jest, even a tiny one, was a positive sign. "So what is your plan? You know you are welcome to stay here as long as you like. Jharna and the boys enjoy your company, even as morose as it has been lately, and we need doctors."

"Thank you for the offer. It is tempting, believe me, and I will keep it in mind for the future. For the present, I need to return to Bombay. It is the right thing to do and for the best. Now that I am on the pathway of learning patience and digging into the frightening recesses of my mind, I might as well forge ahead! What better place than Bombay Island? If nothing else, Dr. McIntyre will keep me humble."

GEORGE'S MEMOIRS
MARCH 27, 1792

I began my day with a surprise I am yet assimilating, Alex. I had finished dressing the wound on Lovett's leg that I swear will never heal if the idiot does not condescend to wash himself more often than once a month, when I looked up and who was standing at the door of the hospital but Dr. Ullas! I was stunned but delighted of course. His last correspondence was over a month past, and he said nothing of visiting Bombay. He is here to discuss in person what he has brought up no less than a half dozen times since I left Thana a year ago. Yes, he is requesting I travel with him for a time. You know that the offer has been tempting, extremely so, but I was determined to practice the art of patience. Staying in Bombay was my penance, so to speak. Or so I imagined it. Oddly enough, I have grown to love this island, the people here, and my work. Dr. Trenowyth is an excellent Physician General and a fine doctor. McIntyre and I enjoy working with him, and with our rank as his assistants, we have the power to enact many changes. Medical care and the facilities at Bombay have improved dramatically under our tutelage. I confess to an abominable pride! The ready access to fresh supplies from the Motherland, including updated literature and the newest instruments, is a marvelous boon. The people have benefitted and that, naturally, is what matters the most.

So I find myself weighing both sides of the issue. If I stay here, I am capable of practicing the best of English medicine and some Indian as well. That aids the residents here. If I leave to travel into the interiors of India with Dr. Ullas, I know I will learn skills I cannot begin to fathom. I will not deny this tantalizes me.

The offer is in conjunction with the Company, by the way. Long have I known that physicians are needed with the British troops and diplomats who conduct business for our Empire and King. Dr. Ullas has already spoken with Commander Doyle, sneaky bastard! He is one determined fellow and that is rather flattering, I daresay! Apparently, my vaunted ego is intact. The plan is that I would accompany Dr. Ullas, the two of us working together as colleagues, on a mission of sorts to the various EIC outposts. We have been granted permission to freely move as we wish, to the point of branching out on our own. There are requirements, as expected with the Company, but nothing too stringent. As I have previously ascertained, Dr. Ullas has a positive reputation with the EIC here in the west and a tremendous amount of clout. I should add that he is taking his family with him. He feels strongly that his sons need to learn about their country, and I know he would never be parted from them for any great length of time. In truth, I gather the main point to this venture is for them. It is admirable. Dr. Ullas has wealth enough to travel in style, yet he prefers to serve others along the way.

So why do I hesitate? In striving to learn patience and trust God for my future rather than control everything, have I tipped the scale the other way? Have I become passive or, heaven forbid, afraid? Or worse, have I become too used to comfort and too English? Perish the thought! Nevertheless, I refuse to be hasty. Momentous decisions need to be thought through carefully and—

Good Lord! Am I sniveling? I just read over my own words and have the urge to rip them from the book! Luckily, no one will ever read this until I am dead. Hopefully, my future deeds will supersede, so any progeny I may have will know I did not wallow in indecisiveness for too long. What am I thinking? I came here to travel and increase my education, after all. If I hadn't sidetracked myself with affairs of the heart, I would probably already be in Madras or Calcutta by now. Working side-by-side with Dr. Ullas for several years is a dream come true. Very well then, Alex. I knew discussing this with you would gain me insight. Dr. George Darcy off on a new adventure! Should I warn India first?

I also must tell you that I now have a personal servant. I know! Do not laugh so hard you fall off your cloud and tumble to earth. I am yet cringing at the concept myself, which I know is terribly un-English of me, but I have never been comfortable with another man doing nothing with his life except being at my beck and call. I can dress myself, thank you very much, and could care less if my shoes sparkled. Remember my writing of Anoop, the youth with the severe trachoma? His right eye was so inflamed and exuding copious pus as I have rarely seen, the conjunctivitis reaching a place where scarring was beginning and blindness inevitable if not treated properly. I thank God that I wandered by the corner where he sat begging—unsuccessful, if you recall, since no one would come near him with his face as it was. I was overjoyed to help him and try the Ayurvedic remedies I had recently discovered. The collyrium of churnanjana and probha vati worked miracles, especially with the drops of mustard oil added. I did need to incise the scar tissue along the lid—delicate surgery that was—and was thrilled that he was left with nothing more than a disruption to his peripheral vision and a slight eyelid droop. Well, he was appreciative to an obsessive degree. As flattering as it is to be revered, it was damned annoying to have him dogging my steps with those puppy eyes of his staring at me as if I were divinity or something. Gah! If he weren't so blasted nice, I would have dropped him off the Bombay pier where the water is the deepest! The gents have mercilessly harassed me over Anoop, McIntyre predominantly, for the past four months while I tried to ignore him straightening my messes, running to fetch things for me, and telling everyone that he is my noker, *that being Hindi for servant. Then one day, he was standing near me as I was tending to a man with an infected wound on his chest and it dawned on me that Anoop was anticipating my every move before I did it, handing me the proper instruments or ingredients without me asking. Then when I finished, I saw that he had a tray of sweet meats and wine, and a clean shirt waiting. Well, it sealed the deal, I confess. I still refuse to have him help me dress or bathe, and would sooner walk naked and dirty than admit I can't care for my personal hygiene, and I will never call him my* noker *and continue to try correcting him on that preferring* madadgaar, *which is translated "aide" or "helper," since that is where he shines. He is smart, Alex, and uncanny in reading my thoughts. Rather eerie but helpful. So he is now being paid and sleeps in my bungalow in that extra room I had no use for other than to throw stuff in rather than deal with it. Anoop organized it to boot. God, my whole bungalow is clean! I always feel as if I have stepped into the wrong one! Now I will need to see if he wishes to accompany me on my travels and leave the only home he has ever known. After my reluctance, I realize I would be sad if he stayed behind. Guess I am still English after all.*

CHAPTER FIVE

Mysore

SEPTEMBER 1796

WITH A GROAN, GEORGE fell into the padded Pidha chair under the shaded porch. One hand reached for the waiting glass of chilled mango juice while the other snapped open the folded fan. Fanning his moist face and drinking large gulps of the refreshing beverage occupied all his attention for a good minute. Finally, he glanced to the woman sitting in the matching chair and gasped, "Your sons are exhausting me! How is it possible for a group of youngsters to have so much energy?"

"Is that truly the problem, dear George? Or have they beaten you at the game again?"

"It isn't fair, Jharna," George whined, pitching his voice like a sulky child. "I taught them how to play so should prevail each time!"

Jharna lifted one corner of her mouth but did not look up from her painting. "Is this game named after a chirping insect vitally important to your pride and manliness?"

"Cricket"—he used the English name then returned to Hindi—"is the greatest sport on earth, an English sport," he declared with mocking indignation. "No Indian, especially a child, should play better than an Englishman."

"Then perhaps you should stop the purposeful mistakes that allow them to win. I would hate to see your pride suffer an irreversible blow."

"I seriously doubt *that* would ever happen," he harrumphed, referring to the second charge and not denying the first.

George was staring toward the grassy makeshift cricket field where a dozen boys and girls of varying ages were laughing and shrieking as they played the unusual game. Three months ago, shortly after arriving in Saliom, a suburb of Mysore City, the tall, lanky English stranger had boldly walked out onto the open area with a ball, six wickets, and four blade-like wooden bats tucked under his arms. While the timidly wary children observed, he gouged lines in the soft turf and pounded the wickets into groups of three at either end of a designated zone, whistling as he prepped the rectangular pitch to his specification with the assistance of the Ullas boys, Nimesh and Sasi. Once done, he turned his attention to the group of youngsters who were by then more curious than afraid and, flashing his patented Darcy grin, asked them in Hindi if they wanted to learn how to play a game more fun than any other. That was all it took. From that day forward, Dr. Darcy was sought by every child in the village nearly as often as the adults sought his medical services.

"No, Komali!" He leapt to his feet. "Stand in front of the wickets... the post things, yes... that's a girl. Now get ready... no, don't look at me! Watch the bowler... Yes!" He whooped when she hit the ball, clapping and shouting encouragement to run. "Ah, that girl is going to be the best player of them all, mark my words. She already has beaten Nimesh in sprinting speed, to his annoyance."

"That must be why he was dashing up and down the hall yesterday. Raveena banished him to his room for making such a clatter. Humility will serve him well, especially after taunting *Sahib* Dutta's daughters for not being able to read as well as he."

"Underestimating the worth of a woman will not be a fault of his for long." George resumed his place on the chair and stretched his bare legs across to a terra-cotta planter, casually crossing his ankles on the wide edge. "He sees you trounce me at chess often enough to know women have keen intellects."

"Winning a game of chess with you is not all that difficult."

"Oh ho ho! Methinks I detect an insult and challenge in those words, Mrs. Ullas! I believe a rematch is in order!"

"Are you sure your pride can take such a hit twice in one day, Dr. Darcy?"

"Probably not, so it is fortunate for my bruised ego that I will not be able to test myself until tomorrow. I am due to meet your husband in an hour," he explained when she looked up from the plate she was painting, teasing eyes asking a silent question. "We are performing the surgery on Bai Dalmiya. That will take all afternoon and part of the evening, but tomorrow I should have time to redeem myself and prove my superiority. Be warned."

"Noted. So that is why you feigned exhaustion and quit the cricket field?"

"Partly feigned. They do possess a stamina I wish I could bottle in some way." Pausing for another deep drink of the sweet juice, George smilingly observed the playing youths for several minutes. "I have decided that my favorite sound in all the world is that of children laughing. Remember when we were discussing that and you suggested I discover it?"

"I do." Jharna sat the paintbrush aside and turned her attention to her companion. "It was nearly three years ago. You said you had to think about it, which is wise. One's favorite sound above all others is not to be hastily decided, although it may change as one grows older. Why children's laughter?"

George shrugged. "Oh, I could name a hundred reasons, but the simple fact is that no other sound gives me such joy." He met her thoughtful stare. "Now I have told you. What is your favorite sound in all the world, Jharna?"

Smiling smugly and cocking her head, she replied, "That is my secret."

"Hey! Not fair! I told you!"

"I never asked you to tell me. I recommended the exercise as part of your life journey. Whether you share the revelation or not is your prerogative. I choose not to."

"You are a damned infuriating woman, Jharna Ullas. Do you know that?"

"I am a woman," she stated simply, smug smile intact.

George glowered for a few more seconds then chuckled and shook his head. Conversation with Kshitij's wife was never boring. No wonder his mentor and friend loved her so profoundly. Nimesh and Sasi were blessed with incredible parents, a fact borne true by the boys' fine characters and delightful personalities. Daily, George counted his blessings at the honor of being an adopted member of their family.

In the four and a half years they had traveled together, George never once regretted his decision to leave Bombay.

The first two months after Dr. Ullas enticed Dr. Darcy away from his comfortable post were passed on Salsette Island as they gathered supplies and finalized their plans. Guides and servants were hired, and medical personnel interested in the excursion were interviewed along with British soldiers, the numbers swelling their party to over thirty before they departed. That number grew when reaching Thana to retrieve the Ullas family and personal servants. Since then the company varied, as some chose to return home or tarry behind while new recruits joined in along the way. Upon occasion, it was only the Ullas household and George with Anoop.

Mysore was always part of the agenda. Partly that was Kshitij's desire to reacquaint himself with his estranged kinsmen and to share his past with his current family, but also due to the busy hospital and school of Ayurvedic medicine in Mysore City. George had desired this since the beginning of their association, but with the third war between Tipu Sultan of Mysore and the British having reached a peace agreement the same year they set out, it was judged sensible to wait for matters to calm. They left the western coast to press east as far as Hyderabad Deccan before veering south two years into their journey, opportunities to practice medicine and learn presenting themselves as they kept moving.

Their longest stay in one place was Madras. The booming city, established as the administrative headquarters of the British East India Company, offered vast educational experiences for all of them. The physicians zealously launched into the work available among the British and native peoples. It was an exciting time, even Kshitij supplanting his personal irritation at the exalted, imperialistic attitude of the British with the positive aspects present in the region. They might have dwelt longer if not for Jharna's yearning to study the famed painting techniques of the Tanjore in Tamil Nadu. That movement further south led to a brief voyage to Ceylon, the physicians heeding a summons to assist the Dutch for a handful of months in early 1796 while Jharna and the boys remained in Tanjore. It wasn't the first time they had embarked on missions of a limited duration away from the others, Kshitij opting to leave his family where it was safe if they were entering an unstable or unknown environment. The jaunt to Ceylon gave George a taste of the unique culture and was not nearly long enough to satisfy his hunger to learn all that was possible, but it was better than nothing.

From Tanjore they diverted west, rather than further south to Cape Comorin, as originally intended. The waters surrounding Tipu Sultan were far from calm, but after four years, the pull of Mysore proved too great to resist. For the past four months, they had resided in Saliom. Kshitij and Jharna dwelt in the residence of his youngest brother and family. George rented a modest bungalow on the banks of the tiny river running to the north, preferring the solitude, although the walk to his friends' abode was less than ten minutes.

"You do intend to wash and don clothing more respectable before you perform surgery, do you not?"

Jharna's query broke into his reverie, George looking over at her with eyes wide with false shock. "Are you implying that this lovely *kurti* is not fit for surgery?" He tugged on the dirt-stained multicolored cloth of the tunic covering his chest. "Or is this an implication that my legs are a problem?" He raised one of the extremities in question off the pot's edge, the hem of the knee-length *lungi* slipping to reveal an inch of thigh. "Admit it, these are fine looking legs. Manly and muscular. All the way around excellent examples of how a man's legs should be."

Jharna quirked one brow over her glittering, dark eyes but said nothing.

"Fine. I'll change." He groaned. "Besides, your husband would skin me alive if I wasn't presentable before getting drenched in blood and yuck."

Not that he disagreed or would do otherwise, as they knew, Jharna laughing and shaking her head. "When are you going to wear the *shalwar kameez* that Vani sewed for you?"

"How did you know of that?" he blurted, truly surprised this time.

"She showed it to me before she began," Jharna answered calmly, daubing her brush into the pot of paint and ignoring his expression. "She was afraid the colors were too bold, which I assured her was impossible for you. I assume it fit well?"

"Yes," he spluttered after a moment, "quite well."

"It should. She does know your size, after all." She glanced upward then chuckled. "Oh, George! Why the embarrassment? You should know by now that personal affairs never remain secret in a close-knit community like Saliom."

"I do. It is just... Well, it is Vani, and I was not sure how... Does Kshitij know?"

Jharna flashed him a look that cleared that redundant question. George winced. "Don't be ridiculous, George. As if Kshitij would care who shares your bed as long as no one is being harmed."

"Yes, but Vani is his daughter—"

"And she is a grown woman, a widow with her own life and the ability to make choices, all of which she has done without her father's influence or permission. You two are good together. Vani is happy and fond of you."

"How fond?"

"You have no cause for concern, *mitra*. As I said, Vani is a grown woman. She understands how it is with you, that we will be leaving in time, and she is content with the situation. Honestly, not to further bruise your fragile ego so soon after a cricket and chess defeat, but Vani would probably not have you permanently if you offered." She burst out laughing at the abrupt wounded cast to his face. "Men! All the same no matter where they hail from. Please do not take it personally, George."

George opened his mouth and shut it without speaking. Few things flustered him and he was not sure if it was the fact that his liaison with Vani was common knowledge—and to her father no less—or that he was discussing it with Jharna! Either way, it was best to close the topic right now. Fortunately, two interruptions served as perfect diversions.

"*Vaidya*! Come play with us. Komali's team is winning and we need your help!"

"Please, *chacha-jee*!" Nimesh and Sasi pleaded in unison, drowning the three other male voices begging for delivery from the girls. "You are our best player!"

"That is because I am taller than all of you combined."

The drama may have gone on indefinitely if not for the appearance of Dr. Ullas, his soft tones cutting through the tumult.

"Dr. Darcy, we have another case of hydrophobia, so I have just been informed, and I am questioning why you halted the smallpox inoculations."

Kshitij shooed the children away. They left with hanging heads and shuffling feet until reaching the edge of the lawn, whereupon they dashed back into the fray on the field, apparently having decided that girls were *not* going to win. George leaned his head back to peer up at Kshitij. Whenever addressed as "Dr. Darcy" among family, George knew it was a sign that he was in trouble.

"Chapal and Loy took ill after their doses, more so than normal, and the inoculation sites are inflamed and ulcerated. I do not think they will die but judged it wise to wait until we know they are well. In the interim, I have Partha and his team concocting fresh inoculant, just in case there was a contaminant or miscalculation. It isn't an exact science, as you know, and that bothers me. The whole idea of inoculation bothers me, as you also know. I definitely want to be as certain of the safety of this batch before we start with the children."

"The risks with inoculation outweigh the outcome of smallpox."

"Usually," George amended. "I concede that it is a principle that has merit and data to support, but there are cases proving otherwise. I haven't forgotten Chittoor. Eight people dead and a dozen infected with the very disease we were trying to prevent. And the scarring?" He brushed his fingertips along the inner surface of his upper left arm where a sovereign-sized silvery mark was the sign of his smallpox inoculation done years ago. Barely visible on his fair skin, the same scar on darker skin was typically more pronounced. In a tiny percentage of individuals, the reaction to the serum containing live smallpox cells increased, with resultant scarring that was unsightly and ofttimes painful and debilitating.

"Scarring from smallpox, if one survives, is far worse, Dr. Darcy. In India we have inoculated for a thousand years."

"Stop 'Dr. Darcy-ing' me, Kshitij. You know I agree with all you say. Still, *you* can't argue that there are risks. Besides, we have exerted caution before in circumstances like this. At the present, there aren't any cases of smallpox here, so we have time. I'll make sure it gets done, Kshitij. Trust me. Now, what about the case of rabies?"

Kshitij grudgingly conceded, reaching for the pitcher of juice and pouring a glass. "A man was bitten by a wild dog while hunting. Three weeks ago. Fool dressed the wound on his hand with some homemade poultice and did not seek medical care because he feared amputation. Sadly his gamble has been lost. Losing a limb is unfortunate, but it is a cure. Maybe draining or cauterizing the wound would have sufficed. Now he is symptomatic and we know the probable outcome."

Kshitij sat on the divan beside his wife, a light caress over her knee the first and only gesture indicating he was aware of her presence. Jharna carried on with her painting. George barely noticed the exchange and spared not a moment's thought to their reserve. He could count on one hand the number of times he had seen the Ullases kiss, and those had been swift presses of closed lips. Long ago, his gift for reading people helped him discern the love they shared, just as he discerned that Jharna placidly accepted her husband's inhibitions, following his preference, though her wish was to be more demonstrative. Curiosity at the relationship between his mentor and wife had once sparked George to observe closely and ask subtle questions, but now they were his adopted family and that was enough.

"We can examine him before we begin Bai Dalmiya's eye surgery," Kshitij continued. "It has not been long since the initial infection, and his symptoms are mild so perhaps we will have luck with the salix leaf and silene root."

"Maybe a stronger dosage this time." George offered a handful of additional suggestions, the physicians discussing the merits of possible treatment plans with cool, clinical detachment. Underneath, the hint of doubt was audible, neither holding much hope of a positive outcome. Rabies was fatal almost one hundred percent of the time.

Kshitij stood. "We should leave soon. You will be washing and changing clothes, yes?"

George lifted a brow at the question that was not a question at all but a command. "What *is it* with you two and my attire? Never have I seen two people so concerned with the garments one wears."

Jharna coughed loudly at that nonsense. Kshitij's expression did not alter. Instead, he crossed his arms over his chest and stared pointedly.

"Very well. If I must don a new suit, I will." George sighed and rose to his feet.

"Don't wear the outfit Vani sewed for you though. That one is too fine. Save it for dinner tomorrow at *Sahib* Rettadi's house. Wear one of your usual gaudy tunics. That will restore Bai Dalmiya's sight as well as our skills."

And with the same inscrutable expression, Kshitij pivoted and entered the house, leaving a stunned George with mouth wide open and Jharna shaking with laughter.

⚜

The surgery to remove the shard of metal from Bai Dalmiya's eye was a success. A week after the delicate procedure, the bandages were removed for the final time and the warrior who had received the wound while practicing battle drills was allowed to open his eyes. His vision was blurred, but the orb was healing nicely. Both doctors were confident that his eyesight would improve, and as the days passed, this proved to be true.

Unfortunately, the outcome for the man with rabies was not as kind. Weeks of treatment with every known medicine only prolonged the man's torture.

George left the hospital at dusk on the evening of his death. Weary, dirty, and heartsick, he opted to walk rather than accept the offer of a horse-drawn cart. Diverting to the sandy trail skirting the edge of the trees and bank of the creek, George breathed deeply of the clean air as he walked at a moderate pace. At times like this, on shady paths covered with moldering leaves and the only sounds those of nature and the dim murmur of laughter and voices from the distant houses, George could almost imagine he was in Derbyshire, strolling along one of the numerous trails cutting through the woods. It was far warmer than in England, the air moist and heavy with tropical smells alien at home, and of course, the vegetation was nothing that would grow in the cool climes of the north. Yet like in Derbyshire, George found solace in the out-of-doors. Perhaps the simplicity of life among the plants and animals that existed without the troubles that beset humans spoke to a hidden need within his soul.

Veering off the path at an unmarked point, George parted the low-hanging branches of a copse of tamarind trees, several of the long, bean-shaped pods yanked off as he passed through and stuffed into the bag hanging over his shoulder. The medicinal qualities were numerous, and although he grabbed handfuls every time he walked this way so that a huge pile of tamarind pods and seeds covered one end of the herb table in his bungalow, it had become a habit. Weaving through the fragrant leaves, George unerringly followed the foot-wide rut in the dirt that feebly passed for a trail until reaching an area of the creek where an ages-past dead tamarind had fallen over to form a dam, the water backing up and eroding the spongy soil until a shallow pond resulted. It wasn't much, especially for a broad-shouldered man three inches over six feet, but enough to lie down in while the steady stream of water cooled by the thick trees flowed over his skin. Dropping the bag to the ground, George stripped and entered the water with a sighing groan. Anoop would be at their bungalow waiting with a washbasin, buckets of fresh water for rinsing, soap, and clean towels. Cleanliness was not attained in a slow running creek, but the refreshment found when floating in water and staring at the stars was unmatched.

George frequently diverted to this secluded spot after a long day. Years of living among Hindus had taught him to relish these opportunities to sink into a relaxed state, where his mind could rest and body rejuvenate. Practicing the deep breathing exercises of yoga, he allowed his brain to grow quiet. He dwelt on nothing in particular and opened his senses to the calming sounds of nature and his heart to the gentle whispers from heaven. Through these processes, George had deepened his faith over time, forging a communion with the God he had always believed in but largely taken for granted. He sensed His presence, not talking to him in a defined way but touching his spirit with a loving, soothing Hand. Disconnected yet strangely attuned to everything, peace fell like a cleansing flood to wash away the bulk of his weariness and heavy heart.

Death of any patient was never easy for him. He knew he took such realities of life too personally. Dr. Ullas was constantly reminding him that, at best, physicians could only serve as helpers to the gods but would never have the final authority on how one's fate was decided. That philosophy wasn't far off the Christian perspective, and logically, George accepted it. However, logic and emotion conflicted, the chaotic aftermath assuaged while floating in the pond. George was able to walk through the door of his bungalow with a consoled heart.

Anoop waited with bathing implements and a hot meal at the ready. After five years, the two had fallen into a comfortable routine, with Anoop nearly indispensable. He was an outstanding cook, that skill the one above all others that George appreciated. Additionally, he was a masterful steward and housekeeper, whatever dwelling place they inhabited instantly organized and kept clean. George had made it very clear that he could take care of himself, was essentially a private man, and finicky about his property. It hadn't taken long for Anoop to figure out what was safe to touch and what was not!

For three years, George had argued with Anoop over their personal relationship, begging him not to refer to him as, "My *haakim*, the exalted *Vaidya* Darcy," or some such similar rot. Anoop listened, smiled, and nodded as George explained his reasoning, and then promptly ignored his orders. It drove George crazy, primarily because he respected Anoop and abhorred the idea of the younger man believing he was nothing but a servant under the boot of the autocratic Englishman. George encountered that attitude among his countrymen, and it sickened him. George paid Anoop a substantial wage, trusted him with great responsibility, and talked to him in an intelligent manner with dignity and friendly humor. The attitude went a long way toward narrowing the self-imposed gap, but for Anoop, there was forever an air of master/servant that he refused to relinquish.

Gradually George came to realize that, for Anoop, it was a matter of honor to serve him, not because he was English but because he was a *vaidya* who served all of mankind. To Anoop, a Hindu through and through, he was lifted high and esteemed due to his faithful service, and would be rewarded in the afterlife. It was never a matter of seeing himself as beneath George but rather the proper position for him to inhabit to maintain the careful balance of life, what they call *dharma*. Once George grasped this—as well as he could, not being a Hindu—he no longer fought Anoop. Their friendship and cohabitation settled after that, their mutual accord established and comfortable.

Therefore, as typical for them, George retreated to the tiny veranda at the back of the house while Anoop cleaned the kitchen area. Sitting on a swinging bench with his legs extended to the railing and gently propelling the swing into motion, George sipped a cup of tea and stared into the darkness. Moonlight and starlight bathed the small yard and faintly illuminated the trees and bushes that swayed in the mild breeze. A lit candle sat on the table, the glow needed to read the book laying on the cushion beside him—a copy of *Ramayana* written in Hindi that he was reading to perfect his command of the language and learn more of Indian history. The peace attained in the pond clung to him, and while tired, he was wide awake. Anoop was singing a ballad, his fine tenor drifting through the open windows, adding a pleasant ambience. Day after tomorrow, George would be traveling to the EIC base in Coorg for a week to two-week engagement with the medical corps, so was enjoying the solitude.

Briefly, he considered walking to the Ullas house where he was never considered a visitor. However, he knew Kshitij was as exhausted as he and deserved to pass the evening sedately with his wife and children. His thoughts drifted to Vani. It had been five days since they last spent time together and that was a family gathering with the entire Ullas clan. It had been longer still since they had been alone together. The prospect was very tempting, although strangely it was not sex foremost on his mind. Vani was a tender and loving woman. Being with her was soothing more than passionate, her sweetly simple nature a great comfort whether they went to bed or not. On a night like tonight, the idea of lying in a woman's arms merely to feel a necessary human connection was enticing, and the only reason he didn't leave the swing was because he never imposed upon Vani in that way. She was an independent woman and not his merely for the taking. If she wanted him, she would ask.

George sighed and reached for the book, but before he cracked it open, he detected movement in the shadows of the trees. It only took a second to recognize the shape outlined by the pale light from the sky, George chuckling under his breath as he rose from the swing and crossed the lawn.

"I made a fresh batch of *gulab jamun*. Mine are better than Anoop's and I thought you might want some."

"Thank you, Vani." George took the covered bowl from her hands. "You do make it better than Anoop, but forgive me if I do not admit that. He cooks most of my other food and washes my clothes. I'd rather not be punished by biting into a *bhut jolokia* pepper hidden in my *puri* or have my *paijamas* starched."

"I understand. I am sorry to hear about the man with rabies, *Sahib*. Dessert is a small consolation."

"It is a better consolation than you might think, Vani. You know me well enough to trust it will do the trick."

Her merry eyes were detectable even in the darkness. "Then perhaps you would be interested in some *rasmalai* as well? After that I can open the jar of tailam oil and massage your muscles. If you wish to stay at my house past that, you are welcome, *Sahib*."

George honestly could not say which item sounded more appealing: food, an excellent massage, or loving. Taken all together, it was a package deal no red-blooded man would reject, so with a smile and gentlemanly offer of his arm, they turned and headed back up the path to her house.

❧

The volatile situation between the British East India Company and the ruler of Mysore, Tipu Sultan, promised to escalate into another war. Diplomatic missions were ongoing, but no one seriously thought the warrior king could be swayed from his prior intent to convert all Hindus to Islam and to drive the English permanently off India's shores, especially after being soundly humiliated in 1792. That war ended with the Sultan forced to cede nearly half his realm and surrender two of his sons as hostage, pending payment for the cost of the campaign against him. That debt had been paid long ago, his sons returned as the EIC promised, and thus far the treaty held. Rumors of his renewed plotting with the French circulated, this a particular threat due to Napoleon's personal vengeance against Britain and desire to rule the world. Largely speculation at this point, taken as a whole, it nonetheless meant the region was not overly favorable to foreigners unless sanctioned directly by the Tiger of Mysore, and naturally, EIC soldiers were not welcomed with open arms.

For this reason, George and Kshitij wisely decided to leave any English members of their group in Dindigul before crossing the border into Mysore. It wasn't the first time they had struck out on their own without military or official company escorts, nor was it likely to be their last. The association between the EIC and the numerous Indian states ran the gamut from absolute control to strong alliance to bare tolerance to frank hostility. Like it or not, George was forced to pay attention to politics and the winds of change far more than he ever intended.

Early in their travels, while still crossing the friendly Deccan Plain of Maharashtra, Jharna suggested he dress in native fashion as a way to blend in, at least as much as possible for a man fairer and taller than most Indians. Additionally, it served to pacify his patients, many of whom, right or wrong, held a less than favorable opinion of Westerners. This suggestion George embraced wholeheartedly. The truth was he loved the loose, comfortable, cool, and colorful designs of Indian garments. Once used to the radical switch from restrictive, hot, layered suits in bland colors, George rarely donned one. He kept his wavy hair long, the Ullases rightfully suspecting it was not so much a sentimental observance of British style but because he liked to tie his ponytail with a flashy strip of fabric as just another way to stand out in a crowd. As if anyone could miss him. As time passed, George adapted to the culture he lived in, mastered the Hindi language and bits of the various dialects, and above all cultivated a true love for the Indian people. The latter, more than anything, was sensed instinctively by the natives he met, so much so that rarely was anyone dubious of him for more than a few minutes.

Therefore, difficulties had been nonexistent. Caution had been applied, Kshitij insisting that his wife and sons dwell in larger cities where the races tended to reside in harmony and where the government, whether British or Indian or a combination, kept the peace. Trips he and George undertook to less-populated zones were done alone and nothing too frightening had occurred. Nor had they encountered problems since entering Mysore, those suspicious authorities dealt with along the way not able to argue Dr. Ullas's right to be in the area nor displeased to permit trained physicians. In order to abide by the treaty, Tipu Sultan could not very well order the immediate arrest of every white man seen in Mysore as much as he might like to. George certainly wasn't the only one wandering about, and once settled into Saliom near Mysore City, he became an oft-seen addition to the population and was forgotten by those in command. Or so he thought.

Days after his return from Coorg, George was working with Dr. Ullas in the hospital when a commotion from the front of the building gained their attention. Leaving the bedside of the patient they were tending, the two men walked around the corner for a better view of the tumult, neither suspecting it had anything to do with them.

A group of Mysore soldiers stood in the entryway, their red turbans and bayoneted muskets out of place in the sterile environment of a hospital. The leader was talking to one of the orderlies, who seconds later glanced in George and Kshitij's direction and, with an expression of relief, pointed at them. The soldier's eyes followed his indication, George's brows lifting when the soldier gestured for them to join the cluster.

"This does not bode well," Kshitij murmured.

"Might be exciting though," George murmured back, earning a sour grimace from his partner.

The leader inclined his head respectfully when they stopped before him, George hoping that was a positive sign. "Honored *vaidyas*, his most high exaltedness Sultan Fateh Ali Tippu requests most humbly your professional services in a matter of extreme delicacy. A carriage waits without to convey you in comfort and honor to Seringapatam."

Sweet words such as "honor" and "request" did not fool either of them. This was a demand, pure and simple, and one they could not ignore. They obtained little information from the commander other than the assurance that it was a medical issue and nothing more. He wasn't exactly the most readable man George had ever met, stony face and iron eyes free of emotion, but the sense was that his words were truthful. Of course, whether because that was all he had been told or because it actually was a medical emergency was another story. A hastily scribbled note for Jharna was written while George gathered their traveling bags, and within thirty minutes, they were wheeling out of the city.

George had never been north of Mysore City nor had he laid eyes on the cosmopolitan capitol of the Sultan's powerful state. The nineteen miles of terrain separating Mysore City and Seringapatam was flat with gentle hills and sparse vegetation obstructing the view. Long before entering the gates, George and Kshitij could see the white walls spanning the breadth of the city with the towering pillars of Tipu's palace, the square pinnacle of the Ranganathaswamy Temple among numerous other Muslim temples, and the twin minarets of the Jumma Masjid rising above. As fascinating as it was, sightseeing was not on the agenda. Their escort traveled at a fast clip and presumably expected the citizens to get out of their way, because they did not slow considerably once entering the gates. George and Kshitij were too busy holding on to the seats to avoid undue bouncing to talk. Shared glances sufficed, however. The haste spoke volumes as to the purpose of the summons.

Therefore, they were not surprised to arrive at the residential palace and be ushered through a secondary entrance with no one greeting them other than servants and a refined gentleman in courtly attire who identified himself with a title in a language George did not know. A whispered translation from Kshitij as they rushed along in his wake revealed he was a sort of seneschal or steward and guessing by the genuflections automatically granted by every person they passed, he was indeed someone of importance to the Sultan's household. Information was scant other than that their medical services were required for one of Tipu Sultan's sons, a royal *shahzada* prince.

There wasn't time to linger on speculations, and upon reaching their final destination, they no longer cared.

The chamber was an enormous bedroom crammed with dozens of people, perhaps more, although it was difficult to ascertain with the heavy drapes shut and the only illumination weak, smoking oil lamps. A boy of approximately seventeen lay on the bed, propped into a half-sitting position that did nothing to aid his labored respirations, each strangled gasp echoing around the tapestry-draped walls. He weakly writhed on the sheets, the dimness not hiding the twisted grimaces of agony etched deeply into his sweating face. Groans and whines of pain were interspersed with his ragged breathing. An untrained idiot could instantly recognize this was a situation of direst extremity.

Immediately, the physicians snapped into their professional roles. Dr. Ullas spoke the Mysore dialect better than Dr. Darcy, so it was he who commanded the drapes be pulled and windows opened wide as the first order of business. The hesitation was negligible, the shine from the sun revealing seconds later what they suspected. The youngster was suffering from pneumonia and some sort of lung collapse with death an approaching certainty if treatment of a radical nature was not performed soon.

George knelt by the boy's side, Dr. Ullas naturally assuming the role of assistant. This was not only due to his ability to translate but because they both knew that when it came to ailments of the heart and lungs, Dr. Darcy was the expert. For reasons that probably related to how Alex died, George's specific interest had lead to studying anatomy and physiology of the connected systems more than the other body organs combined. There wasn't a treatment for a single disease involving the heart and lungs that Dr. Darcy did not know and hadn't used. He fearlessly attempted innovative procedures and had mastered a number of them, gaining a reputation that had apparently migrated to the ear of someone associated with the Sultan.

"He is burning with fever." George laid the back of his hand over the boy's forehead then peeled one eyelid. "Stuporous from diminished oxygen. Ashen and diaphoretic. Severe cyanosis." He rattled off the symptoms so that Dr. Ullas could translate to the medical men observing. The blankets were flipped aside and shirt lifted, baring a broad, well-built chest destined to be that of a muscled warrior. Fine breeding and strength was definitely an asset in this case. George bent to press one ear against the defined chest that was laboriously straining to continue the fundamental act of breathing. Closing his eyes and sticking his index finger into the free ear canal so as to concentrate and block extraneous input, George listened. First to the upper left, then to the upper right, down to the axilla, then the peripheral base, and so on, until the entire chest area had been covered. He was nothing if not thorough, although within seconds he had known the diagnosis and treatment necessary if the prince was to survive.

"They say he has been ill for nearly a week." Dr. Ullas had been busy while George auscultated. Their medical cases were open at the foot of the bed and he was retrieving instruments and medications, servants and healers tending to his orders for boiling water and clean cloths. "Properly diagnosed as lung fever and treated appropriately from what I can gather. The Sultan employs well-trained healers. Three are Ayurvedic *vaidyas* and two Persian *Yūnānīs* from Nepal. There is also a French doctor about. It was he who heard of you and your skills. This is Abdul-Qahaar." Kshitij nodded toward a tall man in blue robes standing on the far side of the bed, the man bowing respectfully when George glanced up. "He is *Yūnānī* and in charge of the patient. Any guesses on what will happen to him if the *shahzada* dies?"

George met Kshitij's expressionless face and bobbed his head once. No need to verbalize further. Two lives were at stake, perhaps more, adding to the pressure of the situation. Luckily, Dr. George Darcy had never been one to crumble under pressure.

"Explain that the prince is suffering from acute hemopneumothorax secondary to the pneumonia. The collection of blood and fluid in the pleural space has increased the thoracic pressure and it is now under tension, displacing the lungs and heart to the right. I must remove the fluid immediately or he will die. Does he understand?"

Dr. Ullas repeated Dr. Darcy's words in broken Persian, as it had been more than a decade since he'd used the language in his travels north. It was adequate to get the point across, Abdul-Qahaar nodding. Another *Yūnānī* healer standing nearby translated in Arabic, other bilingual speakers picking it up and translating for the Hindu speakers until there was a steady stream of languages spoken in soft tones around the room.

Gestures went a long way too, the "come here and help me turn the prince onto his side" pantomime comprehended easily. Three men leaned onto the bed to assist, holding the shaking prince as still as possible while George ripped the shirt away and wiped the sweat-drenched skin with a cloth soaked in an herbal antiseptic solution. The latter was handed to him by Dr. Ullas, George not even looking up but simply holding out his hand in trusting anticipation.

"Opium?"

"Only a drop or maybe two," George answered. "He is close to unconscious as it is, and I don't want to suppress his respiratory drive any further. Keep it handy though. The *tharra* is in the far right bottle. Use it to clean the scalpel and reed, please. That stuff kills healthy stomach tissue so should effectively eradicate any invisible organisms." He gestured for one assistant to remove the pillows so that the prince was flat and to hold his left arm over his head. Hastily, George wiped the wet cloth over the young man's left torso all the way to the breastbone while assessing his pinched, blue face and shallowly rising chest.

Lips pursed and jaw clenched, George palpated down the midaxillary line of the rib cage, counting until reaching the recessed space between the fourth and fifth ribs. Sliding his left index finger along the ridge posteriorly to the precise point sought for, George marked the spot with his fingertip and reached his right hand to grasp the handle of the scalpel Dr. Ullas held out for him. After a swift scan to make sure everyone was alert and prepared, George sliced cleanly through the prince's skin and muscle underneath. A jerk and low moan was the only indication of awareness of what was being done to him.

"Hold him tight," he commanded in Hindi, the message clear even to those not sure of the words.

The hollow reed Dr. Ullas handed George was blunt on one end but shaved to a sharp point on the other. It was the pointed end that George pressed into the bleeding incision, easing through the tissue until resistance was felt. He paused for a second, his broad left hand spanning the rib cage and bracing, and then with a controlled thrust the hardened reed pierced through the tough membrane protecting the lungs. Another jerk was the prince's response, but the helpers had listened well and kept a firm grip on him.

Immediately, cloudy, blood-tinged fluid began to flow from the blunt end of the reed, Dr. Ullas collecting it into a cup for later examination.

"Not too thick and translucent. Odor not foul and minimal blood. All good signs, but I will need to leave the drainage tube in for a while to make sure." George flicked his discerning gaze back and forth from the fast-filling cup, the patient's chest, and then his face. The first cup was replaced with a new one before improvement was detected. Initially, there was a faint increase in the lift to his chest as each inhale grew deeper, the alarming blue tint receding incrementally. Then as the second cup hit the halfway point, the young man gasped and shuddered, his nostrils flaring and mouth opening wide as he drew in a ragged breath followed by another and another. Healthy color suffused his face, not completely but a vast improvement over the deathly cyanosis of minutes prior, and the chest rose higher with each harsh inspiration.

"I have seen this I don't know how many times now and it still amazes me. Well done, Dr. Darcy."

George said nothing. He was too busy wrapping a clean cloth around the puncture site, holding tight to the reed while gently rolling the youth back to rest on a pillow wedged against his back.

"Well, look who is waking up!" George smiled into the fluttering eyes of the rallying prince. "A drop or two of opium," he said to Dr. Ullas while keeping his gazed fixed on the bewildered eyes staring up at him. "Do you understand me, Your Highness? Excellent. I am Dr. Darcy and this is Dr. Ullas. We are *vaidyas* from Mysore City…"

In simple language and cadenced tones, George explained what had been done to him, hands simultaneously checking his pulse and applying pressure to precise points until the prince fell into a deep, untroubled sleep, opium, exhaustion, and Ayurvedic application combining in a sedative effect. Only once assured the critical situation was under control did George leave the bed. Taking the wet cloth from Kshitij and wiping his bloodstained hands, George grinned at his colleague, mentor, and friend.

"See? I told you it would be exciting."

❧

"Yes, that is truly what he said. 'I told you it would be exciting.' And then he laughed."

"It blows off the tension," George explained with a straight face.

The two men were sitting across from each other in the dining room of the Ullas house in Saliom. They had returned home an hour prior, after a week in Tipu Sultan's palace, and of course, the boys had flocked around them with questions gushing. Delaying until settled with food and refreshing beverages in front of them, they were recounting their adventures to a captive audience.

"So what happened next? Did he die?"

"Of course not! Would I or your father allow that to happen? Never!"

Jharna rolled her eyes. Sasi looked vaguely disappointed, as if the death of a prince would be much more dramatic. Nimesh beamed with pride.

"We continued to treat him, with the aid of the other healers. He was an acutely ill young man. Dr. Darcy had to replace the drainage tube once when it obstructed with exudate, but within a day he was able to leave it out. The prince's strength enabled him to recuperate, thankfully."

Interruptions were frequent. Nimesh inquired on the medications and techniques while Sasi attempted to steer the conversation into descriptions of the palace.

"At what point did you meet the Tiger of Mysore?"

"Not for four days," Kshitij replied to his wife's query.

Her expression was serene, showing no overt sign of the intense fear she had lived with for eight interminable days. George could sense her distress, however, as did Kshitij, and it was why they were jesting and painting a glorified picture. Neither had felt overcome with anxiety while residing in the palace, yet the fact remained that they were, for all intents, hostages whose fates were at the whimsical mercy of a tyrannical man not know for being merciful. How he would have reacted if his son had died is anyone's guess.

They had been treated with due respect throughout their stay, with every personal need attended to. Not a soul was rude, yet the guards posted sent a clear message that they were not to wander beyond the designated wing where the ill prince lay. A thirty-foot square garden courtyard was the only allowed exterior area. The prisoner sensation hung over their heads and the curiosity over whether the Sultan was aware of his son's illness or their presence remained a mystery, both hoping they could slink away as quietly as they had come.

Still, as George would later say to Kshitij, there aren't too many people, especially Westerners, who can say they dwelt for a time in the palace of Tipu Sultan *and* entered his throne room to carry on a conversation.

"We did not ask for an audience, that's for sure." George popped a fig into his mouth. "But it was exciting when we were summoned. Well, it was! You can't deny it." He wagged a finger at Kshitij, who shook his head and laughed. "You should have seen it, boys. A massive chamber dripping with gold and jeweled tapestries." He leaned forward, eyes wide and hands gesturing, his voice dropped into an awestruck pitch as he went on, elaborating upon the furnishings with explicit detail only slightly exaggerated for effect. He painted a picture with his words, relating features that Kshitij barely remembered, Sasi and Nimesh open-mouthed and silent. The Sultan he described perfectly, from his attire to physical appearance to changing expressions. Practically word for word, he quoted Tipu's thanks for saving his son and praise for their skill.

"Then he stepped off his throne, descended the dais, and after retrieving a casket from a waiting servant, he walked right up to us. 'Payment for services rendered,' he said, handing the casket to your father. Then, 'Let it be known that Sultan Fateh Ali Tippu treats fairly with his English and Hindu neighbors.' He bowed and we thought that would be the end of it, but he snapped his fingers and another servant hurried forward. In his hands, he held two chains with dangling pendants that he placed over our heads. We were out of the room before we could see what it was."

Reaching inside his kurta, George withdrew a chain of gold. The unadorned links were small but thick, falling to midbreastbone with a two-inch-long replica of a roaring tiger in gold plated with black and orange enamel, the eyes tiny ambers, fastened with three wide rings.

The boys whistled and Jharna gasped. Kshitij pulled his out of his pocket and handed it to his wife. "Keep it safe. It is worth a small fortune, I imagine, but I have no desire to wear it."

"I do!" George shrugged when they collectively gaped at his vehemence. "Not because I care for who gave it to me but because it is incredible. Just look at it!" He dropped it onto his chest, the gold flashing in the sunlight. "Quite the eye-catcher isn't it? Think of the conversations this little beauty will start. The ladies will love it, and then I can tell of our adventure into the tiger's den. Nothing like a man of undaunted bravery to stir up enthusiasm, is there Jharna?"

His cheeky grin and egotistical chuckle sent them all into gales of laughter. Kshitij mouthed a silent *thank you* and George winked. Best to keep the topic light and not let on how appreciative they were to be safely back with their family. Excitement aside—and it had been exciting, as far as George was concerned—coming face to face with a man some considered on par with the devil was not exactly fun.

Kshitij took over answering the endless questions from his sons, George slipping out and returning with the casket given as payment. It was a small chest, approximately eight inches square of polished silver etched and painted with Persian designs. It was a work of art, Jharna's eyes shining and fingertips reverentially tracing the exquisite patterns.

"A treasure chest!" Sasi breathed.

"That about sums it up," George agreed, lifting the lid with agonizing slowness until the contents were revealed to the eager trio. Inside, it was filled with coins. Some bore Persian and Arabic writing, but most were the gold pagoda, silver rupee, or paisa copper elephant coins commonly seen in town. The lesser value coins were overwhelmed by the larger denomination gold ones, it easily calculable without separating and counting that the physicians had been paid more for this one patient than all others combined for the past six months.

"We're rich."

"We were already rich, Nimesh. We do not need this and will not keep it."

"*Pati!*" The wails were in unison. Jharna said nothing, but the stricken look on her face made George burst out laughing.

"Don't fret, Jharna. Kshitij intends to let you keep the casket. Now tell them the good news, Kshitij, before they perish from broken hearts."

"You two can each select five coins to keep. That is all. Sasi, there are some rare ones in there. I think I saw a Persian *safavid* that will make a fine addition to your collection. Once done, we will be donating the money to the hospital. Before we leave permanently, Dr. Darcy and I can make sure they have a new microscope at least."

The boys were no longer listening. Treasure hunting had taken over! They would all end up with souvenirs of their sojourn in Mysore, just as they had from every other place traveled to, but none with a story quite like this one attached.

GEORGE'S MEMOIRS
APRIL 25, 1798

Today brought news that I have dreaded on some level since leaving England. Alex, our father is ill. A letter arrived from James. A letter dated November 13 of last year no less. James's previous correspondences have hinted that Father's age has caught up with him in small ways, such as not riding every day, as he used to, or eating less. But he assured me that nothing was seriously amiss. Father still spent the bulk of his time in the stables, usually with young William, who has inherited our father's passion for horses, and of course, he never misses a Sunday service. Now he says that Father has been diagnosed with a wasting illness. Typical of James to not know the proper medical terms or details. Nevertheless, I know our brother well enough to know he would not insist I come home unless it were of a severe nature. So I am making hasty preparations. I can do nothing about the vast distances between us, but it does weigh heavily upon my heart that months have lapsed while this letter made its way to India and then was diverted a half-dozen times until finding me at Yellapur in Kanara, where we now are working. Fortunately, that means I can sail from Karwar and shave off a bit of time. Pray my luck holds firm on the voyage and that the weather and tides will be in my favor. And I shall be praying with all my strength that Father hangs on until I am home.

Alex, you know I am not one to figuratively flog myself over past choices and actions. I have considered taking a trip home a number of times. Always there were too many reasons not to do so, mainly my desire to be here and continue my travels. Nevertheless, if I arrive and Father has gone, I will be overcome with regrets and have James do the flogging, literally. I can't regret the experiences of these past eight years, and I know I am not done with India and will be back as soon as possible. Even amid my anxiety over Father, I am annoyed that I will miss out on working with the Portuguese in Goa and skirting the edges of the Gaults on the way north through Konkan as we planned. Nor can I pretend I am not dismayed at what the news from Mysore portends. Wellesley has heard of an alliance between Tipu Sultan and the French, and naturally he is not pleased. Rumors of another war are filtering in. Kshitij and I were discussing the ramifications if this happens (and I would bet my inheritance it will) and whether we should delay our plans until we see if physicians are called for, as they always are where battles occur. Now that is a moot point as far as my services are concerned, and I am appalled at how much this distresses me when I should only be thinking of Father. I am a horrible son!

I left home knowing the odds were good that Father would die without my seeing him again. Or at least it occurred to me. Father has forever been larger than life, seemingly indestructible and inexhaustible. Even now, it is nigh impossible for me to imagine him ill.

So I have spent the day packing and making arrangements. Kshitij is supportive, of course, but his desire to return home will keep him moving north. Jharna said a blessing for my safe journey and lit incense to her goddess. At this point, I will take anything I can get, which is what I told her, and of course, she scolded me as she always does when I tease her about her religion! I needed the levity. Anoop was in tears at my leaving, not appreciating my insistence that he stay with the Ullas family. I am sure he is convinced I will perish without him. Nimesh helped me gather my medicines, including some herbs that he thought might help Father. That boy is going to be a wonderful physician, like his father. Captain Andrews has agreed to send an escort with me, which will make the trek to Karwar easier and safer. I was pleased at his kindness. Then he surprised me further by writing letters of accommodation! That assures me passage on the next ship leaving whether they need a physician onboard or not. With luck I shall be on my way within a week. Alex, if you have the ear of God from your seat in heaven put in a request for me, will you? Please let Father be alive.

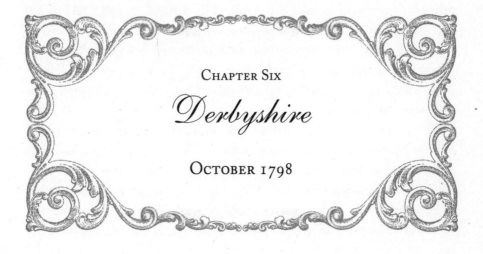

AS SOON AS GEORGE touched English soil, he paid for a fast courier to deliver the message of his arrival. Securing a coach to transport him to Derbyshire was easy, George deciding the quick pace of a public coach with fresh teams of horses every few miles was better than hiring a private carriage. A few hours would likely not make any difference, but the moment George spied land from the deck of the ship a sense of urgency gripped him. At Lambton, he intended to immediately get a horse, even if he had to steal it, and dash the remaining five miles to Pemberley.

Fortunately, theft was not required.

George exited the coach to see none other than his old friend Henry Vernor standing on the stoop with a broad smile on his face. George was never so happy and terrified to see anyone in his life.

Henry opened his arms, George gladly stepping into the manly embrace and then almost fainting with relief when Henry said, "Welcome home, George. Your father will be so happy to see you."

Henry assured him that "the stubborn old man refused to die" but did admit that he was close. So close that James hadn't wanted to leave even to meet his brother, and asked Vernor to be there instead.

The carriage clattered over the stone bridge spanning the River Derwent, the woods that had obstructed George's view of Pemberley left behind. He sat with his face pressed to the glass, much as an overanxious child, and sucked in his breath as Pemberley Manor became visible. How many times had he beheld this exact scene? Hundreds, most often taking it for granted, with rare instances of appreciating his home's majesty. He had seen many grand places in his travels, exotic temples to opulent palaces, yet none of them inspired the deep-seated love of Pemberley.

Sitting on a gentle slope rising from the Derwent, the Baroque manor of beige brick shone in the midafternoon sun. The lawns, hedges, trees, and gardens were brilliant with the colors of autumn. Wooly sheep wandered freely over the wide, grassy expanses near the river, and horses grazed in the pastures to the north, beyond the massive stable complex. All was serene, the only activity aside from the animals a couple of groundsmen weeding and the stable crew moving among the horses.

"Does it look like you remember?"

"Even better. There is no place on earth as beautiful as Pemberley."

"I agree, although if you tell anyone I said that I will deny it vigorously."

George laughed. "Sanburl Hall comes close, Henry. How is that?"

Vernor grunted. "You know it doesn't, but it is mine and I love it."

"Thanks for meeting me, Henry. I appreciate the welcome from a friendly face."

"It was my pleasure. We have missed you, George. I know it may prove difficult, but try to come round for a visit. Mary would like to see you as well."

George nodded but made no promises. Too much was uncertain for him to plan social engagements.

Once over the bridge, they were on Darcy land, from there a short jaunt along the north drive lined with sculptured hedges and thick stone posts topped with iron lanterns, unlit at the present. An enormous stone arch, half covered with ivy, spanned the road that was wide enough for three carriages to enter in a row, the iron gates open and welcoming. Etched into the smoothed rock surface above the arch was one word in tall, bold letters, painted black: PEMBERLEY.

The graveled drive curved slightly, leading to the front façade of the manor. George had a glimpse of James standing on the covered portico, his heart leaping and a smile growing despite the serious nature of his visit. Seconds after the carriage halted, George was out and bounding up the steps. James greeted his brother with a shout and warm embrace, the shorter James engulfed in George's long arms and towering body.

"About bloody damned time, Brother! God, look at you. Browned like a heathen! And where in the world did you get that suit?"

George stepped back, opened his jacket, and struck a debonair pose. "What? Am I not the height of fashion?"

"Sure. About five years ago."

"It is difficult to find a decent tailor in an Indian village. I do have a trunk full of fine native garments, but I thought it best not to shock the family too greatly at the outset."

James clapped George on the shoulder then turned to Henry Vernor. "Vernor, thanks for bringing the wayward traveler home."

"My pleasure, Darcy. I will leave you to your reunion. Please extend my respects to Mr. Darcy. We are praying for his health."

James nodded, the lump in his throat interfering with speech. George chimed in with his thanks, and after assuring his trunk was safely unloaded, followed James into the manor.

"You still have the trunk, I see." James waved toward the piece of luggage being carried by two strong footman, another servant following with a smaller case and portmanteau, the trio heading to the suite of rooms preserved untouched for George.

"Of course. That thing is indestructible and will outlive me. If it could tell tales, they would undoubtedly be better than mine."

They crossed the massive, tiled entryway, George sparing a few precious minutes to gaze to the right, at the ceiling-to-floor tapestries chronicling the Darcy lineage and then to the left, where a fireplace tall enough for a man to stand upright inside was flanked by alcoves displaying priceless statues of white marble. The style was reminiscent of a medieval castle, complete with four armored knights, two by the main doorway and two more on either side of the curved, polished oak stair balustrades. The resemblance stopped there, however, the mansion an obvious masterpiece of Baroque architecture. George glanced upward, to the ceiling painted with Baroque art, as they ascended the blue carpet–covered staircase of white marble that was a central showcase of the two-story foyer.

George was dusty from the road, but thoughts of washing and changing into clean clothes never entered his or James's mind. They veered left at the top of the grand staircase, walked down a long corridor to a smaller but equally elaborate staircase at the far end that lead to the top floor, where the master's suite was located. As they walked, James gave a brief update.

"Father's illness hit suddenly, George. Or at the least it seemed so to us. In retrospect, there had been signs of his increasing weakness and poor health, but you know how secretive Father has always been. The signs were nothing we could point to as more than normal age-related issues. He is eighty years old, for heaven's sake! I confess that we had forgotten that to a degree. Father has forever appeared indestructible, so chronological years meant nothing."

George nodded in agreement and patted James's shoulder to reassure him. James glanced up with a wan smile and blinked back the tears. After a deep inhale, he continued, "Last November he fell when dismounting from his horse. He had been riding with William on his new stallion. Pericles was a gift from Father on William's tenth birthday," James said as an aside, a trace of humor and pride warming his voice. "Anne was incensed and quite vocal in her displeasure. I know." He laughed at George's expression. "It was startling to me as well to hear my wife berate him. Father was his typical implacable self in the face of Anne's ire, explaining in rational language that William was old enough for a grown horse and more than skilled enough to handle it. That much is true, George. William is half horse, I swear. If not yet, he will be, considering how much time he spends in the stable complex. Anyway, the two had been riding and probably doing so in a manner I never want to know about, when Father fell while dismounting. It might have gone unnoticed if a simple stumble, but his ankle twisted severely and he was flat on his back. A stretcher was needed to carry him into the Manor. Lord, you should have seen him!" James chuckled and shook his head. "He was livid in his humiliation."

George could imagine it. The Master of Pemberley *never* showed weakness. The fact that he had no weaknesses to show may have been part of it, but George knew that pride was a major aspect of his attitude. George almost wished he had been there to see it, for the laugh if nothing else. Of course, there was nothing funny about what Mr. Darcy's fall revealed.

"The doctor was called for, a new fellow named Easterman who took over for Doc Meager four years ago. He is young but proficient, although I am thrilled you are here to offer your input. Anyway, he and the surgeon tended to the sprain, but in the process of examining Father and talking with him, the truth came out. I wrote to you immediately."

"You said a 'wasting disease' in your letter. Did Easterman call it a cancer?"

"Yes, that is the term. I know little of medicine, George, but I know that is bad. I never thought he would hold out so long, but you know Father."

"Strong as a bull, ox, and ram put together," George said with a gentle chuckle, using a phrase the Darcy children often used when describing their father, usually when complaining about a discipline they disagreed with.

"Indeed. And in this instance I am abundantly thankful he is." They had reached the door leading to the master's chambers, and James paused with his hand on the knob. "Anne and William are with him. We take turns and never leave him alone. I wrote to all the family, by the way. Our siblings Estella and Philip are here. Unfortunately, Mary is with child so cannot travel. Aunt Beryl was here last month, and we expect her to return any day. The Matlocks are staying in Rivallain, as are Sir Louis and Lady Catherine. Rather disturbing that illness and imminent death is the impetus for a family reunion, isn't it?" James paused but did not turn the knob. When he spoke, his voice was unsteady and he did not meet George's eyes. "George, I am sure in your profession you see many ill people, but I have to warn you that Father looks nothing like you remember. He has changed drastically, and though I have witnessed the gradual alterations, it still shocks me each time I enter the room. I felt it important to warn you."

He said no more, turning the knob and leading the way into the suite.

As a physician, George had indeed seen many horrific scenes and human bodies in every state of malady and injury imaginable, so nothing affected him any longer. This was his father, however, and in his mind, the picture of virile competence was fixed. He steeled himself for the worst but knew before entering the bedchamber that it was bad. Different diseases create unique smells that George was able to detect, those often his first clue to rendering a diagnosis. Those that were of a terminal nature produced a distinctive odor, cancers especially. The stench of devastating disease and impending death emanating from the room slammed into George before he crossed the threshold. Awareness of the truth of his father's infirmity tightened the band of grief about his heart to the point of palpitations, but it also enabled him to prepare.

Lady Anne Darcy rose from a chair by the fire, smiled at George, but did not approach. He smiled fleetingly and nodded a welcome, then swept his gaze over the room in a rapid survey before focusing on the large four-poster bed where his father lay. His eyes were halted by the boy sitting propped against the headboard, a pillow cushioning Mr. Darcy's head supported on his right shoulder and a book open in his lap. The soft murmur of a voice that George had unconsciously noted when entering the room stopped as the boy looked up, azure eyes drenched with sadness and a hint of challenge directed at the stranger.

George sucked in his breath, composure slipping for a second not at the mildly belligerent expression, since George understood that was instigated by love for and a need to protect his grandfather, but rather by the astonishing resemblance the boy—who he knew was James and Anne's son Fitzwilliam—bore to Alex. And, obviously, to himself at ten. Not only was it uncanny, it was unexpected, and the twist in George's gut to see a near replica to his beloved twin while trying to steel himself against emotional assault in regard to his father's illness was almost too much. He blinked his eyes, reaching for that inner core of professionalism that never failed to serve him, and quickly turned his attention to his father.

The elder James Darcy lay on the crisp, white linens in a slight recline on a thick down-stuffed pillow. If George had not already recognized the severity of his father's infirmity by smell alone, his appearance sealed the diagnosis. Mr. Darcy was draped with blankets to midchest, wore a clean nightshirt that covered his body, and had a small, quilted coverlet wrapped over his shoulders, but none of it could conceal the bony figure underneath. The brawny man George had bid adieu to over nine years ago was gone. In his place was a pale, skeletal man with skin thin as tissue paper. Lastly, George looked into his father's eyes and a jolt pierced through him. Mr. Darcy was staring directly at him with eyes cloudy from unremitting pain but at the same time a stark awareness and clarity. Even amid the agony and weakness of his body being eaten from within, the Master of Pemberley's intelligence and strength shined through. Additionally, he was misty-eyed as he gazed upon his second son, love and happiness beaming with the power of the sun.

"George. Welcome home, Son. I am happy to see you."

The simple words uttered in a weak whisper were George's undoing, control sliding further when Mr. Darcy shakily lifted one thin hand toward him. With a swallowed sob, George hastened forward, clasped onto the cool hand that grabbed his with a firm grip, and sat on the edge of the bed. William curled his long legs to make room but did not move away. George barely noticed. His attention was focused on his father.

"Hello, Father. I came as quickly as I could. God shined upon me as the vessel made excellent time."

"I have missed you, boy. You look older but content. Life in India agrees with you, I can tell. No need for you to say how I look. Awful, yes?"

"Moderately so."

Mr. Darcy chuckled. "I like that. Honesty. No point in pretending, is there?"

"No, sir. Although now you have the best physician available to tend to you, and I promise to keep my fees cheap. I'll work for room and board."

"Ah, George, I have longed for your wit. Your presence alone cheers me. Your irreverent humor is almost a cure. Almost. We know that is not possible, even for you."

"No, Father. I am afraid it isn't. However, I am serious in that I have medicines that will ease some of your suffering and improve your strength temporarily."

"Simply prolonging the inevitable, but I do thank you. I admit that the pain is tough to abide." He glanced at the stoic lad sitting rigidly beside him. "I am not afraid to die. I have lived an excellent life filled with love and family. Heaven beckons me and in time I will see my children and grandchildren there. My Emily and Alexander are waiting for me now. No," he sighed, looking back at George, "I am ready. But I needed to see you, George, and will accept any medical assistance you can offer for the interim. Room and board is an easy price to pay."

"William," James interrupted softly. "Come with your mother and me for now while your Uncle George ministers to your grandfather."

"Go ahead, lad." George patted his knee when William did not move. "I promise I will take good care of him."

❧

George's concoctions, brewed as hot teas and viscous elixirs, performed as promised. Dr. Easterman was open-minded and curious about the unique medicines George used, the two physicians conferring for long hours while Mr. Darcy observed with pride and young William with growing appreciation for the uncle he had no memory of. George employed Ayurvedic healing techniques, especially massage and pressure therapy, that enhanced the medicines. The combined result was that Mr. Darcy slept long, cleansing, pain-free hours at a time, waking refreshed and with an improved appetite. It was only a minor, palliative measure but eased his acute suffering, and the borrowed time was appreciated by each member of the family.

Especially George.

He spent hours with his father, sometimes as Dr. Darcy but primarily as George, world traveler with fascinating stories to tell. Nothing of a serious nature was shared. Instead, George used his natural storytelling skills, embellishing flagrantly as he painted pictures with words that had his father laughing and spellbound. Every morning he appeared in a different Indian garment more flamboyant and vibrant until it became a sort of game to guess what color or style he would startle with when sauntering through the bedchamber door. Ethnic gifts hastily purchased prior to leaving India were passed out with lengthy explanations of their use and historical significance, as were the items belonging to George that he deemed would entertain. It became the highlight of each afternoon to see what bizarre piece of jewelry, trinket, woven rug, picture, book, cooking utensil, and so on he would dig out of the apparently bottomless trunk.

One afternoon he brought in a palm-sized jar of Indian ebony, which he used to hold an unguent that repelled biting insects. The jar was beautifully carved with a precise representation of Anamudi Peak in the Western Ghats. George related his visit to Kerala, using the etching as a reference to what he described in living color, but Mr. Darcy was fascinated by the carved wood.

"I haven't been able to whittle this past year." Mr. Darcy ran a fingertip over the lid of the jar before flipping it over to examine the grooves. "My hands are too unsteady to wield a knife for such precise work."

"Sorry to hear that, Father. I know you must miss it."

"I do. I have been teaching William how to whittle." He smiled at his grandson. "He shows some promise, but I know he does not love the activity. No, do not protest, Wills." He patted the boy on the knee. "A hobby should bring pleasure or it is a waste."

"Alex loved to whittle," George whispered.

"Indeed he did, and was skilled for a young boy. So were you, George, my only children who were. Have you taken up the habit again?"

Mr. Darcy spoke gently, his eyes soft as they rested upon his son. Whittling was a skill Alex had excelled at, he and their father passing hours on the terrace with sharp knives and hunks of wood. George had enjoyed the art and shared his twin's talent, but he had always been more active than Alex, so sitting and focusing on a sedentary task had not been a preferred activity. After Alex died, George had been unable to do it at all, a fact his father knew. George shook his head slowly.

"Perhaps someday." Mr. Darcy left it at that, but sent William to retrieve several of the pieces he had created recently, so he could show them to George—tiny animals, flowers, trees, several horses naturally, faces of the family, and a few odd shapes purely from his imagination. It was one of several special memories forged during their time together before his father's death that impacted George.

Another was on November 10. It was Fitzwilliam Darcy's eleventh birthday, and they planned an intimate celebration to take place in the master suite's sitting room. With assistance Mr. Darcy walked from his bed to a cushioned chaise near the fireplace, his presence at the party as essential as William's. Trays of hors d'oeuvres, sweet cakes, and punch were served as the gifts were handed out. The only guests were the immediate family. James and George's siblings Estella and Phillip were there as well as Mr. Darcy's sister Beryl, the Marchioness of Warrow, and two of his three brothers, all of whom had traveled great distances to be near. George donned a simple tunic of white edged with gold and maroon threads woven into an intricate geometric pattern and, to further the fun, a matching *dhoti*—long so that only his bare ankles and lower shins were visible. The outfit was an added conversation piece to a party that was surprisingly festive under the circumstances.

Strangely enough, most days and nights were festive. Sadness could not rule at all times, especially with children running about and relatives who had not seen each other in years. Mr. Darcy did not wish it otherwise. He refused to speak of his impending death or of his illness except as necessary or to discuss estate business with his heir. James had managed Pemberley affairs jointly with his father for over ten years and did so perfectly well, but old habits are difficult to halt, and Mr. Darcy wanted to ensure the final transition would be easy.

Despite the efforts of Dr. Darcy that granted Mr. Darcy periods of lucidity and strength, his decline was unstoppable. The vast majority of the time he was asleep, too weak to talk, or confused from pain or the medicines given to dull the pain. There was little to do but visit with each other while waiting for him to either wake with a need or the desire to converse—or the inevitable of not waking ever again.

"There isn't anything you can do to cure him, Uncle? Nothing learned in your travels?"

George looked up from the book in his lap, fixing sympathetic eyes on his nephew. William sat on the edge of the bed, holding his sleeping grandfather's hand. He was crying silently, enormous tears sliding down his cheeks, vivid blue eyes agonized and pleading.

"If only there were, lad. Believe me when I say I would do anything if it were possible to cure him." George put the book aside with a sigh. "I have learned much in my studies but not how to stop this disease. I'm sorry."

William nodded as he closed his eyes and bowed his head. George's heart broke as he watched the boy's shoulders slump.

"I once thought that if I could learn enough of medicine, travel far enough in the world seeking answers, that maybe, just maybe I could discover the secret to stopping the worst of disease and injury. I was young then, a year older than you are now, and even in my despair, I was confident that I could do what no other had been able to do. Innocence and arrogance gave me that confidence. Of course, it isn't possible to stop death. The best we can hope is to delay it for a while."

"Father says you are the best physician he has ever known."

"Did he?" George laughed, it a mere rumble in his throat. "James is a devoted brother but hasn't met many physicians. Of course, I am excellent"—he grinned, earning a returned wan smile—"but even with my prodigious skills, I am not divine. Only God can perform miracles, William. All I and other skilled doctors can do is heal to the best of our ability and, in some cases, such as with your grandfather, ease their suffering."

"Have you given up trying to find the secret then?"

"No, not completely. To a physician, death is our enemy, as is permanent maiming and so on. We wish for all humans to be healthy at all times. We strive to discover ways to make that happen, realizing that there isn't one secret but thousands, perhaps millions, that need to be uncovered along the way to make it possible. Early in my studies, I understood this truth, not that it stopped me from dreaming I would find a way to speed up the process that I know will take centuries, if even possible, to achieve. For now, I do the best I can and although in this case"—he nodded toward the sleeping man—"I am unable to cure, I have had many successes with others."

"That must be a wonderful feeling, to cure someone who may have died otherwise."

"Indeed it is, William. Each time I am fortunate to do so it is a marvel I thank God for. That is another family who will not suffer through a loss, at that time anyway. That is the most difficult part, you see. Not the one who dies," he explained when William furrowed his brow in confusion, "but the people left behind who must deal with that loss. I wish there were a medication to ease grief but there is only time."

"How long did it take you to not grieve for your brother?"

George comprehended the deeper questions underneath the ones asked and paused for a moment to think how best to respond. William was intelligent, this George had readily ascertained, as well as extremely serious for such a young boy. He was the type of person who examined everything, weighing and measuring with logical deductions reached only after extensive deliberation, and then the conclusion clung to with confidence that would take major counter-evidence to rescind. Order and discipline were important to him. It had taken weeks for George to detect William's inner soul of sensitivity, the heart of a passionate romantic that was buried inside and which he doubted the boy knew he possessed, and if he did would probably deny. George had spent time wondering whom James and Anne's son most resembled. His first recognition was that young Fitzwilliam was most like Mr. Darcy, hence how close the two were. On the face of it, this was true, but George sensed that William was tender and emotional where Mr. Darcy had never been. Goodness knows he was not like his parents. Granted James was intelligent, but James and Anne were demonstrative, playful people with ebullience and humor on the surface for all to see. Finally, he decided that William resembled Alex more than just the physical and was a unique melding of Darcy characteristics. George doubted if William would ever overcome his shy, serious nature to be the outwardly joyful man his father was. The question was whether he would bury that inner gentle soul, the poet's heart that was so like Alex, starving it with pragmatism until it all but disappeared, or eventually allow it to break free. Crushing grief could tip the scale to the former, and George hated to see that happen.

So he answered carefully, "I still grieve for Alex. Grief is a part of life, William. It is the flip side of love and passion. To be truly human, we must embrace both. That is the only way to have a full life. We must express all the aspects of our personality that God granted us, giving of ourselves freely so that our memory will be vividly real to those left behind. My love for Alex is kept alive because of my grief at his absence. Conversely, my grief is strong because of the amazing person he was in life. He remains a part of me, just as your grandfather will remain a part of you for all of your life. And, if like me you believe in an afterlife, as I am sure you do being raised in this family, we shall meet again. I do not know what that will be like to be honest, but I imagine Alex and I as youths swimming naked in a heavenly pond as we did Rowan Lake. I doubt if God will allow us to do some of the mischievous antics from life, but then perhaps heaven will be more fun than we imagine." He smiled and winked. "Whatever the case in the beyond, I know Alex would want me to remember him with affection and hope, and then keep living. We do not cease when a loved one leaves us, which can almost seem cruel at the time, but is how it should be. Of course, it took me many years to accept that after Alex died. Now I am sharing that wisdom with you."

William nodded politely but did not look convinced. George hoped his words would be remembered later.

The discussion with young William prompted George to test his words. Later that day, he entered the chamber that had once been his and Alex's bedchamber. George had never vacated the room for another, but six months after Alex's death, his parents granted his wish to redecorate and rearrange the room. All new furnishings were placed and George had instructed a servant to pack everything belonging to Alex into a chest that sat untouched in a corner of the room.

"It is time, Alex." Kneeling before the wooden chest, George ran his palm over the lid and the name carved with fine script. *Alexander Darcy*. An identical chest sat at the foot of the bed, carved with *George Darcy*. Both had been made by their father shortly after their birth. All of the Darcy children had chests made by their father, Mr. Darcy utilizing his mastery of woodworking and whittling to fashion storage boxes that were sturdy, beautiful, and priceless heirlooms. What they chose to place in the chests was entirely up to them, but much like Mr. Darcy's encouragement to keep a journal, each of them had heeded his suggestion to keep mementoes they deemed significant.

It had taken twenty years and living half the globe away for the pain to be replaced with sweet remembrance. George had sensed the minute he stepped over the house's threshold that the ghost of Alex no longer haunted him. It wasn't the forgetfulness that George had once sought but rather a deep peace with those memories and joy in the special person he had been blessed to share twelve years with.

So he opened the chest's lid with a smile. Tears were shed, but they were the result of belly laughter at some of the items Alex had kept. There was the "perfect skipping stone" that had never been tested because then it would be lost in the pond and unable to save, a child's logic that at the time had seemed sound. The piece of bark Alex swore bore the face of their tutor, Mr. Franks. None of the rest of them could see it, but Alex was adamant the image was there, so they had gone along with his delusion. The play Alex had written and directed when he was nine, the Darcy children performing the awful production for their parents who had been too polite not to applaud and heap praise.

George's favorite surprise was Alex's juvenile poetry, or poems he liked written by others. Here Alex had excelled. George was certain that had he lived, Alex would have been a remarkable poet. There was a stack of neatly tied parchment pages with charcoal drawings on them, most inanimate objects but a few attempted portraits of friends and family. Wrapped in paper were all the wooden pieces he had whittled, exactly twenty-four of them, small and crude but with the promise of talent never realized. Underneath and wrapped in a pouch of tattered velvet was a whittler's set of sharp knives, chisels, rasps, and sanding sticks. Their father had gifted them identical sets, but George had discarded his after Alex died.

He ran his fingertip over the blades, and with a soft smile, he slipped the pouch into his pocket.

It took an entire afternoon, but eventually George examined every last item in the chest. Some he set aside to be packed into his trunk for when he returned to India. Most he returned to Alex's chest. Then he dragged the heavy box across the room, positioning it at the foot of his bed beside his own chest. Standing back, he gazed at the twin chests with a smile. "That is where you belong, Alex. Right next to me. And, yes, I am a sentimental fool, but if you tell anyone, I will pound you when I see you in heaven!"

A few days later, George sat with James in the sitting room while Mr. Darcy's valet bathed the ill man. It was a perfect opportunity for James to broach a topic weighing heavily on his mind.

"George, there is a sensitive matter I want your opinion on, as a physician."

George lifted a brow, then he laughed. "Good lord! Are you seriously blushing? Must be sensitive indeed. I am guessing this involves Mrs. Darcy? Thought so." George sat down his teacup when James nodded and steepled his fingers before his face. "Very well. I am now Dr. Darcy. And because I am damned good as such, I can already surmise this has to do with why you two have no further children."

"How in blazes can you do that?"

"Really, James, it isn't that difficult an assumption. Truth is, I have been dying of curiosity, so even if the topic is otherwise, I am going to be nosy and force you to tell me anyway. I have waited for the past ten years for you to announce a new addition to the clan. I thought you would have a half-dozen little Darcys by now the way you two are. Stop blushing, for heaven's sake! I am not an innocent, but even if I were, it would be obvious that you and Anne have a healthy physical relationship."

James ducked his head, speaking more to his shoes than George—who refrained from teasing his brother about it—and said, "It is as you say, with my wife and I, that is. No problems there." His eyes flickered upward, and he grinned with an unstoppable hint of manly pride. "Like you, we assumed more children would be the result. Anne had no problems conceiving Alexandria or Fitzwilliam, and as you know, their deliveries were easy enough, as those things go. Since William we have not been so fortunate."

"What has been the problem? I mean, does Anne not get pregnant or has she miscarried?"

"The first. She simply has not conceived. Or at least not that we know of. There was one time when Anne was later than usual with, well, you know—"

George quirked one brow and stared solemnly at James's face but said nothing. James rubbed over his mouth and continued after clearing his throat.

"Yes, well, we thought maybe she was pregnant, but then she wasn't, and we did not know if she was merely off cycle or something had gone wrong. Aside from that one time, there have been no signs."

James leaned forward and placed his elbows onto his knees. His embarrassment disappeared and he intently fixed on George's face. "Anne struggles with this greatly, George. I do as well, I admit, since I always dreamed of many children. But for Anne it is a tragedy not to have more babies. It breaks my heart for her more than myself. If ever a woman was designed to be a mother it is my wife. What I am wondering is if you have anything that may help, or any ideas why this may be happening?"

They discussed the topic frankly. George asked a number of highly personal questions that James answered without blushing—not too greatly, that is. In the end, George could not say for certain and saw no need to examine Anne, which would have been too uncomfortable for her, but he did know of various herbs that enhanced fertility as well as practical techniques to encourage conception. James was appreciative and hopeful. George saved his ribbing for when giving the supplies and instructions to James and Anne, using blunt language and sly winks that left Anne red as a beet and stammering. He did notice, however, the glances the two exchanged afterward and wasn't surprised when they retired early that night.

❧

Two weeks after William's birthday, the Master of Pemberley's precarious health took an abrupt turn for the worse. Within a day, his pain escalated to where drugs no longer worked, and two days later, he slipped into a coma from which he never woke. The bulk of his family was with him as he breathed his last on December 3. Pemberley Estate sank into deepest mourning for the man who had been master for over five decades.

A private service for family and Pemberley staff was held at the small chapel on Pemberley land where the Darcy family had worshipped, had been married, and had been christened for generations uncounted. The following day, the public funeral was held at the church in Lambton. People arrived from all over Derbyshire and many places farther away until even the larger building was overflowing. The Pemberley grand ballroom and formal dining room were opened to accommodate the hordes of people paying their respects. James and

Anne, as the official Master and Mistress of Pemberley, did not say their final thank-you until well after dark.

"I had no idea he knew so many people and that they thought highly enough of him to travel to Derbyshire in winter," James murmured from his place by the window as the last carriage disappeared from sight. "I should have, I suppose, but I confess it humbles me."

Messages of sadness from those who lived farther away arrived at a steady pace during the subsequent weeks as the news of Mr. Darcy's demise spread. The constant reminder of their loss was overwhelming, thus it was deemed fortunate that the Christmas season was upon them. The tone of mourning could not be eradicated but having a joyous holiday swiftly approaching prevented grief from taking too firm a hold. As much as possible under the circumstances, they warmed to the idea of gifts and feasting. In an odd twist, it was a special Christmas celebration not seen at Pemberley for several years. The vacant gap left by Mr. Darcy was undeniable, yet having the family together naturally created a festive atmosphere that the adults agreed was a positive ending to an extremely sad period.

By January, everyone but George had returned home and Pemberley was quiet, fitting the mood of winter and continual lamentation. James and Anne struggled to reassert normalcy into day-to-day life and establish new routines after a year of upset. Long hours were spent with Pemberley's steward, Mr. Wickham, as James acquainted himself with those aspects of estate business that his father had handled. Anne and Mrs. Reynolds, Pemberley's house-keeper for the past six years when Mrs. Sutherland retired, methodically sifted through Mr. Darcy's belongings, setting aside those items designated for certain relatives or friends compared to those to be stored or placed elsewhere in the manor. Neither James nor Anne rushed to relocate into the master's suite, but it was the expected tradition, so tentative discussions began as to how they wished to redecorate for their tastes.

On January 6, James entered the library and saw George standing at a window and staring fixedly toward the west meadow. "What has captured your attention, Brother?"

"Your son." George gestured with his teacup. "I have never in my life seen a boy his age ride a horse with such reckless abandon and skill while at it. He truly is remarkable."

James joined him at the tall window. "He is a natural. Father was very proud of him."

George heard the sadness in James's voice, as well as a current of anxiety. "Why are you frowning, James? Does it disturb you that William has a greater affinity for the equestrian portions of Pemberley Estate over the agriculture and... whatever else you do?"

James laughed, shaking his head and flashing a sidelong glance at George. "You never did have any interest in where our wealth came from, did you?"

"Not in the least. But don't take it personally. I am still not interested in business matters."

"As long as you have money for food, right?"

"Well, yes, there is that. I enlisted a bookkeeper in Bombay to keep track of my finances, including the stipend Father would regularly send, which I always told him I did not need and hope you will cease doing, but aside from perusing the quarterly report he compiles, so I know I have enough for food and clothes, since I really do like clothes, I pay scant attention."

"He could be robbing you blind."

George shrugged. "I would think less of him if he did not skim a bit of the excess off the top, but I was raised as a Darcy, so some of the business lectures penetrated my skull. Don't worry, James. He is a legitimate financial wizard. I trust him. My investments are intact, and I have safeguards in place to ensure a stable financial future. Now, what has you bothered about William?"

"Not that he loves horses, I assure you. The truth is, I think Fitzwilliam will eventually be far smarter than me and a better manager for Pemberley when the time comes. I only worry that he finds a balance. He is so damned serious, George, and humorless except for rare occasions or with certain people, such as his cousin Richard or Mr. Wickham's son George. I fear for how Father's death will affect him."

"I was thinking along the same lines, to be honest." He recounted the conversation between he and William prior to Mr. Darcy's death. "Naturally you know your son better than me, but I know what you mean of his tendency toward moroseness. Still, I don't think I would worry overly. He is young and the young are astoundingly resilient. In another year or two, he will discover girls and then you will be wishing he were hiding in the stables."

"I'll lock him in the stables if he is anything like you."

"Hey! I wasn't that bad! And it isn't my fault if the pretty maids thought I was irresistible. But just in case, I wouldn't suggest banishment to the stable complex. All that soft hay and dark corners, you know."

James shook his head in mock disgust and turned away from George's grinning face. "Thanks for the advice," he said drily as he poured a cup of tea. "Now, I was looking for you at the behest of my wife. Anne wants me to exact a promise that you will stay until after your birthday. A major party is not appropriate, but we would like to celebrate with you before you dash away."

"I am touched, James. I hadn't given it any thought, to be honest. Birthdays lose significance after a while. Still, it would be nice to commemorate the day with my family."

"Anne will be pleased. She is fond of you, you know, and has missed you. You liven up the place, even during sad times such as this."

"My, aren't we growing sentimental in our old age!"

"You aren't that far behind me, Brother."

"Thirty-two is vastly different than, what are you now? Fifty? Fifty-five?"

"*That* will get you beaten! Fifty-five indeed. Keep talking like that and you can forget about any presents. I'll toss you out the door onto your ass with your belongings heaped upon your head! Of course, considering how restless you are, your belongings are probably already packed."

George sat on the chair across from James, leaning back and feigning nonchalance. "Restless? Why do you say that?"

"Oh please! You have had one eye on the door since Christmas! I am shocked you are still here, but you don't need to pretend or apologize, George. I understand that India and your work calls to you. You never were good at idleness. Even while Father was ill, I could tell you were uncomfortable and itching to be busy. I do wonder, though. Is it only India and your work, or do the memories haunt you?"

"Only the first, amazingly enough." George told his brother about his feelings regarding Pemberley and Alex, including sifting through the chest.

"Praise God!" James exclaimed with relief. "I wasn't convinced that running halfway around the world would do the trick, but apparently it has."

"I am not sure what it is, James. Maybe simply time. Maybe other heartaches supplanted my grief over Alex. Maybe I just grew tired of dwelling in the past. Rather idiotic to pine over someone who has been gone for nearly twenty years. Not sure what happened, and I don't care. Life is too busy and exciting to analyze the whys. You are correct that I am anxious to leave, though it has nothing to do with Pemberley or Alex." He stretched his long legs onto the low table, nudged the tea tray aside to make room, and swept one hand over his body. "Look at me. I am an English-Indian hybrid! I wear crazy clothes that are unbelievably comfortable, by the way. I speak six dialects moderately well and can read and write most of them. I know so many styles of medical treatments that I no longer recall where I learned them. I am tanned in places that never see the sun on most Englishmen. I have seen panthers mating, handled snakes, climbed a one-hundred-foot banyan tree, eaten creatures that I won't mention because you would vomit, become an uncle to two delightful Hindu boys, have traversed jungles and deserts, and best of all, there is much, much more yet to uncover! I am never bored, James. Never unchallenged. You know me well enough to comprehend how valuable that is to me."

"You almost make me envious."

"Doubtful," George snorted. "You are too much a Darcy and tied to the land to gallivant about. I am the one with wanderlust. And it is very hot there, which you would hate. Do you have any idea how freezing I have been these past two months? I will need a year to thaw out. You would wilt into a puddle of flesh in India."

"I can't argue that. I guess living through your letters will suffice. Just be sure you write frequently so I know you haven't been eaten by a lion or contracted an exotic disease."

"I'll do my best. Now, let's save the maudlin sentimentality for later. Tell me about the presents."

GEORGE'S MEMOIRS
OCTOBER 13, 1800

Father, I wish I had traveled through the Great Rann of Kutch before I visited so that I could have described the wildlife. I am convinced you would have begged for your whittling knives no matter how weak your hands and undoubtedly managing better than I, despite the fact that I am seeing them in vivid reality. My novice figurines of flamingo, caracal, nilgai, *and Indian* ass khur *are not bad but nothing compared to what you would have created. I am practicing, and the demoiselle crane I finished yesterday was an improvement. I never thought myself all that intrigued by nature, but these past few years have exposed me to wonders of flora and fauna unimaginable. Hours slide by with me transfixed by the scenery and teeming wildlife.*

Since I last wrote, after our visit to Kalo Dungar—I am yet in awe over the panoramic view from atop the Black Hill and the temple of Dattatreya—we have been on small boats, floating with the currents on the Rann and continuing our trek inland—when there are currents, that is. The marshland is at its highest water level now that the monsoons are past, but the mudflats and islets are numerous, impeding the forward momentum. We often move at a snail's pace with the boatman propelling us along. When that fails, we walk or ride. We are not trying to stray far from the land and stop frequently as we encounter the villages that are our purpose for being here. Always we are welcomed with enthusiasm, our medical skills happily embraced and put to the test. I have not seen so many strange fevers and infected wounds in all my previous travels. The air is a breeding ground for bizarre illnesses! At the same time, it is a breeding ground for unique herbs and flora, many of which have medicinal qualities that the local healers use. It is dubious medicine at best, but as I have learned, gems of amazing treatments can be uncovered in the strangest of places. I won't bore you with those facts here, since they are in my medical logs, but suffice to say I am endlessly fascinated and learning daily. When I am not miserable and wallowing in periods of gloominess, that is. If it is not raining, it is unbearably hot and humid. I have grown accustomed to the heat of India, but this is taking it to a whole new dimension. I know it would shock you, Father, but wearing anything more than a loincloth is intolerable. Being three-quarters naked does help, but the flip side is that my English skin reacts badly to the sun. And the biting insects adore me. The natives laugh at me as they kindly provide the salves that soothe and protect. Even Anoop is laughing at my grousing, not that he does so in an obvious way. Now that I have a constant tan underneath, the damage is lessening and I am adapting. McIntyre has it far worse than me. His Scottish skin refuses to acclimate in the slightest. Thank goodness it was his idea to accompany us, or I doubt he would ever forgive me! As it is, he has perfected a glower that would slay a lesser man, turning it upon me when I say the slightest word of complaint. Hell, at times I swear he knows I am thinking of complaining, piercing me with that murderous glower before a word passes my lips.

Kshitij has been here before, so between him and our guides, we are accepted in this harsh land. The natives are a hardy stock and as diverse as the wildlife. They speak dialects I cannot master since each tribe is subtly different after eons of relative isolation. Indeed, this excursion is rougher than our years of travel through the east and south of India. That, I now realize, was princely in comparison! But, again, I am not complaining. Well, not too much. Yes, I am physically miserable a good portion of the time but also exhilarated by the experiences. In fact, McIntyre and I have decided to tarry in Rapar for the winter. After traversing the Rann at the height of its wet season, we want to see it when dry. Hearing the descriptions of the vast salt flats has piqued our interest. Kshitij wishes to return to Jharna and the boys. Frankly, I was surprised he agreed to take this trip. We have been gone for nearly five months and it will take another month for him to reach Thana. It was a sacrifice on his part, but I am selfishly thankful he made it. Dr. McIntyre is a great companion, and after years apart it has been a delight to reaffirm our friendship. Yet no one can take the place of Kshitij. I will sorely miss him.

The good news is that he has promised to forward any correspondence from home that has accumulated while we have been in the wilds. It is tortuous not to know what is transpiring with those I love so far away! Hearing that my advice had proven positive with Anne conceiving was wonderful. I still choke up with emotion when I think of my newest niece, named in honor of me. How remarkable is that? Georgiana Darcy. Beautiful! James says she is perfect with golden hair like her mother and the clear blue eyes that appear from time to time, as in me and Alex and young William. I was thrilled to hear of her safe birth and vitality, whooping aloud with joy in fact, which scared Jharna's saintly grandmother, bless her ancient heart. I was not at all happy to read how difficult Anne's pregnancy had been though. James's vivid recounting of her symptoms and continuing weakness is troublesome. I cling to his assurance that she was recovering, albeit slowly, and hope that my letter of further medical advice and package of herbs reached him safely and was beneficial. So I look forward to news and will be sure to jot it down here, Father, not that you probably don't already know what is happening. Unless you are too busy debating with the saints to pay attention to us mere mortals! Selfishly I hope you are, since I would rather you not see me right now since I am "dressed" in a short dhoti *and nothing else.*

CHAPTER SEVEN

Thana

T HE POUNDING ON THE door jerked George out of a dead sleep. He bolted upward, belatedly realizing that he had fallen into his exhausted slumber in a chair tipped back against the wall and with his legs resting on a table at an odd angle. It was not a good position to waken from, his numbed lower extremities not cooperating with the upper portions of his body at all. Combined with a fogged brain, George crashed to the floor in a painful tangle. Instead of jarring sense into him, it only served to confuse him further.

The pounding increased in volume, adding to the throbbing in his head and limbs, someone shouting his name in frantic tones. Clarity was restored only when he distinguished the name "Kshitij" amid the spat of rapid-fire Hindi his muddled mind had momentarily forgotten how to translate.

"Kshitij," he groaned, fear causing his heart to accelerate faster than the fall had. He struggled to speak and move, neither happening easily or as hastily as he desired, but finally he managed to shakily stand and lurch to the door that he had no memory of locking. Fumbling with the bolt, George heaved it open and instantly wished he had not.

Nimesh stood in the corridor, his face ashen and streaked with tears. "*Chacha*, come quickly! *Pita* is convulsing!"

George was already moving past him, rushing as quickly as his legs could while burning with restored circulation, down the hall to the room at the end. The sight greeting him would be forever burned upon his brain.

Kshitij Ullas, jaundiced beneath the pallor, thrashed rhythmically on the sweat-soaked linens of the bed. Spittle foamed at the corners of his mouth, and drool oozed in a viscous rivulet down one cheek. His dry lips stretched tightly across the thick, wooden stick clenched between his teeth, the gap minimal but enough to emit a moist whine. Sasi and Jharna knelt at either side of his body, gently preventing the man they loved from inflicting additional damage by flailing limbs bashing against something or launching off the bed onto the floor, either a distinct possibility considering the violence of his seizure. Like Nimesh, they were white-faced and distraught, but somehow able to retain enough composure to assist the *vaidya* who was also at Kshitij's side administering firm pressure to certain points on the body. Another Indian *vaidya* of Ayurveda was busily mixing a liquid concoction at a small table while a Hindu *sadhu* chanted in the corner. It was a scene reminiscent of the first time George had laid eyes on Dr. Ullas over ten years ago. Then, he had been the physician treating a woman who was convulsing from an unknown pestilence that she had overcome. This time George knew precisely what illness his dear friend suffered from. He also suspected, despite his refusal to admit it, that the outcome for Kshitij would not be as fortunate.

"The fever came on suddenly, *chacha*," Nimesh was explaining as George crossed to the bed. "We dosed with the *sudarshana churna* tonic and the *guduchi*, bathed with the lemon water, but nothing worked. The convulsions started within a half hour of his fever rising."

"Tincture of *cinchona*?"

"I am making a stronger batch now, *Vaidya* Darcy," the *vaidya* at the table answered without turning. "*Vaidya* Ullas received the dose you instructed an hour ago, then we gave another when he began to shiver. Unfortunately, most of it he coughed out when the seizure began."

George nodded shortly as he situated himself near Kshitij's head. He peeled back one eyelid, keeping his face impassive as he examined the patient's yellowed, blood-streaked eyes. The fingers of one hand assessed Kshitij's carotid pulse while the other hand's fingertips dug deep into a notch near the armpit, sensitive hands detecting the faint waning of stiffened muscles.

"It is ebbing," he murmured.

"Yes, but they are growing closer and stronger."

George met Jharna's gaze. He pursed his lips and refused to acknowledge the truth with a visible gesture but his eyes could not hide what they knew to be true.

Kshitij Ullas was dying. Swiftly and soon.

How or where he had contracted malaria was a mystery. The irony of succumbing to a disease common to the jungles of India not during their extensive travels but once surrounded by the modern luxuries of his mansion in Thana was notable. Since the previous December, Kshitij had gone no farther from home than a short family holiday to his father-in-law's *haveli* in Kalyan. And that had been in February. George had returned from his mission to Gujarat in April, after accompanying Dr. McIntyre back to Bombay and passing a month with friends there. Since then he had embraced being homebound with the Ullas family. He had joined a supremely healthy Dr. Ullas as a staff physician at the hospital, the two of them keeping regular hours and performing minimal duties outside of that. Laziness became a sort of joke between them, Kshitij particularly enjoying teasing his energetic colleague for not going out of his way to look for trouble. Neither suspected it to last, and their ears remained unconsciously tuned to the rumbles in the news that might mean an interesting challenge.

All had been well until three weeks ago when Kshitij complained of headache and a fever. George had rarely seen his friend ill and never poorly enough to take to his bed midday. It was concerning, but Kshitij assured it was nothing serious. In truth, it did not seem so in those first few days. The subsequent fever and mild joint pain were relieved with the standard herbal teas and rest, Jharna caring for her husband and shooing George back to the hospital where, "the seriously ill people need your genius and consummate skills." Five days later, George was woken in the middle of the night, called by Jharna at the behest of Kshitij, who was shaking violently with rigorous chills when George arrived. In between noisy clatters of his teeth, wracking coughs, and explosive vomiting, Kshitij barked prescriptions for medicines necessary to treat malaria, as if George had not diagnosed the disease the second he looked at him. Indeed, he had devoted every ounce of his prodigious skill to curing his dearest friend, Kshitij contributing his greater knowledge to the task when lucid enough to speak. Nothing worked beyond short respites, when the worst of the symptoms would recede marginally, granting the weakening man precious hours of sleep. Sadly those brief respites were growing less and less.

The convulsion ended after what seemed an eternity. An exhausted Sasi slipped from the bed and stumbled to his brother, Nimesh gathering the eleven-year-old into his arms for whatever comfort he could provide. Jharna closed her eyes and murmured a series of prayers, her chants mingling with the *sadhu* in the corner. The *vaidya* gestured to two manservants standing near the door who hastened forward with towels and fragrant water in their arms. The routine was standard now, Kshitij needing to be cleansed on a frequent basis but especially after a seizure.

George examined Kshitij comprehensively, one part the detached physician and one part the heartbroken friend. The physician's clinical findings of multisystem failure did not coincide with the frantic yearning for signs of improvement that the friend searched for. Finally, he looked at Kshitij's face, seeing the whole picture rather than the individual parts. It was all he could do not to weep.

"He woke up earlier," Jharna whispered, answering the question she knew George was mentally asking. "Only for a few moments. I could see the pain in his eyes, but for a few seconds he was present. He tried to speak, but nothing passed his lips. Love shone from his eyes, a message to me as clear as his spoken sentiments and farewell last week. Then he slipped away."

George suppressed the wince her tenderly spoken words triggered, instead taking the fresh tincture of *cinchona* from the *vaidya's* hands and bending to trickle drops into Kshitij's slack mouth. He was the physician, damn it all, and she the distraught wife! He was supposed to offer comfort, not the other way around. The problem was that he denied what everyone in the room knew, including Kshitij. The stricken man had accepted the inevitable several days ago, even in his extremity aware as any doctor would be that the infection was of a lethal variety resistant to *cinchona*, the only know curative for malaria.

On that day, he had grasped George's hand weakly, pushed the bitter liquid away from his lips, and in a series of mumbled phrases mixed with raspy breaths, revealed his heart as he never had before. Kshitij told George how proud he was to have worked with him, that he was the finest physician he had ever met, and that he had nothing else to teach him. As if that had not been enough to wrench George's heart out of his chest, Kshitij then went on to encourage him to "let go of your heart... do not fear love... find a woman who brings you joy" and other sentimental rot that he wanted to laugh at but wept over instead. The final straw was when Kshitij said the three words that sent most folks into puddles of emotion, especially women, and although he never gave the idea much thought, George recognized how desperately he had longed to hear them from the man who meant far more to him than he had imagined.

"I love you, George."

Thankful for the remaining shreds of manly pride that dictated one was not supposed to blubber like a baby when thirty-four years of age, especially when a medical expert who encountered death often, George was alone and able to succumb to the sobs he had been holding in. It took a while before he was able to verbalize his love in return and by then Kshitij had fallen into a coma that he would fleetingly rally from in the days leading to his death, but never long enough or with enough coherence for even the scantest conversation.

"Do not doubt that he knows how deeply you love him, *mitra*. We all do, but Kshitij especially." Jharna pressed her fingertips onto the back of his hand, the affectionate caress reassuring as it was meant to be but also to stop him from dribbling the useless tonic into her husband's mouth. "He was prouder of his association with you than any other accomplishment. He told me so many times, in private of course. He never wanted you to stop striving for greater excellence so hid his thoughts on purpose. I saw the light that shone in his eyes when talking of you. I witnessed his renewed vigor and delight since you joined him. These have been happy years for him, George, but now it is time to grant him the necessary rituals for the great departure so that his journey will continue."

George tensed, muscles twitching in his jaw and eyes blinking rapidly. He wanted to scream at her for giving up, curse her for not loving Kshitij enough to fight, rail at her for the ridiculous religious beliefs she clung to, shout his promises to heal so that Kshitij would have many more years to practice and teach his knowledge.

He did none of those things. He couldn't. He knew she was not giving up but merely accepting the inevitable. Her love for her husband was absolute. Their beliefs, although opposed to his Christian ones, were important to them and George respected this. Lastly, George could not promise what was impossible to deliver. Once again death would claim a person he loved and there was nothing he could do about it.

Bitterness and anger welled. It was all he could do not to hurl the small cup of *cinchona* against the wall. Blackness so consumed him that his vision dimmed and his head pounded with the desire to yell. Every muscle coiled with the urgency to inflict violence. Rationality teetered on an edge no wider than a blade of grass. It was a time no longer than a handful of heartbeats, yet George would remember it as one of the darkest, most agonizing periods of his life. What he might have done he could never say, although he was positive it would not have been remotely proper.

One touch changed everything.

"*Mitra*." Jharna breathed the endearment, her tone as dulcet and tender as the palm she laid over his left cheek. "Look at me."

He did, as if compelled by a force stronger than a gale wind. Tears flowed from her eyes that George had once poetically told her resembled the glossy shell of a ripe English oak acorn rimmed with the deep brown of a Pemberley thoroughbred's coat. He had meant it—even if the point had been to make her laugh at his nonsense—and now it forcibly struck him again. The memory of his tease linked with the sensation of home as he gazed into her compassionate, grieved eyes dispelled the anger as if a vapor.

She said no more. She did not need to. George understood all that was in her eyes. He nodded, closing his eyes briefly before planting a glancing kiss to her palm. Bending over Kshitij's unresponsive body, George cradled his beloved mentor's face, tears falling in a wave as he kissed his forehead. "Travel safe, my friend. I shall meet you anon, somehow. Thank you for... everything."

❧

In the weeks surrounding the death of Kshitij Ullas, the house was overrun by family and friends. Hindu funeral rites are a lengthy process, as George knew, and widely diverse among the varied cultures, but always sacred. There were the post-mortem rites of *shraddha* to prepare the body, followed by the funeral ceremony, or *antyesti samskara*, when the body was cremated with due pomp, allowing for the five elements of *prakrit*, or nature, to be properly returned to their source. Purification rituals were ongoing, both for the deceased and his immediate family, in the days leading up to the cremation and for thirteen days afterward. Each person played an integral part in assuring Kshitij's soul was released to move on rather than being lost in between. Outward lamentation was controlled and balanced so as not to create too strong an emotional tie, thus preventing the departed one's journey into the next world. The prime purpose of aiding the loved one to reach *pitr-loka*, that realm where the benefic ancient progenitors of mankind as well as the deceased relatives of the living known as *pitrs* dwell, was dependent upon following rigidly dictated procedures.

Through it all, George maintained a quiet presence. Partly this was due to needing to express his grief in the privacy of his quarters, where he could mourn in the manner of a Christian. Partly it was due to his minimal understanding of the numerous Hindu customs surrounding death. Most of the rituals were spiritual in nature and deeply personal to the family, and despite George's love for Kshitij and close relationship, he was neither family nor Hindu. It wasn't that he was unwelcome. In fact, when he did appear, a kind relative took him by the hand with the intent to include him. George simply wasn't keen on that option. Therefore, he chose to maintain a distance so they could indulge in their religious beliefs without fretting over his presence.

The only time he spoke up, vehemently, was when accidentally overhearing a cluster of elders discussing the merits of *sati* with the clear plan to prevail upon Jharna to perform the ancient ritual.

"Absolutely not!" he thundered. Silence fell as all eyes swiveled to his. In his shock, he had shouted in English, but the furiously disgusted expression on his face, not to mention the tone, left no doubt what he meant. George charged closer until towering over the shorter Indians, switching to Hindi but speaking as forcefully. "Jharna will absolutely not commit suicide! I will never allow that, and if I have to kidnap her to prevent it, I will. *Sati* is a barbaric custom, one that is against all reason and should be outlawed, by God! If any of you so much as breathe of this to Jharna, I swear I will—"

"George! *Mitra!*"

He pivoted to the door where Jharna, drawn by the shouting commotion, was rushing toward him. "Jharna, do not listen to these fools! Kshitij would not want this, and you know it."

"I know. Have no fear, dear George. Be calm and trust me. I could never do that to Nimesh and Sasi, you know this. Now let go of my arm please."

George looked down at his fingers where they were digging into the flesh of her forearm. Still too frightened and angry to feel embarrassed, he did loosen his grip, though not letting go entirely. "I will trust you," he grated, tossing a venomous challenge to the elders, "but I will also be watching. Just in case."

And he did, all through the funeral ceremony. Unable to stand beside Jharna and the boys, George was near enough that if necessary he could leap to her if the stupidity of an idea overcame her reason. Fortunately, that did not occur, and Kshitij Ullas was sent on his way alone.

The immediate period of ritualistic mourning and cleansing ended, the days turning into weeks until eventually a month had passed since Kshitij's death. George remained in the Ullas house in the quarters given to him years ago upon his first visit, resumed his work at the hospital, and spent his free time with Jharna and the boys. Most of Jharna's family returned to their homes, leaving the four of them with a couple of cousins and Jharna's aged grandmother for company, not counting the servants. It was almost as if nothing had changed, but of course there was a glaring hole in what had become their unique family. It was painful and strange. Kshitij's absence was notable every moment, yet at the same time the normal routines carried on woodenly, as if they were going through the motions of life without truly living it.

Under the surface was denial that with Kshitij dead, the changes were huge. Facing that would not be easy.

It began one night toward the end of July, when George and Jharna sat alone in the parlor, a chessboard between them. She was winning, naturally, and after a clever play that left him with few options to avoid checkmate, she made a jest about his pathetic chess skills, to which George had to retaliate that she could only win if cheating. The playful teasing led to laughter, genuine and free, both of them caught up in the sweetness of it, until in the same breath, the reality of the situation crashed over them.

"This is awkward, isn't it?"

Jharna stared into his eyes, her warm smile intact as she shook her head. "No, George. *This* is how it should be. *This* is how Kshitij would wish for us to be, for me and for you to live without his ghost haunting us. For Nimesh and Sasi to celebrate that their father is in *pitr-loka* with our ancestors and remember him with joy. Death is a beginning, not just an end."

"I have lost too many people who are dear to me, Jharna. One would think it easy by now, but it is the opposite." He tapped his king against the edge of the board, his smile grim and eyes dark.

"You feel deeply, George. This is an asset and not to be shunned. Losing one who is loved should never be easy or then the love was not real. Embrace your love for Kshitij, feel the grief as I do because it signifies the glory of experiencing the love. But do not let it cripple you. Do not refuse to live, my friend. Be braver than that."

George stood and walked to the window, his back to Jharna as he stared out into the moonlit darkness.

"George?" she asked tentatively. Then he heard the scrape of her chair. "Oh, George! *Mitra*, please cry no further! I should not have lectured—"

"No, it is fine Jharna. I am not crying. I am laughing." He faced her so she could see, his laughter growing at the surprised expression on her lovely face. "I am sorry. It is just—" He pressed the back of his hand to his lips to stay the threatening chuckles. "Your words are precise repeats of what I told my nephew when my father died. I passed on my wisdom of carrying on and embracing grief as a proof of one's love. I pray he took my wisdom to heart better than I obviously have."

"Do not be so harsh upon yourself, George. It is always easier to speak of wise choices and controlled emotions than to employ them. I am a perfect example." She shrugged one delicate shoulder, the silk of her sari swaying as she bent her head in embarrassment and gracefully sat on the window bench. "I advise with phrases carefully selected from the Vedas, yet I feel little but my pain. I miss him, sorely, and the boys cry each night although they try to hide it from me."

"It has barely been over a month, Jharna. You cannot expect otherwise."

"Yes, this is true. Mourning must be respected and proceed at its pace."

"More quotes from the Vedas?"

She glanced up with a faint smile at his tease. "Not verbatim, no, but close. See how easy it is, George? To inject humor and laugh? These are small steps that must be made as we deal with the sadness."

"So what are you suggesting? I *am* skilled at playing the court jester."

"I am suggesting nothing specific other than that you be the George we love. The George Kshitij loved." Jharna patted the cushion beside her, waiting until George sat before she continued. "Our comfort is in your effervescent, affectionate presence. It is selfish, but we need that George now, especially the boys."

"It isn't selfish, Jharna. I need the three of you as much. You are my family." He stared at his clasped hands and muttered the last, feeling a bit pathetic in admitting he had no one else.

Jharna, as he suspected, read his thoughts. "There is no shame in this, *mitra*. How could it be otherwise? Sasi and Nimesh have known you most of their lives, Sasi for all of his memories. You are their *chacha-jee*. After Kshitij, you are their closest male influence and now more than ever they will turn to you. I am happy for this. Nevertheless, Kshitij would not wish for you to settle for this alone and stagnate here."

"I am not settling or stagnating!"

"Perhaps not yet but you will eventually. And don't pretend that you are not aware of the turmoil brewing in Poona. I doubt either you or Kshitij would be here right now with all that is afoot. For certain you would have accepted the request from Vinayak Phadnavis in Khardi."

"How did you—?"

"Silly man! It is my house so I know everything." She laughed when George's eyes narrowed. "Very well. Learn this lesson: Don't tell Sasi a secret you wish to keep. The boy has no self-control."

George leaned against the wall and grunted. "I should have known. They saw me reading the message and asked. I could not lie, nor did I want them to think I was leaving. Was Sasi upset? I tried to reassure him and thought I had done so."

"He was," she admitted, "until Nimesh reminded him that you are an important man like their *pita-jee*, who was needed to help the unfortunate. Honestly, I sensed that he was somewhat disappointed. Not in your choice," she amended when George's mouth opened in dismay, "but rather because he yearns to follow in Kshitij's footsteps."

"He already is. I assign him the most heinous chores at the hospital and he completes them without complaint. He will be a fine physician. In a couple more years, I will take him with me on one of my journeys with your permission, of course."

"I can imagine no better doctor to train with." She cocked her head, wearing a warm smile that was faintly smug. "And now you are committed to resuming your travels. The cycle of teacher and student, Darcy and Ullas, will continue. As it should."

"I do believe you have tricked me, Mrs. Ullas. Sneaky!"

"Whatever it takes. Now, shall we resume our game of chess, so you cannot claim my victory was by default?"

"I have no intention of defaulting," he declared, jumping up and offering his arm. "All this has been a distraction whilst I plot my next moves. Fell for it, didn't you?"

Jharna took his arm, laughing at his wiggling brows and sly grin. Leaving the serious talk behind, they renewed their contest with the usual mixture of intense strategy and banter, George somehow managing to pull it together and win.

It was the beginning of a gradual process. *Life goes on*, George repeated to himself. Platitudes, Vedic proverbs, adages, and other truisms were also repeated, out loud and within the silences of his mind, offering solace in varying degrees. Yet more than anything, it was not in his nature to be depressed for long. Even in the worst of situations, George was ready with a witty quip or whimsical gesture to diffuse the tension. Years ago, he had accepted that as a vital aspect of his character, as well as being critical to not only deal with the stresses of his profession but also to aid healing in his patients.

The revelation came early in his surgical studies when two of his instructors had summoned him into their office and for thirty minutes lectured him on the importance of maintaining a stern demeanor at all times, especially when interacting with patients. The young George had returned to his rented rooms near the college, heart heavy and mind confused but determined to listen to the words uttered by his wiser leaders. Until he opened his Bible for his evening devotion and quite by accident, or perhaps Divine intervention, the pages parted and his eyes fell on Proverbs 17:22.

"A merry heart doeth good like a medicine: but a broken spirit drieth the bones."

Cross-referencing led him to Proverbs 15:13, "A merry heart maketh a cheerful countenance: but by sorrow of the heart the spirit is broken," and then 16:24, "Pleasant words are as a honeycomb, sweet to the soul, and health to the bones." Several scriptures spoke in the same vein and combined to inspire an epiphany and resolve. Moreover, he would eventually witness the truth of God's words innumerable times in his own soul and in the impact cheerfulness and humor had upon the ill and on those who grieve.

Before the year was over, the shift in how the odd family of Indian and Englishman interacted together was established. Certain patterns already present in their relationship tightened and cemented. Other patterns would develop as a result of the profound changes. Nimesh and Sasi sought their mother for loving consolation when childish tears overwhelmed them, but the boys on the cusp of adolescence instinctively turned to their *chacha* for masculine security.

George resumed his arduous hours at the hospital in Thana, visited the homes of the ill whenever he was called, and traveled four times to villages in the region for short missions. Twice Nimesh accompanied him, the fourteen-year-old learning about medicine as he was put to work as an assistant to Dr. Darcy. Sasi decided that he wanted to learn how to whittle, so George bought him a set of basic knives and it became a common sight for the petite boy to be curled on the cushion beside his tall uncle, both of them with a hunk of wood in their hands. Nimesh lounged with them, his nose pressed into a book. Usually George filled the silence with his resonant voice either recounting a highly embellished tale from his youth or travels with their father, or teaching them English. The tutors Jharna hired taught them of Indian history, mathematics, and science. George passed on the practical knowledge of a man who embodied English culture even in his appreciation for Indian ways. Jharna could not recall the last time she had seen him wear an English garment and sincerely doubted he owned a pair of breeches or a neckcloth, yet despite his browned skin and fluency in Hindi, there was a quality to his bearing uniquely English. He was a strange juxtaposition of both races and cultures. In the climate of the new century, with the rise of the British Empire's influence in India, George proved to be a beneficial addition in more ways than any of them imagined.

❧

A week before Christmas of 1801, George knocked on the door leading to Jharna's studio and then entered without waiting for a response. As he suspected, Jharna was not working on one of her painting projects or other artistic crafts that she excelled at. Rather she was on her knees before a case, carefully wrapping the fragile pottery with paper, straw, and cloth and placing it into sturdy crates edged with additional cushioning materials. It was a painstaking process that she insisted on completing herself.

She glanced up as he breezed in, smiling as she sat back on her heels. "Are you leaving soon?"

"In an hour or so. I promised Sasi I would wait until he returned from his music lesson. I am all packed, though, and the *tanga* is loaded. You need any help?" He reached for a plate and strip of cloth as he asked, winding the cloth around the intricately painted plate until well padded.

"I will accept your assistance, if you are sure you have no one else to see before leaving?"

"Who?" He asked vaguely.

"Mrs. Ganesvoort," she replied in a similar tone, playing along with his false innocence.

"We dined together three nights ago and said our farewells. She understands that I will not be coming back to the area, at least not any time soon."

"Ah, I see. Pity. I was hoping you might have felt differently." She blew a stray strand of hair from her eyes, watching his face closely.

"No need to be coy, Jharna. I know what you hoped for and regret that our sentiments were not serious. Sorry to disappoint. But feel free to continue burning incense to your goddess while praying I stumble upon my true love. Sacrifice a small animal if you think that will help."

"Maybe I will. Small ones only, of course."

"Of course," he replied, lifting one eyebrow. The teasing between them in regards to their religious beliefs was ingrained and enjoyable. Then he chuckled and reached for another plate. "Are these the dining plates you painted for Nimesh? He will be a grandfather before you finish all fifty place settings."

"I have finished Nimesh's set—fourteen place settings—and they are in that crate." She indicated one by the door that was already nailed shut. "Those," she pointed to the one he held, "are for Sasi, a completely different pattern"—she rolled her eyes—"and I only have five pieces left to paint. I'll manage to finish them before he has too many gray hairs."

"Does the house in Junnar have as nice a studio as this one does?"

"Larger with wide windows overlooking the gardens. It may prove to be distracting as the gardens are lush and there is a view of the mountains, but the sunlight will be wonderful. This room never had adequate lighting. I will have space for more than one easel if I wish."

"And you are sure there is an extra room for Nimesh to have a small laboratory?"

"There are several outbuildings, yes, and one has been promised for his use. Best any experiments are conducted away from the main house, don't you think? He can have a garden to plant the seeds you have given him and safely play with the tubes and instruments belonging to Kshitij. We will encourage him, George, have no fear."

George nodded, the creases between his brows deep no matter how hard he tried to present a serene exterior. He methodically wrapped the precious pottery, the task perfect for keeping his mind from dwelling on unpleasantness. Jharna was not fooled, naturally. She always read his thoughts no matter how nonchalant or secretive he tried to be.

"It is a beautiful area and rich with the history of our people, the Marathas, not the least being Shivaneri Hill, the birthplace of Shivaji Maharaj. Lushly green and dotted with rivers and tiny lakes, Junnar is the perfect playground for energetic boys, especially where my grandmother's house is located. With the bulk of my mother's clan there, it will be a wonderful place for them to mature while growing close to family. They will have an abundance of cousins to play with. It is where Kshitij wanted me to relocate when the time came."

"No need to sell me on the idea, Jharna," he interrupted gently. "We have talked of it at length, and you know I approve of your decision to leave Thana, not that my approval is necessary."

"Perhaps not strictly so, *mitra*, but I value your opinion and never wish to cause you unhappiness."

"Thank you. I'll have to remember you said that when, or if, the time comes when I *do* disagree with one of your decisions." He flashed her a calculating grin and arched one brow deviously, Jharna chuckling. "Don't let me whine too much, Mrs. Ullas. You know I am simply being difficult and selfish. I don't like change—"

"Ha! You are the king of change! You change your clothes three times a day and would shrivel into a dried husk if forced to reside in one place for longer than six months!"

"Not true at all. Well, the clothes part maybe I'll admit to, but I have lived here for nearly a year."

"You have been here for eight months, barely, and spent a total of two of those months elsewhere," she corrected, then waved a hand at the stack of plates he had quit wrapping, using his words to tease him into a happier mood. "Now get back to work and cease whining and being difficult."

Jharna resumed her task of packing the breakable items on the wall case, George doing the same after a flippant bow in her direction, which she ignored. Silence fell for several minutes before George again spoke.

"You are going to make me confess to being a sentimental fool, aren't you?" He sighed when she looked up encouragingly. "This house is so closely linked to Kshitij. It is odd to think of others dwelling here besides us."

"There is nothing wrong with being sentimental, George. Perhaps I could use a dose of your tender nature. For me it is merely a house. Yes, I see Kshitij here, since it was his house and where he first brought me as a new bride. Yet due to all our years of travel, we lived here as a family less than we did elsewhere. Even before those years I was often not here, choosing to be with kin when Kshitij was away. Nimesh was born in Kalyan at my father's *haveli* and Sasi in Junnar in my grandmother's house, the same one that we will be living in and which will be mine when she passes. I never felt truly at home here. Thana is too large and populated with people who are too busy to make lasting friendships."

"Large cross-cultural towns with busy people take no interest in a stray white man wandering about or which walls he lives within."

"That is what bothers you! Here in Thana, few notice, and if they do are accepting of you as Dr. Darcy, associate of Dr. Ullas. What of Junnar, you are wondering. Oh, George." She rose to her feet and crossed to where he stood. "You have nothing to fear. My family knows how important you are to us and they adore you. You will be as valuable and delightfully appreciated there, more so in fact, than you are here."

"Thank you. The reassurance is appreciated. And you are right that I do not fear change. I welcome new and exciting adventures, which is a good characteristic considering the unrest in the region now. Britain is flexing her muscles and strife is brewing among the Confederacy. I wish I had a crystal ball to predict the future winds, but I can almost guarantee I will be busy with

Company affairs. I am selfish, though, and hate that Junnar is farther away from Bombay."

"Not that far. A swift horse can cover the seventy miles easily. Once you are done visiting your friends in Bombay and worshipping the virgin mother and straw baby god you will see how near we are."

"Only Catholics worship the Virgin Mary, not Anglicans, and Jesus is God as a baby lying *in* the straw not made *of* straw." He shook his head as if exasperated, knowing full well that she knew the Biblical story nearly as well as he. "And your theory is dependent on having a swift horse. Time to purchase a new steed, I suppose."

A tumult from the corridor interrupted any further conversation. They turned to the doorway just as Nimesh and Sasi crowded through, vying to be first to reach George and ignoring their mother's pleas to be calm in her studio teeming with breakable articles.

"Did you give him his presents yet, *mata-jee?*"

"I was waiting for you two," she answered, not that anyone was listening to her.

"You will be so surprised, *chacha!*"

"Yes, so surprised!"

Voices tumbling over each other, Sasi and Nimesh grabbed a hand and propelled the baffled man out into the hallway. Jharna trailed behind, a backward glance revealing her exuberant smile and that she had retrieved a brightly wrapped box from some hidden shelf in her studio. George's curiosity piqued, especially when they bypassed every room in the house and exited a side door, the boys jabbering in rushed Hindi as they dragged him toward a clearing near the barn.

George saw the horse before his mind registered that they were heading toward the majestic animal who stood proudly off to one side, head lifted and averted in imperious disdain of the groom loosely holding his reins. He was a stallion, easily sixteen hands high, with a deep chest, straight shoulders, and pronounced withers supporting a long, sloping back. He was colored reddish-bay with white patches in a skewbald pattern, tail and mane black, as were his intelligent eyes and tall, pointed ears that curled inward with the tips touching. The combination of traits, especially the ears, left no doubt as to the breed.

"A Marwari! You are giving me a Marwari? He is for me?" The questions were redundant since the boys were leaping about and clapping with sheer delight. George waited for Jharna to nod before he could believe it. "This is too much, Jharna. I know how rare a Marwari is and how expensive. You should not have done this. I can't accept it."

"You will accept it, dear George, because it is not from me. It is a gift from my father. A thanks, he said, for your devotion to our family. You wanted a swift horse and now you have one. Maybe there is something to the magic of your Christmas after all. Straw baby gods perform great miracles, so I am told." She grinned and thrust the colorful box into his arms. "This is a new *sherwani*, *salwar kameez*, and pair of *mojari* decorated by me and my grandmother with your taste in mind. That means it is gaudily decorated with every color of the rainbow. You will love it. The boys helped with the sewing too. Not as exciting as a Marwari stallion, but I trust it will earn you a fair amount of attention at some glittering British East India Company gala, specifically of the female persuasion. The horse will gain you points with the men, so you win all the way around. Happy Christmas, George."

❦

Five days after the new year, George sat across a table from his longtime friend Dr. Searc McIntyre. They were at Henry's, the oldest English-style pub in Bombay and the same place where George attacked the former Physician General Dr. White. The pub had been under new ownership for eight years, and although polished up, the furnishings hadn't changed considerably. The tables and chairs were newer, as was typical in rowdy drinking establishments where brawls were not uncommon, but constructed of the standard wood and arranged exactly the same as they had been for decades. Nevertheless, George didn't pass a second in remembrance of long ago events. Instead, he smiled at his drinking companion, the two men happy to steal away for a private chat—or at least as private as one could get in a loud public room with a dart game in one corner, a minstrel on the tiny platform in the other, and a game of faro at the table by the door, which was promising to become lively very soon based on the angry expression worn by one of the players. The physicians ignored all of it, including the speculative gazes from several ladies-for-hire milling about the room.

"Here is to 1802. May it be a year of excitin' prospects and stoat health!"

McIntyre lifted his mug of ale, George mimicking the gesture but pausing before clinking together to add, "And to the new Physician General of Bombay Headquarters, Dr. McIntyre!"

"Thank ye," McIntyre said after they drank deeply of the frothing liquid, "although I was hoping to make that another toast to drink to."

"I am sure we will find much to drink to before we are too inebriated to care any longer."

"Such as drinking to yer birthday. Oh, dinna look so shocked. Of *course* I forgot. But my wife remembered it was this month. She remembered the date too, although I have already forgotten that, so your low opinion of my sentimental nature is correct. All I am sure of is that it hasn't passed, since Lileas is planning to bake a cake for ye."

George's eyes gleamed. "A cake? With very sweet icing? Ah! Delicious! I shall be there on the twelfth, you can count on it. Supper too, dare I hope?"

"God, ye are a greedy bugger, aren't ye? All right. Dinner too. Just don bring any sweets for me wee lasses. Cake is enough."

"That I cannot promise," George declared firmly. "Your daughters are too adorable not to treat with candies and ribbons. And how ridiculous is it to say that cake is enough? Absurd! To cake never being enough!"

George lifted his mug, and after a moment, McIntyre knocked his mug against the side, joining in the nonsensical toast and laughing as he drank.

"Repeat this and I will kill ye, Darcy, but I have missed ye company. It is good to have ye here and I am sorry it's taken so long to share a drink wi' ye."

"That isn't your fault. I expected the Christmas celebrations to be enjoyable but not the grand affair we have had. Lord and Lady Burgley's invitation mentioned that Governor Duncan was attending the soiree, but not that General Wellesley was a guest of honor. I've never seen such pomp in Bombay."

"And ye loved every second of it."

"Well, of course! Gave me a reason to wear my newest clothes. I was quite the spectacle."

McIntyre lifted his mug. "Here's to Dr. Darcy being a spectacle. Again."

"Cheers!" George grinned unrepentantly as he met McIntyre's mug with a spirited thunk. "Somebody had to liven up the party. Thank goodness I was there and unafraid to make a bloody fool of myself, or it may have ended before the stroke of midnight Christmas morn. I still think you should have danced a

Scottish reel and answered the age-old question of what a man does, or doesn't, wear under his kilt."

"Someone needed to maintain their dignity," McIntyre grunted. Then his eyes narrowed and he pointed a finger at George. "Is that why we are here? So ye can get a start on intoxicating me so I'll dance at the ball tonight?"

George leaned forward, his expression and tone deadly serious. "It is Twelfth Night and the Lord of Misrule calls for folly. It is the law."

McIntyre shoved him back, both men laughing. "God help Bombay if ye had accepted the position of Physician General from Governor Duncan."

"What?" George's mug slapped onto the tabletop, the sound taken as a hint to the barmaid to refill their mugs. She hastened over but neither man noticed.

"Ach, no need to be in a dither, Darcy. I know they asked ye first and I dinna mind. With yer experience it makes sense, aside from the fact that ye have no wish to stay on the island. I ken that and am glad ye said no 'cause ye would be no good at the job."

"That's exactly what I told them! Searc, they never would have thought of me if I hadn't shown up when I did. You were their first choice."

"I said dinna fash yerself. The best man got the job—me!" He grinned and winked. "But they thought of ye first, no mistake. Yer fame has spread, my friend, and well earned to boot. The name of Darcy is whispered with the same hallowed awe as Ullas once was, more so on account of ye being English. 'Course I make sure they know ye don't walk on water and piss like the rest of us mere mortals."

George heard the tease in McIntyre's voice and knew that any jealousy felt was minimal. Aside from a handful of close-to-home missions, like to Kutch, Dr. McIntyre was content to practice his craft in Bombay. Not only were his wife and children there, but he also did not possess the same drive that George always had. No, George knew nothing had changed in their relationship as a result of Dr. Darcy being asked first.

What caused him to stare into his mug with contemplative amazement were the claims of his fame. He had no idea that anyone outside of those he knew intimately ever talked about him at all! Sure, he was recognized and welcomed in every English enclave he traveled to, but he chalked that up to either his family's fame in England, the letters of introduction he carried, or to people simply being thrilled to see a physician. Humbleness was not a trait

George counted among his positive attributes and proudly listed arrogance right on top, yet for some bizarre reason he had never extended that arrogance into the broader scope of far-reaching fame. It was disconcerting because fame was never something he craved. Some accused him of being ostentatious and a seeker of attention with his flamboyant ways, but the better term was audacious, because while bold and uninhibited, George cared not a whit what anyone thought of him. His only desire was to please his patients, and himself, in a ceaseless quest for healing knowledge. That truth was why McIntyre's words were also exhilarating. George was a firm believer in one's education ending only when laid in the ground, but it was nice to know that his skills had reached a level where others noticed because it was a sign he was doing something right!

"So what other positions did they offer ye?"

George started out of his reverie, it taking a couple of seconds to register what McIntyre had asked. Attempting to be casual, he blew on the fresh froth of his refilled mug of ale before answering. "What makes you think they offered me anything? I am the rebel who refused their shackling request as PG."

McIntyre released a rude noise. "I'm no an idiot, Darcy! And I have ears to the ground and eyes everywhere. Yes," he affirmed when George arched a brow, "I do. While ye was out traipsing about the country, I have been here firmly entrenched—"

"Which is why you are a far better choice for the PG job."

"Damn right I am! Unlike ye, I have an interest in politics and that adds to my qualifications. Ye, on the other hand, have something more valuable than that."

Dr. McIntyre paused, but George did not take the bait. He wanted to hear what McIntyre thought and what rumors he might have heard, so he sipped at his ale and stared silently.

"'Tis no secret to anyone with half a brain that neutralizing the French factions in Mysore and Hyderabad bent on causing rebellion, and especially the death of Tipu Sultan, has stabilized matters to the south. Problem is that the War Office back home thinks life is now rosy. The Tiger Sultan was a lunatic but a smart one with power and connections. I can see why eliminating him would seem to eliminate the threats. Yet I tend to agree that there are greater threats yet to deal with. That is the opinion of Lord Wellesley, our illustrious Governor-General, in case you haven't kept up on the news."

George pierced him with a condescending glare. "I am not completely uninformed," he replied drily. "Calcutta and the War Office are primarily concerned with money. How to keep amassing it through uninterrupted trade while not spending so much on military campaigns is the question, and my guess is that they each have different answers."

"That is one way to put it. But the War Office is a long way from here and Wellesley has the authority, and the will, to get the answer he wants."

"I am waiting to see what any of this has to do with me, but since we are talking politics here"—George grimaced—"and you are apparently in the Governor's confidence, does any of this smell of empire expansion to you? Wellesley's doctrine of subsidiary alliance has already gained Hyderabad, Awadh, and Mysore—"

"Territories that were volatile and blatantly threatening the Company. Ye have seen it first hand, Darcy, and said yerself that Tipu was a menace."

"He was intense, that is for sure," George agreed with massive understatement. "We were in Mysore during the years of 'peace' but the currents never disappeared. And the one time we met the Sultan was one time too many for me. Nevertheless, I am surprised to realize you are such a patriot and fan of British control."

McIntyre winced. "I ken the parallels, Darcy. I also see the differences. Scotland had legitimate, competent rulers who wanted to reign in accord with England. Most of the time," he added in a firmer voice when George opened his mouth to speak. "I have reasons deeply-seated in my blood not to trust the pretty words of an English aristocrat, and even if the marquess is honest as a day is long, he is only one man. Who knows what the king is thinking, mad as he is. But he is half a world away and the Company is stretched too thin to exert empiric control. Just keeping the peace will take all they got."

"So, as fascinating as this conversation is, what does it have to do with me?"

"Are ye really going to keep playing the innocent game?" he asked scathingly, but went on before George had a chance to reply, ticking off each condition on one of his fingers. "I am promoted 'cause Dr. Trenowyth is moving up to Surgeon-General of the Bombay Presidency section of the Indian Medical Services. He ousted Dr. Clinton, whom we all know wasn't very competent but not a total failure at the job. It dinna take an augur to predict there will be trouble with the Maratha dynasties in the years ahead nor does one need to be a genius to figure where that may lead. With battles comes the need for doctors and since Jaswant Rao's uprising last June, they have added a dozen or more surgeons to the ranks. The call is out for more and they are looking for doctors, British, Indian, or whatever, who have experience first but also knowledge of the region. I am surprised they bothered offering ye the PG of Bombay Headquarters position. You are needed out there"—he waved toward the northeast—"not here."

George had sat back through McIntyre's speech, mug still in his hands and eyes fixed on his companion's face. He wasn't "playing the innocent game" for the reasons McIntyre assumed. George wasn't a secretive man in general, and one of his main purposes in time alone with his friend was to talk about this very topic. He was genuinely startled that McIntyre knew of Governor Duncan offering him the Physician General position, however. It hadn't been a serious offer, George instantly aware that Duncan was testing him, wanting to hear what his justifications would be for turning the job down. For a second, he had toyed with the idea of saying yes, just to see how Duncan and General Wellesley would react. That would have been humorous! George was too skilled a diagnostician not to read their eyes, and clearly they not only had another preferred plan for him in mind, but also they knew he was not the best candidate for Physician General. Commander Doyle of Bombay Headquarters, who had also been in the room along with Dr. Trenowyth, had known Dr. Darcy since he first stepped foot onto the dock twelve years prior and could assert better than any other that he was not the stay-in-one-place kind of fellow.

No, they had been confident that George would say thanks but no thanks. And of course he had. Then he had waited. Sure enough, they had an alternative. George wasn't one to closely follow politics, that was true, but there were some realities that couldn't be ignored no matter how hard one tried. Like McIntyre, George had seen the signs and suspected trouble on the horizon. Rumors and gossip can never be avoided completely, so he wasn't surprised when Duncan presented him with another post. Nevertheless, he hadn't given an answer. They granted him time to think about it, and he was determined not to be hasty in accepting an assignment with so many potential consequences. Hence the reason he needed to hear McIntyre's uncolored opinion of what was occurring in the region and how Dr. Darcy might best fit into the scenarios.

When McIntyre fell silent, George leaned forward. "They want me to be the Deputy Surgeon-General, working alongside Dr. Trenowyth."

McIntyre nodded, his expression bland. "I figured it was something like that. Might involve a fair amount of administrative duties. Ye up for that?"

George rubbed his chin. "Not sure, to be honest. Oh, I know I could handle the work, that's not the issue. I've been around long enough to understand how the medical corps for the army is arranged and what the attitudes are. And therein lies the problem: I also know where they are falling short. I have worked with various groups, western and native, recognizing what is efficient and what is not."

"That is why they want ye for the job, I reckon."

"Yes. But saying they appreciate my experience and want my authoritative input is vastly different than implementing my ideas if they diverge from the norm. Diplomacy is not exactly my strong suit," he said with a laugh. "I'll probably irritate Trenowyth or someone else in the first month and be booted out anyway, so shouldn't worry over accepting."

"Bollocks, and ye know it, Darcy. Except for a handful of notable persons that we best not mention, ye can charm the worst of the lot. People love ye, men and women. More importantly, they respect ye. As a physician, there are few better and I for one don't doubt ye administrative skills. And as bull-headed as ye are, any obstacles will be rammed right through. Plus, ye know Trenowyth well after yer time here. Ye two have similar methods and get on." He stabbed his finger at George. "I'm no saying anything you dinna already ken; otherwise, I would no be falling over myself with the compliments. So what's the real concern?"

"None really," George admitted with a shrug. "Truth is, the idea appeals to me. It will be a challenging appointment at a challenging time. It's just—" He sighed and ran one hand through his thick, wavy hair, continuing hesitantly, "I guess I've gotten used to my freedom. Being able to come and go as I please is nice. As Deputy Surgeon-General, I will be traveling. I made sure of that because sitting behind a desk preparing reports is not an option and never will be. And I'll be acting as a working physician. But it will be more regimented. I may not be able to set my own pace as I am accustomed or be able to focus on medicine as often. That gives me pause."

"And ye are not sure how often ye can veer off to Junnar."

"Remind me to tell Lileas that you are not nearly as obtuse as you claim to be."

"Never mind that. Best she believes me a simpleton. It is easier that way, trust me. I dinna see the problem with Junnar. It isn't that far away and ye wouldn't be sitting about on ye arse there for long neither. For what its worth, I see this as a smart choice for ye, Darcy. But I've never known ye to care much what anyone thinks. Trust yer gut and it 'twill be the best."

GEORGE'S MEMOIRS
DECEMBER 25, 1802

Merry Christmas, Father! The clock struck midnight not an hour ago, making it officially the day our Savior was born, although I am probably the only person in Junnar who noted it. I wonder if Christmas is celebrated in Heaven? I suppose I shall find out someday, but for the present will imagine a massive feast with Jesus as the Honored One and you sitting at a gigantic table with the other saints. As I wrote in my previous entry in November, I was not sure whether I would be able to extend my planned visit with the Ullas family through the holiday. Aside from the fact that it makes more sense to celebrate a Christian observance with other Christians rather than a household of Hindu Marathi, the turmoil in Maharashtra may not have allowed it. Surprisingly enough, we are experiencing a lull. Let me see if I can sum up, more so that I will remember these events if I ever pick up this journal forty years from now.

It took three of the Bombay Presidency medical corps, with the help of dozens of Indian healers and I don't know how many nurses and helpers, to tend to all the wounded Sindhia and Marathi after the battle in Poona on October 25. Jaswant Rao of Indore did a bang up job in decimating his enemies and sacking the Peshwa's capitol. Too many died, but our combined skills saved many who would have joined them. Let's pray they do not heal only to die upon another battlefield, but more than likely that will be the case. It was a test of how well our organizing and training this year has paid off. We had adequate supplies for the most part, and down to the last man and woman, the medical corps conducted themselves efficiently. I was too busy and exhausted during the onslaught to notice or praise anyone, but once we were able to breathe, I assessed the situation and have to say that my pride swelled considerably. Trenowyth was verbose in his praise, once the reports reached him that is. What is it with bureaucrats and paperwork? Must they substantiate their existence with piles upon piles of documents written so that no one can truly know what they say? I think so. I kept my report as brief as possible, but it still took me days to provide the information I knew they would insist upon. It must have sufficed, thank the Maker, since no one came after me for more details.

Anyway, while we patched up holes and reset broken bones, among other injuries, Jaswant chased after Peshwa Baji Rao II, who fled to Suvarnadurg fort in Konkan for refuge. Rumors ran the gamut from reports of his death and capture by Jaswant to that he was heading east to Calcutta or north for goodness knows what purpose, to wilder stories in between. What we did know for sure was that he had appealed to Colonel Close, the British Resident at Poona, for an alliance with the EIC in exchange for assistance in reestablishing his authority over the Maratha Confederacy. No one with any knowledge of how matters lie with the EIC and Governor-General Marquess Wellesley can doubt that an agreement will be made. Then, a couple days before I left to travel to Junnar and while still in Bhiwandi, word reached us that the Peshwa sailed from Suvarnadurg under British protection, making his way to Bassein for further negotiations. I am sure he is there by now with a treaty probably already signed. British commands in Madras and Hyderabad, just to name a couple, are amassed and quietly waiting the next move. Or probably not so quietly, knowing soldiers like I do. Not that I blame them since Jaswant isn't too quiet either. But at least for the interim, we are at a standstill and I was able to slip away for a much-needed rest.

What 1803 will bring is anyone's guess. Maybe the EIC will have luck in negotiating with Jaswant. Then again, considering he wants Baji's head on the end of a stake, I rather doubt it. He has settled in at the palace in Poona, ostensibly taken command of the Maratha army, and is calling one of his relatives the new Peshwa. Somehow I doubt the Bombay Presidency will take kindly to that. I foresee more bloodshed, Father.

I decided to grasp onto the momentary cessation of hostilities. I have been at Junnar for nearly two weeks now. It is so peaceful here. The Ullas house is located on the outskirts of town, and with Junnar not on a direct avenue between larger towns, we are especially isolated. It is like stepping backward in time, or sidestepping into an alternative universe where war and death do not exist. I can relax here with nothing more strenuous on my docket than a sporting game with the boys. Anoop loves it as well, utterly forgetting that he is a mature man of twenty-some years and cavorts with the children for hours at a time. There is great hunting in the jungles near here, but even that typically enjoyable pastime isn't intriguing to me. I suppose I have heard enough gunfire for a while. I am doing a whole lot of nothing and loving every second of it. Although our makeshift hospitals were always well away from the skirmish lines, one never feels completely safe when with a fighting army. Here I am safe with my only fear another embarrassing defeat in chess at the hands of Jharna.

Oh yes, I almost forgot! I received a parcel of letters from home. I haven't gotten mail in six months, not that I have written all that often either, but it appears that my *correspondence was languishing in an office in Bassein. A clerk who knows me saw the pile by accident and sent them to Bhiwandi with orders to either locate me there (they did) or be sent on to Junnar. Finally, a man in the EIC employ with some brains! He better watch out, or they will make him a general! So, letters from a handful of blokes from school days, one from Malcolm (Lord Matlock as he now is), and another from Henry Vernor, two from young William including scribbles by the hand of my namesake Georgiana—so precious—one from Estella, and five from James. All in all, a major delight for me! Most were filled with typical newsy bits of gossip from the countryside that I love reading about. Estella's daughter was presented at Court this year, which means she may well be married soon, which means I am getting damned old! How the hell did that happen? Sorry, Father, I know I should not swear, but I am shocked and dismayed. Worse though was the news James had to impart. It seems that Anne has never recovered her bloom. James says it is nothing that can be pinpointed exactly. I would tend to disagree with him, arrogantly believing I could detect the problem, yet none of the symptoms he chronicles are definitive. Her muscles are weak and difficult to control with muscle spasms and ataxia common. He says that at times she is her old self and they will hope it is permanent. Yet it never is and she will faint or spend hours sleeping from a malaise that does not respond to rest. Pain is associated, although not consistent or localized. It is odd. I have guessed anemia or a heart weakened from the burden of pregnancy. However, none of my prescribed treatments have worked and with further probing, I have discovered that Anne was displaying some of these symptoms prior to conceiving Georgiana. Not as severely, mind you, so no one thought it serious and I noticed nothing while visiting. I am beginning to suspect a neuropathy of some kind and that is not good news, since there is little that can be done for such diseases. I sent another packet of herbs and a letter with instructions. Unfortunately, they are only of a palliative nature and focusing on the symptoms rather than the cause. I continue to pray that it is not a fatal ailment. The thought of anything happening to Anne is more than I can bear. And James? Well, you know how deeply he loves Anne, Father. I have no doubt whatsoever that her death would destroy him. I must consider a journey home soon. Perhaps this peace will last, Jaswant will see reason and withdraw, and Maharashtra will again be the great nation it once was. If I were an optimist, I might believe my own rhetoric!*

G EORGE PULLED ON THE reins and murmured a gentle *whoa*. The horse obeyed reluctantly, sidestepping and tossing his head impatiently. "I understand, Rathore," he soothed, bending to rub the silky, white neck of his faithful mount. "You can smell the fresh water and grains from here. Bear with me for a minute, *vafādār*, and I promise we will be home soon."

Rathore snorted, conveying his displeasure with waiting but did lean into the firm caress of his human friend. George had named the Marwari stallion gifted to him by Jharna's father after the rulers of the Marwar region of India who were the first to breed the exquisite animals in the twelfth century. Together the two had traversed the length and breadth of Maharashtra and the Deccan Plain, growing in their mutual respect with each passing month. George was a Darcy, and thus a man who loved horses as if a kinship was buried inside the fabric of his bones and muscles. It had taken no time at all for him to bond with his new mount and vice versa, Rathore sensing that this man was a worthy one to allow the privilege of sitting on his back. Therefore, trust was an aspect of the partnership forged, so Rathore relaxed in the shadows of the overhanging trees and waited.

George continued to rub Rathore's neck, but his attention was on the sprawling house nestled in the verdant valley below the hillock they stood on.

Designed as a rectangular structure encompassing an open central courtyard of stone, the large, two-level building was impressive, even in the half light of dusk. The receding illumination from the sun muted the effect of high noon but was adequate enough to discern the elegant architecture and geometric designs of stones painted in vibrant colors. Lamps glowed welcomingly from the windows above the cusped arched of the main entrance and strategic niches carved into the outer walls. From his vantage point, George could see the entire house and most of the outbuildings where the animals were lodged and supplies stored. A few servants milled about, tending to late afternoon tasks before the light was gone. A brisk breeze caused the tall trees to sway, adding a pleasant play of shadows to the tableau and lifting the natural smells of flowers, grass, river water, and moist earth upward into the air.

Inhaling, George closed his eyes to greater appreciate the aromas. Individually they were common to any dwelling place in India. Combined, they were unique to the residence of Jharna, Nimesh, and Sasi Ullas in Junnar. The place George called home.

Home.

Since arriving in India, he had never stayed anywhere long enough to think of it as home. If asked, he would have answered that Pemberley in Derbyshire was his home, yet the truth was that his ancestral estate hadn't *felt* like home for decades, even before leaving England. Another truth was that George, for all his sentimental nature, hadn't cared all that much. The itinerant life was what he had happily chosen, so such perks as having a home with all the emotional ties that the word conjured weren't part of the package.

So why did the word now fill him with such peace and longing? And when had he started thinking of the house where the Ullas family lived as home? George could not pinpoint the day or the month. It had happened gradually, the term spoken inside his heart a dozen times before he realized it.

Perhaps the better question was, "Why this house?"

It was a beautiful house designed flawlessly and constructed well. It was a perfect blend of modern conveniences and old-world ideals. Not overly ornate, comfortably furnished, spacious, and airy, accented with lush gardens inside and out, the house now owned by Jharna Ullas since the death of her paternal grandmother five months prior was worthy of being loved. Nevertheless, George knew his affection toward the place was not because of the structure itself.

It was home because his heart lived there. It was home because his heart was utterly and irrevocably captured. It was home because Jharna lived there.

George had fallen in love with Jharna Ullas.

The gradual acknowledgement of the Junnar house as home had occurred simultaneously with his gradual awareness of altering emotions for Jharna. There wasn't a specific day or month when that had happened either. He had simply come to a point of admitting that the feelings inside were no longer ones of friendship but of passion as a man has for a woman. He had not consciously sought more. It had happened of its own volition.

George shifted in the saddle gifted to him by Jharna last Christmas. Rathore took it as a signal and stepped forward, the sound he made when George tugged on the reins clearly expressing his annoyance in more waiting, although he complied and stood still. George continued his contemplation of the house and his situation.

Aside from a two-day layover in early March when traveling east to Ahmednagar, George had not visited since December. At that time, the Ullas family had hosted a surprise holiday celebration for George complete with foods from his country prepared quite well, considering they were cooked by Indians who had never heard of wassail or plum pudding, and Christian carols sung in mispronounced English. It was an overwhelmingly emotional experience that moved him profoundly, but when Nimesh brought in the gleaning saddle fashioned specifically for Rathore, it had taken every ounce of George's self-control not to kiss Jharna. The entire two weeks of his visit had been an agony of repressed longing as he hopelessly fell deeper in love with a woman who responded to him precisely as she forever had.

"I am indeed unlucky in love," he murmured.

After the failure with Lady Ruby Thomason, George had asserted this conviction to Dr. Ullas. To a large degree, it had been the claim of a man agonized from a broken heart. Twelve years had passed, his heart had healed, and rarely had he given the matter of his luck or lack thereof much thought. Casual affairs fulfilled his physical desires and provided a semblance of intimacy that suited where he was in his life. If asked, he probably would have said he was lucky *not* to fall in love and suffer the complications.

It wasn't guilt or betrayal he felt for loving Jharna. Kshitij was dead. George was a practical man and had never assumed that a woman as young and beautiful as Jharna would remain unwed forever. He couldn't imagine that Kshitij would want that for her. There were no other suitors yet, but how long would that last? Would he be able to sit calmly by when another man married her? Honestly, he did not think he could. So instead, he avoided visiting until the pain of missing her, and Nimesh and Sasi, was too great to bear. He loved them and needed to be a part of their lives, no matter the agony it may cause him. The agony of never seeing them again or not being a part of their lives was worse.

Still, he sat on the hillock and watched the sun set until the house was immersed in the shadows, with only the entrance lit with smoking oil lamps. He may have sat there indefinitely, but the clomp of hooves alerted him to the approach of Anoop.

"*Sahib Vaidya* Darcy, you waited for me! Thank you! You should not have though. You could have eaten already and be at rest. I know the way myself!"

"I know you do, Anoop. Ready then?"

Anoop nodded enthusiastically.

"Stop being a bloody coward," George muttered to himself, following with the command Rathore had been waiting for. The horse leapt a foot off the ground in his eagerness, jarring George's teeth together at the impact. His curse was lost in the clatter of hooves striking hard-packed dirt. Guards alerted by the sound rushed to intercept the unexpected visitor, drawn swords sheathed at recognition that it was Dr. Darcy arriving. Shouts of *Darcy Sahib* rang through the air as servants hastened to assist the respected guest of the Ullas household. George's feet barely touched the ground before he was surrounded by two pairs of youthful arms, squeezing tight.

"*Chacha-jee*! We have missed you! Where have you been? Have you seen many battles? Have you eaten dinner? Have you cured many sick patients? Have you missed us too? How long are you staying? Where is Anoop?"

And on the questions went, tumbling on top of each other so that he could not tell who asked what, nor begin to formulate answers. Instead, he smiled and hugged until the air whooshed out of their lungs, momentarily halting the babble. The caesura was brief, but enough for Jharna's softer voice to penetrate.

"*Namaste, mitra.* We are so happy to see you."

George lifted his head, his heart already pounding from the effect of her voice alone, and willed his expression to remain neutral as he bravely looked at her. She wore an emerald green sari of silk, edged with a wide trim woven with gold thread into an intricate design of flowers, the garment hugging the curves of her hips and generous breasts before falling in a cascading drape down her back and over one arm. Her black hair was pulled away from her face with a gold circlet, the heavy tresses loose upon her shoulders and spilling in waves to just above the slope of her buttocks. She was smiling happily and her eyes were luminous in the lamp-lit courtyard, shining with friendship and sincere delight. Then suddenly they widened with alarm, the lips that George had been staring at fixedly opening as she mouthed a troubled *oh*.

"You are bleeding!" Her exclamation was accompanied by a tender brush of her fingertips across his lower lip, the shockwave of her touch making him gasp and jerk his head backward. "Sorry"—she pulled her fingers away—"I am sure it is painful."

Jharna sent a servant for water, towels, and medicinal ointment, her attention momentarily diverted, allotting George the time to recollect the wits that scattered the second she touched him. Gingerly pressing a finger to his lower lip, he belatedly realized that it was in fact bleeding.

"Rathore took one look at the house and set off at a fast gallop. I guess it rattled me more than I thought. It is nothing," he assured the woman whose concerned eyes were staring at him. "I didn't notice it in my excitement to see all of you. And get some food! What does a man have to do to be fed around here? Is that tandoori I smell?"

Anoop rode into the courtyard at that moment, his slight body bouncing crazily on the back of the pony that had bravely tried to keep pace with Rathore. In no time at all, the two men were ushered into the house amid laughter and endless streams of conversation as food was brought into the dining area on large platters. The various kinsman that lived in the house with Jharna poured through the open archways, everyone delighted to welcome Dr. Darcy and join in the lively meal, even though they had already partaken of their evening repast. George's jovial nature took over, his happiness to be among people he cared for genuine. The only tense moment was when a servant brought the requested medicine for his split lip, but George was able to relax when Nimesh assumed the task rather than Jharna. It was humorous how Nimesh adopted a serious expression while meticulously tending to the wound, as if performing the most delicate of surgeries. George held the smile in, partly because the cut did sting a bit, but mostly not to insult the boy's heartfelt intentions. He did wink at Jharna from above the boy's bent head. Her return smile was warm, expressive eyes conveying her appreciation for him tolerating Nimesh's fussing.

It was a brief exchange, a small moment and insignificant on the face of it, but in that short span, George sensed the cords binding his heart into knots loosen. More important than the love he felt for Jharna was the friendship they shared, and he refused to do anything to jeopardize that. As he gazed at Jharna and then down at Nimesh and across to the laughing people clustered about the low table, his eyes sweeping rapidly about the spacious room with palms and colorful flowers adding to the beautiful decor, George knew that this was *home* in more ways than just his love for her. As long as she was here, as long as Sasi and Nimesh were here, as long as he was welcomed into the family fold, he would do nothing to compromise the situation. It might be painful but losing them would be far, far worse.

It was a good plan and one that worked well until the day the topic of love and marriage was brought up.

Groups engaged in various household tasks were scattered about the enormous roofless courtyard in the middle of the house. Some were sewing and mending while others laundered soiled garments. Near the entrance, a cluster of men and boys polished swords and leather saddles while watching a half-dozen brawny, sweating guards spar. Gardeners tended to the numerous potted trees and flowers while craftsmen bent to repair broken tiles and service fountain pumps. Cleaning servants wandered about with brooms and scrubbing cloths in hand. More than half the household, family and servant, were in the central courtyard, harmoniously milling around each other with conversation flowing and laughter frequent as they worked. Yet the area was designed so well that the voices rose in the air, drifting up and over the high rooftops of the living quarters so that tranquility was maintained.

Under the shading palms and porch roof in the corner near the kitchen sat tables laden with assorted edibles as the women cut fruits and vegetables, spiced meats, and rolled dough for breads and desserts. They were all familiar with George and his appetite, it having become an old game to try to catch him as he sneakily pilfered from the piles of food while charmingly distracting with a toothy grin and witty joke. Of course, he was unrepentant when caught, merely slipping another slice of something between his fingers as he shook the hand that had been slapped. The fact that stray bits of food were left lying about was no accident, naturally, but the charade continued.

Today he was sitting cross-legged on a large cushion near a table where two women were rolling dough for naan, a small girl on each leg. Three-year-old Ihita sat on his left knee, her face scrunched as she waited to explode into another series of loud laughs when he would abruptly jerk the leg and nearly send her tumbling backward unless she was quick enough to grab onto him. Two-year-old Treya was perched on the right and not as happy about it. She would rather be running amok around the feet of the women but kept to her confinement with borderline contentment as long as the big man kept tickling her and feeding her bites from the tray of victuals on the floor just beyond her reach. Several young girls and a few boys sat close to him, children gravitating to the affable George. Two other girls stood behind him, Tvarita and Dhanya, ten years of age and doing goodness only knew what to his long, thick, wavy hair. George had lost count at three braids and six flowers, but then he wasn't paying too much attention. He was busy entertaining Treya and carrying on a conversation with Gita, Jharna's elderly aunt, about various medicinal treatments for preventing miscarriage. One of Jharna's sisters was pregnant for the fourth time, the previous three lost midway through term and since she was early in this pregnancy, they were hoping to prevent another tragedy.

Suddenly one of the girls glanced up from the basket she was weaving, her curious gaze resting on George. "How is it you know so much about birthing and babies, *Vaidya*? That is work for a *dai*."

"A *dai*, or midwife in my language, does deliver most babies, that is true, Esha, but as a doctor I have substantial experience. I have cared for many women during their pregnancies, births, and afterward. Your *chachi* Gita is a skilled *dai* and hopefully with our combined knowledge we can help your cousin."

"Will you deliver your own baby, *Vaidya*? Or have a *dai*?"

"Well now"—George scratched at his chin—"that is an idea I have given no thought! Perhaps, if I ever am faced with the matter, I will decide then."

"Your wife will decide," one of the girls added with a sage nod. "It is her choice."

"Do you have a wife, *Vaidya*?" This from a wide-eyed child confused by the last sentence since she was sure Dr. Darcy did not have a wife.

"No," he began, but was cut off by Esha.

"You should have a wife. A man your age needs a wife."

"Oh yes! You should have a wife, *Vaidya*!" chimed in several young voices all at the same time. "That is the proper thing! We can help you find a wife." And this was followed with a flood of options from among the household females as well as other names he had never heard.

"*Daaktar* Darcy can marry no one, since he has promised to marry me, haven't you?" The tug on his hair brought his eyes in contact with Tvarita, her expression a mix of seriousness and teasing. Then Dhanya's face came into view just as she said, "He cannot marry you, Tvarita, because he is going to marry me!" This claim was taken up by several, while additional names were tossed into the ring for his matrimonial consideration.

The adults were all laughing. Mercilessly laughing. George was flummoxed that he had proposed marriage to so many without remembering a single one and that there were this many unattached women in the Junnar household!

"Silly girls," Gita's voice pierced the refrain of marriage options, "he can marry none of you because he is a Christian and you are Hindu."

As if *that* were the main reason and not the huge age difference or that they were children! George grunted and shook his head. Gita's words did sting, however, although he shoved the immediate thought of Jharna from his mind. For a while, this was easy to do, since the determined youngsters quickly redirected their marriage candidates.

"Then he must pick from the Christians at the mission house. *Memsahib* Maria is pretty and so is *Memsahib* Anna. She is nice, too, and always has sweet cakes."

"She does have a big nose though, but maybe that would not bother you, *Vaidya*?" This from Tvarita, who was pointedly staring at George's generous proboscis.

"I say *Memsahib* Corina or Marcie."

"*Memsahib* Stukas is the perfect choice."

"Hey, wait a minute! She is at least fifty if a day!" All eyes turned to George, as if seeing him for the first time, and then they shrugged in unison and went on naming prospective brides irrespective of age or the fact that most of them were Catholic nuns!

Into this chatter Jharna emerged from the kitchen, depositing a bowl of chopped onions and garlic for the naan next to her aunt. "Why are you discussing the physical attributes of the missionary women?" Jharna asked as she picked up a ball of dough.

"We are finding a wife for *Daaktar* Darcy," Esha answered, "since he is not accomplishing the job himself and it must be done."

Jharna dropped the dough, it hitting the table edge and falling to the ground by George's foot. Ihita kindly picked the dough ball, handing it to Jharna when she bent over and with trembling hand took it from the toddler without meeting George's questioning gaze. "I am sure *Daaktar* Darcy can find his own wife if he wanted one," she said, her tone clipped. Her rough attack on the dough as she commenced kneading brought a curious lift to George's brow.

Esha noted none of this, waving her hand airily and snorting disdainfully as she added, "Women are better at arranging these matters, are they not *chachi* Gita?"

"Oh yes," Gita agreed. "Arranging a proper wife for a man is a time-honored tradition best approached with cool rationality."

"Well, call me a sentimental fool, but I would rather have a wife I chose myself with affection as a prime factor, thank you. I appreciate the recommendations, however, and if I reach a point of desperation, I'll consider the viable options."

The topic changed, thankfully, but in the week ahead, George noted a marked increase in the number of speculative glances from the ladies in the house. At first he thought it just his imagination, but as the days passed with hardly an hour going by without one of the unmarried women smiling at him provocatively or engaging him in a conversation about something inane, he knew it wasn't. Clearly word had spread that Dr. Darcy was in need of a wife and just as clearly the fact that he was a Christian and English did not bother them all that much!

Of course, foreigners had taken wives from the Indian population for years. It wasn't precisely embraced with full endorsement, but when white women were in short supply, a man naturally looked elsewhere, love and attraction occurring as a result. Liaisons of all types were common, marriage included.

Vani had not been George's first Indian lover or his last. None of them had captured his heart enough to contemplate a serious commitment until Jharna, and with her the issue was not their differing faiths but that she did not love him. Fervently, he wished for her to gaze at him with eyes of love as none of the others had. His heart would spiral into heights of ecstasy if she did.

The uncomfortable feminine pursuits forced George to vacate the house to preserve his sanity, leaving one day shortly after the morning meal and walking a narrow path through the trees toward a small pond a half mile from the house. He strolled with his eyes to the ground, searching for stones of a certain shape, those found to be just right tucked into a sturdy sack. The first order of business once at the pond was to strip naked and dive into the cool water. After ten laps from one end to the other, George turned over to float. With eyes closed, he tuned in to the hum of nature underneath the silence, peace calming some of the inner turmoil.

Hunger lured him out of the pond, the bread and cheese confiscated from the kitchen eaten in spaced bites while he stood at the edge of the pond and methodically picked one stone at a time from the heavy sack sitting on a boulder beside him. Each smooth stone was tested and rolled between his fingers for several minutes before he bent and, with expert technique, pitched it out over the surface of the still water. By the time the food was gone, he managed at least three skips on each stone tossed, the record of six skips unlikely to be beaten, although he intended to keep trying. His hair was still wet, the slow drip of cool water sliding down his back and shoulders a pleasant reminder of the pond's waiting delights when the stones were gone.

It had been a decade since April 17 and the memories of his twin distressed him. Somewhere during the day, he would retrieve the miniature of Alex taken from Pemberley, smile at the childish face staring back at him, tell Alex to keep saving a place on his cloud, and then wrap the precious item in the thick velvet before storing it away until the next year. The ritual gave him a sense of peace but that was the end of it. Then he would write in his journal, now addressed to his father, covering whatever he previously might have missed recording and expanding on his thoughts. If time allotted, he would catch up on correspondences. The anniversary of Alex's death had become a habitual day of family remembrance and introspection on his life and goals.

The latter was what occupied the portion of his mind not focused on achieving another six-skip toss.

The flirting females at the Ullas house would soon grow weary of his indifference and set their gazes upon other men. It *was* moderately annoying but also quite flattering. George was not dissimilar from any other man, his ego pleased that so many women saw him as marriage material. The real surprise was that suddenly he was viewing the disinterest of the women in his past in a new light. Arrogantly, he had relied on his charm, physical appearance, and, in some cases, wealth to attract women and had assumed that the reason none of them fell wildly in love with him was due to his caution in choosing ladies who did not want such entanglements and the fact that, because of his lifestyle, the affairs never lasted long.

What if he was wrong? Was there something fundamentally un-marriageable about him? The prospect was much more disturbing than he would have imagined.

A second surprise was that the concept of being married was appealing as it had not been in a decade. What he could not unravel was whether this was due to his feelings for Jharna or simply because he liked the idea of being married in a general sense. Had he finally matured? Was he weary of the itinerant life?

What he did know was that his opinion of marriage was different than it had been when he had wanted to marry Sarah or Ruby. In both cases love was present, as well as intense passion, with marriage merely the natural way of things. Isn't that what respectable Englishmen did? Get married and produce offspring? It wasn't that he ever took the idea of committing to one woman lightly or that his vows would not have been honored. However, George now realized that while the idea of *marriage* was one he grasped, he had never considered being a *husband* as a different concept. Was pursuing his selfish whims compatible with being a husband?

It was no longer enough to have a woman waiting for him at a house somewhere while he traveled about. He didn't just want a bedmate. He wanted something deeper. He wanted a partner to his soul. He wanted to give more than he received. He wanted to *need* someone who in turn needed him as completely.

All of it came back to Jharna. For ten years, their friendship had grown, George delighting in her intelligent conversation, gently teasing humor, and maternal nature. There had always been a connection between the two of them, innocent as it was while Kshitij was alive. George knew deep in the marrow of his bones that this connection added a dimension to his love for her greater than anything he had ever experienced. They complemented each other, and he had no doubt that the heights of passion attained if she recognized the same would rock them to the core.

The unfairness of discovering this with a woman who did not consider him in the same light was painful in the extreme. Yet, as odd as it seemed, he was hopeful. Maybe he was a bloody fool doomed for overwhelming disappointment, but he clung to the notion that in time Jharna would recognize the truth of their connection. He was determined to be a friend to her, as he always had, and perhaps her sentiments would shift. As a strategic plan, it wasn't much. However, if vague optimism was all he had to grasp, then he would do so with both hands.

"Better than nothing," he muttered as he stooped to dig the last two stones from the sack. With one in each hand, he gazed at the calm surface of the water, gauging the odds of matching that six-skip toss. George flexed his back muscles and ignored the tingling sensation that flickered between his shoulder blades. It was the combination of increased itchiness climbing up his neck and the faint crunch of gravel that finally grabbed his attention and caused him to glance over his shoulder.

Standing twenty feet away and partially concealed in the shadows of a tall tree was Jharna.

And she was staring straight at him.

George turned toward her, surprise momentarily rendering him mute. For what seemed an eternity they stared at each other while George struggled to wrap his mind around this apparent apparition, his thoughts so focused on Jharna that he wondered if he had fallen asleep and was dreaming. George was unable to decipher her expression, but he could detect the direction of her gaze. First it was centered on his face, and then a slow glide across the broad expanse of his shoulders, down the center of his chest to his belly, and finally resting on his groin.

With a jerk and audible gasp, he spun about, the stones dropped as he grabbed for the cloth piled on the rock and, with fumbling fingers, tossed it around his waist, automatically wrapping the *dhoti* to cover the nakedness he had forgotten while spellbound.

"Jharna! What are you doing here?"

"Enjoying the view."

George yanked his eyes upward, mouth agape. Jharna had stepped further into the clearing but was turned away from him, her eyes now cast toward the pond and vegetation on the far shore. He could see her face fully, noting the soft smile playing about her lips and casual demeanor. Precisely what she had meant was unclear, and he did not trust his judgment at that moment. *Good God! I'm blushing!* He touched his cheeks, stunned beyond belief. He hadn't blushed since a green adolescent. Lord, how she unnerved him! The image of her eyes boldly examining his physique and manhood was burned into his brain, likely for all eternity, and he was abundantly thankful that *dhotis* were capable of being tied loosely. Normally skilled at recovery under the strangest of circumstances, George was dumbstruck. Thankfully, Jharna lead the conversation.

"I know I should not bother you, *mitra*, when you are seeking solitude. Especially today of all days. Yet for that reason most of all, I did not wish to see you suffering alone."

"That"—he cleared his throat—"that is kind of you, Jharna, but I don't suffer as I used to. Alex is my past. This is my present, and my future."

"I am happy to hear that." She moved closer. George had the distinct impression that she was amused at his discomfiture.

"I was seeking solitude, as you say, but only to enjoy the peacefulness of nature and clear my mind."

"This is a fine place to accomplish both. I have often visited here when I needed utter peace. That can be problematic with a home full of people seeking your attentions, as I assume you are discovering and was what drove you away. At least in part."

She was teasing him, clearly as aware as everyone in the house that he was suddenly the hot commodity. Her tone was light yet with an edge that made him frown in confusion. Try as he might, he could not decipher her emotions. "Well, yes," he answered slowly, watching her face closely, "it is exhausting to fight off so many gorgeous women all at once. I needed rest and relaxation."

George ended with a devilish grin and a wink. Jharna pursed her lips, the corner of her eyes tightening. George nearly missed the hint of displeasure before she smiled the teasing smile he loved and cocked her head.

"I am pleased to hear you are relaxed and rested. Surprising after your efforts." She waved toward the pond. "You are very good at skipping stones."

His eyes narrowed. "How long were you watching me?"

"Long enough to know why Sasi is forever gathering round, smooth stones." Her dark eyes conveyed more than maternal interest, especially when they slipped across his bare chest.

"It was a favorite pastime of my brothers, Estella, and I. There is a lake near Pemberley, Rowan Lake, that was our preferred swimming place. We spent hours there almost every day during the summer. Endeavoring to beat each other at skipping stones was only one of our challenges."

While speaking, he reached for the discarded *kurta*, moving slowly as he shook the wrinkles and pulled it over his head. He could feel the burn of her gaze and the heat flaming over his cheeks. If he didn't know better, he would say this is how it felt to be shy. He could not be sure, since *shy* was one thing George Darcy had never been. He wasn't an exhibitionist by any means, adhering to standard English rules of propriety which dictated that a person's body should be kept largely clothed when in public or the presence of women. He had learned to relax and was comfortable in loose Indian attire that displayed some skin, but blatantly baring himself was not a habit—unless in a bedroom—and this was a direction best not veered toward while alone with Jharna in a secluded, romantic setting. He was struggling to control his desire for her as it was and the effect of her teasing visual inspection was fueling his passionate hunger. Imagining them alone in a bedroom was taboo if he was going to maintain his reputation as a gentleman. He had his pride, however, so was not going to let her know that she rattled him so. Besides, if she wanted to examine his body, he wasn't going to stop her!

He rambled on about his siblings and childish antics to distract his mind from weightier thoughts. Jharna listened and asked the occasional question. As they talked, he gathered his belongings, Jharna falling into step as they traveled the path back to the house. George was a superb diagnostician. It was a true gift he possessed, one utilized mostly in a professional capacity. Frequently, his ability enabled him to read a person's emotions and to detect hidden problems of a psychic nature. Numerous times during this visit to Junnar, he sensed Jharna was troubled or preoccupied with a nagging concern, the nebulous feelings gone before he mustered the nerve to ask. As they walked, the sensation was strong. Outwardly she was calm as typical, but George felt sure she was on the verge of changing the casual conversation to one of greater import. She didn't, though, and as the house came into view, his annoyance grew.

"Jharna, I need to ask you—"

"*Vaidya* Darcy! I have found you!"

George and Jharna stopped short, bodies swaying at the abrupt interruption. Instinctively George encircled Jharna's waist when she stumbled into his side, the shockwave of the contact ripping through his entire body. He heard her gasp and felt her shudder in his arms. Instead of twisting away, as he might have expected, she melted against him. It was a marvelous sensation, and one that he desperately wanted to explore the meaning behind, but Anoop was babbling on, and despite his reluctance to do so, George could not ignore what he was saying.

"A message from Captain Masters?"

"Yes, *Vaidya*. Please forgive me"—Anoop bowed hastily—"but the courier said it was of vital importance that you receive it immediately. I still did not wish to disturb you on your day of grief"—he bowed again—"but he insisted."

George took the folded parchment and was forced to release Jharna to open it. To his dismay, she moved several paces away, eyes downcast and hair shielding her face.

"General Wellesley is gathering his cavalry to retake Poona from Jaswant's false *peshwa*, Amrutrao. They plan to attempt negotiations, naturally, but that seems unlikely. Amrutrao has vowed to burn Poona to the ground and Peshwa Baji Rao has pleaded with the English to secure his family's safety. The Maratha forces alone are insufficient to deal with Amrutrao, so it could get ugly. The medical corps is preparing and needs me to return as soon as possible."

"Will we leave right away, *Vaidya*?"

"I believe we must," George answered, his eyes fixed on Jharna's face rather than Anoop's. "Run ahead, Anoop, and begin gathering our belongings. I will be right behind you."

Anoop's bow and swift pivot flashed in George's peripheral vision. His focus was on Jharna. That she comprehended the gravity of the news, including the added awareness of friends and family who would be involved in the conflict, was apparent in the serious cast to her face. Her coffee-kissed eyes spoke of her broad knowledge and numerous concerns, yet somehow George sensed that her fears were predominantly directed toward him. The fierce emotion emanating from her round eyes struck him with an impact nearly as intense as a physical slap to his chest.

"I will make sure your horses are readied. Time is waning, but you should make Umbaj by nightfall if you hurry."

"Jharna, I am sorry. I hate that all of my visits lately have been cut short."

"You have a duty, *mitra*. I understand."

"The boys! They are at school, so I cannot say good-bye!"

"They will understand." Then she turned and briskly continued on the path toward the house.

At the house, George veered down the corridor to his room while Jharna set to the task of instructing the staff for a hasty departure. Anoop had already packed half of their belongings, George automatically assisting with the procedure that was an established system after the past year of constant travel. In less than thirty minutes, he had packed, hastily washed, and changed into riding clothes. Saddlebags and portmanteaus in hand, they left the luxurious, cozy chambers with rapid steps but heavy hearts.

George felt the sting of departing the place that was home worse than he ever had. He always missed the large quantities of delicious cuisine and luxurious comforts in exchange for slim army rations and narrow cots among smelly men. Saying good-bye for he knew not how long was getting rougher each time, yet never as harsh as now, when on the cusp of the in-depth conversation he had sensed looming.

A servant informed him that the mistress was in her studio, George sending Anoop to load the horses before ascending the stairs two at a time. He burst through the open door and stopped short at the sight of Jharna pacing and wringing her hands. He had never seen her so distressed.

"Jharna?"

She whirled about, barely breaking stride as she crossed the room to where he stood.

"Jharna," he soothed, "there is no need to fret so. I know the situation seems bleak, but Wellesley is an extremely capable leader and has a large army at his disposal. And the Marathas are strong as well. It may not come to that if negotiations—"

"George, you must promise me that you will be careful! Very careful. Promise me!"

He looked down at her hand where it had clasped on to his wrist, frowning at the desperate intensity of her grip and tone of voice. Every muscle on her face was twisted into an expression of severe anxiety. Eyes usually warm as liquid chocolate were black, shimmering with tears and fear as they pierced into his soul.

"Don't worry. You know me. I am strong and know how to take care of myself. Avoiding danger and work that is too strenuous is an art form for me!" He smiled and spoke lightly, attempting to inject his typical humor and flippancy into the reply.

It didn't work.

She squeezed his arm tighter and stepped closer. He could feel the waves of tension emanating from her body, the awareness of her angst causing him literal pain. Yet at the same time, her nearness sparked other reactions that, no matter how inappropriate under the circumstances, could not be suppressed. The combination, including the musky scent of her perfume, made him lightheaded. Still, he heard her insistent response.

"Do not jest. Not this time, *mitra*. Promise me you will be careful. You must come back to me."

Instinctively, he reached up and touched her cheek, fingertips delicately lying against her skin. "What is it, Jharna? Why are you so afraid? Do you have a premonition of something happening?"

His physical contact was a gesture never done before. The few times they had touched over the years were always glancing and platonic. This was intimate and they knew it. Yet rather than step away from the intimacy of his caress, Jharna covered his fingers with her entire hand and pushed firmly. Briefly, her eyes closed.

"No premonitions," she whispered, "only that..." She opened her eyes and George sucked in his breath at what he saw revealed there. "I need you to come back. I can't lose you, George." And then she lifted on her toes, eyes slipping shut as she closed the small gap between them to press her lips to his.

Their first kiss was but a chaste brush of soft lips designed to gauge the reaction. Hesitancy was present, awareness of the line being crossed with so much at stake if the response was not positive. And if it was, what did that mean for their future relationship? Currents of these weightier realities flickered between them as they leaned into the kiss, the heartbeat span of time lengthening and then obliterated by the rush of tidal force sensations instigated by one feathering touch of unparted lips.

George groaned and Jharna gasped. She tried to that is. It was impossible to draw a breath when instantly covered with an insistent mouth greedily seeking more, especially when she willingly granted what was sought.

Their second kiss was an utter contrast to the first. It was long and passionate with lips parted and every portion of their mouths employed. There was nothing hesitant about this kiss, and the mutual reactions were staggering. No further concerns over crossing lines or future consequences entered either of their minds. After all, the line between friendship and love had been crossed long before the kiss sealed their fate. If coherent thought had pierced through the haze of rapturous happiness, they would have resolutely declared that moving forward was the only option.

George was soaring the heights above heaven. He was relieved, ecstatic, joyous, giddy, and more. A kiss alone was fulfillment greater than he had ever imagined. So much so that the pounding lust to possess Jharna ebbed to a degree. Feeling her lips under his, her pliant body pressed against his chest, and her hands tangled in his hair were enough for now. His heart heard every sound of love she made as she poured her heart into the kiss. It was the answer to his prayers and the completion his soul had sought. Moreover, he knew it was only the beginning of something amazing stretching before him. Leaving now, when on the cusp of attaining joy unimaginable, was harsh, but far better than leaving with no hope. Postponing bliss was preferred over never finding it at all.

With these realities floating through the fogged happiness infusing his body with each rapid beat of his heart, George gradually slowed the kiss. It wasn't the easiest act he had ever done, not by a long shot, but duty did call. Besides, he wasn't about to vacate the house without telling her of his affection in words as well as action.

"Jharna," he breathed between small kisses, "I love you. I have loved you for the longest time."

"And I you, dear George. My *priya*."

My priya. My love.

These words were almost his undoing. It was all he could manage not to back her onto the divan and make love to her that second. He had never wanted anyone more in his life! How he resisted was a mystery involving strength of will he did not know he possessed. He did kiss her again, hard, using the intensity to expend a particle of raging need, but when she responded in like manner, it fueled his desire to the point of drowning the last vestiges of restraint. If not for the sudden clatter of hooves from the courtyard below, followed by shouts in rapid Hindi, George was sure he would have taken those last steps to the cushions. He was also sure Jharna would not have minded one bit.

Pulling away from her caused true physical pain. He buckled slightly, his hands running down her arms to clasp her wrists, serving as a stabilizing anchor so he did not collapse. Jharna appeared to be suffering as acutely. She was swaying and panting, heavy-lidded eyes locked on his face as they stared in silence.

"You must come back to me, *priya*. Safe and soon as possible."

"I will, I promise. And then we will do more than kiss, Jharna. My love. I promise that as well."

She smiled and reached up to touch his cheek with tender fingertips. The hand still clasped around her slim wrist held on for the journey, turning her palm to meet his lips for a firm kiss. Seconds later, George pivoted and left the room. He had to or he never would, duties be damned. His last vision before galloping out the gateway was Jharna standing at the second story railing looking at him with radiating love as she bowed with hands clasped before her chest, the murmured *namaste* followed by *I love you* not audible but read on her lips and felt in his heart.

General Arthur Wellesley with the British cavalry and infantry behind him reached Poona on April 20, 1803, and found the city intact. Amrutrao had vacated the day before, precipitously pulling his troops out rather than face the fury of the British. Haste saved the capital of the Maratha Empire from destruction but not so fortunate were the lands around. Anything edible or usable had been either consumed or plundered by the invaders. Most of the residents had scattered, deserting their homes and seeking shelter elsewhere.

Peshwa Baji Rao II left Bassein and arrived in Poona on May 13, entering his palace and resuming his seat on the *musnud*. Ostensibly in control and safe, with a host of British and Maratha soldiers entrenched for miles about, the Peshwa launched into the work of reestablishing his government.

Bloodshed on a major scale had been avoided. However, tension was high throughout the region. The situation between Jaswant of Holkar, the Sindhia, the Nizam of Hyderabad, and the Peshwa—just to name the principle players of the splintered Maratha Confederacy—was volatile in the extreme. Dispatches flew hourly as new intelligence was shared and decisions were made about the best plan of action. Minor skirmishes and recaptures of occupied forts and towns were frequent. The power of the British under the immediate leadership of General Wellesley, who was in constant communication with his brother, the Governor-General of India, Marquess Wellesley in Calcutta, kept matters tenuously at bay.

Medical personnel, including Dr. Darcy who was stationed in Poona, found themselves treating patients suffering from exhaustion and overexposure more than battle wounds. The oppressive heat and rough conditions felled many a strong soldier, especially those not long dwelling in India or familiar with the jungles of the Deccan plain. It wasn't the critical doctoring that George had anticipated when leaving Junnar, but it did serve to keep his mind occupied and not dwelling upon Jharna and the Ullas boys.

The Ullas house was tucked into a shallow valley on the outskirts of Junnar, thankfully a small town not on a main avenue. Nevertheless, with hostile factions swarming across the breadth of Maharashtra, George could not suppress the rising panic each time a courier galloped in. He knew that Jharna's father, the Sardar of Thana, had men guarding his daughter and other family members living at the Junnar house. He hoped it was enough and that any passing troops would respect the office of Sardar. He wrote often to let them know he was well and hear of their well-being in return. Neither he nor Jharna wrote a word of what had passed between them, instinctively sensing it was best to discuss their feelings in person.

Administrative duties kept Deputy Surgeon-General Dr. George Darcy very busy in the weeks ahead. George focused on the daily problems that arose, dividing his time among reports to Dr. Trenowyth in Bassein, managerial tasks for all the medical corps for the Company, and tending to patients. A handful of people deemed it inappropriate for the deputy to roll up his sleeves and perform surgery. Of course, those people thought Dr. Darcy odd in a number of ways, especially in how he dressed, since George wore Indian garments unless forced to do otherwise, even opting for one of his many elaborate *sherwanis* over a constricting English ensemble for formal occasions. Add to that his habit of spending a period of each morning in a quiet place practicing *hatha yoga*, dining with the natives on their cuisine, speaking Hindi as well as one born there, and a host of similar oddities. Still, none could argue his superior medical skills, superb health, inexhaustible stamina, excellent supervision, and fine personality. He could be relied upon for relieving humor or empathy or firm command or whatever else was perfect for the situation. To the majority of those in contact with him, Dr. Darcy was a rock depended upon and highly admired. He could not deny that authority sat well on his shoulders, no one more surprised than he at how naturally he had assumed the mantle of leadership.

A month passed before he saw a break in the madness wide enough to maybe, just maybe, allow him an opportunity to slip away. Negotiations had concluded, an apology and reconciliation between the Peshwa and Amrutrao, this agreement settling the interior as well as possible under the present circumstances and rattling the composure of their enemies. Jaswant had moved to the northwest, closer to the territories held by the Nizam, his intentions unclear. Politically, the treaty with the Peshwa held but was shaky at best. General Wellesley was not pleased with the Peshwa's lack of support in regards to supplying troops and the aid of the Sardars. Nevertheless, bolstered by native soldiers or not, the bigger concern was Company business and the need for stability in the region. Thus, the general planned to march north by early June, hoping to continue the quest for peaceful negotiations. War was certainly not best for trade, but neither was the disintegration of the Maratha Confederacy.

Luckily for George, the standstill meant that his services were not essential. A year of hard work paid off in that the medical corps was now running flawlessly with a large number of skilled professionals. George knew they could handle their assigned duties without needing the Deputy Surgeon-General breathing down their necks. Leaving orders to send for him if anything changed in the next two weeks, George mounted Rathore and Anoop his pony, the two men joining three soldiers tasked to ensure their safety reaching Junnar.

They traveled the fifty miles at a swift pace, arriving at the house as dusk was falling. Every last inhabitant of the manor was standing in the inner courtyard when they rode through the open gates. Servants and family alike swarmed around them, greeting as if welcoming returning heroes not seen for years, Nimesh and Sasi at the forefront. It was flattering, Anoop especially loving the attention.

George was unsure of his emotional reaction to the place he called *home* and he doubted whether remaining nonchalant was possible when every scenario involved sweeping Jharna into his arms and kissing until neither could breathe. He tried to find her in the swirling crowd and suspected she hung back, probably doubting her own poise as well as his. *Good call*, he thought as he engulfed the Ullas boys with his long arms, squeezing tight.

"God, look at you two! I swear you have grown another foot in the past month."

"I am almost as tall as Nimesh!" Sasi declared. Nimesh had inherited his father's build and at sixteen was an inch or two over five-feet tall and likely not to grow much more. "You missed my day of birth, *chacha-jee*. I am thirteen now!"

"Yes I know, Sasi. I have a gift for you in my bags. I would not forget."

"I have news, too, *chacha*." Nimesh's voice was calmer than his brother's but with a tremor of ebullience evident to George amid the clamor. "I have been accepted as apprentice to *Vaidya* Rajani. He wishes me to begin immediately, but *mata-jee* is insisting I wait until I am seventeen. You must speak with her and convince her otherwise."

George laughed at the young man's earnest face. "Oh, I must, must I? And what makes you think I have any influence over your *mata-jee*'s opinions?"

"You are a doctor, too, and started your education at my age, just as my *pita* did. You can make her see reason!"

"I shall do my best," George nodded, ruffling Nimesh's hair.

Over the youth's shoulder, he spied Jharna standing on the stone steps before the main dining area, far enough away not to have heard the words spoken, although George suspected she knew what Nimesh would blurt out first. She was smiling, her dark eyes soft and tender as they caressed his face, yet one delicate brow was arched and she winked after sweeping her gaze briefly to Nimesh. The message made George laugh and served to defuse the tension coiled inside.

This is how it feels to come home.

All through the evening, as they sat around the open table in the loose manner of Indian dining and fellowship, George and Jharna shared warm looks filled with promise. Purposefully, they kept distance and people between them, yet it wasn't a matter of not trusting themselves to act as mature adults rather than randy adolescents. It was the sweetness of enjoying his homecoming and contentment with their fledgling relationship while their mutual anticipation built. Nevertheless, George was happy to bid good night to everyone, the dispersal gradual until he was alone in the parlor waiting for Jharna.

She crept silently through the door, closing it behind her and treading on bare feet to where George stood by the patio threshold. A gentle breeze blew off the river, not enough to notably cool the heat igniting his skin but brisk enough to stir his hair where it fell loose on his shoulders. Jharna's hair was twisted and pinned at the nape of her neck. The jeweled clips twinkled in the low lamplight, beckoning to George to remove them, a task he intended to perform as soon as possible. Right after he slowly removed the multicolored sari draped over her lush body, that is. No longer restricted by the presence of others, George allowed his eyes to convey his desire. Hungrily he watched her graceful approach, sweeping over the swell of her breasts and sway of her hips with visible appreciation.

"You are so beautiful."

Neither reached for the other. Instead, they enjoyed the moment of simply *feeling* the myriad emotions spinning between them. It amazed George that this could feel so perfectly right when not yet having officially begun. How much better would it be once they had taken the step of expressing their love physically? How incredible would it be to be one in mind, body, and soul? George shivered in anticipation.

Jharna interpreted that as a signal. Or perhaps her plan was already formed. George did not know, but when she clasped his hand, smiling with a divine mixture of sensuality and teasing lilt as she led him from the room, it did not matter. He was unaware of the stones and carpets under his soles as they traversed the corridors and steps until reaching her chambers. George had never been inside her private quarters and should have been curious how she decorated her inner sanctuary. Not tonight. He didn't care to see where the bed was or what it looked like. He was sure she had one and that was enough for now. No, he could not and would not remove his eyes from her. Jharna was all that mattered.

Without a word, he cupped her face between his palms and bent until so close to her lips that he could smell the spices carried on each of her panting breaths. "I love you, Jharna." And before she could answer, he engulfed her mouth lightly but insistently, expressing the depth of his love with a kiss.

Passion kept at bay flared instantly. Hearts already beating fast increased to a painful tempo. Warmth flowing through heightened nerves burst into a flaming inferno that miraculously did not scorch the sensitized endings but increased the impressions. Breathing already quickened leapt until harsh rasps were audible between the muffled exclamations of enjoyment as they kissed.

The reaction was blissful and overwhelming. George flew with the tide, embracing Jharna and drawing her close to his body as his head whirled in the grips of savage craving. It was Jharna who restored a modicum of clarity when she stiffened ever so faintly before wiggling out of his arms.

She only moved a half pace away, one hand curled around his shoulder and the other pressed against her lips. She stared at him with eyes dilated and wide. Wild passion radiated from her, a hunger every bit as uncontrollable as his written on her face. Yet there was something else that confused him.

"What is it, Jharna?"

"You," she wheezed, "us… surprise me."

And then he understood.

George recognized the depth of passion between them as something he had never experienced. He had known many lovers, some of whom were skilled and capable of instigating zealous excitement leading to immense satisfaction. Only one had he loved and that was so long ago and he so young that the memory was vague. He yearned for a mature relationship based on intense love, knew he had found that with Jharna, and relished discovering how that would affect the act of lovemaking.

Jharna had only been with Kshitij, but they had loved deeply. From the startled cast to her eyes, it was clear that their love had not translated to uncontainable passion behind closed doors. George had assumed that what he felt with Jharna as new to him would be familiar to her. Obviously that was not the case. The abrupt rush of relief and rising gratification in knowing that together they would discover the secret of loving the one who owned your heart was heady.

George tugged gently on her waist, bringing her back in contact with his body. He arched one brow and poured every ounce of his arrogant charm into his grin.

"You should know by now, Jharna love, that I am full of surprises."

Her giggle quickly transformed into a gasp when he pressed his lips to the pulse at her neck. George was no less affected by the nearness of her than before—more so as he traveled leisurely along the delicious slope of her neck, tasting the jasmine and musk bathing her silky brown skin—but a measure of control had asserted itself.

"This is one night of hundreds we shall share, *priya*," he whispered against her ear, pausing to draw the lobe between his lips for a gentle suck, "but it is our first. Surprises are only beginning for us, and they shall all be wonderful."

While he spoke, one hand glided over her back with feathering pressure designed to soothe as well as thrill. By the susurrate noises she was emitting and dreamy writhing of her body, he knew she was responding positively to his lazy maneuvers and reassuring words. The pin holding the folds of her sari at her left shoulder was released, the satin sliding sensuously through his fingers as he lowered the fabric until it draped over his arm. He couldn't resist leaving the pleasure of her neck to gaze down at her chest. The *choli* Jharna wore under her sari covered her torso to just above her navel, the linen dyed a bright blue and edged with the matching fabric of her sari. It was tight, as *cholis* typically were, and thus displayed the perfect contours of her full breasts and hard-peaked nipples, leaving little to the imagination. Desire to bare her completely so the final mystery of whether the flesh was as smoky as the rest of her made him salivate. Would her nipples be crimson as pagoda flowers or perhaps dark as ripe figs? His hands trembled with the urgency to rip the thin material away. Instead, he met her eyes, grinning once again before stepping back a pace and, with a small tug and push, made her pivot around as he unwrapped the sari from her waist.

Jharna was caught up in his silliness, lifting her arms above her head and laughing as she twirled. Each circle added to the pile accumulating in George's arms until the sari was undone, leaving nothing but her *choli* and thin drawstring skirt riding low on her hips. He could see the outline of her legs underneath, slim and shapely all the way to her curved buttocks. Snapping his eyes away from the dimly visible triangular patch at the apex of her legs before reason vacated his mind, George focused on her face. Jharna, to his surprise, seemed to have lost her momentary nervousness. She was standing tall and proud, not a hint of a blush on her cheeks and no attempt to hide her assets from his scrutiny. Rather she was unconscious of how her breasts rose and fell enticingly with each pant or that the sheen of perspiration moistening her skin caused the gossamer material to cling. She was too busy drinking in his body, George realizing that although still clothed in a loose *kurta*, sweat had dampened it against the hard ridges of his chest and the form-fitting *shalwar* worn for riding provided minimal room to hide the evidence of his arousal.

Noting the unrestrained avarice washing across her face, George doubted at this point that Jharna wasn't as excited as he and that any residual hesitancy would evaporate the second he touched her. Still, this humorous foreplay was rather enjoyable! With a grand flourish, he flipped the sari in the air and let it float down until covering his entire body, only his face visible.

"Your turn."

She smiled, this one pure lust, and walked to him—the short space taking an incredibly long time to George's reckoning—undulating her hips with each step and never losing contact with his eyes. Proving that she had arts of seduction at her disposal despite the revelations of several minutes earlier, Jharna tortured him by unraveling the sari with painstaking slowness. The *kurta* followed the path to the floor only after teasing his chest and back with hands gifted with magical powers. At that point, George lost the battle of remaining passive. They did not rush or unleash the growling animalistic passion quite yet, but they did relent to the demand for more.

First he removed the combs holding the thick, twisted sections of her hair. The scent of jasmine tickled his nostrils as the heavy plaits fell to below her waist, the sweet aroma increasing when he unraveled each portion and fluffed the silky strands between his fingers. Jharna shook her head, the cascading blanket of amber-highlighted black hair floating around her face and bouncing against her back. Fisting large clumps in both hands, George pressed his face into the mass, inhaling deeply and rubbing the sleek tresses over his whiskers. The tactile contrast was electrifying and George gave in to the thrill of it. Kissing through the sheet of hair tumbling over her neck, he made his way gradually to her mouth, claiming and plunging deep. Possessively he thrust his tongue inside, meeting her with each rhythmic stroke, moans mixing with their sharp breathing.

God! He had never known such ecstasy! It was a struggle to restrain the beast inside. With an effort he pulled away from her lips, his hands still balled at the nape of her neck with tangles of hair twined around his fingers. Raggedly breathing, George rested his forehead on hers, eyes closed for a second before opening to discover he had a stunning view of her round breasts and aroused nipples straining against the confinement of her *choli*. It was as if they begged for freedom and the pleasure of his touch.

More than happy to comply, George doffed her *choli* with minimal fanfare and immediately delved into the lush fullness with greedy hands and mouth. Jharna arched against him, harshly clutching his head to her chest and crying loudly at each tease of his tongue and nip of his teeth. It became a sort of dance. Moments of tenderness tempered the rhythm and softened the caresses, followed by aggressive attacks. Intervals of creating gaps between their bodies so they could appreciate the visual enticements flowed into intervals when they succumbed to the tactile. It seemed to last a very long time, but George later suspected that the time they spent kissing and embracing in the middle of the room wasn't lengthy at all.

He wasn't sure when he became aware of the bed's location and wondered if it might have merely been blind luck, but when Jharna finally slipped his pants down his legs and stroked one hand firmly over his hardness from head to hilt, murmuring, "Indeed you are *full* of surprises, *priya!*" he growled and picked her up into his arms. The beast was unleashed and they knew it. A second later, he had her spread on the cool sheets with his entire body hot and taut as it crushed her into the downy mattress. If she had not still been wearing the skirt, he would have entered her instantly and after releasing a wail of frustration was thankful the garment had somehow not been removed. Probably because he was too busy at her breasts, a pleasant diversion he did not regret one iota. As annoying as it was to be stymied in his quest to be inside her, George did not wish to rush their lovemaking. The thought of her exquisite breasts provided a stabilizing focal point and impelled him to straighten his arms and lift up from her body.

"Oh god, Jharna!" he choked when able to speak. "You are magnificent! Sublime. I ache to possess you, to make you mine wholly, and in a way you will never forget." He ran his fingertips delicately across the sharp ridges of her collarbone, down the valley between her breasts, and onward until dipping into the well of her navel, his husky voice continuing, "I want to brand myself upon your skin, so deeply that I live inside you, breathing with you and beating with your heart. I want to love you as I have never loved another, giving pleasure and giving of my soul."

"Then what are you waiting for?"

He looked up at her eyes. The teasing glint he knew so well was there, laced with heaps of love and passion. While he paused to absorb the emotions pouring from her gaze, Jharna wiggled out of her skirt and kicked it away.

She was bared to him completely. Voracious eyes examined her head to toe, burning a trail over her dusky-hued skin and missing nothing. Not the parted lips gasping for air. Not the fluttering pulse in the notch of her throat. Not the puckered nipples still wet from his kisses. Not the impatient squirms of her body. Not the tight muscles of her belly quivering in anticipation. He missed nothing, including that she was examining his body as fully. He knew precisely how she felt as her gaze started a fire, racing over his hair-scattered chest, muscular arms and thighs, solid abdomen, and groin, the latter throbbing with need and growing unbearably harder by the second. The weak thread restraining the ravenous beast snapped when Jharna lifted one sinewy leg, sliding it over his calf until it wrapped around his waist, with her heel and toes teasing his rump.

"No waiting, *priya*."

After that, he didn't. He took his time, burying himself within her welcoming depths gradually and then moving with deliberate strokes designed to heighten and prolong the fervor. No rush. Clarity and control worked in tandem with hazy rapture and wildness. George would remember every touch, every sensation, and every move vividly. Time stretched, and each second was counted as he soared through heaven in unison with the woman he loved. But time, after all, was uncountable when soaring through heaven in unison with the woman you love.

Sleep did not touch either of them during that blissfully long night. It was too special to waste on the oblivion of sleep. Most of the time was passed in the wide bed—a massive piece of ornately carved and painted furniture draped with crimson gauze and piled with colorfully embroidered pillows, George eventually noted—but not exclusively. They did move to the veranda at one point, lying on cushioned mats spread over the hard stone with moonlight as the only illumination.

"You laid these here specifically for us tonight, didn't you?" George was propped on one elbow and leaning over her supine figure, the other hand tracing a cluster of grapes along the flickering shapes of light dancing across her thighs.

"Of course. I would not want your back to suffer from rough scraping on rock."

"My back?"

"Yes. Your back." And in one lissome movement Jharna lifted up and pushed him backward, rescued the grapes from his surprised grip, and straddled his thighs. George's chuckle turned into moans of pleasure as Jharna cleverly utilized the grapes in sensual play. Few words were spoken for a while, unless one counted shouted names and one-syllable exclamations.

"When did you fall in love with me?"

His warm breath wafted across her shoulder, Jharna shivering. She drew his head away from her neck, engaging his eyes and toying with the wavy hair sweeping across his brow.

"I have always loved you, George."

"That isn't what I meant."

"I know. I am uncertain I can answer. I am not sure that the beginning wasn't long, long ago. Your friendship has been precious to me, *mitra*." She used the term for *dear friend* that had slipped into their conversation during their travels together years prior, but the tender caress along his cheek and lips expressed the deeper intimacy they now shared. "But especially these past two years. I have come to rely upon your presence, to desire your visits as if a special holiday yearned for. We all did, so I thought my feelings no different than the boys. I know now I was falling in love with you well before I recognized the emotion. The day I first recognized a physical response to you and could no longer remain blind to it was that day last autumn, when you were so blatantly flirting with Indira."

"I was not!" But the denial was accompanied by laughter, George remembering the day, and although it had meant nothing serious to him at the time, he couldn't argue that he had been pouring on the charm.

"Oh, you most certainly were! You are a rogue, George Darcy. Do you know that? Women should beware!"

"Henceforth, all women shall be safe because my roguish days are past. Except with you in your chambers where I intend to be an absolute scoundrel as often as I can until you cry out with elation." He accented his threat with a well-placed probe, Jharna gasping and squeezing her thighs tight to still his magical fingers.

"Do you want me to answer the question or give in to your current proposal?"

"That is not a fair choice." He frowned mockingly. "I say both. Continue please"—he nudged her legs apart and commenced a lazy series of intimate strokes—"with the part about how you were jealous and wanted my manhood all for yourself."

"Arrogant and a rogue! I hardly said that, but will admit that I did not like the idea of Indira being with you, although it was none of my business who you bedded."

"For the record, Jharna, I have bedded no one for well over a year. Closer to two."

She looked genuinely shocked. "Why?"

"Initially because of my work, to be honest. There simply wasn't the time and I have never been as casual about my relationships as some, despite how it may appear."

"No, I know that is true. All jesting aside, you are not a rogue, my George."

He smiled and leaned to kiss her, taking his time and continuing the stimulating motions of his fingers. "I love when you say I am yours, Jharna. I have wanted to be yours for months."

"When did you fall in love with me, *priya*?" Her heavy-lidded eyes were alight with arousal but also curiosity.

"I cannot answer precisely either. I too have always loved you, Jharna, and think the greater feelings snuck up on me. I can tell you that when I flirted with Indira, it was in part to deny how I felt for you and in part because I knew you were watching. I wanted to make you jealous. I had visions of you storming into my room in a rage. The dreams of how we would make love were vividly spectacular."

"More spectacular than this?" She curved and thrust her hips to meet the increasingly deeper drives of his long fingers.

"The reality is always better, love. And we are only beginning."

Increasing the tempo and pressure, George trailed wet, hot kisses down her neck and chest until reaching her breasts. Instantly she arched into him, her whole body straining to feel more of him. Giving her what she sought, George played the game of love skillfully, drawing out the inevitable until he knew she could take no more. Only then did he release her nipple with a long tug, his eyes lifted to her face as she reached her peak with a scream and convulsive clenches around his moving fingers.

Sweet Lord! In her rapture she is transcendently beautiful! So glorious that he nearly lost control and spilled where he slid against her inner thigh. Gritting his teeth he rapidly shifted. Removing his fingers, he grasped each wrist, raising her arms over her head and stretching fully with all his weight on her, and with one swift impale, filled where his fingers had been. The still-contracting muscles squeezing the new, much bigger intrusion, pulling and welcoming. Jharna whimpered, bucking upward to encourage his wild thrusts, crazed as they had not yet been the two times before, with lunge after ferocious lunge driving waves of piercing pleasure head to toe. No kissing or caressing. Eyes closed and senses zeroed to where they merged, neither thought coherently. They only felt the building ecstasy radiating outward until the cresting wave broke, the shattering euphoria unmatched.

George rolled away to gulp lungfuls of oxygen. He knew his heart was strong, thankfully, because the way it was pounding inside his chest might have been alarming otherwise. It was difficult to hear over the blood surging through the veins in his ears and the harsh gasps escaping his open mouth, but he dimly heard Jharna's labored respirations. Her trembling hand was loosely clasped in his, perspiration slick where their skin met. Taken as a whole, it was immensely gratifying! It was a matter of pride to a man to be able to satisfy his woman. At least George felt that way. He turned his head, one look assuring him that Jharna was miles beyond merely being satisfied. For several minutes he stared at her profile and soaked in the myriad details that revealed how lost she was to the joyous pleasure they had shared. Finally she opened her eyes, sightlessly gazing at the ceiling for a while before turning toward him. The smile that lit her face was indescribable.

"Do you have any idea how much I love you, Jharna?"

"As much as I love you, George."

"I am never letting you go, you know."

"I would not let you, *priya*."

He brought her hand to his lips, chuckling as he pressed light kisses. "We sound like giddy youths spouting bad poetry."

"Bad or well written, the sentiments are valid."

They were still and silent for a time, eyes glued to each other and communicating a wealth of emotions and thoughts. George broke the silence first. "So what happens now?"

"Probably we should sleep. Dawn is less than two hours away."

"That isn't what I meant." He knew she understood his question and nipped at her inner wrist for teasing him.

"You worry too much, *priya*. Trust your god as I trust mine. Our paths are now merged, as was fated to be. Our hearts beat in unison. We have no choice but to walk forward together."

George smiled and nodded. Then he rolled back to her and cupped her face. The kiss was tender and long. Their passion was momentarily spent, giving them the opportunity to sweetly delight in the beauty of a kiss between joined souls. Eventually he broke away, rolling again onto his back but bringing her with him. She burrowed close to his side and nestled her head on his shoulder. With arms surrounding each other, they succumbed to satiated exhaustion. With a last kiss to her brow, George closed his eyes, murmuring before sleep took him, "I am yours forever, Jharna, and am never letting you go."

GEORGE'S MEMOIRS
OCTOBER 3, 1804

It is official, Father. Five days ago I signed and filed my last document as Deputy Surgeon-General of the Bombay Confederacy and handed over the keys to Dr. Perry, so to speak. I never stayed in one place long enough to need physical keys. I didn't expect to weep and wail but thought it might sting a wee bit to be stripped of my authority and revert to being plain Dr. Darcy. You know me too well, Father, so I won't pretend I didn't relish the attention all these years! I prefer to believe that is an inherited trait as a Darcy, rather than a manifestation of my inflated vanity. Remind me not to ask James's opinion. I know how he would vote! Whether conceit or an inborn characteristic, I did flourish in the position, surprising myself, and we both know that is a rare occurrence!

Ah, Father, I wish you were alive to meet my lovely Jharna. Ten minutes in her presence would erase any disapproval at our relationship. She is my joy and light. I am a better person because of her. I know those are rather inane statements and at one time would have sent me into hysterical laughter, yet they are true. I am lighthearted more than I already was which is, I admit, frightening. I never comprehended how having a worthy woman who loves you and a family who depends upon you alters your outlook of the world. It alters you inside as well. Profoundly. I am skilled at verbal medical explanations but cannot place into comprehensible words how this love feels. The desire to share my life with her is a magnetic yearning. I hunger for her in the primal ways a man hungers for the woman he loves. That alone is intense. However, it is more than our physical intimacy that is astounding and powerful. I long to discover how much stronger all the facets of our relationship will become as the years pass and we live together for longer than days at a time. Stolen days every month or two is intolerable, but I am often too busy to dwell upon my misery. I know it has been far worse for Jharna. She maintains her serenity, outwardly accepting the dictates of fate. She almost fools me. Then I see her face at unguarded moments and know she is suffering as acutely as me. This is complimentary and a nice boost to the ego that needs no boosting. That selfishness aside, I don't like knowing she is sad, especially because of me.

Jharna worries that I will miss the excitement. Bah! My proficiency and appreciation for the job is all well and fine, but what I cannot convince her of is that I am sick of patching up sword and gunshot wounds and treating dysentery. I am done with living in tents and sleeping on hard mats. I won't mention the food or will embark on a rant that will fill this new book to the final page. I can no longer muster the energy to pretend I care about EIC policies or Maratha intrigues, let alone keep track of the particulars or latest treaty. The bulk of the time I forget what faction we are fighting and which soldiers are wheeling through my hospital. Perhaps I am feeling the need to be pampered. Can you blame me? Sleeping in Jharna's bed with her body draped over me is vastly preferred to this! Her bathing chamber alone would tempt the most devout monk to renounce his vows. I am certainly not a monk. What I am is a relatively normal man of thirty-seven who knows exactly what he wants at this time of his life.

And what is that you ask? Glad you did, Father! As hinted above, I am weary of battle wounds despite all that I have accomplished. I have learned more about how to treat penetrating injuries and amputation than I ever imagined I would. My skills as a surgeon have increased fiftyfold at least. When devastating trauma and imminent death are the usual business, a doctor has the freedom and obligation to experiment. I have perfected the art of resetting broken bones, even a few that were compound, so that amputation was not required. I am proud of that, to be honest. Statistically I am at 50% for thoracotomy working to relieve crushing chest wounds and the drainage system we have been using is effective. Head injury is the worst, and I have decided neurosurgery is not my forte, but I have improved and seen more positive outcomes. Infection and the resultant death thereof remain major sequelae, but we have discovered certain techniques and herbals that do wonders. Viewing so many bodies in varying states of dismemberment and dissection does provide the benefit of comprehending anatomy and physiology more than I ever have. So while all of that is the upside, the cost of witnessing suffering and death on a massive scale has soured the enthusiasm. I pray that will change once I am able to apply my advanced expertise in a more controlled environment. That will be the hospital in Junnar and caring for the locals as they call for me. This sounds like pure heaven. I can live with my family, love Jharna as she deserves, and ply my trade in a leisurely manner. Of course, "leisurely" isn't exactly a word one would ever use to describe me, at least not for long, so I only mean in comparison.

Anoop and I arrived home yesterday. We were greeted with a bit of fanfare, I must say. Delightful! I only wanted to whisk Jharna to bed—forgive the imagery there—but was happy to gather with the others for a while first. Nimesh is living in Junnar near the hospital so I will see him later. If I had my way, Jharna would have *stayed in bed with me all day, but she has to prepare for her father's visit next week. I decided to be lazy and am currently reclining on the terrace with a tray of food and drinks beside me as I write. I am hoping Jharna comes back so am staying near the bed. Told you I wasn't a monk! I also said I knew what I wanted in my life. That is Jharna. Maybe I'll have better luck convincing her to marry me now that I am constantly underfoot. How can she resist my myriad charms indefinitely?*

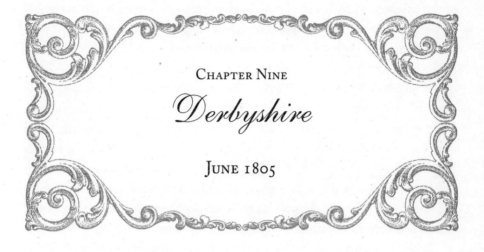

THE WIDE PATH THROUGH the tall brush and wildflowers led to the woods north of Pemberley Manor. One of the numerous divergent trails ended at Rowan Lake, another at the cave, while others skirted areas prime for hunting birds and rabbits. The trails were familiar and traversed so often that after two decades, George could have reached any destination on the vast estate without watching where his feet fell or heeding to the passing terrain. It wasn't geographical uncertainty that made him pause at the fork bearing to the left hillock.

Unfortunately, George knew this pathway equally as well.

When he was young, before Alex died, it was usually taken in the dark as the result of a dare. Much like bravely dwelling in the dank cave overnight served as a sort of initiation, so too had staying past midnight in the gated cemetery. As George stood and gazed at the iron gate and stone wall in the distance through the waving grass, he recalled Alex's resolutely stubborn face as he flatly refused to be goaded into accepting the challenge from his siblings. Eventually they had relented, especially when George flipped sides and supported his twin's stance. Later, watching Alex's wooden coffin lowered into the ground, the irony had struck George and incited fresh tears. Since then, he hadn't been a big fan of cemeteries, and thankfully family deaths weren't too frequent.

Frequent or not, George knew this path. He knew the precise dimensions of the cemetery. He knew the layout of every plot and how each of them would lie beside his father, mother, and Alex. Therefore, he did not have to guess what bench James was sitting on, the spaces allotted to he and his wife decided on long ago although never imagined to be used so soon.

Pemberley's butler, Mr. Taylor, had welcomed George as if his unannounced arrival was nothing unusual. His professional aplomb had brought a smile to George's weary face. It was a smile that vanished minutes later when Mr. Taylor informed him that Mr. Darcy was at the cemetery. The butler's tone was bland, but the hint of tragic acceptance and unspoken "as always" was detectable to George. He hadn't asked where Fitzwilliam or Georgiana were in the huge house with the palpable air of depression. No point in coming all this way to be sidetracked with greetings and introductions.

Inhaling deeply and sending a silent prayer skyward, George ascended the gentle rise to the entrance and pushed open the gate. Not the tiniest squeak from the oiled hinges. Not a bit of rust or decay was to be found. The groundsmen included the cemetery in their duties, so there wasn't a single weed among the fragrant flowers and manicured trees. Natural grasses and clover grew over the graves and open expanses, but they were controlled so that the graveled footpaths were clear. George veered to the right, weaving past the Darcys from the 1600s and the crypt where a whole family from the late 1400s rested. Three enormous oaks shading graves where his great-great-grandfather and contemporaries were buried obstructed his view for a few yards, but then he moved past and, sure enough, spied James where he imagined.

James sat on the stone bench with his elbows on his knees and head bowed. George could not see his brother's face, nor did he hear weeping. In fact, it was deathly silent. No breeze to ruffle the leaves and apparently the wildlife gave the cemetery a wide berth. Quiet and still it may have been, but George could feel the grief of his brother. It was as if a dark cloud rolled off of his slumped shoulders, thickly drifted on the immobile air, and slammed into anyone or anything nearby with the force of a hammer. Wetness stung George's eyes, and he swallowed against the assault of emotions. Waiting until he had some control, George stepped out of the shadows and purposefully scraped his heel into the pebbles.

It was faint but enough to alert James. Nevertheless, he lifted his head sluggishly, eyes unfocused for several heartbeats before widening.

"Hello, James."

"William?"

"No, it's George. Your brother."

"George?"

"Yes, it's me. And I am really here. I haven't died in an Indian jungle as predicted and probably wished for by some. I'm not a ghost here to haunt you, so don't start screaming like a girl."

"Am I dreaming? I can't believe my eyes! You look... good."

"You sound surprised!"

"I suppose I am, on many counts. Something is different about you. I can't place my finger on it, but you just look... good."

James hadn't risen from the bench and was peering bemusedly at George. All things considered, George didn't blame him for believing he was dreaming. He came closer until feet away. "Thanks for the compliment, James. I wish I could say the same about you, but you look ghastly. When did Pearson shave you last?"

James rubbed over the stubble on his cheek then shrugged. He didn't answer, the topic clearly not of any concern to him. He was still staring at George as if expecting him to disappear any second. "Did we know you were coming, George? Did I miss the message?"

He asked the question but absently, as if the possibility of being a bad host meant nothing. There wasn't much in the way of enthusiasm at George being there at all, for that matter, but George did not take it personally. It was a fair bet that James showed little if any enthusiasm these days, meaning the abyss of grief he burrowed further into each day was consuming him. George's heart constricted, but he forced a grin onto his face.

"Oh, you know me, popping up uninvited whenever I can. I like to make an entrance. I tried to scare old Taylor but nothing rocks him. Maybe I'll have better luck with Mrs. Reynolds. She did take a shine to me last time I was here so will probably weep with delight."

While speaking, he sat on the bench beside James, forcing his brother to scoot over, which seemed to startle him partially out of his haze. Apparently touching the apparition had some impact on making it real! He was now staring at George's profile with a confused frown, knitting his brows. George ignored him and continued to babble.

"You still have Mrs. Langton as your cook? I sure hope so. God, she is fabulous! Contends with the best I have ever had at an English table including the Bombay Governor, just don't tell him I said that 'cause I know he pays the man a bloody fortune. If I have to go without native cuisine for a bit, I can happily do so with Mrs. Langton's food. You should avail yourself of the table more, Brother. I think you have lost twenty pounds since last I was here. A few pounds you could go without—all that good eating and laziness hitting you around the middle a bit—but not this much. We should go hunting for a fat buck. The venison here is the best in the world and when fresh?" He closed his eyes and made a series of satisfied appetite sounds. "Nothing better. I miss the trout from our pond too. And the wild grouse. And plum pudding. Think Cook will make some for me even though it isn't Christmas? I need to make a list of my favorite foods so that—"

"Anne died."

George turned his head and met James's eyes. They were black and drowning in anguish but free of tears. George suspected tears no longer sufficed as a way to express James's grief. One glimpse at the stricken man's face was frightening. A longer scrutiny was terrifying. George had witnessed and dealt with grief. Lots and lots of it. Never had he seen this degree of utter despair, not even in his own eyes after Alex's death. James's once boyishly handsome face with the inner light of gay optimism and love was gone. Now it was lined, sallow, aged beyond his forty-five years, and dull. The brown eyes perpetually warm and shining with humor were flat and dead, the only emotion a vague confusion as if he couldn't comprehend how he managed to live with the unrelenting pain.

George had anticipated that Anne's death would rock his brother. He had spent the past six months preparing himself for confronting James in his sadness. It wasn't enough. What he observed shocked him profoundly, and it took a very great deal to shock Dr. George Darcy. It was a mystery how he wrestled the strength not to cringe when the urge to remove his gaze from the empty, agonized shell that was his beloved brother was more powerful than any urge he had ever felt. It had to be of a divine source because George knew he was not that strong.

"Yes," he said in a calmer voice than he expected, "I know Anne died. I am very sorry, James. More sorry than I can express. I wish I could have been here."

"She just grew weaker and weaker. Day by day and month by month. Her body refused to respond, as if her muscles were disconnected from her brain. It was the strangest thing." James's eyes had glazed over and were unfocused somewhere over George's left shoulder. His words were ethereal, whispered in a voice without emotion. "Nothing could be done. We tried everything, even the remedies my brother suggested. She was in so much pain." James blinked and swallowed at that, pausing and inhaling against the tendril of feeling tickling his senses. Then he visibly slumped. "It was gradual," he resumed in the same dead tone, "and took so long. She tried to fight... it... but couldn't. Then one morning she was gone. I held her in my arms as tightly as I could. I begged her to stay but she was gone."

George laid one hand on James's shoulder and repeated, "I wish I could have been here. I don't think I could have prevented Anne's death, but I would have tried with all my might."

James said nothing. He bent over with his elbows on his knees and rested his eyes on the headstone etched with the name of his wife. He hadn't twitched when George touched him and showed no further awareness of his brother's presence. The past ten minutes replayed in George's mind and, visualizing it from a different perspective, increased his alarm a thousandfold.

Word of Anne Darcy's death had reached George in Junnar, shattering the cocoon of bliss he was living in with Jharna. It was distressing to leave his home for a trip that could easily separate them for a year, and he did struggle with the decision for a few days. Yet no matter how many arguments he made for not going to England, some of them completely rational, he could not shake the nagging sense of urgency felt inside. Illogical as it seemed, George knew he had to go. The sensation grew every time he read the notice of Anne's death, penned not by James but by his sixteen-year-old son, William.

Dear Uncle,

I pray this letter reaches you safely and is delivered into your hands in a timely manner. I further pray your health and circumstances are excellent. I regret that this missive, written on behalf of my father, your brother, is of a grievous nature and thus may instill melancholy into your heart

and upset your daily affairs. These concerns notwithstanding, I believe
you would wish to be informed that, this month past, my dear, sainted
mother lost her battle with the ailments besetting her and has gone to be
with God. Pemberley is deeply immersed in a state of mourning, most
especially my father, who is unable to write to you directly. If I may be
so bold, I request your devotionals include appeals for his health and
emotional well-being during this immediate season of crisis. Perhaps
written words of encouragement and comfort from you, his most beloved
brother, could be sent in response? My father holds you in the highest
regard, Uncle, so I know your presence, albeit from a distance rather than
by his side, shall appease his heart and lighten his spirits. With affection
and esteem,

> *Your nephew,*
> *Fitzwilliam Darcy*

George could not claim to know his nephew well, but one thing he was
sure of after meeting the lad five years ago and reading the six letters William
had written to him since was that the youth was extremely careful in his choice
of language. Usually George laughed aloud at the precisely phrased sentences
and paragraphs written with an economy of words distinctly picked to convey
the proper meaning. William lacked overt humor in his correspondence yet
constructed sentences in such a way that nuances, witticisms, and deeper inter-
pretations were evident if one was intelligent enough to discern them. In this
case, George was affected on several points. One, it was odd that even while
sunk in grief, James had not written himself. Yet James was "unable to write"
and the pleas in regards to his "health and emotional well-being" pointed to a
serious problem. The references to George offering words of encouragement,
the comments as to his importance to James, and the subtle remark about his
presence were clear. Fitzwilliam wanted his uncle to come to England and felt
it was vital to James's recovery for some reason. He was simply too polite to
come right out and say it.

Try as he might, George could not silence the tug at his heart. He had sat
down a dozen times in the space of four days and attempted to write to James.
Never could he finish the letter. He told himself he would wait a bit to see if
James wrote to him or if William did again. He told himself that with time

James would rally, but his anxiety only grew more pronounced. Finally it was Jharna, she who read into his soul better than anyone alive, who all but insisted he leave.

Five months of monotonous travel was spent reassuring himself that after nearly a year James would be healing, even if just a little. The plan was for a month of brotherly camaraderie maximum and then he would set sail on the fastest ship back to India and Jharna.

James, however, was far worse than George's wildest imaginings had envisioned. Aside from his appearance—and it truly was ghastly—he was disconnected from reality. George's abrupt presence after nearly six years away hadn't startled James one iota. Instead, he was staring at the gravestone as if George were not there. Words were not penetrating the self-installed barrier but maybe action would.

"Remember at the Summer Festival when Anne was seventeen and Millie Hent tried to kiss you? Lord, I have never seen a woman so furious! There she was, a diminutive sprite spitting fire, and she charged right up to Millie and punched her in the nose. Remember that? Millie fell flat on her hind end. It was hysterical. But we sure learned not to anger Lady Anne Fitzwilliam after that. She always had a temper, that one, especially about you. If she could see you now, it would be you with a bleeding nose and dirt on your ass. Then she would stand over you for an hour, delivering a good tongue lashing."

James had turned and was staring at George with the same vague expression. George stared right back, this time with visible disgust and irritation. "Not sure if Anne can see you from Heaven, and while normally I hope for that sort of possibility, this time I pray she can't. Still, on the off chance she can, and since she can't deliver the slap you deserve, I'll do it for her." And without any preamble, George balled his fist and punched James square in the nose. He controlled the blow so that James wasn't hurt too much—no blood or crunched bones—but enough of an impact that it stung and knocked him off the bench onto the hard-packed gravel.

"What the bloody hell!" James roared.

"About damned time you showed some emotion, Brother," George roared back. He stood up and loomed over the supine James. "Now get up off your sorry ass so I can do it again. Or is once enough to wake you up from your pathetic bout of self-pity?"

"You hit me! I can't believe you hit me! That's just... Wait. What are you doing here? When did you get here?"

"We have been sitting here for the past half hour, James. Where the blazes were you?"

"I..." The shock and anger on James's face was replaced by confusion, and then after a glance toward the gravestone now inches from his eyes, the glazed mask of sadness began creeping in.

"Oh no you don't!" George reached down and grabbed James's soiled, loosely tied cravat, yanked him to his feet, and raised his other hand in the air.

"Wait! Don't hit me again, George. I take your point."

"Do you? Because if I hear you sniveling and sinking into your grief like that again, James, I will beat you until you're bloody."

"Why all the hostility? And where is the compassion, damn it all! Did you come all this way to harass or commiserate?"

"I have a suspicion you have gotten far too much commiseration." He let go of James's cravat and stepped back with a sigh. "Listen, James, I have oodles of compassion for your loss. Believe me. I feel it too. I loved Anne and can't believe she is gone. I also knew your wife well and am sure she would not want you to curl up and die of mourning her. That isn't the Anne Darcy I knew. She was a fighter who was full of life. She loved Pemberley. She loved her friends and family. And she loved you too much to want you to suffer so."

"I don't know how to make the pain stop," James choked.

"It may never stop. You have to come to grips with that. But it will become tolerable. It will lessen in time. If, that is, you quit ignoring life to come here and stare at a cold grave. Anne isn't here, James. She is alive inside you and inside your two children. Don't let her die completely."

"I'll try, how's that for now?"

"I'll accept it, mainly because I am starving and tired of lecturing you. Come on. Show your guest some hospitality." George slung his arm over James's shoulder and steered away from Anne's plot, his grip firm enough that James could not look back and had no choice but to walk with him. "I came directly here from the house. Didn't even grab a drink. I'm parched and it is all your fault."

"Did we really sit together for a half hour?"

"Yes. We talked too. You told me I looked especially handsome and debonair and in the prime of my life."

"I did?"

"Well, you said I looked good. I knew what you meant though."

James laughter was music to George's ears. "You also thought I was William for a second there. I suppose that means he is as dashing as I am?"

"Not sure how I can mistake you for him with that get up." James waved at the blue *sherwani* with braided gold and red trim George wore over yellow *shalwar* trousers. "He does look like you though. It is uncanny at times. Wait until you see him, George. Or did you?"

"No. I came straight here to rescue you from digging a hole and climbing into it."

"I am glad to see you, Brother. I might even forgive you for hitting me. Eventually. And you do look good. What is your secret?"

"I'll tell you later. First, tell me more of my nephew and niece."

With gentle prodding, George kept the topic away from Anne as they walked the familiar path back to Pemberley. He felt it best to avoid mentioning Jharna and his own felicity for the present.

Mr. Taylor had alerted Fitzwilliam of his uncle's arrival, so the youth was waiting on the rear terrace. He bowed in George's direction as soon as he and James mounted the steps.

"Uncle George, welcome to Pemberley. I apologize for not noting your arrival and greeting you properly."

"I snuck in, lad, so as to avoid any polite greetings. The lengthy falderal is a waste of time. Besides, I needed to search out your father so I could punch him in the nose. Got a nice lump starting there, James."

"Pleased with yourself, I suppose?"

"I daresay I am! Rather impressive overall, although I was holding back. Didn't want your ugly mug to look any more ghastly than it does already."

William's eyes had widened and he was staring between the two men in astoundment. "Father, I shall send for some ice and soothing ointment immediately."

"Never mind that, William. He'll be fine. Do him good to feel it as a reminder of what will happen if he indulges in another bout of self-pity. Now, I think food is in order. Maybe tea too, unless you have some illegal whiskey hidden about?" He raised his eyebrow in James's direction, then nodded when James shrugged, trying to look innocent in front of his son. "Thought so!

Go fetch your stash, Brother, and make it quick but clean up. You look like you have been rolling around in the dirt. It's disgusting. Now, William"—he clapped the gaping youth on the shoulder, turned his back dismissively on James, and headed into the house without skipping a beat—"you do realize how fortunate you are to resemble your grandfather and me? Stunning hand-someness is advantageous, let me tell you. Ladies fall over themselves for a man who can dress well and dazzle with his appearance. Height is a plus, too, and you are nearly as tall as me! You will have every lady at Almack's vying for your favors."

"If you say so, sir." William looked terrified rather than enthused, blushing furiously and fidgeting with the edge of his tailored coat.

George resisted laughing by greeting Mrs. Reynolds, who was in the parlor bent over a tray of food and beverages on the low table surrounded by several settees and chairs. He heaped on the charm, Mrs. Reynolds laughing and teasing in return. Judging by the slack-jawed gape on William's face, Mrs. Reynolds engaged in frank coquettishness was unheard of.

"By the way, Mrs. Reynolds, one of the bags I brought with me is a smaller portmanteau with red handles and green clasps. I assume the excellent Pemberley staff has taken it to my chambers, but if it is not too much trouble, could someone bring it to me here? I am led to believe there is a young lady in the house, a particularly beautiful miss with a lovely name and golden curls. Is this true?"

"Yes, Doctor. This would be Miss Georgiana Darcy you refer to," the housekeeper confirmed with a sage nod. Neither glanced to the chair across from the one George fell into and pretended not to see the glimmer of blond hair or corner of a sky-blue eye peaking from behind the tall back.

"Would I be correct in assuming that this angel from heaven is fond of colorful ribbons, fine cloths for dresses, glittery jewels, and pretty trinkets?"

"You would be correct, yes."

"Excellent! The case I requested is stuffed full of surprises that should delight this mysterious, as yet unseen girl."

"I will get it straightaway then." And with a bow and a wink, Mrs. Reynolds left the room.

Georgiana disappeared from view when George looked at William, where the boy was standing in the middle of the room in confusion. "Have a seat,

William, please. I honestly deplore formality and I want us to have a quick man-to-man chat before your father returns." He leaned forward to pour a cup of tea. As he sat back, cup in one hand and fruit tart in the other, he shot a rapid glance to Georgiana and winked before she ducked back behind the chair. Seconds later, he saw her peeking at him, more of her face showing and a tiny smile at the edge of her mouth.

"I know I have startled you with my words and actions, lad. I apologize, but it was necessary. I am going to speak obliquely due to small ears listening and will be quick before the master returns. I need you to trust me, William. Understand that I have years of experience in dealing with situations like this, as well as personal knowledge of losing one very close. Plus, I know him very well and in a manner different than you. Anything I say and any way I act is because I love all of you and want to help. Do you believe me and understand so far?"

William was staring at him in the intense manner George recalled from his previous visit. Patiently, he waited and submitted to the scrutiny. Finally his nephew acknowledged with a single short nod, but his lips were pressed into a tight line and creases marred the clean ridge of his brows.

George continued in the same level tone. "I know this is a difficult time for all of you. I am not minimizing the impact of loss to you and your sister, nor is my intent to offend when I tell you that the impact on your father is a million times worse and of a critical nature. I am trying to be careful with my words"—he jerked his head minutely toward the lurking Georgiana—"and I appreciate your doubt in light of my reaching these conclusions in a matter of minutes. Nevertheless, you must trust me and follow my lead. Can you do that, Fitzwilliam?"

This time William's nod was swifter and more confident. The frown and serious cast remained, but a dose of dawning hope inside his blue eyes revealed to George the youth's awareness of his father's acute depression. Shoulders straight and broad with the promise of mature masculinity were visibly drooped under the weight of being forced to deal with sadness and other negative emotions. Eyes that should have been gay and free of care were haunted and older than seventeen years. George's heart wrenched. The effects of trauma and death upon a person, especially a sensitive adolescent, George understood better than most. For one like William, who was also far too somber at the best of times, the ramifications were potentially multiplied. For George, it meant the stakes were even higher. He would pray fervently that his temporary presence and influence set the stage for everyone's healing.

A servant entered the room at that moment, interrupting the topic and worrisome contemplations. In his hand was the portmanteau. "Ah! Thank you, my good man. Now, let me see what I have in here that might pique the curiosity of a pretty girl." George opened the case and pursed his lips. "Hmm... I may need your input, William, as to what the hitherto unseen Miss Darcy may appreciate. I would not wish to burden her with a, oh, blue silk ribbon with glittery gold threads if she would hate such a thing." He pulled the ribbon out with a flourish and let it flutter to the floor. "We can throw it in the rubbish heap if offensive to her."

From behind the safety of the chair, Georgiana, biting her lip with tiny white teeth, watched with one wide eye as the ribbon curled on the carpet. George rummaged inside the big bag, making a show of it before withdrawing a long, ivory and pale-blue scarf with a sewn beach and foaming surf scene, the pattern so intricately woven that one could imagine the sound of the ocean and smell of salt water. "This ugly thing would surely not delight a little girl, would it?" He draped the scarf over his head and shoulders, the satin flowing in a rippling wave, and pretended not to hear Georgiana's breathy squeak. "I am assuming she likes dolls, yes? Probably has several dozen, yes?" He looked at William with each question, pleased to see the young man smiling and playing along with the charade. "As I expected. Not sure if she would want another to clutter her room then. Especially one as unattractive as this."

The "unattractive" doll was a hand-stitched fabric lady wearing a brilliant hued sari and beaded *mojaris*. Glass gems adorned the horsehair, dyed raven black and styled into intricate braids. Her face was painted and sewn, the painstaking detail bringing life to her eyes. The craftsmanship extended to her fingernails and toes, the plush toy a true work of art.

George held it up for William to see, twisting his wrist so that the sari swayed around the doll's legs. "Probably nothing that would interest Miss Darcy. I'll just put this away then," and he started to rewrap her in a swatch of colorful cloth.

"No! I want the lady, please!"

"My word!" George exclaimed, clutching his chest and gasping. "Where did you come from? Are you a fairy creature who can appear from thin air?"

"No. I'm Georgiana." Her eyes were drilling into the pretty doll that George held purposely close to his body and out of her reach but turned so that she could see it. Fear that George might stuff the doll back into his bag of miraculous treasures overcame her shyness, a rapid dart at his face followed by two steps nearer.

"You are Georgiana? Impossible! Georgiana, my namesake, is but an infant. Not a young lady such as yourself, magical miss."

She flashed another quick glance at his face. "I'm not magical," she giggled, adding as she lifted her chin and held up her fingers, "and I'm almost six!"

"Hmmm... I have no reason not to believe you if you say you are Miss Georgiana Darcy, although you, little princess, are far prettier than I was told."

Georgiana blushed and giggled at that, but she was looking at her uncle with greater interest and less fear. He held out the doll, still keeping it close so that she had to step forward, his smile friendly and wink jaunty. Ten minutes later, James walked into the parlor to see his painfully shy daughter sitting on his brother's lap with not one but two Indian dolls in her arms—the second a groom dressed in full marriage regalia to match his stuffed bride. Her forearms were adorned with several metal and bead bracelets clinking musically together as she moved, and her head and shoulders were covered with at least four layers of shimmering silks and satins. He could barely see her under the flood of color! Even her tiny feet were encased in rainbow shades, a different jewel and embroidery encrusted shoe on each one.

Presents opened the door, but it was George's unique blend of eccentricity, effervescent personality, magnificent storytelling skills, boyish playfulness, and generous affection that effortlessly won the bashful but gay Georgiana over completely and for life. She was glued to him every second they were in the same room together, usually held in his arms or curled in his lap.

Fitzwilliam, on the other hand, was a youth entirely too severe for seventeen. Hints of his levity were detectable at times, and additional clues to his lighthearted character were revealed when he interacted with his friends George Wickham and Gerald Vernor and cousin Richard Fitzwilliam. Unfortunately, George's need to devote the bulk of his attention to James did not allow him to focus on establishing a strong bond with William and the boy's austere, introverted nature added to the difficulty. George came to the conclusion that Fitzwilliam Darcy would be a man of uncommon strength of character, exacting morals, temperance, wisdom, keen intellect, and deep compassion, but a close relationship between the two of them appeared unlikely.

One punch on the nose was not enough to break the spell of mourning James was under. For a week they hunted, fished, trekked about the vast estate grounds on foot and on horseback, explored the caves and hills and rivers and lakes as if never seen before, and visited the gamekeeper compound and stables for hours at a time. Inside the manor, George challenged him to cards, darts, games of sport such as tennis and shuffleboard, and billiards, the latter almost always won by William who was typically involved with their activities. George sent messages to old friends, family, and acquaintances all over the shire. Every day, someone rode up the curved drive to visit George Darcy, and by extension James as well.

"Lowell Stine? Who is Lowell Stine?" James glanced from the serene face of Mr. Taylor to George, where he stood by a row of freshly planted pots of herbs in the orangery. A sudden desire to dig in dirt and teach members of the kitchen staff and Mrs. Reynolds on the culinary and medicinal properties of six herbs indigenous to India was that morning's activity, George insisting that James tag along as his assistant. James could care less about herbs, no matter how miraculous they were, but he appreciated what George was doing so played along. The message delivered by the butler was another matter, however.

George did not look up from the pot he was helping one of the kitchen girls plant, answering as if the question were not important. "Oh, he is a fellow I knew in boarding school. Be careful to bury this seed so that it is far down into the soil or the weak stem will fall over."

"I have never heard the name, so how could you have known him so well to invite him to dine with us today?"

"I don't know all your friends, James, so how can you reasonably expect to know all mine?"

"Fair enough, I suppose, but this is the fifth man to visit that I have never heard you mention. Ever."

"There is also Herbert Malone and Giles Nye from Alfreton who I don't think you met. They should arrive soon as well. Malcolm and Henry are coming by too, and I told Wickham to put the books away for the day so he can join us in tracking that stag we spotted two days ago. Mr. Burr knows the rough vicinity where he grazes and is planning to accompany us."

"You told *my* steward to not work for the day?"

"Don't be testy. Wickham wouldn't go if anything vital needed attending. Call it a suggestion if it makes you happier, but he is one of the best hunters I know, after Mr. Burr of course."

"And when were you going to tell me about these fine plans of yours?"

George shrugged. "I'm telling you now."

James sighed exasperatingly. "*After* people have arrived! A little warning would be nice!"

George looked up from the pots and seeds, one brow lifted over wide, innocent eyes. "Did you have other plans for the day, Brother?"

"No, but that's not the—"

"Then I am not sure I see the problem," George interrupted. He smiled at the flushed James, then concluded his herbal lesson for the day before blithely leading the still-irritated James into the parlor where Mr. Stine awaited.

This was one of several typical conversations during those early days of George's stay. Pemberley's main door was revolving with constant visitors. When done entertaining gentlemen in various masculine pursuits during the day, they socialized with friends over dinner. Three nights at Pemberley, one night at Sanburl Hall with the Vernors, and one night in Matlock at Rivallain with Lord and Lady Matlock. Fine food and spirits augmented by lively conversation and pleasant activities, such as music and games, was distracting. And exhausting. George made sure James was too tired at the end of the day to lay awake dwelling on and crying over Anne. James needed to get on with the business of living, and George intended to remind him of the joys to be had in life even without the woman you love to share them with.

This truth aside, George also understood that James had not been able to talk through his grief. Crying produced partial catharsis but too much emotion remained bottled up inside. It was during the quiet, alone periods when George and James sat in the library or on the shaded terrace as Georgiana played on the lawn that the topic of Anne, in life and in death, was gently broached. Subtly, George steered the conversation to reminiscences of Anne as she was when healthy and vibrant rather than the frail, sickly woman who dominated James's mind. Increasingly, the depressing images were replaced by pictures from happier times.

It was while having one of these brotherly interludes that James crossed his arms over his chest and nudged George's leg with his foot. "So, when are you finally going to stop coddling my frail sensibilities and tell me about the woman you are in love with?"

The whittling knife clattered against the stones of the terrace and missed George's bare pinkie toe by an inch.

"Oops!" James bent to retrieve the sharp instrument and handed it back to his stunned brother. "Didn't mean to cause an accident. Good thing the blade missed, since your digits are just hanging out there and not encased in protective leather like they should be."

"They are hanging out there but cooler than yours, I imagine." George took the knife and then used it to point at James. "What makes you think I am in love?"

"Oh please! I may be a bit preoccupied but I'm not blind. Despite the years apart, I still know you fairly well, Brother. Not that I think one needs to know you well to see the signs."

"What signs exactly?"

James ticked off on his fingers. "One, the use of the word 'we' here and there. Two, the dreamy expression on your face at unguarded moments, particularly when fiddling with that mysterious medallion you wear around your neck. Three, that you haven't dallied with a single maid since arriving and ignored Mrs. Hurt's brazen seduction. We were all shocked at that, by the way, both her attack and your dismissal. Four, your evasion when I ask about your current living situation in India. Five, there is a look about you that is different. Don't laugh but you have a glow, for lack of a better term, that I can detect, having seen it in my own countenance. I know a man who is in love, George. Six, the carving you are working on is shaped like a woman. Seven—"

"Very well. I get the point. I am transparent and not the smooth deceiver I thought I was. Damned annoying, that is, and a blow to my ego. I'll need to practice my acting skills. Who is the 'we' sitting around gossiping about the amorous Mrs. Hurt? I was taken aback by her demeanor, I shall confess. Considering her husband died, what, eight years ago I think she said, I imagine—"

"That is not a topic which interests me nor does it interest you. What is the big secret here, George? Why the hesitation to tell me about your life? It is because of Anne?"

George sighed and set the whittling knife and wooden figurine onto the table. He rubbed over his chin and avoided James's eyes. "It would not be kind for me to prattle on about my happiness when you are suffering the loss of Anne, James. It still makes me uncomfortable, so we should change the subject."

"Nonsense! Maybe if you had opened with that news seconds after arriving I may have punched you instead of the other way around. I still owe you for that, just so you know and aren't taken unawares. But to not tell me at all is ridiculous." James leaned to the right until in George's line of sight, forcing him to meet his eyes. "Brother, do you have any idea how often I have prayed for you to find a woman to share your life with? It is the greatest blessing, and I was beginning to lament that it did not appear to be in the cards for you. This makes me very happy!"

"I feared you might grow bitter at the whole concept of love. It makes *me* happy that you can see past your pain."

The cloud of grief perpetually lurking over James's head grayed his skin for a moment, but with a visible shake he cast it off. The smile directed toward George was wan but genuine. "There are times, I won't deny it, when in the deepest of my despair I wonder if the love was worth all this pain. I am *not* changing the subject here, so you aren't off the hook." He wagged his finger at George, who could not help but laugh. "I am telling you that despite my fury at God or fate or whatever for taking Anne from me so soon when I wanted another thirty or forty years with her, I would not change anything. Every hour I miss her. Every day I wake feeling lost and wondering how I can survive the years of my life without her. It has taken me a while to climb out of the pit I was in and I am not on solid ground as yet, but I am struggling to get there. I owe you a debt of thanks for your intervention, Brother. You motivated me and I appreciate that. What will keep me from falling back into the pit are memories of the incredible blessing that was my wife, the hope that we will be together again, and the two amazing children created by our love." He paused to blink away the tears and inhale past the tightness in his chest.

George observed his brother's grief and wondered what disturbed him most: that he might someday be the one overcome by paralyzing sorrow or that he wouldn't. Losing Jharna was a prospect he cringed from imagining, yet he could not help but consider it when the reality of death was square in his face. Would his happiness cease if Jharna died? Would he be frozen in an icy existence? Frankly, he could not envision himself losing all will to live or being so depressed as to stare at a cold grave for hours on end. It wasn't in his nature. Even after Alex and the powerful melancholy, a small part of his mind knew that he would have rallied in time. Maybe it was different with the woman you give your heart too. Somehow he did not think so, at least not for him, and this was both a relief and unsettling.

He shook his head, shoving that character study aside for the present to attend to what James was saying.

"What I am trying to say is that love is a wonderful emotion. Rather than distressing, as you feared, hearing of your felicity is soothing. So quit tiptoeing around me like I am made of glass and tell me about your lady."

George removed the braided cord from around his neck and handed the pendant to James. Hanging from the thick cord was an oval disc made of porcelain, fired until glossy and bright. On one side was the portrait of a woman painted in such fine detail that she appeared about to speak, or more likely to laugh, with the way her dark eyes sparkled and plump lips curved upward.

"Is this her? She is beautiful! What is her name?"

"Jharna."

"Jharna," James repeated. "Lovely name. How did you... wait. Wasn't that the name of Dr. Ullas's wife?"

"Yes. And it is the same Jharna."

"Well, well. I see you have a story to tell!"

"Trust me. There is nothing improper to it. Well, at least not in how we fell in love." George proceeded to tell James the tale of their gradual dawning feelings toward each other, including the way they finally admitted their love. "We laugh about it now. We were as unsure as adolescents with a first infatuation rather than mature adults."

"It is a unique circumstance, so I can understand the hesitation. I am sorry you had to leave her to come here, George. It must have been a difficult decision and sacrifice on your part. I am touched."

"Don't nominate me for saint of the year yet. It wasn't easy, I'll be honest. If I was still with the Presidency, I would not have been able to come even if I could have left Jharna. At least we have not had that interference since last October when I resigned."

James was frowning. "Hold on. How long ago did all this happen with you and Jharna?"

"Two years ago." George did not flinch from the truth and remained calm as James processed the information, his face flashing through several emotions.

"Let me get this straight. You have been with Jharna for two years and never told me? Not blurting it after Anne's death is one thing. I can understand that. But to not tell me at all? I have received a half-dozen letters from you in the past two years! How could you not tell me of this?"

George did wince at the hurt tone. "Please, Brother. Hear me out. I wanted to tell you in every letter, believe me. I simply did not know how. It is a long story. I have only told you a third of it, and I did not think I could explain our relationship well enough in a letter. To be honest, I was not sure how you would react."

"React to what? That she was your friend's wife or that you are not married? I am assuming the latter or you would have addressed her as your wife, yes?"

"Yes. And no, we are not married."

"Hell, George. I am not that much of a prude. Father would have had a seizure but not me. Most of the men I know are unfaithful to their wives and had relationships before they were married. I am the odd one for loving my wife and never having been with another woman. As repugnant as the idea is to me now, even I can't swear I will live the rest of my life without a female. Marry again? Highly doubtful. Abstain? Not so sure. You don't have to explain yourself to me, Brother, although I am curious as to why you don't marry her. I have never heard you express disdain for the idea and you wanted to marry other women long ago."

"That is where it gets complicated, James, and why I never wrote about it." He retrieved the pendant from where it lay in James's lap. "Jharna had this painted for me and gave it as a gift on the first anniversary of when we..." He glanced at James's amused face and grinned. "Well, you can guess and already have. Abstaining isn't something I do well either and never have, although no one has compared with Jharna. For the first year, I was away from her home in Junnar more often than I was there. It was agonizing but I was very busy. I wanted to marry her and had every intention of asking but wanted to wait until the timing was right. Maybe the real reason is that I knew she would say no."

James gaped. "Why? You said she loves you so... why? I don't understand."

"Like I said, it is complicated. James, I have lived in India for a long while now. It is a unique culture, and I do love it, but there are aspects that are difficult to grasp and accept. It isn't a big secret that Englishmen marry Indian women. It happens far more than you hear about, trust me. But each situation is different and each woman is different. Jharna is a devout Hindu. I respect that, just as she respects my religion. We view marriage as a sacred vow. The problem is our vows and sacred beliefs regarding marriage are with different gods. As much as I want to argue with her and say it does not matter, I can't honestly do that. I couldn't ask her to renounce her religion any more than she could ask me to reject mine. In a practical sense, as she explains it, what is the point of us marrying? How would we do it? Who would marry us? What would it mean if one did not hold to the same philosophy as the other? On top of that, Jharna was married to Kshitij and to Hindus that is a bonding that lives on in the afterlife. Actually, that is not much different than what Christians hope for, but to Hindus it is defined."

"You make a strong case, George, but I sense you are not happy about it."

"God no, I am not happy about it! I love Jharna as I have never loved another woman. I had given up on the whole idea of love and marriage, told myself it didn't matter all that much and I probably would have been fine if not for Jharna. She changed everything. Now I want a wife and perhaps children of our own. I want the assurance of God's blessing and to see our names written in a parish book. I want to address her as Mrs. Darcy and introduce her as my wife. I want the whole damned package!"

He broke off and ran a hand through his hair. He stared out at the glistening water of the pond and counted the blasts from the fountain as a way to calm. Minutes passed before he was able to continue in a level tone. "The irony is that Jharna wishes for the same. Yet it isn't possible. At least not in a traditional manner. The other irony, or perhaps surprise is a better word, is that when we are together, it does not matter. I may not be able to call her Mrs. Darcy but she *feels* like my wife. I have no comparison as far as being legally wed, but I know for a fact that the bond we share is stronger by a million than with the other women. Jharna feels the same and she has been married before. She won't say it directly out of respect and love for Kshitij, but her connection to me is deeper and her love powerful."

"Listen, George. This may sound heretical, but I truly believe that marriage is more than just a blessing from the Church. Am I saying God's hand upon a union is unimportant? No. What I am saying is that when I fell in love with

Anne, even when she was sixteen and we were forced to wait three years before our wedding, she was my wife inside my heart. Our love grew, especially once able to express it physically, and time added to the dimension. But we belonged to each other long before. What you have with Jharna is real, so if you are devoted to each other and faithful, I believe God will bless you. I don't think He is as rigid as the preachers teach. Just don't tell our reverend I said that or he will excommunicate me!"

"Thanks, James. I hope you are correct, although I will face eternal damnation if that is the price to pay for loving Jharna in this life."

"Eternal damnation? Indeed she must be remarkable then."

George laughed and nodded. "You have no idea, my brother."

"Then enlighten me."

After that, George was open with his feelings, the topic leading to many conversations about women, wives, family, intimacy, and so on. As hesitant as George had been to broach the subject, his relationship with Jharna and accompanied appreciation for romantic sentiments brought the brothers closer and helped James refocus his thoughts on Anne during their happier years. George persisted in teasing him for his whimsical sentimentality, James always the poetic type ready with a maudlin verse or fanciful gesture. George was too practical for extreme displays of affection. He did jot a few mental notes, however!

The remaining three weeks of his month-long sojourn in England were spent in London. George arranged for their sister Estella and her family to meet them at Darcy House on Grosvenor Square, unbeknownst to James. His brother was in the dark about most of George's machinations during that first week, as it turned out. Messages were leaving the gates of Pemberley several times a day and heading to destinations all over the country. George was rather proud of how well his sneaky agenda paid off, even to the point of enlisting Georgiana and William to his cause.

William claimed that since he was planning to begin his studies at Cambridge in the fall, it was logical to prepare in advance and acclimate to the new environment. It was a sensible proposition, as it turned out, which was fortuitous because William was a horrible liar and even the tiniest hint of deception, especially toward his father, was beyond his capabilities! George had to convince him of the necessity before the young man was able to use the argument to sway James. It was an exhausting piece of scheming.

Georgiana was easy. A few cleverly dropped comments about Town and how he had not been there in decades added to seemingly offhand remarks about the shopping, beautiful parks replete with ducks and ponds and colorful gardens, breathtaking activities such as Astley's Circus and horse racing, grand palaces with potential glimpses of royalty, and the crowning perk of ices at Covent Garden sent Georgiana running to her father with pleads to visit the magical city called London.

James's heart melted as it always did with Georgiana, and he concurred with William's reasoning, but he glared at George, not fooled one bit. It took more finagling and a fair amount of bullying to ultimately convince him. Even then James never would have left the cocoon that was Pemberley if George hadn't handled all the arrangements and all but shoved him into the carriage.

By the time James embraced George at the East India Company dock before he embarked on the return voyage to India, there wasn't a shred of residual pique.

"I love you, George. You will be missed, by all of us. Keep the letters coming and try to return for another visit before too many years slide by. I will be counting the months."

Partings of long duration are inevitably bittersweet. Yet as George bid adieu with his patented blend of lighthearted banter and serious emotion, he was encouraged by the renewed vigor James showed. The haunted sadness of loss would never disappear from his countenance, but it had lessened. His eyes were clear and smile intact. He had put on weight and no longer walked as if trudging through quicksand. A month prior, George had been sure his brother was on a short path to his own death. As he waved from the ship's railing and shouted a final farewell, his heart was light with relief that James was on a solid path to health and long life. Neither of them fancied for a second that this would be the last time they laid eyes on each other this side of Heaven.

GEORGE'S MEMOIRS
APRIL 10, 1806

Father, this time I swear it was not my idea. I was fine with residing in Junnar with Jharna for the duration of my life and could envision myself working at the hospital until my hands were too decrepit to hold a scalpel. If there is any doubt, you can read every journal entry for the past two years. Never a word about embarking on another mission abroad. Then last week, Nimesh comes to dine with us and breaks the news that he has accepted a post with Drs. Reddy and Desai for a two-year assignment studying and practicing Yūnānī *medicine in northern India between Delhi and Agra. Now, I confess that this was intriguing to me. How could it not be? I have longed to learn more of the blended Greek and Persian healing system created by Avicenna a thousand years ago. I have read* The Canon of Medicine *a dozen times and sought out every* Yūnānī *practitioner during our travels. I have been fascinated by those techniques and medications that are undeniably Ayurvedic yet incorporated with unique methods that must be of an Islamic or other root. Indeed, I have long wished to travel into the north where* Yūnānī *physicians are thickly located. Nevertheless, I am content with the knowledge and skills I have. Truly I am! So I was listening to Nimesh and politely asking questions about his travel plans when Jharna interjects, "I have long desired to travel north. Kshitij traversed the breadth of northern India from Punjab to Nepal to Bengal, even to the roots of the Himalayas, and the stories he told were spellbinding. It filled me with yearning. Oh, to see the Taj and stroll the banks of the Ganges!" At this point, the drama was running high, I have to say. I was taken aback by the emotional velocity she was employing but thought it was to placate Nimesh that she wasn't too upset over him leaving for two years. Then she looks at me and says, "George, we must accompany him. My wanderlust is reasserting itself, and you are growing musty." Musty? ME? I was severely offended! I don't intend to ever be musty until moldering in a box six feet under! Nimesh jumped on the idea faster than a grasshopper, saying that he intended all along to invite us. He yammered on about it being a dream of mine followed by additional nonsense that he "needed my expertise and superior comprehension to decipher the finer nuances" of the techniques, etc. Schemer! I sat there stunned while they laid the entire agenda. Jharna was jotting notes and barking orders like a general! As if there is a major rush.*

Once I was alone with Jharna, I dug in deep. I had to be sure she wasn't sacrificing for me. Honest to God, Father, I am not unhappy in Junnar! How could I be?

I love my life with Jharna and the boys and love my work at the hospital. It is more than I have ever dreamed of. She insisted that her desire to roam was real and I know her well enough to know when she is lying. She wasn't in this. Her heart was sincere and I admit that surprised me. I never knew how much she enjoyed moving around with Kshitij, assuming she did so as an obedient wife rather than with her own hunger to experience new places. After all this time, I am yet learning new facets of this incredible woman God has gifted me! She did add as proof that we should accept the offer that, "Your eyes were glowing and lit up brighter than a flame." Nicely poetic I suppose, but I am a physician and can assert with confidence that both of these are physically impossible! They may have sparkled a bit, I'll concede that point, especially when Nimesh said they would be spending time with Moḥammad Šarif Khan. Now THAT is an opportunity I can honestly say I would hate to miss!

So now we are up to our eyeballs with packing and preparing for a lengthy absence from the house in Junnar. Gita and the others will remain, of course. Jharna has insisted on new clothing for everyone. I wish I could argue that as a necessity, but alas, I am apparently too like a woman in that regard, as Jharna teases. Merchants are flooding through the gates all day. Crazy! The Sardar has sent a handful of soldiers to add to the escort. I am not sure that was vital now that the British have control of the area and we are part of the medical contingency, but when it comes to the safety of Jharna, I am as rabid as her father. Sasi is beside himself with glee. He cannot stop talking about the Agra Fort, Taj Mahal, and so on that he can explore. He is 16 now and as enamored with ancient history as ever.

So there you have it. And, yes, I will finally confess that while not looking for it, I am thrilled beyond words. Dr. George Darcy is on the move! Again!

WHEN DID THE SIMPLE act of waking in the morning become so exciting?

Sun filtered through the curtains shielding the latched windows. Peeking with a half-opened eye George ascertained that the light was undimmed by clouds which boded well for the day being warmer. Since the onset of winter in Agra, he had come to realize how thin his British blood was after dwelling in the year-round tropical climates of midland and southern India. In the north, with the Himalayas two hundred miles away, the cold of winter hit hard and was a sharp contrast to the heat of the summer they had enjoyed. It was not anywhere close to the chill of a winter day in England, but a shock to the system they were learning to cope with.

His favorite way to cope was to languish abed under a pile of blankets with Jharna's warm body curled in his arms or draped across his chest. Either position was fine by him, and since she suffered from the extreme cold worse than he, cuddling to leech from his internal furnace was a constant. Rarely did either of them have early appointments or duties to attend to now that they were for all intents on holiday in Agra. George was discovering the joy in freedom from intense activity, especially the pleasure of sleeping until well after sunrise.

They had left Junnar the prior May, the initial weeks weaving north through Sindhia, Holkar, and Rajpootana before veering east for Delhi. Three months they lived in historic Delhi, Sasi busy exploring places of historical significance while George and Jharna settled into a life of relaxation. He worked with the *Yūnānī* physicians in the city, accompanying Nimesh most days if not choosing to indulge in a different activity with Jharna. Additionally, he joined the doctors for two short jaunts to villages nearby and gave a series of lectures to the British medical corps stationed at the expanding complexes attached to the Red Fort of the Mughals.

Before the cold of winter, they relocated to Agra, settling into a fashionable, new house built by the English. Anticipating a longer stay, George selected a house comfortable and modern that was located in an area with a healthy mix of foreign and native residents. Thus far in their time together, he and Jharna had encountered little difficulty as a cross-cultural family. His fluency in Hindi and several other dialects, coupled with his ease with the customs, ethnic attire, darker hair, and tanned skin, allowed him to blend in easier than the average foreigner. Only his startlingly blue eyes gave him away, but most Indians shrugged that off as an anomaly. Besides, Englishmen were crawling all over the place since gaining control in 1803. Nor did most care that he lived with an Indian woman or vice versa, pairings of this nature common enough to raise few eyebrows. George was utterly indifferent to what anyone thought of his relationship with Jharna, but he preferred to avoid any controversy or gossip for the sake of Jharna and Sasi. In Agra, they were merely another family among the populous.

George didn't bother glancing at the clock. By the minor rumblings in his stomach, he knew it was midmorning, which meant they had slept for eight hours more or less, so he could wake Jharna without feeling too guilty about it. No need to rush into that either, however.

Jharna was lying on her back with one shoulder propped against his chest and her shapely rear resting on his inner thigh. Blankets covered their bodies so that he could only see her relaxed face and raven hair tumbling thickly over her neck, the pillow they shared, and his upper arm. A minuscule shift and George was able to reach the side of her face closest to him, his lips skimming lazy kisses along the sweet curves from ear to neck. Identical gentle caresses of his hand occurred unseen under the blankets from delicate shoulder blade to thigh. Waking Jharna incrementally and undemandingly was the wisest course at the best of times, George having discovered early in their relationship that while she tended to rise earlier than he in the morning, she did so grumpily. If he desired morning loving, or even rational conversation for that matter, waiting an hour or so was the only way it was going to happen.

This day was special, however, so he hoped for success in starting with a pleasant interlude under the sheets before embarking on the planned agenda of fun.

Jharna stirred under his leisurely assault. "You think because today is special you can wake me and not suffer the repercussions?"

Her morning voice was sultry, the husky tones increasing his shivers of promised pleasure. George smiled into her hair. The sentence was uttered with a tint of irritation, but the teasing overruled, as did the backward press of her rear into his thigh and playful glide of one foot up his leg.

"It is my birthday, a momentous one at that. Would you be unkind to me today of all days? Especially when I intend to bring you pleasure unmatched?"

"Unmatched? Now that is a promise you may be hard pressed to uphold. I have known spectacular pleasure in your embrace, *priya*. Has something magical occurred now that you are forty to create a lover of unparalleled proportions? Have you learned a new technique?"

Jharna turned her head and gazed at him with sleepy but mischievous eyes. Better yet, there was a gleam of hunger within the dark depths that took his breath away. Seconds later, when she cupped his groin through the fabric of his *paijamas* and slid a firm palm along the length of his arousal, he exhaled in a gush. The corners of her mouth curled upward, smugness dancing over the surface of each rosy lip. Passionate desire bathed her entire countenance and was felt in the sinuous wiggle of her body against his.

Taken all together, George was happily stunned. Jharna was a passionate lover, receptive and incredibly skilled. The physical relationship they shared was beyond his wildest dreams not only in how intense the sensations when they made love, but also in the level of spiritual affinity. With Jharna, there was a pure form of love that had only grown over their years of living with each other. She was his wife in every way except legally, as far as he was concerned, and although he still desired her to be his in that way as well, to wear the name Darcy, he now understood what it fully meant to be committed to one woman and he adored everything about it. From the physical to the spiritual to the day-to-day realities of life, they were a union of two souls.

"Perhaps I *have* learned new techniques." He lifted one brow and grinned cockily. "Or perhaps I am simply determined to prove that your forty-year-old mate can perform better than ever, loving you thoroughly until heaven is reached and you are delirious from the overwhelming pleasure is my gift to you." He leaned in and bestowed a consuming kiss teeming with evidence that this was a promise he could and would fulfill. When he pulled away, Jharna was panting and had turned fully toward him, a soft moan escaping when he broke off the kiss. "But first," he continued as if nothing had interrupted the discussion, "I want to talk about your gift for me."

"You can't seriously want to leave our bed *now* to see your present?"

George chuckled at the returned tone of irritation. "I have no intention of letting you out of this bed, my dear, until I have tasted of your succulent flesh and shown you what I am capable of. A promise is a promise and I am a man of my word." He smoothed one hand up her thigh and underneath the gown, gliding slowly over her rounded buttocks and up her spine before traveling along the curve of her rib cage, fingertips brushing the underside of her heavy breasts as he completed the circle down her torso to the soft mound of her belly. "The only gift I truly desire is you, Jharna, now and forever, and what you have hidden away here."

Gently, he palmed the tiny bulge below her navel, his broad hand cradling the area. He was looking straight into her eyes so did not miss the brief flash of reserve amid the shining happiness and heightened ardor. He reassured her with a delicate kiss to her lips, his voice weighted with joy and confidence.

"Oh, my sweet love! I know you are superstitious. You believe talking about this baby is ill luck after losing our other last year. I know you have hesitated to tell me, as if I could not detect the signs weeks ago. You forget I am a physician, and how intimately familiar I am with your luscious body." He accented his tease with a perfectly placed tweak at the juncture of leg and hip, Jharna twitching automatically at the tickling. "See?" He laughed, pleased at the responding smile and retreating anxiety in her eyes. "I know you carry our baby and that you are well into the second trimester. I can almost feel the flutters deep within you. You can feel them too, can't you? Yes, I thought so. I have seen the expressions cross your face, my love. Already you are past when the other miscarried, so I am confident all is well this time. Either way, however, we must share this together. And since it is my birthday, you must grant me whatever I want!"

His arrogant grin and arched brow did not have the effect he hoped.

Jharna shook her head and laid one hand against his cheek. "I haven't meant to keep secrets from you, George."

"I know. And I understand why you wanted to wait, Jharna. I am not angry, not in the least." He kissed her palm and drew her closer to his body. "But aside from wanting to rejoice with you and share our blessed news with Nimesh and Sasi, I could not permit you to linger in a state of denial or false forebodings. That is not healthy for you or the baby."

"I want to give you a child with all my heart, *priya*." Jharna's eyes clouded with tears and her lower lip began to tremble. "It pains me that I have failed and I fear—"

"Shhh," he soothed, brushing the moisture from her cheek. "You have failed at nothing, sweet. And if I did not know for certain you were pregnant before, I would now. One minute burning with desire and a hairbreadth from ravishing me and the next in tears. I predict next you will say you need to visit the privy. Ha! I knew it!" He laughed harder as Jharna slithered out of bed and dashed away without a backward glance.

Flopping back onto the pillows, George crossed his arms over his head and waited. The elated smile splitting his face was felt down to his toes. Naturally he had hoped the result of their liaison would be a child. Being a father wasn't a prospect George spared considerable thought for while still a single man, and even after falling in love with Jharna, he tended to focus on the thrill of their relationship rather than immediately wishing for more. Finding her and being with her was a dream brought to reality. Anything above that was more than he cared to tempt fate over. Yes, he too had his superstitions!

Then, shortly after his return from England, she conceived. The signs were evident early on, mere weeks after, yet before either had time to glory in their boundless excitement, Jharna miscarried. It happened so quickly, the rapid high of happiness followed by the swift blow of sadness. Physically Jharna recovered speedily. Emotionally the impact was bitter. It was at that time George learned Jharna had lost one other baby, that miscarriage happening after Nimesh. He pointed out that women miscarry often, probably a sign that something is wrong with the baby, and since she had later successfully carried Sasi, it was unlikely the problem was with her. Of course Kshitij had told her the same. On the other hand, as she pointed out in returned logic, she had never conceived after Sasi, with Kshitij or with George for nearly two years, and at thirty-seven she was no longer young. She added the pieces up as a divine message that she was not destined to have another child. Despite her attempts to accept this interpretation, she was devastated. George devoted all his energy toward convincing her that he was content with their life, which was true, and that while having a baby together would be wonderful, it was not of the utmost importance to him. This was also true.

A year had passed since that difficult period. Then, over a month ago, he had seen the subtle hints that Jharna may be pregnant. Empathizing with her feelings, he buried his jubilation and waited for her to tell him when she was ready. Last night when they had made love, he had distinctly felt the firm bulge of her belly and faint quivers against his abdomen. He yearned to launch from the bed and dance a jig, no longer capable of waiting to shout his joy.

"I am going to be a father."

He whispered it into the air, rolling the words across his tongue. His heart began to pound. When Jharna had conceived before, he had said the words and he remembered how his spirit had leapt at the idea. Sadly the full joy never penetrated completely.

"I am going to be a father."

Spoken louder this time and followed by a broader smile. Everything about this pregnancy felt different. For a month, he had silently watched the woman he adored more than life blossom as the precious life within her grew. She was grumpier in the morning, but not ill. She tired quicker and slept longer, but radiated health and energy in between. Traces of fear edged her demeanor, but an uninhibited optimism that she could not squelch shone through.

"I am going to be a father."

Conviction imbued the sentence. For too long he had denied his wish to be a father, appeasing the longing as *chacha-jee* to the Ullas boys. He too had experienced the pain of Jharna's miscarriage, hesitating to trust and believe this time would be different. There were never any guarantees, but so far all was well and that was enough to allow him to release the full extent of his euphoria.

"I am going to be a father!"

He shouted it, extending his arms into the air and performing an odd jiggling dance while still laying supine. He laughed aloud, a vigorous whoop added for good measure.

"Happy, are you?"

"Absolutely!" He turned his radiant grin toward Jharna, where she stood in the middle of the room and instantly lifted up onto one elbow.

She wore the same generic sleeping tunic covering her body to just above her knees. Her face was freshly washed and hair brushed to a shining cascade of satin reaching to her buttocks and draping her delicate shoulders and full breasts. No jewels, cosmetics, or elaborate garments. Only Jharna, the wife of his heart, keeper of his soul, and now mother of his child. Lust crashed over him like a storm to join with the indescribable sensations of completeness already surging inside.

"How could I not be happy? I have you, the most beautiful, amazing woman on the planet, and a baby on the way. First a husband and now a father. I am ecstatic! Now come back to bed, so I can show you just how immense my joy is."

She laughed, crossing the short space with a sinuous gait and kneeling on the bed next to George. Leaning until barely an inch away from his parted lips, she whispered, "Was that a euphemism? The 'immense my joy' phrase? Mmmm... I do believe it was. A truthful euphemism." She stroked over his groin, laughing huskily at his gasping groan. "Happy birthday, *priya*. I love you."

"I love you, Jharna, *priya*. Always."

Closing the gap, George kissed her teasing mouth, drowning her laughter with a voraciously seeking tongue. Rolling her smoothly under his body, he hungrily deepened the kiss, one hand snaking into the inky silkiness of her hair while the other slid up her thigh beneath the gown. For a long while they kissed and caressed. Excitement rose with every touch and taste. Generated heat dispelled the crispness of the winter air, the blankets and garments cast aside without a thought to being chilled. That was impossible with the searing flames racing through their entwined bodies. Desire was a fierce current, yearning to be satisfied.

Yet George felt a greater urge. A magnetic need that drew him again and again toward her belly where their baby slept secure in his or her cocoon. He cupped the tiny mound, kissed along the bronzed skin dozens of times, and whispered sweet words of love to the unseen ears. Then he would return to her lips and attempt to convey his boundless appreciation with fervid kisses. When he finally sheathed himself within her warm body, the sensation was powerful as it never had been before. Acknowledging the life between them that had been created by their love was a fierce aphrodisiac as it turned out!

"George?"

He grunted an affirmative, trusting she would hear him since he was nibbling her earlobe in time to each steady thrust.

"Are you listening?"

Another affirmative grunt, this one accompanied by a nip to her jaw.

"Is the sound of children's laughter still your favorite sound?"

Why is she asking this of me now? She had his attention though. Nevertheless, he kept to the rolling rhythm of lovemaking as he lifted onto his elbows and studied her serious face. "Yes it is. I have other sounds I love as well, such as your voice and the scrape of my whittling knife shaving wood and Rathore's hooves racing over packed turf." Long kiss. "But I can honestly say that children laughing brings a joyful smile to my heart. Very soon it shall be our child eliciting that smile. It will be euphoric, I have no doubt. Thank you, *priya*, for that gift as well."

Another consuming kiss followed, George increasing the tempo and perilously close to losing control. He was deliriously unaware that Jharna had more to say. She arched into his skilled fingers, signally for him to carry on. She panted and rode the undulating momentum of his body. Lithe legs wrapped around his waist and slid over the flexing muscles of his rear. Greedily she reciprocated the penetrating kiss. The tide of blissful sensations surged upward on a sheer wave. It was heaven! George plunged his tongue further into her mouth and groaned deep inside his throat.

Harshly she grasped onto his jaw and pushed him away. "George," she wheezed, "I need to tell you my favorite sound in all the world."

"Now?"

She smiled at the petulant whine in his voice and rubbed one fingertip over the creases between his perspiring brow. "Yes, now. It is important. You see, before, in Mysore, when you asked me, I was merely teasing you by not answering. It wasn't a secret what my favorite sound was. It was the song of the shama bird. They were plentiful in my childhood home and nested in the tree outside the window of the sleeping chamber I shared with my sisters. The song reminded me of my home and all that it meant to belong to a family."

"All right, Jharna. Thank you for sharing that with me." He honestly did not care at this particular moment and to say he was befuddled would be putting it lightly.

"I am not finished. You see, I have known for a long while now that the song of the shama bird is no longer my favorite sound."

She circled her fingertips over his face, her own countenance serious as she held his gaze. "It is you, George. When we are here, like this. Loving each other and you express your pleasure with me, with us. The sounds are far sweeter than that of a songbird. They are spontaneous and raw and real." She swayed upward, George sighing at the sudden rush of scorching heat. "I hear your rapture with every move and know it is felt within your soul because it touches me. And when you attain your peak and relinquish all control, the shouts and cries transport my being to a place higher than the heavens."

George absorbed every word she said, his body immobile yet pulsing with a fiery passion he had never known. He could form no words to respond to the phenomenal gift she was giving him. Ah, to know such love! He was truly speechless, but what she said next utterly floored him.

"You must understand, *priya*. It is only you." She inhaled and laid the tips of her finger onto his lips before continuing. "I loved Kshitij. You know I did. We were happy together and enjoyed each other. I never wanted for more or thought there could be more. Until you. You are the *more* I desired without knowing it. That is why hearing your love in return, equal with mine for you, is my favorite sound in all the world."

Thankfully, she did not wait for a reply because he could not have articulated if his life depended upon it. Instead, she hastily pulled him back to her lips, her entire body commencing a furious assault on his senses that overcame his astoundment. Perhaps later he would manage to tell her how profoundly her confession affected him. Later. For the present, he would show her. And if it was sounds of passionate ecstasy she wanted, by God he could manage that!

His last coherent thought as he unleashed the final thread of control was that his fortieth birthday was by far and away the best one ever.

～✥～

January rolled into February, March, and April. The warmer weather of spring in Agra was heavenly and these were the glorious months. Jharna blossomed, her health extraordinary and energy boundless. The typical discomforts of pregnancy, most of which she had suffered to some degree with Nimesh and

Sasi, were minimal. The baby grew and was active, and the vestiges of her superstitions were allayed.

George's joy during those months was incomparable. He was giddy as a sparrow and proud as a peacock, to quote Jharna. "Indeed I am!" was his beaming reply. Never had he imagined the delight to be found in these months of waiting. His professional knowledge of gestation in no way affected the miracle of observing his child's development. Feeling her kicks and lazy rolls under Jharna's expanding belly became an obsession. Jharna teased that if she allowed, George would follow her everywhere with his hands on her abdomen. It wasn't far from the truth. He rarely passed her without reaching out to rub over the visible bump, and when they were sitting stationary, he was right beside her with a hand at the ready. His face that was usually lit with humor and mischief now wore a ridiculous grin that never seemed to fade.

They went to Delhi to accompany Nimesh on his relocation to Agra and to tell of their news in person. Twenty years of age and caught up in his medical studies, Nimesh was distracted but of course he was thrilled for them and excited at the prospect of welcoming another sibling. At seventeen, Sasi was distracted by girls and his ongoing quest to study Indian history, but considered it the most marvelous development of all time. He insisted the baby was female, for no reason other than he wanted a sister, and after weeks of referring to his unborn sibling as "she" or "her" the habit caught on. Neither Jharna nor George had a preference or inclination toward either sex and figured the feminine direction was better than saying "it" or some other vague term.

In March, they welcomed George's longtime friend Dr. Searc McIntyre, his wife, and their two daughters. The physicians maintained their correspondence but had not crossed paths since George returned from his last visit to England two years prior. It was a wonderful reunion and to George's delight everyone got along famously. Together the two families embarked on a journey through Mathura and Barsana for the Lath mar Holi spring festival of colors. For nearly a month, they were away from their temporary home in Agra, leisurely weaving through small villages and larger towns dotting the region on a holiday that offered a few medical opportunities but was mostly pure entertainment.

By mid-April they were back in Agra and bid adieu to the McIntyres. George resumed working in the Indian hospital as well as the British hospital under control of the East India Company's Indian Medical Service. The name

"Dr. George Darcy" was well known, his history with the Company and reputation for excellence preceding him wherever he went. After seventeen years, George was used to walking into a medical facility, field office, or even makeshift hospital tent and being instantly recognized. He was rather proud of his fame, but mostly it was nice not to waste precious time in long explanations or testing probations. His roguish, itinerant ways were looked at askance by some, but no one could argue with his professionalism or skill.

Between work and preparing for the birth of their baby, George was never bored. Jharna settled into life as a physician's mate and soon-to-be mother of an infant. Necessary items were purchased and nursery quarters were decorated. The cradle was made to George's specifications and then enhanced with designs he carved into the wood himself. George discovered himself reverting to English customs and concerns, one of which he thought he had accepted.

"Marry me, Jharna."

She looked up from the tiny shoes she was sewing, her startled eyes meeting George's intense gaze. "*Priya*, we have discussed this—"

"I know. And I know I promised to accept the situation, and I have, Jharna. I truly have. But that was before this." He touched her abdomen, the baby jabbing into his palm as if listening and encouraging. "You are my wife in all the ways that truly matter. In here"—he placed her hand over his left chest—"and inside the invisible spirit God has given me. I am asking now from a practical standpoint."

He paused and shook his head slightly. "Not entirely, I will admit. I will never lie to you and say that being married, truly married as in blessed by the Church and God, isn't something I long for. But in this case, I want to make sure our child is a Darcy legally. I never want her or him to suffer as a result of being a..." He swallowed, unable to say the word. *Bastard.* It made the gall rise in his throat. In his mind and heart, their child was legitimate. The world would look at it differently and the thought killed him. "Please, just think about it. That is all I am asking for now."

Jharna said nothing for a long while. Then she nodded. "I will."

They left the topic there. George could tell she was thinking of his request in the days that followed and that was enough.

A sudden rise in temperature as Jharna entered her last two months dramatically sapped her strength. With waning energy came an increase in irritability. Between the two extremes, George was busy doing all he could to soothe and assist.

"Hoping to catch a breeze?"

"At this point I am actively praying to any god who may take pity upon me, even yours."

George chuckled, the vibration thrumming across the nape of her neck as he pressed a series of kisses to her damp skin. He encircled her waist, resting both hands over the swell of her belly and placing his chin on her shoulder. For a time they stood silently gazing out the open window. The sun had set hours ago, the crescent moon high above the horizon and stars abundant in the black sky. Unfortunately, the temperature had not dropped appreciably with the sun's absence. Even if there had been a breeze, it would be a scorching one. Heat sat heavy on the air, making breathing difficult and exertion beyond walking from one shady corner to another an exhausting endeavor.

George was sweating and he wasn't seven months pregnant!

"I shooed Sasi out of the pool and sent him to bed. I ordered it kept vacant for us and have a tray of fruit and cooled juice being prepared. Come, let me help you cool down." She nodded, numbly taking his hand and following him out of their bedchamber, down the stairs to the ground level where the bathing pool was located in a walled, private courtyard.

One of the many reasons George had selected this house when they arrived in Agra last autumn was the pool. It was a common feature, the Persian-designed, subterranean bathing chamber or outside pool of stone with fresh water piped from the nearby Yamuna River in this case. The British builders of newer houses in Agra, as well as many other larger cities in India, employed aspects of native architecture, especially those proven to provide relief from the climate that was opposite of that in England.

The brick walls encompassing the courtyard ended above George's head, square pillars rising another three feet before meeting the domed roof shading the area. Carved arches and colorful mosaic tiles in a simple pattern added an aesthetic pleasantness. The pool was not overly large or deep, but adequate for two people to immerse themselves fully.

Jharna sank into the water with a groan of relief. "If we did not have this here, I am sure I would perish. I would be forced to live in the river. In fact, I think I will stay here for the next two months."

"As nice as that sounds, you might not like shriveling up into a prune shape."

"I would be cool. That is all that matters."

Jharna laid her head onto arms crossed over the stones at the pool's edge, closed her eyes, and let her body float weightless on the surface of the refreshing water. Their nights in the pool were becoming a routine as the temperature increased in pace with Jharna's advancing gestation. George grasped each swollen foot with one of his strong hands and commenced a thorough massage from sole to shoulders. It was one of a multitude of ways he could serve her and express his adoration for the gift she was giving him. He had always considered himself an attentive partner, but daily his need to protect and nurture grew. Happily, he did all that he could to ease her burden so that together they could share in the miracle. The result was a swelling within his soul that could not be explained and an evolution in their intimate relationship, one area he thought impossible to improve upon.

George kneaded her muscles until the last knot of tension disappeared. Sliding his hands over her arms, he gently tugged her off the pool's edge and pulled her onto his lap, his hands immediately spread over the rounded ball of her abdomen where their baby lived. Jharna's head fell back onto his shoulder as she bonelessly relaxed into his embrace. She was smiling up at him, her eyes dark in the dim illumination from the four smoking torches in each corner. He gave her a glancing kiss and with a shove of one foot sent them into a lazy glide backward.

"She is quiet tonight," he whispered.

"Earlier she was dancing the *odissi*. No wonder she desires rest. Or perhaps she is as hot and miserable as her mother."

"Her nest is a perfect thermal environment. I wish I could arrange the same for you, love. Only six, maybe seven weeks more, if my calculations are accurate."

Jharna closed her eyes. "It sounds like an eternity," she whined.

"I should have foreseen your discomfort and moved us back to Junnar."

"It is hot there as well, so I would be complaining as vigorously." She patted his cheek with a wet hand. "Forgive my peevishness. It is unfair for me to unload my childish temper upon you, *priya*."

George cupped her breasts and rubbed his thumbs over her ultra-sensitive nipples. Her appreciative gasp was encouraging so he continued the erotic play, his mouth adding a sensual assault to her neck. "For better, for worse, and all that," he murmured. "I shall buck up and handle it somehow."

She smiled at his dramatic sigh and shivered at his breath dancing down her moist skin. "We have yet to make those vows, remember?"

"I did, while you weren't looking. You must have made them too because you tolerate me."

"Yes, you are tough to endure at times."

"I misbehave on purpose so that you will better appreciate me when I am wonderful. Is it working?"

"Apparently so, since I think you are wonderful a good portion of the time."

"Very sweet. Now you have gone and swelled my head even more than it already is. Be warned of the monster you create with such praise!"

"A game of chess will humble you."

"True. Tomorrow, lets plan for that. Tonight, I would rather you carry on with the 'George is wonderful' accolades and if that involves high praise for my virility, stamina, and virtuoso performance at loving you, I will accept that as well."

"Then it will take two chess defeats to properly humble you."

"More like three. I intend to be quite spectacular."

This time Jharna's laugh was easy and sincere. And her fondling hand extremely direct! George gave himself over to the glory of her body and the frenzied arousal that ensued. He fully intended to fulfill his promise.

Later, as they crawled into their bed under one light sheet and with hands clasped but otherwise not touching due to the heat precluding full-body cuddling, Jharna declared with conviction that he had indeed performed spectacularly. So much so, she said, that she would allow him to win at chess as a reward. "Besides," she murmured as she drifted into sleep, "I want to keep my spectacular, wonderful husband happy."

George's eyes flew open and for a second he could not breathe. Jharna had used the word *pati*, the Hindu word for husband, and she had never used it in referring to him. He was always *priya*—my love—and that pleased him immensely. *Pati* sent him into spasms of joy! Had she slipped unconsciously? Or had she intentionally uttered it as a promise? Suddenly he recalled her turn of phrase earlier, "We have yet to make those vows." *Yet.* Had she meant that as a clue to a change in her thinking?

He almost woke her up to ask. He had to know! But one look at her peaceful, sleeping face held him in check. The conversation could wait until tomorrow, but by God if she had changed her mind, he was dragging her to the nearest priest, rector, holy man, or Buddhist monk they could find! Sleep was difficult to reach, and once he did, his dreams were of Jharna wearing a dazzling wedding sari and jewels as she walked toward him where he stood in a fine English suit beside an Anglican priest. It was an odd scene but beautiful nevertheless. So overwhelming that his dream-self was at a loss for words. The priest kept nudging him in the shoulder to regain his attention. Jharna was staring at him with a face growing in concern at why he could not repeat the vows until finally she grabbed his arm, shaking harshly as she shouted, "George!"

George jerked and launched upward in bed. Jharna held on to his arm, her fingers a vise digging into the muscle. She was sitting propped on a pillow, eyes frightened and wide, her other hand lying on her abdomen.

"I am having pains, George. Not often, so I thought they would go away, but the last three have been stronger and closer. I am afraid! It is too soon!"

George had already jumped out of the bed and was wrapping a *dhoti* around his waist. One benefit of being a physician was the ability to snap to awareness in an instant. He had his clothes on and three candles lit before she finished the sentence.

"Stay calm, Jharna." He spoke in his low, resonant voice of professionalism. Panic and fear bubbled in his breast, but in no way was he going to let her see that! He sat on the bed beside her and laid a hand over the bulge. "How long since the last pain?"

"I am not sure. Two minutes, maybe four."

"Breathe. Just breathe. You must stay calm. Practice yoga and meditate, do you hear me? I am sure it is nothing, but just to be safe I am going to brew a tea and prepare a tonic to stop the contractions. You stay here, in bed. Do not get up. I will return in a few minutes." He bent and kissed her forehead. "Stay calm," he repeated, and then left the room.

Outside he dashed pell-mell down the stairs to the kitchen. Waking the girls who slept there, he ordered water boiled for tea, then dashed back up to the chamber where he kept his medical supplies. Over and over he kept telling himself, as he had told Jharna, that it was nothing. He didn't believe that inner voice. In the same way he had always been able to diagnose an illness or pinpoint the cause of pain after the briefest of glances, George knew Jharna was in labor. And it *was* too soon. Therefore, the focus was on stopping further progression.

Throughout the subsequent hours, George as Dr. Darcy administered every herbal treatment and Ayurvedic remedy he could think of. The *dai* Jharna had chosen was called, an elderly woman with considerable experience, her advice adding to George's. The women of the household assisted and stood vigil when he left the room where Jharna had been moved. Hindu custom warned against giving birth in the chamber one slept in, it considered ill luck and polluting. Fortunately, they already had a room prepared down the hall and furnished with a simple but comfortable bed, birthing chair, and other implements George was fervently praying would not yet need to be utilized.

Several times Jharna's pains ebbed, once for six whole hours. Each time, they would restart, the spans between growing closer. She managed to sleep during the periods of inactivity, aided by George's soothing voice and gently massaging hands. Keeping her tranquil was as important as the medications he served on a regular basis. His goal of postponing the delivery of their baby for weeks dwindled to a hope for days. When her water sac broke twenty-eight hours after she had roused him from the dream of marrying her, the hope for days was lost.

He wasn't sure what would have been worse: Jharna filled with crazed panic and fear or Jharna wearing an expression of resigned hopelessness. While the women cleaned her, George sat beside her and clasped her hands. Holding them to his mouth, he waited in silence for the intense pain to run its course. When she opened her eyes to stare at him with abject sadness, he transferred her hands to his chest, pressing them flat against his heart. Cupping her jaw with one hand, he leaned close.

"Jharna, I never lie to my patients and I won't lie to you. You know as well as I that our baby should stay within you longer. She is coming early; this is a fact we cannot change. What I need you to do is trust me. Do you trust me?"

"Yes, *priya*. I do."

"Then here are the facts. I have seen babies born early who survive. It isn't the best way, and I cannot promise all will be well. I won't promise that. What I do promise is that I will do everything in my power to help her. What *you* must do is not give up hope! Pray, Jharna. Pray and have faith. Cry if you wish. But do not give up. I need you to be strong, but most importantly our baby will need you to be strong. Do you understand?"

Tears slid down her cheeks and her lips trembled. Seconds later, a grimace marred her brow as another labor pain pulsed over her abdomen. But in those moments before she closed her eyes to concentrate on breathing, George had seen the returning obstinacy flashing behind the moisture. He smiled grimly. Jharna's tenacity was formidable, this he knew. She was by far the most capable woman he had ever met. Furthermore, she possessed a core of serenity and a backbone of steel that would help her cope with the difficulties ahead.

He only hoped he would hold up as well.

For four hours, George held her, comforting through each pain and keeping her focused. The *dai* assumed her normal duties and rituals now that the birth was imminent: chants to the gods, massages with oils, encouragement to consume warm beverages per tradition, and the intermittent physical exam to note her labor progress. George had practiced medicine long enough in India to appreciate the various customs associated with childbirth. As long as the process advanced smoothly, he was fine with allowing the *dai* to be in charge.

At the point when the birth was near, Jharna asked to deliver in a semi-sitting position. They helped her into the chair, and at that juncture, George took over. The *dai* raised her thick eyebrows and pursed her lips until they disappeared, but she said nothing. He ignored the birthing attendants who made gestures against bad luck, his focus on the woman who was about to present him with his firstborn child.

"Push, Jharna! I can see the head crowning now. Very good! Now breathe and do it again. Harder! Here she comes. Look! Can you see her, love? You are doing so well. Yes! This is it now, *priya*. We shall see if Sasi has the sister he predicted. Once more will do it. Ah! A girl! Oh my God! Look at her, Jharna. She is beautiful! A blanket, quickly."

George grabbed the warmed cloth handed to him, vigorously rubbing his daughter until she let loose with a series of wails. Jharna had collapsed onto the pillows piled behind her back, tears streaming down her cheeks. The baby continued to cry, her color gradually transforming from ashen gray to ruddy pink. George was crying too, his steady doctor's hands trembling. The helpful *dai* cut the cord, freeing the infant to be placed onto her mother's bared chest as George moved to sit on the stool beside the birth chair.

"She is so small." Jharna's voice was rough from her efforts.

"Yes, she is small. Very small. Three pounds and a bit more, I guess. But she is breathing, love. That is the important part. Keep rubbing her back. Do not let her stop crying yet. She needs to strengthen her lungs and press the fluid out. We must keep her breathing and warm above all. Warm should not be an issue in this heat, but no ritualistic bathing yet. Sorry."

The last was directed to the *dai* positioned between Jharna's knees. George expected an argument, but to his surprise she bobbed her head in agreement. Peripherally, his physician's awareness noted that the *dai* adequately assisted with the final stages of Jharna's birthing process and that she showed no signs of trauma or problems. This was a boon because he did not wish to remove his discerning eyes or stimulating hand from his daughter. One second he was Dr. Darcy, and the next he was a novice father, the emotional vacillation between concerned clinician and overjoyed papa making his head spin.

His first chance to fully examine her came when it was time for Jharna to clean and return to bed. Hindu purification rituals following childbirth were stringent. Some of these made sense, especially those involving the cleansing of her body with fragrant water laced with healing herbs and spiced oils for massage. Some were ridiculous to his Christian mindset, but they were not harmful and would ease Jharna's heart so were vital in that respect. He carried the tiny bundle to a small, padded bed near a lit brazier in the corner. It was after noon, the temperature in Agra as sweltering as ever, but George was taking no chances with his fragile daughter's life. Cautiously, he peeled the blanket edge back, his fingertips brushing over her delicate skin to test for warmth.

"There you are, my precious girl. Ah, look at you! Adorable."

He bent to kiss her tiny forehead, another light press to her cheek added before pulling away. Absently, he swiped a tear from his cheek and forced the choking emotions down so he could study her clinically. This proved much more difficult than he ever would have imagined when he saw her eyes staring directly at him. A bolt shot through his heart, scorching his entire body with a sensation of such profound love that stinging tears clouded his vision. His exhausted muscles began to quiver, and he may well have collapsed into a weeping puddle of emotion if not for two timely distractions.

One was the woman who arrived at that moment with a bowl of warm, aromatic water for the ritualistic cleansing necessary for newly born babies. The second less welcomed but more powerful distraction were the grunting exhalations the baby suddenly began making. Instantly, Dr. Darcy snapped to attention. George's experience with newborns in trouble was not as vast as patching battle wounds, but he recognized the ominous sounds of an infant struggling to keep her lungs exchanging oxygen.

A rapid general glance revealed that she was indeed small but perfectly formed. Her tiny body was proportional and not unhealthily wasted. All of her digits were present, the minute toes so adorable that he momentarily slipped into spellbound-father mode. Her skin was intact, the honey-brown tones matching the tanned skin of his hand rather than the almond shades of Jharna's skin. The grunting sound that had so alarmed him was not constant but intermittent and not accompanied by additional signs of severe distress. He knew this could change, but for the present, she was breathing adequately if a bit too fast. He was not overly anxious. Yet. So much could change with an infant this premature.

The critical reality clenched his heart, squeezing painfully. He could not allow himself to be overwhelmed by fear and irrational emotion. It was imperative that he remain calm and in control, not only for his daughter but for Jharna as well. Swallowing the lump lodged in his throat and blinking away the tears, George commenced washing the baby with the fragrant water. Her loud cries were music to his ears.

While he cleaned the blood and birth fluids from her skin, the woman aiding him began chanting in Hindi, calling upon the gods to watch over the new life. George added his own prayers, the ladies in the room accepting this as wise and a beneficial aspect of the *jatakarma* ceremony of welcome. A drop of ghee was placed onto her tongue, the clarified butter and honey mixture a hope that the parents' good qualities would be passed on to the child. George may not have ascribed to the belief in the same way tradition intended, but he was open to anything that might help her to be strong and healthy.

All of it was done swiftly, the baby dried and wrapped in a clean, warmed cloth to be taken to her mother. Refreshed as much as possible after nearly two days of pain, Jharna lifted the blanket and cuddled their baby against her breast with a sobbing sigh of relief. George stretched onto the bed beside her, tucking them both under his arm, and pressed them to his side. Later they would note that her hair was thin and wispy, and that the color was brown rather than the ebony tresses of her mother. Who she resembled most was impossible to ascertain, her features immature and diminutive, but they would memorize every inch of her from head to toe, the image never to be forgotten.

It wasn't until she wiggled her way to Jharna's breast, her tiny mouth seeking and then, with some direction, grasping the nipple for her first sucks that Jharna bravely asked the question haunting her.

"Will she live, *priya*?"

"I will never lie to you, my love," he reminded her, whispering the words as he tightened his grip on her shoulder, "so I have to confess that I do not know. She is very small and immature. She breathes on her own, but it is slightly labored. Not as badly as I feared, however, and that is a positive. We can keep her warm easily enough between your body and mine. She will stay in contact with the people who love her most. That is essential. My greatest concern is weakness and inability to nurse."

"She knows what to do but tires already."

"Yes. But often times mature infants do that at first, is that not true, *dai*?" The midwife nodded at his hopeful query, her eyes unreadable. "We will be diligent. And I will do everything I can think of, Jharna. You know I will!"

"I know."

Her weary, sad tones broke his heart. He desperately wanted to make promises and instill hope. He wanted someone to say the same to him, to tell him with confidence that their tiny baby would be just fine. For one of the few times in his life, he wanted the delusion, wanted to toss fact out the window and cling to ignorant optimism. If only he could.

"She is beautiful, isn't she?"

Jharna's declaration broke into his dark thoughts. He peeled the blanket away from his sleeping baby's face, studying her closely for the first time as a father and not a doctor. Despite the resident fear, his heart leapt and he smiled.

"She looks like her mother. Beautiful. Delicate. A flawless angel. Cherished. Always and no matter what, she is cherished."

He laid his hand over her head, the whole of her round skull fitting underneath his palm, and caressed one satiny cheek with his thumb. Jharna traced her fingertip alongside his.

"You have chosen her name, as is custom." Jharna tilted her head back and smiled at the startled expression on his face. "The *pita* chooses the name. Bhrithi. Cherished. It is perfect."

George nodded slowly. "Yes, it is perfect. Bhrithi. Our cherished daughter. Bhrithi Alexis Dhamdhere Darcy."

⁓ꙮ⁓

There were several times in George's life when he would struggle to accept fate. During those times, he held on by a thin thread to his faith in a God who was in control, loving, and omnisciently seeing how everything works for the best. Not permitting the thread to break so that he fell into a state of despair and disbelief became the greatest of trials. Afterward, when the thread did not break but was miraculously reinforced with renewed fibers knit into a stronger mesh than before, he would know that God was real, because only a divine being could have saved him from the fall. Only a God who personally loved him could have kept him from the darkness. Only a God who touched his heart, speaking to him in a quiet but persistent manner could help him see beyond the pain to what was beautiful. Learning to be thankful for what *was* rather than what *might have been* could only be taught by a loving, wise Creator.

In the weeks and months that followed the death of his daughter, Bhrithi, George would again see this truth come to pass. It was a bitter truth, one he would rather not learn since it meant losing her in the process. Nevertheless, amid the pain he was aware of his God's presence and thankful for the comfort mercifully granted.

Bhrithi lived for eight days.

It wasn't enough. Not nearly enough.

But it was more than he had imagined a year before.

For too long, most of his adult life, in fact, the possibility of having a child did not appear to be in the cards. George had given up on a dream he had not even been aware he held. In comparison to nothing, eight days was a glorious blessing. Not that he accepted this immediately. While dangling on the thread of his consuming grief, he did not see this at all.

Gradually, in some ways almost against his will, when self-pity sounded like the preferable choice, George started to see the blessings. Every time he whispered or cried her name—Bhrithi—he would *feel* the meaning underneath.

Cherished.

Oh! Indeed she was cherished!

He cherished every time she opened her thickly lashed eyes, the midnight-blue orbs scanning over his face and reaching into his soul.

He cherished every cry, whether of hunger or vexation, whether robust or feeble; her voice was unique.

He cherished all the minutes of every hour when he held her naked body cuddled warmly against his chest. Her slowly weakening heartbeat and shallow breaths were bolstered by his sturdiness. Her tiny fingers curled around the hairs on his chest and her miniature toes pressing into the skin of his abdomen the sweetest of sensations.

He cherished the vision of Bhrithi nestled against Jharna's breast and the beatific expression that would wash over his precious lover's face as she nursed or even when she merely held their sleeping baby.

They had known from the beginning, deep inside, that she was not destined to dwell with them for long. It was bitter indeed, and not openly verbalized for days while George fought to improve her stamina with all the knowledge he possessed. Tonics dribbled carefully into her mouth, Ayurvedic massage with healing oils, Jharna's breast milk fortified and given to her when she was too weak to suck. All this and more was done.

Was it pointless? Or had it given them the eight days that would forever be viewed as a blessing? Eventually, George and Jharna would agree that the latter was the truth. She was a blessing. Her short life touched them and was a gift that enhanced the love they shared. If ever George doubted this—and he rarely did—he would remember the day when Jharna proved the extent of her understanding of his soul.

"George, I know you do not wish to leave, but you must do something for me. And for you. No, listen. You must go take Bhrithi to the church you attend for worshipping your God and you must have her baptized. You have permitted all of my Hindu customs, performed some of them yourself, but none that are vital to you. It must be done or you will regret it later. I cannot bear to witness your sadness in thinking your daughter will not be in your heaven with your ancestors. Or that your God does not know her if her name is not written in the church's book."

In the end, the rector came to the house and blessed Bhrithi without the need for her to go far. George was not overly superstitious about such things, his heart sure that her soul would ascend to heaven, probably joining Alex on his cloud, as he had always joked. It wasn't only the ceremony itself that moved him but that Jharna had been willing to part from her baby and risk further damage to her health for the sake of George's peace of mind.

He had never loved her more and did not think he ever would. But Jharna was a woman who had forever surprised him and surpassed his expectations.

They were together when Bhrithi breathed her final breath. Their daughter was cradled in Jharna's arms, Jharna cradled in George's, and both their hands were touching her when she quietly passed. Sasi and Nimesh sat nearby, their tears joining in. Together, the family grieved. Together, they tended to the Hindu purification rituals, dressed her in a colorful gown, and wrapped her in a white linen shroud before laying her in a beautifully wrought casket of rosewood and silver. Together, they insisted on upholding George's wish to have her buried as a Christian. Together, they made the trip back to Junnar so she could rest at their home. Together, they comforted each other.

On a sultry evening in late June, George sat on the bench located near Bhrithi's grave in a shady plot under a giant, flowering ashoka tree. The location had been chosen purposefully, not only because the area was tranquil and secluded, but also because the tree, known as the "sorrowless tree" and planted around temples, was revered by Hindus as a symbol of love. Oddly enough, this place was one he frequently had retreated to when he sought solitude and did not feel like walking to the stone-skipping pond further on down the trail. He had a letter in his hand and his journal on the bench beside him. He had no intention of addressing the journal to his daughter, however. She was missed profoundly but had died too young for him to share his adult musings with. He would continue to tell his father of the latest events in his life and unload his innermost thoughts. If the departed Mr. Darcy wished to share with his granddaughter in heaven—the two probably sitting with Alex and laughing together at the antics of George Darcy—that was fine by him! It comforted him to imagine it, as nonsensical as the vision was.

Instead, he read the letter that had arrived from James that day. It was filled with updates on Fitzwilliam's success at Cambridge, Georgiana's skill on the pianoforte, news of extended friends and family, and the usual daily activities around Pemberley.

"Your Uncle James still sounds sad, Bhrithi. At least he has moved on and learned to overcome the worst of his grief. I know how difficult that is—a wife or beloved daughter. I am not sure it is easier either way." He paused, sighing deeply before shaking himself and continuing in a lighter tone. "I do wish you could have seen Pemberley, *beti*." *My daughter.* "You would have adored Pemberley. I can see you dashing across the meadows banking the River Derwent. I am sure heaven has marvelous fields of green grass, probably so vividly green they would hurt mortal eyes. Yet I cannot fathom any place lovelier than Pemberley. Don't tell God I said that though, or he may not let me enter the pearly gates! I would have taught you to ride a pony, a gentle mare like the one Georgiana was learning to ride when last I visited. James says that they had nearly a foot of snow in one fall this past winter. Hard to imagine. I think I have forgotten what snow feels like, which suits me just fine if you must know. I never was all that fond of the frigid cold of winter in England."

"May I interrupt?"

George looked up with a smile. "Of course!" He patted the bench, Jharna sitting down and instantly leaning into his side. "I was reading James's letter aloud. Silly, I know, but it comforts me to talk to her."

"It isn't silly at all, George. We know she is not here, not really. But wherever she is, your heaven or in *pitr-loka* with my ancestors, I think she is listening. And don't tell my gods I said this, but I think they may well be the same place."

George chuckled and then kissed her forehead. Jharna lifted her face and moved into the kiss, covering his lips with hers in a tender but pointed exchange that left him breathing a bit heavier than normal.

"I came to tell you dinner is waiting. Sasi thinks he is going to die if forced to wait longer than another ten minutes. But that is long enough for me to also tell you that after dinner, I wish to retire straightaway to our bed and have you all to myself."

He was smiling, grinning actually, and, despite his own rumbling stomach, would have willingly foregone food if she demanded it. But he had to be sure. So he clasped her chin and tilted her face away so he could better see her.

"Are you sure, Jharna? It has only been five weeks since the birth. And not a normal five weeks, as we know."

"I am fine. My heart will take a long while to heal, as will yours, *priya*. I believe loving each other will help. I have missed your touch and never want to lose the pleasure found in your arms."

They kissed far longer than the ten-minute limit Sasi and his adolescent appetite had set! Finally they pulled apart. Passion simmered with desire shooting sparks across their skin and love burrowing deeper into their wounded hearts. Together, as always, they would heal.

They rose, hand in hand, and after a brief pause to stare at the marble cross that bore their daughter's full name, they turned and walked into the house in Junnar that was their home.

George's Memoirs
May 27, 1811

James, I have seen innumerable paintings of the Himalayas and none of them have done justice to the reality of seeing them with my own eyes. Remember when we traveled to Austria with our sister Mary and her new husband Baron Oeggl? The Alps are amazing, no question about it. I remember feeling small and insignificant. Of course, I was not as tall then as I am now, but I do not think that makes much difference when compared to mountains that must be tens of thousands of feet high. It boggles the mind. There are a few persons in our party who itch to veer closer or even climb to the snowy peaks. Insane if you ask me. I can't fathom that one will ever be able to manage such a feat. Not sure one should try, to be honest. I pride myself on being a brave man, but getting any nearer to all that snow isn't a challenge my psyche needs to prove my manliness! This whole trip has been a bit too cold for my taste, not that I would change a thing. Well, maybe wearing that horrid suit while in Kathmandu. I still can't believe I consented to do such a thing. And a cravat too. Gah! Anoop was panicked that I was going to expect him to tie the bloody thing. I panicked a bit as well when I could not for the life of me remember how to drape the nasty thing, let alone knot it so that it wasn't a mess. Luckily, Colonel Fisher volunteered to assist, which was humiliating. You would have been in hysterics, James. And there was Jharna looking divine and comfortable in her sari. I may have actually hated her for a second or two there. How I manage to become entangled in these diplomatic, political affairs when I hate them is beyond me. And you can just shut your mouth right now, Brother! No comments are welcome!

We left the Kathmandu Valley behind and climbed northward into the mountainous zones. Our Sherpa guides know the Khumbu region and villages well. Thank goodness for that. I am picking up the Nepali language in pieces. Certainly not well enough to manage on my own. Hindi speakers are rare and English speakers nonexistent, so we definitely need our Sherpas for translating, but also to serve as mediators. Even with that, we are encountering a great deal of suspicion when it comes to medicine. The people are unfailingly polite and hospitable, but simply not trusting or interested in our healing skills. So we do more standing back and watching their techniques. I have learned a few new useful skills and there is a wealth of unique vegetation that I am collecting for later study. But for the most part, their methods are crude and in some cases downright barbaric. Yet, somehow they have survived in this harsh climate and elevation for eons so who am I to be overly judgmental?

So it has evolved into a laggardly trek through lush terrain with visually stunning vistas every direction you gaze. Ah, James! I am forever amazed by my adopted country! Initially I didn't relish being dragged away from the comfort of Junnar. I admit I liked being relatively stationary with the only traveling the times McIntyre and the EIC enticed me to Bombay. And yes, I confess I have grown a bit soft and am anxious to reach civilized cities if for no other reason than a cushioned bed to better love Jharna in. Nevertheless, I am abundantly thankful that this expedition presented itself. I can't imagine living in India, traveling as I have, and then to say I did not enter Nepal and touch the foot of the greatest mountain range on earth. The tallest mountain, the one called Sagarmatha, looms on the northern horizon. It fills the sky! Unbelievable, it is. I am not an adequate writer to describe it so won't try. Jharna has drawn a dozen pages of Sagarmatha alone, from various angles, so forgetting it won't be possible.

We are now at a village named Jubbing and will leave on the morrow. The air is thin at this elevation. We are better adapted to the atmosphere, cold, and ruggedness than when we started this journey, yet it does require recuperation periods in between. I refuse to accept that my age may have something to do with it! I wrote that mainly to beat you to the insult first, James. I know you were planning it. In truth I haven't felt this fit in a few years. I think I was growing weak in my cozy life in Junnar. Happy, yes, as I still am, but adventure was necessary to keep the mind sharp and body strong. Jharna is as tough as me, I am proud to say. We are invigorated. Of course, I would be embarrassed to admit otherwise when some of our guides are older than us and the Sherpas live to a surprisingly advanced age.

All that being said and true as it stands, we shall leave here and head south, catching the Koshi River near Dhulan. Jharna is firm on reaching the Ganges in time to celebrate the avatarana. *A river is a river as far as I am concerned, but I know the Ganges is more to Hindus. It has been her dream to partake of the* avatarana, *or Descent of the Ganges, and you know I can't deny my lovely* priya *anything if it is within my power to grant it. We will take our time with it, but if all goes well and we do not change our minds, should be in Calcutta by the end of summer. Or sooner. Who knows? I am opting for sooner, mainly in hopes that I have had correspondence from Pemberley. Sasi has promised to forward anything I receive to the EIC headquarters.*

I need to hear from Fitzwilliam that he is well. Georgiana too. He was so devastated at your death, James. Hell, we all were! I still am. I address my journal to you as has become my custom for whatever bizarre reason, but it feels wrong. Seriously wrong. How can you be dead, James? A few years ago, after Anne died, I half expected you to follow her. I suppose you did, in a sense. It just took six years. Your heart never healed, did it, my brother? Well, you have it good now, so I should not begrudge you being with Anne and Father and Alex. Hopefully you are sharing a bit of love with my Bhrithi. If it is any consolation, I will do my best to help your children. Not sure how when I am so far away. I am writing as often as I can. Silly ramblings of Nepal and so on. I have nothing to offer in regards to estate management, God knows! Luckily, William has Mr. Wickham. He is an excellent steward who will teach him well. And of course William is an exceptional young man. I know he feels overwhelmed. I can read it between the lines of his letters. He pretends otherwise, naturally. Far too much pride to confess he is drowning! Then again, a man as intelligent and strong as your son will do just fine, I am sure of it. Probably not much that would break his steel core of discipline unless it is a woman. Women can turn the mightiest of us into poetry-spouting lapdogs! It doesn't help that we like it that way. Ha! I'll pray romance for William holds off for a spell though. One head-spinning problem at a time is enough.

And speaking of women, my delightful enchantress is calling my name and the tug upon my heart cannot be resisted. Poetry! See what happens? Kiss Anne for me.

CHAPTER ELEVEN

Calcutta

NOVEMBER 1812

G EORGE STOOD NAKED BEFORE the tall mirror in the corner of
his dressing room, turning his face side to side. One last scrape
of the razor to a missed whisker patch and he was satisfied. The
blade he laid neatly onto the commode tray before grabbing the wet towel
and wiping the soap away. For a minute, he held the cloth over his face, eyes
closed and breathing steady as the warm moisture seeped into his skin and
through his nostrils. It was a daily routine and had been for years. George
rose from bed and started his day with body stretches and breathing exercises.
This activity was a signal to Anoop, who then poured heated water into two
bowls sitting next to a tray with his *haakim*'s toilette implements, soap, towels,
and various lotions and colognes. Anoop insisted on preparing everything
but did honor George's command to be left alone and tend to his personal
needs himself. It was a system that worked, and the truth was that George
liked it.

Putting the towel down, George unstoppered one of the five bottles situated in a precise row. He took a whiff of the liquid, even though he knew it was
his favorite fragrance, and proceeded to apply it to his smooth cheeks, adding a
bit to his freshly washed neck and chest.

Next came the comb to his hair, but after three strokes he paused, lips
pursed and brow furrowed, as he submitted to a brutal visual analysis. *I need*

a haircut, was the first honest appraisal. George had finally bid farewell to his last-century ponytail, Jharna cutting and styling his thick brown hair so it ended at the nape of his neck. When the wavy locks behaved themselves, his part was on the left side, hair sweeping heavily over his high forehead and joining the rest of his hair that flowed in natural, loose curls. He had mourned his shorn locks and absence of a colorful tie for about a week before realizing he loved the looser, freer style. It took him another month before he relinquished the pretend sadness that garnered some sympathy. Not a single gray hair as yet, the brown a rich chestnut with a few lighter streaks from the harsh sun. No balding spots or receding hairline, and considering his father had possessed a full head of hair all his life, the odds were in his favor.

More for the sake of clinical assessment rather than vanity, George continued his scrutiny, ticking items off one by one.

A couple of tiny lines at the outer corners of his azure eyes but no other wrinkles. Bone structure as sharp as ever with prominent cheekbones and squared jaw unchanged. Teeth straight, white, and all still present. *Thank goodness.* George was definitely vain about his smile, full lips and large teeth proudly displayed in that cocky grin he knew well was infectious and charming. Apparently, tough bones and teeth went together, a thorough scan over his body affirming that his skeletal structure was unbent and sturdy, all six feet, three inches of him standing tall. George had never experienced a broken bone and only one tiny chip to a tooth, the latter a result of Rathore insisting on jumping a ravine without being one hundred percent sure the terrain on the other side was safe. Okay, George had wanted to jump the ravine too, but shouldn't animals have better sense in these matters?

Ever a man not overly muscular but more on the lean side, George did not expect a time in his life when excessive weight would be a burden. There was a deception here, however. George's angular lankiness gave the impression of weakness, especially with the loose garments he wore, as opposed to the excessively tight breeches and padded jackets Englishmen were wearing these days, thanks to the Prince Regent and his dandified cronies. The truth was that while thin of physique, George was stalwart and tough with an athletic nimbleness. His vivacity frequently exhausted men half his age and his strength surprised everyone. The mystery was revealed in the muscles that while not bulky as some, were defined and sinewy.

Taken as a whole, George was satisfied with what he saw reflected in the mirror. Flaunting a pompous, arrogant attitude was a hallmark of George's personality, as was being ostentatious and eccentric. He cultivated the demeanor, but despite how it may have seemed, it was more ruse than who he truly was. Oh, Dr. George Darcy was tipped to the prideful side, no doubt, but mostly in regards to his medical talents. He wasn't nearly as eccentric as he was simply unconcerned with what anyone thought of him. This was why he flagrantly mocked his idiosyncrasies and pretensions, knowing full well that while doing so, he was putting people at ease and spreading joy.

Still, it was comforting to know the body was holding up against the stresses of life and ticking time.

"Not too bad for a man of five and forty!"

"No, not bad in the least. I personally believe you have improved with age."

He glanced over his shoulder at Jharna, lifting a brow. "Improved?"

"Maturity suits you."

He turned around, tossing his head so that his hair fluttered. "Are you intimating that I am even more outrageously handsome than I was in my twenties?" He grinned, raising his chin and posing like a Greek statue.

"You were passably acceptable when I met you, if a terrible fop."

"A fop? Me? Never!"

"Is that not the correct English word?"

"If you mean a man who is vain and overly concerned with his appearance and attire, then yes, although I have no clue how that applies to me."

She had reached him by then, laughing as she clasped his face between her hands, fingertips lightly tracing the wrinkles by his eyes. "Maturity in your exterior but just as silly within."

"You mean boyishly charming and irresistible, right?" George pulled her close, opening the robe she wore and slipping his hands inside.

She encircled his shoulders, sighing at the sensation of his warm hands sliding over her waist and the pressure of his smiling lips on her jaw. "As much as I hate to contribute to your conceit, I must say yes."

"As I suspected." Clutching her bottom, George drew her tightly against his body. "Shall I show you all the ways I have improved with age, my dear? I know you can't resist these charms."

"I need to add incorrigible to your character list as well."

"As a positive or a negative?"

"It depends on the moment. Are you not supposed to be at Native Hospital early this morning?"

"The new EIC physicians won't be there until closer to noon, and it isn't like they are going to terminate me if I am late. Besides, it is too late to worry about that now, my love." And indeed it was. George had already removed her robe, sat her on the cushioned stool he used when donning his shoes, and was on his knees between her open legs, kissing his way down her body. "You should never have entered my dressing area. Admit it, you knew I was naked in here and the vision was a magnetic enticement you could not resist."

"I would try to deny it if I thought you would believe me."

George's laughter was a rumbling roll over her breast. Appointments and hospital timetables shoved aside, he leisurely played with her flesh, knowing she was receiving double enjoyment due to the tall mirror situated at an angle where she could see as well as feel. It hadn't been arranged on purpose, the discovery an accidental one made months ago but since utilized to great advantage numerous times. Of course, he was correct that she had come here specifically for this purpose, the teasing they enjoyed part of the fun.

Lifting the leg closest to the mirror over his shoulder, George eased his way inside her, their eyes on the reflected image of bodies joined and moving together.

"Ah, *priya*," he groaned, "the irresistibleness goes both directions, as does the improving with age. I love you, Jharna. More today than ever."

Dr. Darcy was whistling when he entered the front doors of Calcutta Native Hospital nearly two hours later.

George Darcy in a feisty, ebullient mood was nothing surprising. Nor was the finely woven *sherwani* of navy blue with maroon trimming worn over a paler blue *shalwar kameez* anything worth noting. This was the East India Company hospital exclusively for the care of Indian citizens, so most of the staff were natives, thus George's attire was not all that unusual. What was rare was to see an Englishman as vibrantly dressed and rarer still to find one who possessed his verve and forceful personality. Nevertheless, the bulk of the people who worked at Native Hospital, as well as those at Calcutta General Hospital where Europeans were treated, had grown familiar with Dr. Darcy. A few shook their heads or pursed their lips, but the vast majority at either facility smiled when he appeared, hearts lifting as if a cleansing breeze had blown in with him.

"Good morning, Mr. Bhatt! How are you this fine day? What have I missed?" He snatched two apples off the basket sitting on the front desk, tossed one blindly over his shoulder to Anoop, who caught it deftly, and bit into the other as Mr. Bhatt, the receptionist, greeted them with *namaste* and a bow before answering pleasantly.

"Good morning, Dr. Darcy. Or should I say 'good almost noon'? I am well, thank you for asking. And all you have missed is Dr. Parsall's weekly visit."

"Drat! Was that today?"

Mr. Bhatt hid his smile and did not look at Anoop, who was rolled his eyes and shook his head. "Yes, *Vaidya*. It was today, as it is every Monday and has been for a number of years now."

"Has it? Extraordinary! How did I not know that? Anoop, be sure to make a note so I won't miss the director's visit next week. Is Shoolbred in his office? I am sure he will fill me in on the critical information I missed by not being here earlier. As long as we are still open for business, I can save the valuable enlightenment for later. We are still open for business, aren't we?"

"Indeed, Dr. Darcy. We are, and your patients await. Dr. Koneru is in the infectious ward prepared to update you."

George nodded, clapping the receptionist on the shoulder before grabbing another apple and heading into the hospital ward.

Waving and halting for brief chats with a number of orderlies, doctors, and patients along the way, George and Anoop finally parted the thick curtain at the end of a long hallway blocking the large building assigned exclusively for those patients with obvious illnesses of a type known to be transmittable. No one fully understood the intricacies involved with contagion but there wasn't a doctor alive who had not seen diseases like measles or typhus spread as a wildfire to whole families or communities. Furious debates raged as to how or why, and there were far too many men of science who flat refused to accept that they were the cause of directly transmitting infections, especially those within wounds. However, gradually, advances were being made in understanding, and although isolation served more to contain a possible epidemic rather than cure the individual patient, it was a place to start. Thus the enormous wing was sectioned into smaller areas either curtained or separated by walls for the various diseases.

Dr. Koneru was standing next to Dr. Maqbool, sheaths of papers in their hands. In unison, they glanced up when George approached.

"*Namaste*, Dr. Darcy. We have three cases of a pox that came in over the night." Dr. Koneru handed the paper to George with one hand, pointing to the beds on his right with the other. "All children, as you can see, and from the same family. Parents panicked, sure it was smallpox."

"You think otherwise?"

"The smaller lesion size and lack of overt illness other than a mild fever and malaise suggest the so-named chicken pox variety. Their worst complaint was pruritis, which we have relieved with a paste of kasaundi root and kanji. Now their complaint is boredom."

George laughed. "Yes. I know how rapidly boys grow bored, even when ill. Keep them here for the day, just in case. If the itchiness grows unbearable even with the paste, try juice of amaltas leaves or zinc oxide. If nothing else, they can alleviate their boredom by painting themselves white. Then you would really scare the girls, right?" The latter addressed to the youths, who laughed and nodded.

They moved to the next area, and then onward around the ward. Collaboration in most cases, Dr. Darcy needing only to be informed of changes and offering new orders when appropriate. Unafraid to touch patients, George frequently interacted by examining, asking questions, changing dressings, and whatever else he deemed necessary. Anoop took notes while others scurried to fulfill his instructions or fetch requested items.

When Dr. Shoolbred, superintendent and chief surgeon of Calcutta Native Hospital, found Dr. Darcy, the lanky physician was sitting cross-legged on a bed with a five-year-old girl in his lap. George had his *sherwani* open and the little girl was leaning with her ear pressed against his left chest. Crossing his arms after an amused exchange with the girl's mother, Dr. Shoolbred waited and observed.

"What do you hear? Galloping camels?"

"No!" She giggled. "Boom booms like a drum."

"Fast and at a beat you can dance the *bihu*?"

"No, silly." More giggling. "Slow and dull."

"Dull, am I? Well, that is disconcerting. Hopefully your chest provides better sounds. Can I listen now?"

She nodded, standing up so Dr. Darcy could easily reach her thin chest. "Take as many deep breaths as you can. Oh my! You will not believe what I hear in there, Ekaa!"

"What, *Vaidya*?"

"A strong, fast heart. Perfect to dance the *bihu*. And better yet, lots of whooshing air. When did you last cough?"

"In the night. Woke me up," she said with a pout. "Not today though. Am I better now? Can I go home with *mata-jee*?"

"I think you can. I will send medicine with your *mata-jee* just in case the whooping cough happens. Continue to rest for a few days, promise me, Ekaa? Good. Your siblings can pamper you for a while, how is that?"

He stood, ruffling her hair and patting one rosy cheek before turning to the superintendent as he buttoned his *sherwani*.

"Dr. Shoolbred! Excellent to see you."

"Glad you found your way into the hospital today, Darcy."

"I have been here for hours and hours. Tending to patients. Sorry we didn't encounter each other sooner. It is easy to miss people in a facility this grand."

"Yes, I suppose it must be since you missed the director's inspection and apparently have not seen the cluster of men standing at the end of the ward."

"Oh I saw them! They are rather conspicuous after all. I figured they were enjoying the respite from boring lectures, directions to places they won't be able to find tomorrow, and endless introductions to people they won't remember. Besides, they probably don't know Hindi, so I only would have confused them."

"You confuse everyone, Darcy, English or Hindi, but you are the Chief of Infectious Diseases and Liaison for Ayurvedic Medicine—"

"Both titles I resisted, if you recall, John. I was perfectly content to be the Handsome Physician of Fine Garments, but you wouldn't allow it."

"You are incorrigible."

"I am hearing that quite often lately. I rather like it!"

Dr. Shoolbred chuckled and gestured with his head toward the eight men standing in a semicircle and watching the exchange they could not hear. "Just get it over with. It won't be too painful."

George grimaced but started walking, Dr. Shoolbred alongside. "Not so sure about that. They are going to ask me incessant questions and expect hand-holding for the next month."

"Didn't you when you first arrived in Bombay?"

"No."

Shoolbred started a bit at the automatic, peremptory answer. He looked up at the taller physician, expecting to see a jesting expression, but George was studying the new EIC recruits with the fierce, eagle-eyed gaze they were as familiar with as the jocular one. *No, he probably didn't,* Dr. Shoolbred decided. Rarely had he met a medical person as confident as Dr. George Darcy, and while it was logical to assume it the result of twenty-plus years practicing, Dr. Shoolbred's association with the renowned physician for the past year had revealed a genius that he knew transcended the normal. More than that, in the superintendent's nearly forty years as a surgeon in multiple capacities, he had only met a handful of physicians who possessed the gift for diagnosis Dr. George Darcy did.

With that in mind, he carefully watched the exchange that took place over the subsequent minutes as he introduced each of the eight men.

The recruits were of varying ages and experience, four barely finished with their education and the other four ranging from three to ten years practicing. Five were English, one Welsh, one Frenchman, and one Spaniard. All of them had arrived in Calcutta over a month ago, working since then at General Hospital so as to acclimatize to the Indian environment while treating in a style familiar to them and on people they could converse with. As with everywhere in life, gossip filtered through the halls of a hospital, and it was normal for one to ask questions and listen, especially when new. Therefore, Dr. Shoolbred knew before looking at any of their faces that they had heard of Dr. Darcy or even caught a glimpse of him since he was popular there as well. Most likely, they had assumed the stories were exaggerated, just as previous new staff had. They had been standing here for forty-five minutes watching him in action, but if that weren't already enough, they would soon learn they were wrong in their assumptions on all fronts.

Dr. Darcy greeted each one as they were introduced, inclining his head respectfully. All traces of flippancy were gone, his face firm and eyes penetrating. The air about him was professional and friendly at the same time. He was polite, serious, and unthreatening. The questions he asked of each man were more conversational than direct, his queries on their education and background general. He didn't lecture or talk about the hospital or the medical personnel. He didn't drill them on diseases or surgical techniques. *That will come later*, Dr. Shoolbred thought.

Shoolbred noted the subtle signs of Dr. Darcy already forming opinions of their potential, opinions he would be willing to change if proven wrong—Shoolbred knew his colleague to be fair in that regard—but then he was rarely wrong and his impressions gave the administration vital information for assignments. It was one of the reasons new recruits were brought to him, a fact Dr. Darcy was aware of.

For the next three hours, Dr. Darcy toured the surgeons around the hospital. He didn't show them a single storage cabinet or linen closet. How they learned that was of no interest to him unless they didn't learn swiftly, at which point they would be excused. Nor did he translate very often. They would either learn the language, asking for help in the meantime, or end up catering to European patients. Either was fine by him. He simply wasn't going to waste his time at the present on someone with zero aptitude. What he did do was tend to his patients and had them assist. In doing this, he taught about the unique illnesses and injuries they would see in India, and gave an overview of indigenous treatments and therapies they would be expected to respect at the least. In this he was crystal clear, the look he gave each man allowing no room for confusion over what his tolerance was if this rule was broken at Native Hospital.

"We treat the Indian people here, employing exactly the same standards and medications and skills as at General. What we also do is work with the local, native physicians and holy men. It is a cultural melding of medicine, some that work and some that don't, but until you try it, you will never know."

Each surgeon was dirty and exhausted by the time they left, piling into the three *tangas* that would convey them back to the residential compound. George stood in the foyer, his arms crossed over his chest and eyes watching the wagons wheel away. Dr. Shoolbred remained silent, waiting for what he suspected was coming after trailing along most of the afternoon. Still, the individual interest surprised him.

"Tell me about the Spaniard. Penaflor, was it?"

"Correct. Dr. Raul Penaflor Aleman de Vigo. I think there is more to his name than that, but I can't recall it. As he told you, he is not but two years out of university. His credentials are excellent, what we know of them that is."

"What do you mean?"

Dr. Shoolbred shrugged. "Nothing worrisome. Merely that being a Spaniard, he didn't come through Company Headquarters in London. He connected through representatives in Madrid, so the documentation isn't as complete as usual. Want me to dig a bit more?"

George waved his hand, turning to head back into the ward. "Don't care. Send Drs. Penaflor, Gwythur, and Lumley back tomorrow. The others are competent but not for Native Hospital."

Then he was through the doors, leaving a grinning Dr. Shoolbred behind.

George had been to the Calcutta Government House once before in October of 1811, two months after he and Jharna had arrived in Calcutta. At that time, they were on holiday, spending their time exploring the city and region surrounding while George volunteered in a number of medical outlets, some EIC controlled and some not. He had not met Governor-General Lord Minto, the controller of foreign policy for the British East India Company, and was mildly surprised the important man knew of him, let alone wanted to speak with him. Few would accuse Dr. Darcy of being humble, and they would be correct, yet when asked by Lord Minto personally to accept a permanent position with the Bengal Presidency of EIC, not only as a staff physician but also in a managerial role at the hospitals and as a professor of languages and medicine at Fort William College, George was unexpectedly touched. Nevertheless, it was after discussing the commitment with Jharna and then negotiating for only a two-year contract that he agreed. Since then, his interactions with Lord Minto consisted of a handful of social engagements and nothing else.

This sunny morning in March of 1813 began as every other except for Mr. Bhatt greeting him with an envelope bearing the Governor-General's seal with a summons inside for an audience with Lord Minto that afternoon at two o'clock.

Interesting!

He wasn't worried though. He knew his record was excellent, for one thing, but mostly because, like everyone in Calcutta, he was aware of the political changes on the horizon. Sure enough, the chamber he was escorted to contained several men, including Lord Minto and his soon-to-be successor, the Marquess of Hastings. Having assumed they had another position of some kind they wanted him to fill, George was taken aback when the request was of an entirely different nature.

After the typical pleasantries, introductions, and serving of refreshments, Lord Minto opened the topic. "Dr. Darcy, as I am sure you know, I will be vacating these offices soon. The Council and I are in the process of orientating Lord Hastings to ensure smooth transition into his leadership. He has agreed to honor an ambassadorial expedition the Council has been discussing for a number of months now and that is to Hill Tipperah, or Tripura as they prefer."

"We have a stable relationship with the prince and there are British contacts in the area," Lord Hastings explained. "Nothing official, nor are we seeking this. We are not exerting our influence, Dr. Darcy. Tripura is neutral and sovereign. They are, however, nestled between Burma and Assam, two principalities not as stable. Our goal is to extend our hand, so to speak, and assure we are closely monitoring the situations without."

"Your role," Lord Minto took over, "is as it ever has been: that of a medical practitioner. Your services would include overseeing the health of our envoy as well as an outreach to the Tripuri people if possible. You have, by far, the most experience when it comes to that sort of activity. Now, your questions for us."

"How long?"

"Two months at the most."

"Can my lady accompany me?"

The two lords exchanged glances, Lord Minto answering, "It is unusual to include a woman, Dr. Darcy. However, I am aware that your lady is of the royal Maratha house and that she has accompanied you on your travels. I suppose we can arrange this then, if it is the contingent?"

George nodded. "It is, my lord. And I have one other. I wish to take an associate. Dr. Raul Penaflor."

Again the two men exchanged glances, Lord Minto answering, "I am not familiar with Dr. Penaflor, but if in your judgment a second physician is sensible, or even a third, we trust your choice."

"No, one will do and Dr. Penaflor is the best choice. Thank you."

Dr. Shoolbred was the only one not surprised by Dr. Darcy's decision to include Dr. Penaflor. Even George wondered at his spontaneous request.

"I had no idea what they had up their collective sleeves, Jharna, so it isn't like I consciously was thinking of Dr. Penaflor. I blurted without thinking and I never do that!"

"You have spoken highly of him on several occasions."

"Have I?"

Jharna laughed at his wide-eyed gape. "Yes, you have. You rarely mention those you work with, unless it is to criticize their incompetence. Dr. Penaflor must be unique. Reminds me of another young doctor who once impressed an older, experienced doctor, so much so that he was hunted down until accepting his destiny."

"This is nothing like Kshitij and me," George grunted. "I am thankful he pursued me to be sure. I simply have no desire to have an apprentice or a partner so won't be doing any hunting. Anoop tagging along is worry enough! No, Penaflor is on his own. If he wants to thank me for the opportunity, that is fine, but he better not expect more."

"Somehow I doubt it is young Dr. Penaflor who will be the one expecting more, *priya*. You are the exacting one, as I am certain he knows. And if he reaches or exceeds your standards, you may well change your mind."

George waved that nonsense away, turning the topic to his elation over an adventure to a new region with her.

As for Dr. Penaflor, Dr. Shoolbred was correct that the new doctors had heard of Dr. Darcy well before meeting him four months prior. Raul Penaflor hadn't been an accredited physician for long, but he did have a lifetime of exposure to commanding, proficient leaders so had instantly recognized that the doctor with the eccentric demeanor and daunting reputation was of the same mold. Therefore, being chosen to tend patients at Native Hospital was an honor he fully appreciated. He intended to prove himself worthy of the assignment and to learn all that was humanly possible in however long fate granted him with Dr. Darcy as well as the other healers. So naturally, he jumped at the chance to join the expedition to Tripura. It was an opportunity to observe Dr. Darcy up close and personal for an extended time, and he was abundantly thankful for that. However, equally important to him was the exhilarating prospect of using his excellent healing skills to help those who may not have been fortunate in having access to competent doctors.

It was this drive and confidence that intrigued George no matter how forcefully he denied it. Dr. Penaflor was unique, George having detected it within the first fifteen minutes of meeting him. The Spaniard impressed him, and that was not an easy feat. In time, the level of impression built, as did his respect for Dr. Penaflor as a person. The two months traveling together hardened the foundation laid in those first months. After their return from Tripura, George assigned him increasingly difficult patients, selected him for tricky surgeries, scheduled him longer hours, grilled him with complicated questions, and challenged him with complex dilemmas. Every test George threw at him, some downright brutal, was met head on and overcome. George ignored the rumors that he had taken Dr. Penaflor as his personal project since he had never advanced such an arrangement and had zero plan to do so. What he didn't deny was that while he held high expectations of every physician he encountered and suffered no fools, whatever their rank or experience, there were those special ones whom he respected. Earning the esteem of Dr. George Darcy was a coveted prize. Dr. Penaflor was the only new doctor to have gained that level of recognition. It had not come to him easily, but it was deserved.

"He never blinks. Never. He may not know the answer immediately, but he finds it. He asks for help rather than attempting something he doesn't know how to do, which is wise, and then never forgets. But you know what is most amazing, Jharna?"

"That he has a gift for diagnosis."

"Yes!" He nodded his head, forgetting in his excitement that this was about the hundredth time they had talked about Dr. Raul Penaflor in the year since his arrival in Calcutta. "That is true. I have encountered others with my gift, but not too many European doctors. It is like the education sucks it out of them to be filled with pure science. Nothing wrong with science of course. Thank God for it! But why the fear of trusting one's instinct? Why the automatic retreat to microscopes and instruments rather than patiently listening to a person and diagnosing with your senses? It is an art that I fear will be lost, Jharna. Cultivating it when a physician has it is vital. But that is not the amazing thing I refer to this time."

She looked up from her painting, George having finally captured her undivided attention. He scooted his chair closer and leaned in with elbows on his knees. "You know him, Jharna. I have always sensed that there is more to Raul Penaflor than meets the eye, but he is so unassuming that I figured I must have been wrong on that score. He is a handsome fellow, young, well mannered, articulate, and clearly of excellent breeding. He never flaunts his wealth, but I know he has money. I nosed into his records and the lack of information is glaring. One could suspect his evasion hints of something nefarious. I have suspected the opposite for a host of reasons, not the least of which are the letters from Spain he receives on a regular basis that are all written on fine parchment with a seal I can never get a good look at but appears grand, for lack of a better term. I concluded his connections were high, or at least rich, meaning he has integrity greater than most if he would turn his back on the easy life to work as a physician in India."

"Just as you did."

George sat back in his chair, rubbing over his chin as he considered. Then he shook his head. "No, not really. I suppose there are similarities, but I left England for lots of reasons, selfless integrity not really high on the list. Besides, my family may be wealthy, and I guess I could have tapped into the Darcy prestige for my benefit"—he shrugged—"not my way though, but even if it was, the Darcys can't match what I now know about Raul Penaflor."

"And?"

George chuckled at the curiosity she was attempting to hide. "We were sharing a meal after surgery today. Dr. Shoolbred performed another brilliant cataract removal, by the way. This was the topic of our chat, and Penaflor makes an offhand comment about his uncle being nearly blind from cataracts and how this interrupts his duties at court. I may not have caught it if he hadn't stammered and tried to cover his slip. Well, that did it! I couldn't stand it any longer and asked him point blank who he was."

"I am surprised it has taken you so long. You usually aren't so polite and incurious."

"Incurious? Hell no! It has been driving me crazy! You know what a busybody I am. In this case though..." He paused for a moment, continuing slowly, "You were right, you know, when you said months ago that I may end up expecting—no, hoping—for more. That this was similar to Kshitij and me, although not quite. I see potential in Dr. Penaflor that he doesn't yet comprehend. Watching him this past year without any preconceived notions or unimportant background facts clouding my judgment seemed wise. And it was. You see, Raul Penaflor is the son of Duke Manuel Penaflor Aleman de

Vigo of Palencia. It means nothing to me, in that I don't know who his father is precisely. I can't keep track of English aristocracy, let alone Spaniards. But obviously the son of a duke is special, even if the third. Then, to make it more dramatic—and he really didn't want to tell me this but I bullied it out of him— his mother is not only a duchess but also an Infanta of the Royal House. Our little Raul is a bloody royal!"

Jharna was nodding her head and not looking as shocked as George expected. "Yes, I can see that. He has the air of a *raja* about him."

George threw his head back and laughed aloud. "Ha! What about that? Prince Raul. Raul the *raja*! And I had him spend the entire afternoon treating patients with dysentery. Wonder what Papa Duke would think of that?"

It was a letter from Sasi dated February 3, 1814, in which he informed his *mata* and *chacha-jee* that he was to be wed that compelled them to leave Calcutta. In truth, it was past time and both had sensed their fascination with the area waning. Or perhaps it was a matter of being homesick.

During their three-year absence, Sasi had stayed in Junnar, dwelling at the family home and assuming a teaching position at the Brahmin school. His passion for India's history was an inspiration to the young boys of the community, and although a mere twenty-four, the Brahmins were impressed by his knowledge. His betrothed, Daya, was a distant cousin, a Dhamdhere met while visiting his grandfather in Kalyan the previous winter. The tentative plan was for the wedding to be held at the grand *haveli* of the Sardar in May, provided, of course, his mother and surrogate father could be home by then.

Nimesh was living in Junnar with his brother and had been since January. He had taken a position at the hospital after traveling extensively through North India for eight years. By all reports, Nimesh was also in love with a young lady named Ziana that he met while in Lahore. At twenty-seven, he was far past the point of being wed, according to Jharna that is. Nimesh hadn't seemed in too great a rush, writing to George that he wanted to fulfill his goals of learning before progressing to the next stage of husband and father. Nimesh was methodical that way, so rather than laugh at his clinical approach to life, Jharna and George simply nodded. Nothing was official as yet, although Jharna hastily dispatched a letter to her eldest son strongly hinting at how lovely it would be to have a joint wedding ceremony for the Ullas sons.

"Subtle," George declared with heavy sarcasm when reading it over her shoulder. Jharna's elbow into his gut reply enough.

Finagling George's contract with the EIC required some negotiating. He had signed on for an additional two years when his initial contract expired with the added clause that he could transfer to the Bombay Presidency jurisdiction if requested. There were always ways to wrangle new deals, most of the administrators willing to appease a valuable asset rather than irritate to the point of losing them entirely later. Even with the second contract's caveat, it would have been easier to break it and walk away rather than renegotiate, but two reasons stopped him.

One, he had come to appreciate the high standard of medical resources available to those attached to the Indian Medical Service. Better equipment, the newest technologies, and quality medicines combined with his staunch belief in Indian healing philosophies benefitted the native people and the English. Nothing gave Dr. Darcy greater joy than to pass on his amassed knowledge so that it wasn't just he providing the best possible treatments but other healers as well. He didn't want to relinquish that. Plus, he looked forward to seeing how changed Bombay Island was after so many years away and to working with Dr. McIntyre, who was still the Physician General.

Two, he insisted that Dr. Raul Penaflor accompany him. Meaning, of course, that Raul's contract would need to be renegotiated. If, that is, he wanted to come. George had no doubts and vocalized his requests to Lord Hastings before talking to Dr. Penaflor. When he did the conversation went something like this:

"Raja"—the pet name had stuck and Dr. Penaflor no longer flinched or argued—"Jharna and I are moving back to Junnar next month. Our son is getting married, and naturally, we need to be there for that, but also Jharna is homesick. As am I, in fact. I have all the legal nonsense being taken care of, so no problems there. Anoop can help you pack if you want. He is a genius at organization. You will love Junnar and Bombay, Raja!"

And that was the extent of it.

GEORGE'S MEMOIRS
MARCH 20, 1815

I gave my last lecture today, James. Received a standing ovation! Nothing quite like that to boost one's ego, now is there? No, I shan't pretend that accolades aren't something I adore. No way you would let that pseudo-humbleness slide by, even if I tried. However, my frightening arrogance aside, I will assert that it moves my heart to have my countrymen and colleagues of my alma mater vociferously expressing their appreciation. To stand on the raised dais at the Royal College of Physicians in London and lecture to a jammed room of avid listeners has been a thrill. It has been over five and twenty years since I was a student here, yet I can vividly recall being the fresh-faced novice sitting in that audience, listening in awe as one of the great physicians spoke—Thomas Beddoes, Erasmus Darwin, James Lind, and John Hunter to name but a few. All of them captivated me with their intellects and drive. Oh, how I dreamt of being like them! I can't say that dream has come true precisely. I haven't discovered the cure for tuberculosis or solved the mystery of contagions or invented a new medical device. What I have done is advanced my skills and saved many lives along the way. When it comes down to it, illusions of grandeur notwithstanding, that is all I have ever wanted from my career. And if some of what I experienced impacts a handful of novice physicians, or maybe one of the masters, then I have excelled. There, you see how puffed with pride I am? It is fortunate that I am done and leaving soon before my swollen head prohibits me from fitting onto the ship back to India. In this one instance, the horrid months of sailing—gah!—might prove fortunate in calming my zeal. Best I not bounce onto the Bombay dock and immediately bombard Raja with manic raptures. On the off chance he remains miffed at being left behind, I best not say anything that could earn me a punch in the face! Not that it was my fault he broke his arm two days before we were set to sail. He should be thankful I was present to set the bone instead of some hack. Searc promised to keep him pain free until healed—that code for "blistering drunk"—and then too busy to lament missing this trip to England. I suppose I'll have to make it up to him somehow.

I will depart in three days. I was tempted to stay longer, believe me. As lovely as it has been to tour London after all this time and immerse myself in the memories surrounding Darcy House, I desperately wanted to visit Pemberley and know I shall berate myself for not taking the time. But I miss Jharna. I know you can understand that, James. Six months is far too long, and I have the interminable voyage home.

Thank God and some clever humans for the new ships that reduce the sailing time. I do so wish she would have come with me, but of course I understand. She has never been on a ship and while faster, they are as smelly and cramped as ever. I shuddered at the vision of my dear priya suffering so, especially when I spend too much time bent over the railing, losing my dinner. The fact that Sasi and Nimesh are undoubtedly new fathers by now was the clincher though. I hate missing that myself. Another reason to rush back rather than divert to Derbyshire.

My month with William and Georgie has been fabulous. It has soothed my heart to see the man your son has become. James, you would be immeasurably proud! He is devilishly handsome, naturally. No offense, elder brother of mine, but his resemblance to me is remarkably fortunate. Ha! The ladies swoon over him, not that the sorry lad appreciates his fortune. Not sure what he is waiting for, but I fear it may be your fault. If I didn't comprehend the glory of a worthy mate, I would kick the boy in the ass good and hard. A bit of female fun would benefit him. Then again, I certainly learned the hard way that waiting patiently is the wiser course. Best I leave him to his own devices. He is managing capably enough in every other way, and his tendency to shy from overt female machinations is a blessing when it comes to Miss Caroline Bingley. Oh, she is a pretty miss, no question. Cultured and all the other boring traits the ton seem to value. God, was it that bad when we were young? I honestly can't recall. But then, I was more interested in cadavers and sick people than the pointless games of Society. She so clearly wants Mr. Darcy for herself it is nauseating. Personally, I think it is Pemberley she wants instead of William. Whatever the case, he pays her little heed and I pray it stays that way. With luck, he will meet a nice girl before CB gets her claws into him. Strange how irritating she is when her brother is a delight. Charles Bingley is good for William. He needs a friend who is lighthearted and fun now that Richard Fitzwilliam is away at war. God knows I have tried to loosen him, but he resists. Perhaps I am too brash, shocking as that is to imagine, yes, James? Ha! Georgiana loves my sunny personality and I think for a few moments there I almost charmed Miss Bingley. Who knows? Maybe she is compatible with William. I love your son, James, so don't misunderstand. He is simply an enigma to me. Far too serious, as I have always noted, as well as reserved to the point of insularism. He really needs something dramatic to break him out of his shell. I tried but apparently my ebullience wasn't enough. I can't quite place my finger on it, and that drives me insane more than anything. I am usually better at diagnosing situations and people, but I honestly cannot decide how William feels about me. He is polite down to the tiniest degree and would sooner die than say I am unwelcome. I am sure he considers me part of the family with every right to be here, but I also don't think he has enjoyed having me here. I am poorly explaining it and maybe it is all in my head. Maybe I am too vain and used to people universally loving me that it bruises my vanity not to have my nephew delivering a teeny bit of hero worship!

James, it is rough to be here now that you are gone. All of my past is just that: past. Yes, seeing Malcolm and Henry has been marvelous. They are dear friends but not family. I did hope to see Estella, but her husband took ill so she could not leave Exeter. The memories are here, yet so much has changed. I suppose it isn't a big mystery. India has become my home. I just never thought it would, as ridiculous as that sounds. Or rather, I thought I could somehow have two homes: England with Pemberley and the Darcys; India with Jharna and my work and the boys. I never consciously imagined one wholly taking the place of the other. In a strange way it makes me feel adrift.

Oh bother! Far too much self-analysis going on here! I must be tired. Or more likely missing Jharna and her kisses and warm body. Yes, surely that is it. Denial of anything deeper suits me just fine.

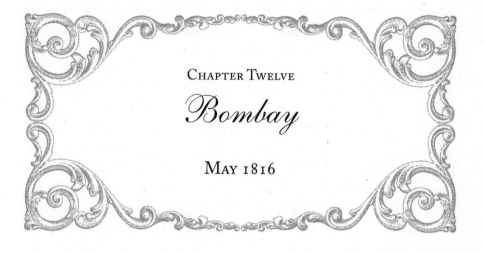

CHAPTER TWELVE

Bombay

MAY 1816

W HAT DO THEY CALL this thing?"

"A phaeton. I assure you it is perfectly safe, Jharna. No need to clench so tightly."

"Have you driven one often?"

"Hundreds of times!" Ignoring her disbelieving glare, George clapped the horses with the reins to speed them along.

Jharna squeaked and held tighter. "Must we race and tire the horses? Are we in a rush? What if they collapse?"

"We are barely moving. The horses will not collapse. And while not precisely in a rush, I am anxious to arrive."

"Where are you taking me?"

"Goodness! You ask more questions than a child! And if you think to trick me into answering that last question when I haven't answered it the previous ten times you asked, you will be disappointed." She shot him a second irritated glare, George not ignoring it this time but grinning as he leaned to kiss her cheek. "It is a surprise and you will love it."

"Watch the road before we topple off the edge into a ditch." She shoved him away but did smile, albeit wanly.

They were wheeling at a swift pace, and while George's claim to have driven a phaeton hundreds of times was an extreme exaggeration, he wasn't a total incompetent. Bombay had been left behind and the Hornsby Vallard crossed. The curved road hugging the coastline toward Worli offered a stunning view of sandy beaches, lush vegetation, and the Arabian Sea stretching to the horizon. Occasionally they passed carriages and native pedestrians, but that ceased when he veered onto a secondary road. More a wagon trail than a true road, this one was narrow and rougher in places. Fortunately for Jharna's frayed nerves, it was short, dumping into a tree-lined clearing barely large enough to fit the phaeton and two horses.

George leapt to the ground and turned to assist Jharna. She had stood the second the carriage halted and probably would have risked ripping her sari in a dozen places or landing in a briar patch just to escape the death trap! Fortunately, George was there, and he clasped her slim waist and lifted her to the earth as if she were a feather. Taking advantage of the situation, he pressed her against the phaeton's hard side with his whole body, his hands running from her cheeks to upper arms to breasts. The latter he cupped, rubbing his thumbs over her hardening nipples, and then engulfed her mouth for a penetrating, heated kiss. Her instant response fueled the excitement he had been dampening since leaving Bombay. Merely thinking of the afternoon he had planned for them thrilled him. Now that they had arrived, more or less, and she was in his arms with her amazing body crushed against him, hands in his hair and one leg stroking the backside of his leg, George's passion flared. With a groan, he ground into her pelvis and for a crazed five minutes considered making wild love to her right there. The vision was immensely appealing, and he knew Jharna wouldn't resist based on the noises she was emitting and how she clutched him.

It was an effort to be sure. George lightened the kiss and pulled away from her lips. His hands and body he did not move, waiting until she returned to reality and opened her glazed eyes.

"Feel better now? No longer scared about the dangerous ride?"

Her laughter was shaky, although not from the ride, and she nodded.

"My devilish attack worked then. Fabulous! Grab a basket, and after a brief, leisurely stroll to the beach, the real fun will commence."

The beach he led her to was at the end of a short but steep path that did not live up to the image he had painted. Jharna needed some assistance, not due to the physical difficulty but rather from her sari's lengthy fabric. Her offhand comment that taking it off would make the trek easier was met with an anticipatory gleam in George's eye. She kept it on, though, at least until they were comfortably settled with blanket spread on the sand and basket of food safe in the shade. At that point, they both removed their clothes, George every last stitch and Jharna down to her thin skirt and *choli*, and raced into the warm water. If anyone could have seen them, it would appear as if two giddy adolescents were frolicking. They splashed each other, rode the waves, and swam into the surf. As they played, they remained close to each other and often entwined as they floated and kissed.

George had imagined this as just one portion of how he planned to celebrate their special day—holding a wet, sun-glistening Jharna in his arms, leisurely bobbing with the gentle surge as they kissed. Her limbs wrapped around him, and her body slowly gliding against his chest as she took him inside her. Sheer heaven. Thirteen years to the day since the first time they made love and each time as wonderful.

After Bhrithi's death, they never spoke of marriage again. George's desire to wed legally had not died completely, but it no longer concerned him. To Jharna he was committed, in every possible way a man can be to a woman and vice versa. Over time, he had come to consider the night they first declared and consummated their love as their wedding. The man who eschewed formality a good portion of the time possessed a compulsion to mark a certain day to honor their relationship. For George, this date was when his entire life had aligned into a perfect pattern. Noting a day as their anniversary was not about placing a stamp of legitimacy on their unorthodox situation but to celebrate the pureness of their union and show her how abundant his thankfulness and abiding his love.

"How did you discover this quaint cove?"

George handed her a plate with a *papad* roll, *samosas*, *pakora* bread, and assorted Indian snacks—all of them cooked by him—before glancing around the tiny, tree- and brush-shrouded beach. "It was an accident, sort of. Lord Bingham's house is just over that rise. When I was there last month delivering his daughter's baby, I went for a swim. After the infant was born, of course. A perfect boy."

"Did they name him George?"

"No," he grumbled with mock anger. "I am still waiting for that. It is the least one should do, don't you think?"

"Absolutely," she soothed while trying not to smile.

"It was a rough delivery. I thought for a time I was going to need forceps. Marvelous invention though they are, they are delicate and have the potential of damaging. I was dirty and exhausted after, so a swim sounded appealing. I saw this little cove, asked Lord Bingham about it, and he said I could come here as a thanks. Not quite the high honor of naming the baby George, but I can share it with you, so that makes it better. Furthermore, after the amount of fun I intend to have with you here, *priya*, I don't think a child named for me can compare."

"That sounds promising. We have already experienced a stupendous bit of fun." She glanced out to the foamy blue waves, then back at him, the arch lift to her brow and sultry smile assuring him she did not mean the swimming or splashing. Leaning closer to his lips, she purred, "What else did you have in mind?"

George grinned every bit as sensually as she had, closed the narrow gap until a scant inch from her mouth, and huskily rumbled, "Why, gathering seashells and building sand castles of course. What else could we do?"

Jharna playfully shoved him away. George was prepared and grabbed her, falling backward onto the blanket so that she half sprawled on top of him. They were laughing, again like two giddy adolescents, until he silenced the vocal mirth with a kiss. Skillfully, he encompassed her lips, his tongue tracing and seeking in a pattern proficiently blending gentleness with demand while his long-fingered, sensitive surgeon's hands stroked over her upper body with the same dizzying combination. Currents of love and lust charged, sparks present at each point where their flesh touched. Food was forgotten, their hunger now transferred to a different physical need.

All part of the plan, he thought. Today was his gift to her, George plotting the day as well as one could prior to it taking place. Jharna's action, while not precisely foreseen, had been anticipated. So he twisted his hand around her flowing, damp hair and tugged her away from his lips. At the same time, he commenced a slow slide of the other hand down her body. The impassioned cast to her face and harsh breathing was exhilarating!

"Tell me, *priya*," he whispered, "how many ways are there for me to show you my love? How many ways can I love you and bring you pleasure? Hundreds, I know. How many can I manage in one day? How many times can I hear your cries of ecstasy in one glorious afternoon?"

If she had considered attempting a reply, George did not allow it. On the edge of harsh, he drew her back in for a kiss, the second with an intensity multiplied tenfold. At the same moment as he wrest her breath with the fervid onslaught to her mouth, he slipped his hand between her legs and plunged into the moist heat waiting within. Jharna gasped, or tried to, and bucked wildly in time to his stroking fingers. Tightly he held her, maintaining total control of his movements and playing her body as a virtuoso musician. Not until he was certain the crescendo was near did he pull her away from his lips.

"Scream for me, Jharna. I want to hear how I make you feel."

And with a minuscule shift and flawlessly executed sweep of his thumb, Jharna did scream.

During that lazy afternoon into early evening, they built castles of sand, gathered seashells in a basket that would eventually be taken to Junnar for the grandchildren who had yet to see the ocean, ate of the scrumptious cuisine George had prepared, picked wild berries and herbs, and romped in the refreshing water. At random junctures, George would abruptly squeeze her rear or nuzzle the bend of her neck or brush across a bared breast or nip the inside of her wrist. Several times he tumbled her to the sand or crushed her against a tree, kissing and fondling until she was breathless. Three times he did nothing but stare silently, his blue eyes smoldering with raw potency and hypnotizing promise until her breathing hitched and eyes glazed. The majority of the time, he then pulled away, chuckling hoarsely and grinning salaciously before resuming whatever they were doing as if nothing had occurred. Jharna never knew when he was going to carry on with the arousing activity, which heightened the expectation to agonizing levels so that when he didn't stop, they were so insanely enlivened, the interlude was cataclysmic.

They dozed for an hour in the late afternoon, waking to the sun hovering inches above the horizon. As they made love the final time, the sun crept over the edge, bathing the endless sea in orange and crimson light and their cove into dusky twilight. The sun's gradual dip created an atmosphere of timelessness. George and Jharna loved slow and steady with measured strokes and tenderness. Pretty words were uttered and meant from the heart. Their pinnacle was attained together with bodies entwined and synchronized, as the rush of pleasure swept over and through them.

Weary and enervated at the same time, they bid adieu to the pristine cove with only the last beams of the disappearing sun illuminating the path back to the phaeton and horses. Jharna nestled against his side as they drove back to Bombay. All her previous anxiety over the strange carriage was gone, replaced with tranquility borne of extreme satisfaction and energy expenditure.

"Do you think we will have an opportunity to come back here before we leave Bombay next month?"

George laughed at the fiery gleam in her eyes noticeable even in the diminished light. "We can certainly try, but the cove won't go anywhere. If we don't make it back before returning to Junnar, we will make a point to visit when next we come to Bombay."

"When will that be?"

He didn't need to see her face to know she wasn't asking because of the cove. "Not too soon, *priya*. Raja is going to stay here when we leave in June. He and Searc are busy overseeing the addition to the surgical wing, so he asked to stay for a while. I am fine with my duties as a provincial officer, since it keeps me closer to home. Baji Rao has requested some assistance in Poona. I am already assembling a team for that and will send them ahead. Probably Drs. Tolman and Beckwith will lead it up. They have the most experience with Marathas and don't mind working with the native doctors, plus they don't need me breathing down their necks and directing every movement. I'll meet Raja there in July after spending time with the family and spoiling our grandbabies. I miss them too."

He kissed her forehead, then fell silent with thoughts drifting across the miles to their home in Junnar where Sasi and Nimesh lived with their wives and children. Aside from his months in England, the past two years had passed split between the Ullas house in Junnar and the beautiful home he had purchased in Bombay. It sat near the ocean and, while not large or of grand architecture, was perfect for the two of them. At forty-nine, it was the first house he had ever owned and he loved it. With Jharna, it was home, as was the dwelling in Junnar, because she was his home. It was nice to be able to call a place his, and he liked the pace they were setting these days. He couldn't promise the urge to travel somewhere new wouldn't hit him and with the EIC constantly evolving and expanding, it was unlikely the pattern of moving between Bombay and Junnar with his job as a provincial medical officer would last forever. For the present, however, they were content with the situation.

The three weeks following their anniversary, George was busy. No matter what his official job description, Dr. George Darcy had his hands involved in a dozen additional tasks. He gave lectures whenever asked, some of them officially planned while others spontaneously arose at the end of a patient's bed or across an operating table. Research had never been a huge interest, but he did peer into a fair number of microscopes or visit the laboratory or experiment with medicinal concoctions. He always had a medical book in his lap or secured in the leather satchel slung over his shoulder wherever he went, either the latest text from the Continent or an Indian volume. A day did not go by without him tending to the ill or performing a surgery. Many nights did not go by without him being called to an emergency. Jharna had long since grown used to that and merely rolled over and returned to sleep.

There wasn't a single soul in any of the medical facilities and few anywhere else within the EIC departments that did not instantly recognize him. The towering Englishman with the thin body, dressed in Indian garments inevitably in the brightest collage of colors and designs possible was easy to spot and remember. His infectious, booming laughter and resonant voice that could slip from perfect, aristocratic English into accent-free Hindi midsentence was known by all. Other Europeans had adopted native dress or learned the language, but not a one with the complete audacity of Dr. Darcy. There was no one with a smile as humorous, eyes as warm and intelligent, features as handsome, or personality as charming and kind. Energy bubbled forth as a fountain, none believing for a second that he was fast approaching the end of his fifth decade. There were many excellent physicians and surgeons in Bombay who excelled in certain areas, but none came close to his far-reaching expertise, diagnostic skill, incalculable knowledge, and unflappable confidence.

Taken together, it was a sad occasion when Dr. Darcy and the exquisite Indian woman who all but a handful assumed to be his wife, planned to leave. Therefore, Dr. and Mrs. McIntyre decided to host an afternoon luncheon at their lavish home in Parel as a farewell. A dozen physicians and officers with their wives filled the open salon, rear terrace, and gardens. George sat on a settee next to Jharna, a glass of brandy which he would sip at all night in his hand, and together they savored the merriment.

"Darcy, come over here and tell Perkins why he is dead wrong about Midnight Jewel taking the title from Houdon in tomorrow's horse race!"

George kissed Jharna on the cheek before rising, crossing to Searc and the others. The discussion grew lively, Englishmen, even physicians, taking horses and racing very seriously. Being raised at Pemberley, where thoroughbreds were as much a staple as the sheep and crops, gave George an advantage over some when it came to comprehending the finer nuances of breeding. All those lectures from his father, a lifetime member of the Jockey Club, came in handy.

Out of the corner of his eye, he saw Jharna continuing her conversation with the ladies sitting near her, the topic destined to shift from flowers to cooking, children, or clothing eventually. She had never experienced trouble connecting with people whether male or female, native or foreign. She was nowhere near as flamboyant or outgoing as George, her gift a sedate humor and honesty that appealed to others. Watching her mingle was never out of protectiveness or fear but due to his pride and happiness. Such was the case now, as she stood and gracefully wandered to a far wall, the ladies trailing behind as she spoke words he could not hear and gestured fluidly with her hands.

Indian art, he thought, smiling. *One of the many subjects my incredible lover is versed in.*

To his reckoning, she was a rare, priceless jewel among lesser gemstones. No offense intended to the wives of his friends, many who were lovely, and naturally he knew he was prejudiced. Nevertheless, Jharna was special. There she stood, pointing out the details of the magnificent painting hanging on the wall when she was a living work of art. She was dressed in a fine sari, a true masterpiece of craftsmanship, and exquisitely wrought jewelry adorned her wrists, neck, and forehead. The window dressing enhanced rather than overwhelmed the flawless beauty of her regal features and curvaceous body. George had recognized Jharna's attractiveness while she was an unknown woman dancing at the Sardar's birthday party. In all the years that had passed since, while Kshitij's wife and his friend, up to this day twenty-five years later, Jharna had only grown more beautiful as far as he was concerned. Physically and spiritually, she was breathtaking to him.

Sensing his regard, she turned from the painting, met his eye briefly from across the room, and smiled warmly. It was one of those fleeting exchanges that was electric and spoke volumes. She lifted one brow when he winked and then glanced away toward one of the ladies. She nodded at whatever the woman said and opened her mouth to speak. At that second, George was about to redirect his attention to his comrades, but Jharna snapped her lips closed and an odd twitch of her head stayed him.

No matter how often he replayed those moments in his mind afterward, George would never know precisely what launched him away from the men, the brandy flying from his hand as he shoved bodies—he never discovered how many—out of his way in a mad bolt to Jharna's side. It only took two, maybe three seconds, and each one was an eternity etched upon his mind and heart with a razor-sharp knife.

Jharna pressed two shaking fingertips to her left temple, her body shuddered a half heartbeat before her head jerked backward, and her frantic eyes swung toward him, all in the time it took him to traverse the room, skidding to a halt just as her legs buckled and arms dropped boneless to her sides. Catching her in his arms and falling to the floor in a semicontrolled heap, George screamed her name and grasped her chin. Wrenching her face toward him, he bent to engage her eyes, helplessly watching the awareness slipping inexorably away.

"Jharna! *Priya*! No, no! Look at me! Please!"

"*Priya.*" A wisp of air through slack lips. "Love you…"

And then she was gone.

The only sound audible in the stunned silence was George's screams and sobs—wrenching, disconsolate sobs as he held her lifeless body to his chest and rocked back and forth for minutes, hours, maybe days. He was never sure how long before Searc knelt beside, his ruddy Scottish face stricken and tear streaked, and laid one hand on his shoulder. He barely noted Raul Penaflor checking for a pulse in Jharna's wrist. Nor did he remember exactly when a hysterical Anoop knelt on the other side of Jharna, Hindu chants for the deceased barely audible amid the weeping.

George did recall the flare of fury and urge to yell for Anoop to stop because Jharna could not possibly be dead. Then this momentary madness was replaced by plunging despair. Even in his shock, George was a physician. He knew an aneurysm or similar insult to the brain when he saw one. Worse yet, he knew when a person was dead and past the point of revival.

Jharna, his love and light, the wife of his heart and soul, was gone. Consummate healer that he was, George could do nothing but hold her, cry, and pray to his benevolent God that somehow he would find a way to live without her.

～❧～

A month later, George sat on the bench in the small garden at the house in Junnar, staring at not one but two graves.

Jharna was cremated in the Hindu custom, her remains then gathered and reverently placed in a silver and jeweled casket similar to the one that held the body of their daughter, Bhrithi. She was laid to rest in the Christian way, beside their daughter, under the shade of the ashoka tree. An identical cross bore her name, the dates of her life, and the inscription, "Beloved mother of Nimesh, Sasi, and Bhrithi. Adored and eternal wife of Kshitij Ullas and George Darcy." All at the insistence of Nimesh and Sasi, George so overcome that he had dissolved into tears.

The tears still came from time to time, and he knew they would for a long while. Grieving never got easier, no matter how many loved ones a person lost. Bitterness and anger consumed him upon occasion. He knew better than most how fragile life was. There were no guarantees. Yet he never imagined not having at least another ten or twenty years with her. Hopefully far more than that, damn it all! At that furious curse to the heavens, he realized it never would have been enough. If blessed to be with her until ninety, he would still rage at the injustice of it.

Was he at the point of being simply grateful for the time they had spent together? No, not quite. He *was* grateful, the pain of loss not so profound he could not understand that loving her for a short time was better than not at all. He hoped he would eventually embrace the peace God offered in that understanding, but for the present, he wanted the anger. If nothing else, it kept the sorrow at bay. With severe sorrow came weakness. With anger came strength of a sort.

"What are your plans now, *chacha*?"

George looked at the young man sitting beside him on the stone bench. The boy he had first met as a one-year-old baby was now a father himself. It should have made George feel ancient, yet oddly it was comforting. *Is that a glimmer of joy I am feeling? A sensation of belonging to something wonderful that will live on forever?*

"I am going back to work, Sasi. The Peshwa is expecting me in Poona, and Raja will be there in a week or two."

Sasi nodded and held his uncle's eyes. George knew what he was not verbalizing. Managing a weak smile, George patted him on the knee. "This is my home and I am forever welcome here, I know that, Sasi. Rest assured, I am not leaving for any reason other than that through my work I can heal." He shrugged. "That is the hope anyway. She would scold me vehemently if I sat here all day staring at her grave and didn't keep moving."

"She was great at scolding, in her serene way that is."

"It was far more effective than if she had raised her voice," George agreed, a sad chuckle escaping. "A day did not pass without her chiding me for dropping my clothes to the floor, using one of my favorite English idioms against me. 'Ah, I see you *were* born in a barn,' or 'Clearly your mother taught you nothing.' I know it drove her crazy but did it on purpose to hear which expression she would use. Now I fold my clothes." He inhaled shakily and closed his eyes. "God, I miss her, Sasi."

The younger man draped one arm over George's slumped shoulders but remained silent. George fought the stinging tears with effort and was thankful when Nimesh strolled into the clearing at that moment. In his arms, he carried his four-month-old daughter. "Onelia was asking for her *dādā*."

"Was she now? Far be it from me not to give Onelia anything she wants. Come to your *dādā*, wee one. There's my sweet flower. It is a grandfather's duty to spoil a baby until stinking rotten, you know."

"And then leave them with the parents to deal with, yes, we know."

"See"—George looked at Sasi while jerking his head toward Nimesh—"that is why I can't stay away for long. Someone has to do the spoiling if for no other reason than to make sure you two perfect your disciplinary skills."

❧

Jharna had often teased George for having a lazy streak within him that with the slightest provocation emerged and reigned for a spell. It was true, as he had discovered multiple times in his life. George could lie about and soak up the sun while reading for days on end and not feel the teeniest bit guilty over the behavior, even when she referred to him as a wastrel or some other jesting slur. The fact was, she had loved it when he relaxed, because no matter how thoroughly he embraced inactivity, he followed those brief spans with his typical ceaseless action.

This was the life of Dr. George Darcy and it had been so since he was in the schoolroom and long before grief touched him. It was not within George's nature to sit on a bench and stare at a grave. Wallowing in unhappiness was out of the question.

Thus the latter half of 1816 unfolded in many respects no differently than George had planned it prior to Jharna's precipitous demise.

He left Junnar to meet Raul Penaflor in Poona in July. Their medical team conferenced with the Peshwa, George relieved when the audience was conducted in a business-like manner. His relief ended when the prime minister and royal descendent of the Maratha Empire later paid homage to his relative Jharna Dhamdhere with a solemn ceremony that wreaked havoc on George's professional control. Jumping into his assignment with both feet restored his equilibrium, and since he had often traveled for jobs without Jharna, it was almost possible to forget that she was gone.

George's passion for medicine and intense work ethic were legendary. Few recognized anything different in how hard he pushed himself or the lengthy hours he kept, and for the most part they were correct. The yawning hole created by Jharna's absence wasn't filled by work nor was his melancholy cured, but at least action kept the pain at bay. Roughest was when his job took him back to Bombay or when his yearning to visit the Ullas families took him to Junnar. There, the acute attacks of agony were around every corner or in every room when she did not appear. At least in Bombay he had work to attend to, books to read, research to conduct, and anything else that avoided dwelling on the leisurely dinners they had shared followed by tranquil evenings and sweet lovemaking.

In late August, a visit to Kalyan offered a needed boost as well. George's friendship with Jharna's father, Pandey Dhamdhere, had taken root decades ago. Pandey was seventy-five and no longer the Sardar of Thana—that honor having passed to his eldest living son—but the one-time warrior still possessed a daunting aura of power and influence over the region. If nothing else, his grand *haveli* continued to be a favorite locale for celebrations and official business. Over the years, George was a frequent visitor, before and after Kshitij died, alone and with Jharna. Pandey had accepted his relationship with Jharna, never once expressing displeasure, but George had never known how the nobleman with staunch Hindu beliefs truly felt deep inside. He hadn't thought it mattered to him until this visit after Jharna's death.

"You were good together," Pandey declared. His cloudy eyes were wet with tears but fixed decisively on George's face. "I am thankful to the gods that she enjoyed your love until the end, George. The gods shined upon my watering spring, my precious Jharna, with two worthy men to drink from her life-giving water and replenish with their devotion and praise. Ah! How blessed she was in this life! Oh, how the joy she was showered with shone from her skin! Her light and reservoir of water increased as those who adored her increased! Too few can claim this honor in life and I thank you, dear friend, for bestowing your love as a gift to her. How the gods and our ancestors must be relishing her in their presence!"

The aged Hindu's flowery way of speaking brought a smile to George's face. Whimsical as it may be, George was moved by the beauty of Pandey's phrases.

Jharna meant "a spring," as George knew, yet he never had given the meaning much thought. It wasn't an English custom to do so. Hindus were different, and for the first time, he saw his beloved Jharna in that light. She was a spring of fresh, pure water filling his soul and heart with love and so much more every day of her life, the ceaseless stream flowing into him still.

Pandey's words were a comfort and a revelation. Placing George on the same plain with Kshitij was profound, and being praised for his influence upon her spirit being visible in the Hindu afterlife was an honor George had no words for.

It was a good thing that Pandey did not overdo the nostalgia and praise, the warrior leader conquering the sentimental father with their talks mostly about politics during the days of his visit.

At George's invitation, which sounded suspiciously like an order, Dr. Penaflor moved out of the bungalows near the hospital and into a suite of rooms in George's Bombay house in September. Raul's stubborn stipulation was to pay room and board at a fair market price. George's attempts to negotiate were met with a stony face and immovable arms crossed over the Spaniard's burly chest until finally George threw up his hands and signed the contract Raul had drawn up.

"I don't need the money," George groused. "What I need is the companionship. I am a lonely, old widower, pining away in a huge, empty house, wandering the echoing corridors like a forlorn ghost."

Raul grunted, responding to that nonsense with a mocking rebuttal in heavily accented English. "You aren't old and appear hale enough for a man pining away. You have Anoop, a cook, and two houseboys living here. I am here a good amount of the time already, as are dozens of other doctors, including Dr. McIntyre. Furthermore, your house, while spacious, hardly qualifies as huge enough to have echoing corridors."

"Ouch! The insults are dropping like monsoon raindrops. Where is your compassion? Are all royal Spaniards so heartless?"

"Most of them, yes." Raul scrutinized his friend's signature with dramatic intensity.

"It is legible and doesn't say Dray or Darry, I promise."

"Making sure. You did note that it is delineated that you cannot refuse the monthly specified rental nor return it to the tenant in a furtive manner?"

"Yes, yes! The tenant has nothing to worry about." George rolled his eyes and sighed, then after a moment, his eyes narrowed and he pursed his lips. "Although, the contract does not specify what the landlord can do with the money, now does it?"

Raul shrugged, trying not to laugh. "You can do as you wish, George, and that will most likely be donating to charity. As long as I am paying my own way, I don't care. Now, how about we seal the bargain at the pub. You can use my rent payment to buy us drinks if it makes you feel better."

"Ho! Not so fast there, Raja Pay-My-Own-Way. Don't be too hasty spending my money. This is enough for an entirely new outfit with shoes too. Hassieh received a new fabric shipment from Madras with some stunning patterns and those yellow *juttis* have been calling my name…"

The money Raul paid to live with George was given to the Bombay orphanage, as Raul figured it would be. Between children and the ill, George was a generous giver, plus it was true that he did not need the money. His income, the stipend his father had added on, and a series of wise investment combined with minimal personal requirements—clothing an exception—meant that George had amassed a small fortune. He did admire Raul's stance, the teasing simply for fun and to make sure he wasn't moving in out of pity. Those who knew George Darcy well knew he was far too practical and cheerful to bemoan his fate and whine for sympathy. The occasional query on how he was faring or a heartfelt reference to missing Jharna was appreciated, but nothing more. As harsh as the reality, time did not stand still and George knew he had to move forward along with it. Nothing good came of miring in the past.

Slowly, he relinquished the unconscious expectation of hearing her voice or seeing her smile or feeling her touch. Incrementally, the verve for living and passion for medicine overwhelmed the sorrow.

After a three-week sojourn in Junnar, George and Raul returned to Bombay for Christmas. The town had tripled or maybe quadrupled in the twenty-seven years since George stepped foot onto the dock. Houses, churches, offices, stores, and barracks—you name it and there were more of them. Yearly, the EIC-controlled port town was transforming into a British-appearing outpost, not that the exotic Indian atmosphere could ever be erased. During the Christian holiday season, to celebrate the birth and epiphany of the Savior, the inhabitants strived to create a festive ambience as close to home as possible. It was a poor imitation when the temperature was higher than a summer day in England and pine greenery or mistletoe did not exist, but that didn't stop the cooking of mincemeat pies and wassail or the giving of presents. Every family of means hosted a dinner or ball, their finest attire of a lightweight construction rather than velvets and broadcloths, but the minstrels played as loudly and the dancing was continuous.

The Ullases had always honored the day for him with their version of a typical Christmas, and George had attended a Christmas Day worship service if there was an Anglican church available. However, it had been years since he last spent Christmas with Englishmen, celebrating in the traditional way. George was invited to dozens of parties and attended the majority of them. Why not? He loved to socialize and he certainly loved great food. The vigorous exercise and endless entertainments were good for him and it made no sense to sit home doing nothing.

Before he turned around, the calendar flipped to 1817. Twelfth Night arrived with a massive extravaganza at Governor Nepean's mansion complete with Mummers, a Shakespeare-themed costume ball, performing singers and dancers, a stage production of select scenes from *Twelfth Night*, and steady streams of food and spirits. George remembered having a marvelous time. He also remembered the incapacitation experienced the next day that took three days to recover from.

On an eve five days after, George entered the house owned by his longtime friend Dr. Searc McIntyre. Walking unerringly to the room Searc referred to as his "Scots Sanctuary," he knocked once and twisted the unlocked knob before the bellowed, "'Tis open!" This was followed by a redundant, "Yer early."

"As if you care," was George's laughing response. "I did wash and change so be thankful for that much. I was too excited to wait for dinnertime!"

"Ye do seem in a dither. Dinit think me wife's cooking thrilled ye so. Sit. Whiskey?" McIntyre stood from his desk and crossed to the sidebar where an array of glass decanters and glasses sat.

George sat on the chair indicated by a casual wave of the Scotsman's hand, but perched on the edge rather than flopping into a sprawl as typical. "No thanks. Tea will do."

"Still a wee peaked, are we?" Searc glanced over his shoulder, grinning evilly.

"Sorry to disappoint, but I feel fine. Nevertheless, I think I drank my quota for the next six months, and I never trust your whiskey."

"Probably for the best considering yer delicate English constitution. Where's Dr. Penaflor?"

"He was finishing up a procedure but will be here later. I left a note with Anoop for him to come as soon as he can. And for now, I shall allow the delicate constitution insult to pass. I have to share this." He withdrew an envelope from the inner pocket of his lavender *sherwani*, holding it so that McIntyre could see the Darcy seal. "I haven't heard from William in over six months, as you know, and was worried especially when the letter I received from Georgiana dated June hinted that he wasn't well or something. She was maddeningly obtuse, probably because she didn't know what was wrong with him. My nephew is reserved to a fault and insanely protective of his sister. It had to be bad for her to notice and then comment to me."

"I presume all is well or ye would no be smiling. Do ye now know what ailed the lad?"

"No. He says nothing of being ill and from the tone of this letter any sufferings, whether physical, financial, or other, are gone." George scooted even further onto the edge of his seat and waved the papers covered with precise lines of penmanship in the air. "He is in love! And to be married! Or rather, is married by now. The date was set for November. Ha! Nothing like the love of a great woman to cure a man, eh, Searc?"

"I needed no curing, thank ye, but I shall agree that a guid woman is a pretty boon." The older physician joined George, taking the chair across and sipping his whiskey. "Is it the red-haired wench 'twas pursuing him? His friend's sister?"

"Praise God, no!" George shuddered. "Miss Bingley could never inspire the passion in William's writing. He is fairly gushing! And he never gushes. I have been receiving letters from him since he was twelve or so, and you know how stifled he was when I was there two years ago. This person"—he again waved the letter—"isn't the same man I saw then."

"Are ye gonna give details, or do I need to snatch the pages and read for myself?"

George grinned. "Intrigued, are you? All right!" He laughed at McIntyre's glare and raised fist. "Her name is Elizabeth Bennet, the daughter of a gentleman in Hertfordshire. Apparently, they met last year when Mr. Bingley, the wench's brother, was living there. Why the long delay I am unsure. He does not say other than a reference... where is it, ah, that, 'Miss Elizabeth was unsure of her regard for him' and that 'they were separated by unfortunate circumstances' until meeting again in Hertfordshire in September. Clearly, he did not delay this time."

"Smart lad. Snatch the fine lassies before someone else does."

"Indeed. He wrote this the day after Miss Bennet accepted his proposal, which, I might add, he refers to as 'this proposal' giving the impression it wasn't the first! Can you imagine any woman rejecting a man of his wealth and station, not to mention incredible good looks?"

McIntyre snorted at the last, knowing George claimed his nephew greatly resembled him. "Unless she wasn't impressed by all that and wanted a man of character. No offense, Darcy, but ye said yerself the lad has a tough shell and a less than sparkling personality. No all lassies care for property and possessions over heart and fun."

"Precisely my thought. There is a story here, mark my words, and I long to hear it. This is not the William I have known." He tapped the pages with a finger. "This is the William I knew to be buried inside. A whole page devoted to describing 'my lovely Elizabeth' in vivid detail. The color of her eyes, how she smiles, the tone of her laughter. On and on. Searc, if I wasn't a man who knew the delights of love, I would be retching from the nauseatingly high sugar content!" He sat back into the chair with a sigh and tender smile, reading through the words he had nearly memorized even though he had received the letter an hour before dashing over to the McIntyre house. "William married," he muttered dreamily. "And married well to a worthy woman he loves. From what he says, unless completely blinded, she is as enamored. Ah, how I would love to see this!"

"Then why don't ye?"

"What do you mean?"

McIntyre did not respond immediately to George's baffled gaze. When he did, George was stunned.

"I mean, perhaps ye should consider another visit to England. Close yer mouth before the spittle falls on yer chin and hear me out." McIntyre rubbed his graying brow, eyes soft but serious, as was his tone when he resumed. "George, I been holding back on ye. I dinna want to spoil yer holidays, and to be frank, it's been guid to see ye smile agin. I ken ye well, my friend, more than most. No point pretending these months no been hard, and I dinna want to add to it but can no longer be secret. Lileas and I are moving back to Scotland. Next month."

"Next month?"

"I ken it seems sudden, but we been hashing it over for a while now. We miss the Highlands. I haven't traveled home once in all these years, and truth is, I am tired of India and the work here no longer interests me. I am over sixty, by God, and wanna be laid in home sod when I die. Kenna wants to marry a Scot and Lorna's man has accepted a position with the EIC in London. I want to see my grand bairns romping in the heather. All the pieces fell into place."

"I… well, I am shocked of course, and sad, but… well, I do understand Searc. I truly do. I just… God, I am going to miss you terribly! I can't imagine Bombay without you and Lileas."

"Don't try then. Come with us."

"Are you—? You can't be serious!"

"Verra serious. Not to Scotland, of course, although ye can visit anytime. But ye can sail with us. Ye said ye wanted to see yer nephew and his lady, to hear the story. And you missed Pemberley on yer last visit. Mostly though, and this is coming from a friend who loves ye, I think a bit of distance would be guid for ye. Don't misunderstand. Ye did well in carrying on with yer life, George. Jharna would be proud of ye for it. But like I said, I am yer friend and have been a long while. So let me ask ye, are ye here doing the same as always 'cause it was the plan and thus easier? Ach, I no saying ye should have done different, but what about this year or the next? Can you see yerself here in Bombay, content in this position without Jharna and the stability she gave ye? Or do ye see scurrying off on another trek with Penaflor? Maybe ye do, and 'tis yer life to lead, George. No saying ye should even ken the answers yet but are ye asking the questions?"

George couldn't readily think how to respond. Searc did know him well and he was an insightful friend to be trusted. George was sensible enough to admit that, when it came to being rational after suffering a profound loss, he was no different than anyone else. His future beyond the immediate was a hazy area that he had not considered when there were still too many days when it was a struggle to get out of his empty bed, the only impetus being the duties and routines he was sure of. It was a comfortable, reliable crutch that he needed. Nothing wrong with that. But for how long?

He was still attempting to assimilate it all, McIntyre placidly sipping his whiskey and saying nothing further, when Dr. Penaflor was escorted into the male sanctuary. One glance between the two silent physicians, neither of whom rose or offered a greeting, and Raul knew something serious was afoot.

"My apologies, gentlemen. Should I wait outside?"

"No, of course not, Raja. Have a seat. We were discussing... well, I am not sure where to begin."

McIntyre chuckled at George's confused expression, so rarely seen on the confident man's face. He took over, giving the brief rundown while pouring Raul a glass of wine. George said nothing, his eyes staring at his hands and the letter from William until McIntyre finished.

"I see," were the first and only words out of Raul's mouth.

George looked up, one brow arched. "'I see'? What is that supposed to mean?"

"It means I see. I understand. That is all. It really has nothing to do with me, now does it?" He took a sip of wine, black eyes peering calm and steady at the wide-eyed George over the rim of the wine glass. "Unless, of course, I was to remind you that you do owe me a trip to England."

"I *owe* you," George sputtered, ignoring McIntyre's snicker. "Who's fault was it that you stumbled over your own clown feet and broke an arm? Owe you, my ass!"

Raul shrugged, it a regal lift of one shoulder and followed by another sip of wine. "You did promise you would take me on your next trip though."

"Maybe, although I don't recall the word 'promise' in there anywhere. And nothing about when that would be. Hell, I might have meant twenty years from now."

"True. But here is an opportunity for you to fulfill your *promise* and not be beholden to me for twenty years."

George cast a glower at each of them. "Is this some sort of conspiracy?" Neither deigned to reply. "You know Governor Nepean will have a seizure if we all leave at once?"

"He has a strong heart. I know because I assessed his physical health last month. He already has my replacement picked out—Dr. Ertham—so it would just be ye two, and it isn't like the EIC isn't used to ye rewriting contracts, George. I wonder why they bother wasting the paper after all this time."

George couldn't deny that truth, having often wondered the same, but like all bureaucracies, they weren't capable of surviving without stacks of documents to prove their worth. Desperate, he tried a different angle. "Anoop will be devastated if I leave him. I can't do that to him again."

"Take him along. An adventure will benefit him as well. He has become as stodgy an old man as ye."

"Nimesh and Sasi are planning a major celebration for my fiftieth birthday. At Pandey's *haveli* in Kalyan. Impossible for me to cancel that."

"Are ye deaf or so old ye canna remember the months? I said I was leaving next month, which is February, and ye birthday is in two weeks. I know 'cause we are invited to the party. Are you done making excuses?"

George gaped at Searc, who was grinning, and then turned to Raul, who continued to sip his wine as if bored by the whole conversation. The gleam in his eye proved otherwise. At a loss for words, George stared from one man to the other. Then, as the panic rose to the point of choking his air supply, George glanced down at the letter still clutched between his fingers.

Uncle,

I now have hope where none existed before that Pemberley shall once again be the joyous home of my youth, and as Father recounted from his child-hood. The ancestral Darcy abode filled with laughter, children, and the touch of a devoted mistress who loves the manor as she deserves to be loved. I pray this image warms your heart as it does mine.

It did warm his heart and brought back fond memories. Mostly, however, he wondered who this Elizabeth Bennet, now presumably Elizabeth Darcy, was that she possessed the magical powers not only to transform a house too long mired in grief, but also a man's entire being. His curiosity was sparked, and if there was one unstoppable force in the world, it was George Darcy when he was curious!

GEORGE'S MEMOIRS
DECEMBER 5, 1817

Jharna, I am staring at this page benumbed and attempting to clarify my churning emotions. I have often thought a man's life is defined by the highs and lows with the humdrum periods in between not as important. While I do still believe we are impacted by the momentous, I now comprehend that those humdrum days combine and truly shape us. Yes, I am in an introspective mood, my dear! You are duly warned. You know how I have struggled with my feelings since your death, especially in these months since returning to England and Pemberley. I am no longer sure what drove me away from India this time. All of the reasons for my "visit" were valid on the surface and I would have sworn I had every intention of returning. Even now, with the recent developments of which I will write soon, there is a part of my soul crying for India. I long for the warmth, smells, sounds, all of it. I do miss Nimesh and Sasi and the children. It is painful accepting that I may well never hold them and hear their voices. Perhaps I never should have come back, I find myself thinking at times.

Then I walk into a room to see my Darcy family smiling at me with true joy and I experience a rush of completeness. Indeed, so dramatic but this is the truth of it. You were warned, priya! *I have missed you, my lovely Jharna, unbearably so, and honestly did not know if it was merely grief and loneliness clouding my judgment or a real affection. Was my growing love for them in any way false? Those Darcys whom I knew I could rely upon are gone. Would this new generation of Darcys fill the void or was I wishing for what cannot be? I have tarried in a place of joyous relaxation on my extended holiday, wallowing in the comforts of my ancestral estate and the acceptance that has surprisingly surrounded me, yet always with a slight reserve. Afraid to give in to the love I felt growing daily for William and Elizabeth and my sweet Georgiana. Afraid to embrace life at Pemberley or think of it as home. How does one utterly reinvent his life and focus at my age? Yes, even I, who trod through jungles teeming with hazards and embarked upon life-saving excursions to the farthest reaches of the East knew fear. What a bitter tonic to swallow!*

Yet all that doubt and fear was wiped away in a second. Today, William accosted me in the library for a pointed chat, expressed his love for me in direct words, and asked, nay, begged, that I not leave! His words precisely, as I will never forget them, were, "I need to tell you in the clearest words imaginable that the heartfelt wish of us all is that you would choose to reside here forever. Simply put, I do not want to lose you." And then the moment that truly sent me over the edge and sealed my fate: William and Elizabeth have asked me to be Alexander's godfather. Of all the possible imaginings that have flit through my brain, this one was an utterly unprecedented surprise! Knowing William's strong religious convictions, his protectiveness for his family, and serious nature… well, I am overwhelmed. And honored beyond comprehension.

Tears yet again! Old age is creeping! Cloying sentimentalism indeed! We Darcys are a romantic bunch for all our strength of character. It isn't enough that I have been walking on a cloud since being present at the birth of William and Elizabeth's son last week, but now this? Yes, I am well aware that I more or less insisted I deliver their firstborn. As if I could have idly sat by and let another do what I am imminently skilled to do, risking Elizabeth's life or the babe's. Never! I would have stormed into the birth chamber at the first scream. Fortunately, they wanted me there, and both William and Elizabeth performed brilliantly. Sweet Alexander is perfect and precious. He is a handsome lad, I can state emphatically. You would scold me, Jharna, when I spoke of ugly babies, convinced that all are gorgeous which I know not to be the case. Alexander, I state with unprejudiced assessment, is truly adorable and greatly resembles his father. Being an integral part of their union and honored with serving them at one of the most intimate events of their lives has branded my soul in a way I never anticipated. As cloying as it is to say, Jharna, I am happy.

If offered a chance to change history and be with you in India, would I take it? It is a nonsensical question, naturally, and I only ask it of myself as a sort of test. A year ago, my yes would have been swiftly rendered. Now? Jharna, forgive me, but I am not so sure. Certainly Raja would beg me to say no! He and Miss de Bourgh are to be married in February, by the way. Another sign of how fate works for the best. Even Anoop, who I had to practically hog-tie to board the ship, is happy here. Indeed, God's Hand has been upon my life every step of the way. Only in looking back can I see the pattern, and since I have no intention of saying farewell to life on earth for a long while to come, I must trust that He has my future woven as well. I believe my fate and future in England have been joyfully closing upon me since the day in June when I stepped over the Darcy House threshold. Probably before that, when Searc badgered me into accompanying him. All this leads to my earlier reference to the humdrum moments. Grander, pivotal occurrences hold weight because of the tiny hundreds happening daily.

Philosophy, theology, or any other -ologies aside, it has been decided. I will take the position at the Matlock Hospital and establish myself as a country physician. Not sure how William will feel about messengers banging on the door all hours of the day and night, but he did beg me to stay after all. The folks hereabout don't know how blessed they are to have a competent physician in their midst! Me, hanging a shingle and making house calls. How strangely traditional is that?

THE DINING ROOM AT Darcy House on Grosvenor Square in London was located toward the rear of the white-stone townhouse. The windows and doors stood open to the terrace and garden beyond, affording a lovely view of the lush vegetation, narrow lawn, and musical fountain while also allowing in what breezes of fresh air were to be found in Town on a warm morning in early May. The Darcy family sat at one end of the long table eating their breakfast and engaging in friendly conversation. Fitzwilliam Darcy, the master of the house, sat at the end with his wife, Elizabeth, to his right and sister, Georgiana, beside her. Dr. George Darcy sat on his beloved nephew's immediate left and between bites of egg and jam-smeared toast was nodding rhythmically to Darcy's instructions while sharing amused glances under his thick brows with Elizabeth and Georgiana.

"Remember, Uncle, your primary responsibility is to escort Georgiana, and that means—"

"Keeping the slavering hounds at bay, yes, William, I know. I shall do my utmost to cut a formidable figure. Are swords allowed in Almack's? I do have a wicked *Rajput khanda* that was a gift from a grateful *raja* I healed in Rajasthan. It would certainly keep all potential suitors away, and it looks quite dashing with the outfit I plan to wear tonight."

Elizabeth and Georgiana laughed, Darcy's glower cast at all three of them.

"No, swords are not allowed in Almack's Assembly, and I do wish you would take this responsibility seriously."

"I am quite serious!" George lifted both brows, his face the picture of innocence. "It is a wicked sword, and I do look especially dashing when wearing it. Ah well," he sighed, "I suppose my mere presence must suffice. No worries, William. I promise to cross-examine and screen every applicant who asks for the privilege of dancing with Miss Darcy, and you, my dear"—George pointed a stern finger at Georgiana—"must promise not to elope the second I leave the ballroom to visit the lavatory."

"I promise."

"Are you sure that is allowed as part of the chaperone agreement, George? Visiting the lavatory? Best to be sure of these details before you depart tonight."

"Ah, good point, Elizabeth. Thank you. I should reread the contract, to be sure. If necessary, I shall eschew the punch and orgeat, just to be on the safe side."

"And if I need to visit the powder room? What then?"

"Oh dear! So many points to ponder! I suppose I could enlist the aid of a severe older lady to substitute as your attendant in that case. Surely even the boldest young man would not storm the women's quarters to spirit Georgiana away. Would they, Elizabeth?"

"I never attended a dance at Almack's so would not know. Dearest, is this something George should fret over?"

"Yes, William, is it? I mean it is doubtful you ever did such a brazen assault to propriety, but you know how some impetuous men in the throes of passion can be."

Darcy was sitting back in his chair, arms crossed over his chest and a resigned expression on his face. "Are you all quite finished? The point has been made, thank you."

George patted his nephew on the shoulder. "You do worry too much, William. I have faced down wild animals and managed harsher crises than a dance assembly. Georgiana will dance and flirt as she wishes, all under my watchful gaze, I assure you."

George proved as capable a chaperone to Georgiana Darcy as her brother, who had escorted her for her debut Wednesday appearance in April, and her cousin Colonel Richard Fitzwilliam for the next two. The colonel had submitted to the identical series of stern warnings from Darcy, listening, nodding, and then harassing his cousin much as George had. "Apparently, surviving battles against Napoleon's troops isn't validating," Richard said to George at one point, his teasing eyes resting on Darcy. "Bayonet-armed Frenchman aren't as terrifying as Englishmen bearing cups of ratafia, Dr. Darcy. Be careful. It is a true jungle within those glittering, gas-lit walls!"

Fitzwilliam Darcy was a hundredfold less intense and reserved than prior to his marriage to Elizabeth Bennet, but that did not make him the loose jester his uncle and cousin were. Hence the reason the two loved to torture him. Nevertheless, George appreciated the need to guard his beloved niece and was not nearly as blasé about the task as he pretended to his overprotective nephew. All was well, as it turned out. Georgiana Darcy's fourth appearance at Almack's Assembly in London passed without a single marriage proposal or untoward advance. She danced every set, socialized with her friends, and even flirted a little, not that Georgiana Darcy would ever be comfortable with the latter.

George attended to his duty but also had a marvelous time. He *was* a fabulous flirt, of course, and loved to dance. His exotic garments, even without the *khanda*, drew attention from males and females. It was a familiar phenomenon, England or India, so George thought nothing of the tickling sensations instigated by stares from all quarters of the room. There were three times during the course of that night, lasting until dawn, when the impression of scrutiny caused him to search the teeming masses for who was examining him so intently. He never could figure it out and shoved it out of his mind. By the time he stumbled into his bed at five o'clock, the mystery was a vague niggle, and by the time his empty stomach woke him at noon, he had forgotten all about it.

His morning ritual of stretching and yoga breathing occurred later than usual, followed by the grooming tasks necessary to make him feel human. Dressed in one of the few simply adorned *kurtas* he owned, a dark brown a shade lighter than the *shalwar* loosely covering his legs, George re-entered his bedchamber and greeted Anoop with a smile that turned into a yawn.

"Lord, I think I am too old for late nights and wild shenanigans. Coffee with lots of sugar, please."

"You should have slept in the afternoon, *Vaidya*, as I suggested."

"Lesson learned." He took a large gulp, the scald on his tongue worth the rush of stimulating coffee. Biting into a warm roll smothered in butter and honey, he waved at the seat across from him. Anoop sat and poured himself a cup of coffee.

"Will we be visiting the hospital today, *Vaidya*?"

"No. I told Dr. Runge I would be out late and not to expect me until tomorrow. I was planning a quiet afternoon in the cool of the stillroom. The ashwagandha roots are dried enough to grind and the bhuiamla I planted last fall is blooming. There are still some seeds brought from India I want to plant, so we will have a replenishing supply once my stores are gone. Can't get giloya or real turmeric here, so have to plant those."

"Did you send the list to *Vaidya* Ullas?"

"Yes, but that will take some time to get here and some need to be fresh, as you know. Nimesh can send seeds at the least. The gardens and orangery at Pemberley are better for serious growing, of course, but the stillroom here is adequate for a few of my favorites. Plus, the pretty stillmaid, Hortense, likes my company." George finished off the first roll and reached for another, his eyes on Anoop. "I think she likes your company even more though."

Anoop flushed beet red under his brown skin. "She is English. Not for me."

"She is a negro ex-slave who happens to live in England. There is a difference." George chewed and drank his coffee, obliquely watching Anoop try to pretend disinterest in the topic. Finally coming to a decision, George sighed. "Listen, Anoop. You are my friend, no matter what label you put on it. You have been with me for, God, what is it? Twenty-five years? I have dragged you all over the place, never giving you the chance to make a life for yourself—"

"Not true, *Vaidya*. I make my own choices and that has been to serve you."

"But what about Diviya or Tanzil? Both wanted you to marry them and don't deny it."

Anoop lifted his chin and met George's eyes. "They were not my destiny. If they had been then I would be married and not here."

George returned the calm stare, finally nodding. "You are right, Anoop. I apologize. I forgot my years of Hindu lessons for a minute there." He smiled and was rewarded with a returned smile and humorous nod from Anoop. "But you know I am a busybody, so will take the next in stride. All I am saying is that I want you to embrace your destiny without any concern for me. I love you, my friend, and will support whatever the gods have planned for you."

"I appreciate that, *Vaidya*. Now, are you done, so I can return this tray to the kitchen? We have work to do if you want to crush all the ashwagandha roots."

As the two men were crossing the entryway toward the rear doors leading to the backyard, where the stables and other outbuildings were located in the old mews, Elizabeth and Georgiana exited the front parlor. They were pulling on gloves and tying bonnets, their conversation animated, so they did not see the gentlemen.

"Entertaining plans, ladies?"

George had pitched his voice in a low rumble designed to startle them. To his disappointment, they merely looked up with sunny smiles.

"George! You look rested this afternoon. Slept well, did you?"

"I am surprisingly chipper considering I nearly died of boredom last night."

"Ha! He danced nearly as often as I, if one can call it such when the steps are wrong."

"I heard not a single complaint. And, let's be honest, this standing in a long line and circling each other is yawn inducing. Lady Jersey and the Princess von Lieven adored the Indian dance steps I taught them, and my waltz with Lady Beauchamp was inspired."

"It was indeed highly entertaining," Georgiana agreed. "William would have been mortified!"

Elizabeth laughed. "That proves the truth of the evening right there. Boredom indeed! How many lovely ladies did you dazzle with your charms, Dr. Darcy?"

"I lost count after forty," he answered with aplomb, and then turned toward the women coming from the corridor leading to the private quarters. "Ah! I presume a walk to Hyde Park is on the agenda. Greetings, Mrs. Hanford, Mrs. Annesley."

Mrs. Hanford curtsied, her cheeks rosy and smile vaguely flirtatious. Even the grandmotherly nanny was not immune to the allure of Dr. Darcy. She was pushing a perambulator within which lay a wide awake Alexander, the five-month-old chewing on a silver rattle and staring at his tall grand-uncle with bright-blue eyes. George exchanged pleasant chitchat with Mrs. Hanford as he bent to tickle the baby. Mrs. Annesley had said nothing, and as George straightened after eliciting a series of throaty chortles from Alexander, he swept his eyes toward Georgiana's companion, she hastily averting the gaze that had been resting on him.

Mrs. Annesley had been hired by Darcy three years prior to serve as chaperone and friendly companion to his sister. After the disastrous previous companion Mrs. Younge had arranged the plot with Mr. Wickham that had come perilously close to culminating in Georgiana's seduction and elopement at fifteen years of age, Darcy had chosen carefully. He told George that the widowed Mrs. Annesley was not only reliable and with impeccable recommendations but claimed she was kind, educated, and possessed a delightful personality. George had trouble believing the personality part, since she refused to speak more than two words to him. Whether that was because she did not care for him or because she was withdrawn by nature he did not know. Normally, it might have bothered him or been taken as a challenging puzzle to solve, but he so rarely saw her that he simply forgot her existence the bulk of the time.

George would have been hard pressed to say what her facial features were, although his impression was that she was attractive. He had no idea what color her eyes were or any other defined detail except that her hair was a pale blond similar to Georgiana's. Today, like always, she wore a well sewn but rather drab gown of pale gray with matching bonnet pulled far forward so that only the tip of her nose and tightly coiled hair at the nape of her slender neck were visible. She stood several feet away and, as typical, attempted to fade into the background.

"Would you and Anoop care to join us, Uncle?"

"Thank you, but no. We have work of a serious nature to attend to in the stillroom. However, if I may impose upon you to cut some dried bulrushes for me, I would greatly appreciate it."

"Do they have a medicinal value, Doctor?"

"No, Mrs. Hanford, not that I am aware. I simply like them!"

"You and my husband both. He is such a child when it comes to blowing the cottony bits."

"It is the simple joys of life that keep us young, dear Elizabeth." He bent to administer another series of tickles that had Alexander squirming and burbling, and then bid them adieu and happy hunting as he assisted out the door. "Have a lovely day, ladies! Be careful. Watch out for attack ducks. They are rampant in Hyde Park, you know, as are killer butterflies. Don't forget the bulrushes! Watch the wee one, Mrs. Hanford. He is a Darcy, and we are an unpredictable lot. Enjoy your afternoon, Mrs. Annesley."

He tipped an imaginary hat as she scurried through the door, last in the line of women. "I will, sir. Thank you," was her softly murmured reply, a rapid glance upward revealing a flash of blue before she moved hastily past and down the steps.

George stood on the threshold watching them stroll away. *What an odd woman,* he thought, his eyes lingering on her lithe gait and slightly swaying hips. Then he shrugged, closed the door, and forgot about it.

Three hours later, George and Anoop were done with the roots and on to hanging an assortment of medicinal herbs, some Indian and others obtained in England. George chatted with Hortense, the shy young lady giggling at his jokes but listening to his instructions as well. When she wasn't sneaking glances at a silent Anoop, that is. They were enjoying themselves, yes, but it was a chore George took seriously, so being interrupted was not appreciated.

"Dr. Darcy, pardon me for disturbing, but you have a visitor."

Mr. Travers, the Darcy House butler, impeccable in his black suit and white gloves, stood at the door looking out of place amid the rough tables and piles of dead plants. George knew he would not have interrupted if the visitor were unimportant, but it still annoyed him to be bothered at a critical juncture in the harvesting process.

"Send him out, Mr. Travers. I can diagnose what ails him here as well as inside."

"It is a lady, sir, and I think it best if you meet with her inside the house."

George raised a brow. Mr. Travers's tone was regulated, but George detected a hint of seriousness. He glanced at Anoop and then the maid, who shrugged unhelpfully.

"A lady, you say? How extraordinary." His curiosity was piqued, but he removed his gloves and leather apron reluctantly.

"Yes, sir. A fine lady, I might add. I have taken the liberty of ordering tea."

"Have you now? Well, then I suppose I better step up the pace!"

"I can bundle these for ye, Doctor," the stillmaid offered. "I been watchin' and know how it done. Mr. Anoop will help. I'll be careful, promise."

"Well! Aren't you a peach! Thanks, my dear." He handed the basket to Hortense, patted her rosy cheeks in a grandfatherly gesture that made her blush, gave a smattering of Hindi instructions to Anoop, and, after dipping his hands into a basin of water and cleaning as best he could, turned to the waiting Mr. Travers.

"A fine lady, you say. Fine as in handsome?"

"I cannot say, sir."

"Cannot or will not? Are you blind or diplomatic?"

"As you wish, Doctor."

George laughed and clapped the butler on the back. "Lead the way, Mr. Travers. If I must be interrupted in my task with one lovely lady, there is no better way than with another beautiful woman." He winked at Hortense, who blushed even more and then looked to see if Anoop was even slightly jealous. He wasn't, too aware of George's personality to take it seriously, but he was caught boldly admiring her rosy cheeks and pretty white smile. George stifled his laughter and stepped hastily after Mr. Travers.

Fitzwilliam had left early in the morning and the women were still at the park. Privacy was not an issue anywhere in the house, yet Mr. Travers led him down a corridor to the room that served jointly as the library and Darcy's office.

"Why is she in here and not the parlor?"

"She requested a place where the two of you would not be disturbed. I gathered her visit is of a sensitive nature. However, if you feel threatened simply cry for help and a footman will rescue you."

"Cheeky scoundrel! I knew you had it in you, Mr. Travers! Rescued indeed! Rest assured that I never ask for rescuing from a beautiful woman."

The butler inclined his head, George catching a glimpse of a smile before he turned away. Chuckling, he entered the library. Seconds later, his laughter stuttered to a halt when his mouth dropped open in shock.

The woman stood near the window, turning as he entered and fixing him with an affectionate gaze he had not felt in a long, long while.

"Hello, George," she greeted in a husky purr that sent tingles up his spine.

"Ruby?"

"Yes. I wasn't sure if you would remember me after all these years."

"How could I forget? I... Well, you have me speechless, and that has forever been a rare phenomenon."

The Duchess of Larent, who was once Lady Ruby Thomason and the second woman George had loved, smiled at his words. "Yes, I know. Very little surprised you."

"This definitely has. Good lord, how long has it been? Twenty-four, twenty-five years?"

"Twenty-seven years, two months."

George's brows rose at her exactness. Perhaps she had performed the math before arriving. Goodness knows he didn't remember precisely. "Indeed. I would not have thought it so long. You are as lovely as I recall, Ruby. The years have barely touched you."

"Oh, George!" She chuckled, the amusement a rich vibration of sensual promise. "You always were a charmer. Thank you, but we know that is not the truth."

It wasn't far off the mark, although if he was honest, he would admit it was difficult to be certain, Ruby's face long since a dim two-dimensional image. Standing before her was strange, as if one of those hazy dreams of some forgotten place or person was transpiring during his waking hours. She had aged, of course, just as he had, but was still beautiful. Rather than the petite, buxom girl in his faded memory, her figure was voluptuous with curves to her flesh that tipped her toward the edge of heaviness but only increased her allure. The aura of sensuality was there under the surface, but muted from what he remembered. Whether that was due to his maturity and the effect of many years or a change within her was impossible to say.

"I see Indian culture has affected you." She indicated his attire with a sweep of her hand. "It fits you well. You are as handsome as ever, George. Older, as am I, but age has only enhanced your attractiveness. Why does that seem to be the way of it for men while we women lose our bloom?"

George laughed and shook his head. "Now who is the charmer? You have lost nothing, Ruby, but have only amplified what was there in youth. Sorry, I am a terrible host. You have shaken my usual composure and gentlemanly conduct. Please sit and be comfortable." He gestured at the sofa and moved to sit on the chair across. "I apologize for my appearance. I was working in the stillroom. I believe tea and refreshments are on the way. And I do realize I should say, 'Your Grace,' but it feels unnatural. Do you mind?"

"Not at all. It seems unnatural from you as well." She sat on the edge of the sofa indicated, arranging her skirts with hands that trembled ever so slightly.

A knock at the door interrupted the uncomfortable pleasantries. Mr. Travers delivered the tea and refreshments as promised, the ritual of pouring and serving allotting George time to observe Ruby and gather his thoughts.

Last year while in Devon visiting with his sister Estella, George had read of the Duke of Larent's death. The news jolted him, not out of regard for the duke, goodness knows, but because he had never once considered encountering her, or Sarah for that matter, at a social function while in England. It was pointless to fabricate scenarios, but at least reading of the duke's death planted a seed of possibility, so he wouldn't be utterly flummoxed if it happened.

However, none of the scenarios involved Ruby brazenly walking into Darcy House! Why had she? The skills that made him a masterful diagnostician sensed she was here for a purpose, and that was not to reminisce about the past. She was serene, her gestures and expressions controlled and composed, but he sensed her nervousness. This was definitely not a casual social call between two old friends, although what other reason she had for seeking him out he could not fathom. Unless, he suddenly wondered with alarm, she was ill!

He altered his study, scrutinizing her as a physician rather than a former lover, and quickly diagnosed that nothing major was amiss. She was a picture of health, so unless it was something subtle indeed, he doubted it was a professional call. Whatever had brought her to his door, the ball was in her court so he allowed her to lead the conversation.

"I heard you came back to England just last year. Is that correct?"

"It is. I thought I was merely coming to visit, as I had before. After a few months, I realized I had no desire to go back to India. Still I hesitated to commit. After all, India had been my life for nearly thirty years. Finally, though, Fitzwilliam and Elizabeth begged me to stay, and you know I adore being indispensable, so here I am."

A half-hour passed as George told her of his adventures in India, leaving out anything personal. She asked if he had married, that the closest they came to touching on intimate matters, and he simply answered no without mentioning Jharna. She kept the conversation focused on him, cleverly evading his attempts to inquire of her life, a ploy George grew annoyed at.

Putting his teacup onto the tray and leaning forward with his elbows on his knees, George halted her midsentence. "Why are you really here, Ruby? As pleasant as it is to play catch-up, we both know that is not your purpose. Sorry if that sounds rude."

"No," she answered, the faint shake in her voice notable. "I appreciate your bluntness, George. You are much more perceptive than you used to be, for which I am grateful."

He frowned, sensing that she meant something he did not understand in the statement. Ruby set her teacup onto the tray and folded her hands in her lap. Clearly she was struggling, and he waited as patiently as he could muster but his curiosity was growing. Inexplicably, he experienced an abrupt current rush through his body, settling in the heart that was beginning to beat faster. He could not explain it, and never would, but suddenly he knew that whatever she had come to say was monumental.

"I have practiced this conversation a hundred times, yet I am still not sure where to begin," she murmured.

"Usually I would suggest at the beginning, but in this case, I am suspecting the middle, or even the end, may be best."

Ruby lifted her eyes from her lap after a deep breath. "Yes. Much more perceptive. Very well then, from the end, or the present I suppose. George, I came here to tell you that you have a son. Our son."

Perceptive he may be, but nothing had prepared him for that. For the second time in a matter of an hour, his mouth dropped open and he was speechless. Truly speechless. Words could not have passed his lips at that moment if his life depended on it.

"I lied to you, about many things. None of it I am proud of and all of it caused me tremendous pain. Under the circumstances, I doubt you wish to hear of my suffering, nor would I expect you to care. I am prepared for you to hate me forever and know that I am destroying whatever kind thoughts you have held for me in your heart. So be it. That price I willingly pay for you to know, finally, that we created someone amazing during our time together. Our son who is now the Duke of Larent. His name is—"

George jumped from his chair, stalked to the window, and stared sightlessly into the garden. If Ruby spoke further, he did not know. The churn of emotions could not penetrate the fogged paralysis in his mind, George too stunned to hear anything. He was not sure whether to cry, collapse, scream, strangle the woman on the sofa behind him, run wildly from the room for the nearest ship to India, or perhaps all of the above in that order. Nothing coherent rose to the surface to overcome the sentence cycling and clanging in his ears.

You have a son.

The one yearning desire he had never been blessed to satisfy was having a child and being a father. Bhrithi had lived no longer than a vapor. He had learned to be content as "uncle" and surrogate father to Nimesh and Sasi and to give his affection to many other children over the years up to and including Alexander. Long ago, he had convinced himself that the desire was behind him. Now he was being told that for twenty-six years he had been a father! The implications of all he had lost slammed into him, grief nearly bringing him to his knees, but anger won the battle and steeled his spine.

"Does he know?" He turned as he spoke and noted her wince at the seething fury in his voice. He did not care. "Does he know about me?"

"He does now. I told him shortly after his fa… after Larent died. He always suspected something was not right and was relieved to learn why. I held nothing back. I told him everything, all my sins. I told him of you, how we met and why, and how I fell in love with you—"

"Don't say that!" George slapped his palm onto the top of Darcy's desk, the sound sharp and jarring. "You cannot say that! You do not have the right. Not now! I refuse to listen to your excuses and claims of affection, Ruby. I only want to know how this happened and why you kept it from me. Kept *him* from me. How could you do that to me? And what do you expect me to do with this information? As if the high and mighty *Duke of Larent* would want anything to do with a lowly physician from the wilds of India!"

Ruby's eyes swam with tears, but she lifted her chin and met his irate face with a dignified stare. "You can rail at me all you want, George, and I will not argue one point. But do not cast aspersions of character onto Alexis. He is a remarkable—"

"Alexis? You named him Alexis?"

"Yes. I had to fight for it. 'George' was out of the question, obviously, but *he* never knew why I insisted on Alexis."

She referred to her husband, naturally, and George heard the tone of dislike. It did not surprise him that their marriage was not a happy one. How could it have been with such a cold man?

She named him Alexis.

As much as he wanted to hate her, it suddenly became too much to sustain. Weakly, he staggered back to the chair, dropped into it, and stared at his clasped hands. Too many thoughts jumbled together so he chose the simplest.

"Tell me," he whispered.

And she did. She confessed the entire tale of her selfish desires and hunger for power. She revealed how she met the Duke and explained about their secret marriage a month before the Sardar's birthday celebration, where Larent pointed out the man she was to seduce: a doctor who bore a striking physical resemblance to him.

"It seemed so easy, George. I was honest when I told you that I liked men. I always had, although never taking it to an improper place. Having my husband order me to bed another man sounded like a gift. Men enjoy such freedom and are respected for it. Why shouldn't I have the same liberty? I had never met a man in my life who would not have gleefully taken me to bed. From before puberty, men had been drawn to me, and I knew that what they wanted was my body. Never had anyone wanted my heart or cared for my feelings. I am not excusing my actions," she amended when George glanced up with a dubious glare, "but you must admit that it is true. Few men are decent, at least not in the circles I traveled in. I am older now, wiser I hope, and I know not all men are rogues and scoundrels. There are honest gentlemen out there. Sadly, the first one I met was after I belonged to another."

She spoke sparingly of the months following her desertion of him, saying only that it was the baby growing inside that kept her from madness. Despite his wish to hate her, George was too skilled a diagnostician to ignore the subtle clues that spoke of the heartache she endured. She had told lies, but not about her love for him. He had believed it then and he believed it now.

They had returned to England immediately, she told him. The Duke of Larent proudly squired his pregnant wife to a multitude of Society functions before retiring to their country estate for her lying in. His virility and potency was affirmed to the entire world, doubly so when she birthed a boy.

"Alexis was a perfect baby, George." The smile and brilliance of her eyes touched George's heart, and he smiled too. "I could see you in his face instantly. He was the light out of the darkness of my heartache."

George nodded and that simple gesture spread relief over her face. With a sigh, Ruby continued and talked about their son, details upon details. He could have listened for days, never interrupting, but then she mentioned Alexis's sister.

"Sister? How did you—?"

The answer was written on her face, but she had promised to tell him everything.

"Larent was not content with one child. I have three children, each of them special and loved with all my soul, although only Alexis was from a man I cared about. The others were chosen for a task, and I refused to allow myself to think otherwise. I received a bit of pleasure, and then, when I was fortunate to conceive, another son and a daughter."

She boldly held his eyes as she talked of her illicit relations, clearly unapologetic for her actions. *I like men.* George had dwelt for too long among the less-inhibited Indians to be appalled by her statement or the fact that she had enjoyed her promiscuity. She was absolutely correct that men exploited their carnal freedom, and although George tended to be a moral traditionalist, he was not a saint either. No, he could not condemn her.

"I adored being a mother and Larent, while largely indifferent, was not a bad father." She drank from her tea, as if needing the strong drink to wash away the memories. "Ours was not a marriage of affection, but he treated me well and gave me the life I wanted. I enjoyed freedoms few women do. I wished it could have been different. I wished for the life I imagined you and I would have had, but wishing for something that isn't to be serves no purpose. I am, above all, practical."

Ruby offered no additional explanations, and George respected that. It was not his place to judge her life, and to be honest, Alexis was all that mattered to him.

I have a son!

"Did you ever consider contacting me?"

"Hundreds of times. But I had no idea where you were, and how could I tell you of Alexis in a letter?" She reached across the low table to clasp George's slack hand. "George, you must understand there was no way I could take the risk. My guilt has eaten at me, but my loyalty is to Alexis. He is the Duke of Larent and nothing can jeopardize that."

"Then why are you here, Ruby? Why tell me any of this now if it means nothing? You say not to cast aspersions in one breath then in the next tell me he wants nothing to do with me!"

"You misunderstood me, George. I never said Alexis wants nothing to do with you. He has been anxious to meet you, meet his father, since I told him the truth. I was only stressing that his parentage must remain our secret."

He didn't draw his hand away and searched her eyes for the tiniest hint of deception. There was only honesty in the direct gaze staring back at him.

"He is anxious to meet me?"

Ruby smiled at the tightness in his voice. "Yes. He wanted to come with me today, but I felt it best to talk with you alone. Additionally, I can sneak about more easily than the Duke of Larent. When you see him, you will know what I mean. He is a stunning figure of a man. The handsomeness of his father and a considerable dose of his mother's magnetism make for quite a combination."

George chuckled at her boasting. "Yes, I imagine so. He resembles me, you say?"

"His eyes are darker, more like mine, as is his hair. He isn't quite as tall as you and is thicker built. Most see my husband in him, naturally, but I, who knew you both intimately, see that he has your features. For one, he loves to smile and his eyes are animated."

"Not cold like… him."

"No, not ever. He is more reserved than you, but humorous and charming. He may inherit those traits from both of us. He has your mouth and smile, a smile that is lovely on its own and enhanced by how it lights his face. That is entirely you, George. And when Alexis is especially enthused or happy, his joy is contagious. I remember that in you, and when I spoke with him this morning and saw that light brighter than ever, I knew it was time to tell you. Alexis insisted anyway."

"He did?"

She laughed at his almost childlike delight. "Yes, he did. It was all he could do not to speak with you himself last night. He was at Almack's and recognized you instantly. I am sure your attire tipped him off as well."

"That's what I was feeling! I had the strangest sensation of being stared at but could not pinpoint the person."

"He remained unobtrusive, preferring to watch you."

George winced, remembering his antics on the dance floor and while socializing, any of which could easily be misconstrued from afar as ridiculousness. Hell, it was ridiculousness up close for that matter, not that George ever cared one whit how people judged him. This was his son, however.

His son!

Ruby laughed, reading the thoughts flickering over his face. "Have no fears. He was impressed by your carefree spirit and admires you for grasping an adventurous life. I have always seen that yearning inside him and know it comes from you. Alas, there are drawbacks to being a duke."

"Is he happy? Has… this… knowledge upset him?"

"I think you should save your questions for Alexis. Trust me, you will not be disappointed."

George bowed his head and ran one hand through his hair. "What happens now?"

"We would like you to join us for dinner tomorrow, if that is amenable to you. It will only be the three of us."

"Yes, of course. I will be there."

She stood then, George doing the same, and handed him a paper retrieved from her reticule. "Our townhouse in Kensington. Seven o'clock."

George took the slip automatically, his eyes on her face. For a long while they stared in silence, neither knowing what to say.

"Ruby," he finally choked through a thick throat. "I am still unbelievably angry at you, yet I also want to say thank you, which makes no sense."

"I know, George. I am asking for nothing for myself. Hate me forever, forgive me, have compassion or not, it makes no difference as long as you do not blame Alexis. I cannot change the past, and to be honest, I wouldn't if I could. I can't give you the little boy you deserved or the legitimate place you should have as Alexis's father. I am sorry for that. However, I can give you a remarkable young man who can be your friend. We shall see you tomorrow. No, stay here. I can show myself out." And after a glancing brush of her fingertips across his knuckles, she was gone.

Eventually, George sat back down, but he was still staring blindly at the slip of paper when Darcy entered the dark room an hour later.

"Uncle? Are you in here?"

"Yes, William. I am here."

"We were worried. Dinner is in an hour and no one knew where you were. Are you well?"

Darcy lit a lamp and carried it to the circle of chairs where George sat slumped. Darcy sat on the seat vacated by Ruby. Was it really only an hour ago? George felt like five minutes and twenty-seven years had passed at the same time.

"What is it? Do you wish to talk, or shall I leave you to your solitude?"

George smiled and lifted his head. "You are a remarkable young man, William. Clearly concerned over my disturbed state and desirous to help yet also respectful of my privacy. Have I told you lately how blessed I feel to have you in my life? How deeply I love you? Good." He nodded at Darcy's affirming incline. "Of all the life lessons I have grasped, one is not to be afraid to tell a loved one how you feel."

He sat back into the chair, the one lamp casting just enough illumination to reveal the confusion and worry etched on Darcy's face. "I know I have told you that you are everything I would have wished for in a son, that our relationship is all I could have imagined had I a son of my own. It took us a while to get there though, didn't it? For a long while, I didn't think you liked me, and even after I knew that was not true, I was unsure we would ever be more than friends. Just being your friend would have sufficed, but I longed for more and am thankful God planned more. No, lad, I haven't lost my mind. These deep thoughts and apparent rambling sentences have a purpose. Today, I found out something that has rocked me, yes, but my brains aren't wholly addled. Monumental enough to send me into an introspective spin, however, and I really hate that!"

George laughed, part mirth and part irony. "The point of all this is that I need to prepare myself honestly for what will come of what I learned today. Our relationship gives me hope, you see, that something wonderful can result from the most bizarre of circumstances."

George inhaled twice in a cleansing manner. "I learned today that I have a son. A twenty-six-year-old son I never knew existed who just happens to be the Duke of Larent."

For the remainder of the evening, the two men stayed in the library. Dinner was brought, and while eating and sipping wine, George shared the entire tale with his stunned nephew. Darcy helped in a host of ways, partially his serene presence and ability to say nothing while George talked, but also the tidbits of information he knew about the present Duke of Larent. Darcy did not know His Grace well, but he had met him on numerous occasions over the years and heard others talking of him. The conversation calmed George, helping him to form a clearer picture of the man he would meet tomorrow.

After twenty-four hours of what he insisted pass as any normal day, meaning a long shift at the hospital, George stood on the lower step before the enormous double doors of the elegant townhouse in Kensington. He had dressed in one of his finest *sherwanis*, woven silver threads adding a shimmering effect to the black fabric edged with silver and forest green braid. The *salwar* trousers were fitted more than some, dyed an ashen gray with trim matching that on the *sherwani*. Jeweled and beaded *mojaris* completed the exotic ensemble that could easily have been worn by an Indian prince. The pendant gifted to him by Tipu Sultan hung around his neck, the gold chain and roaring enamel tiger the perfect accompaniment. He struck a fine figure, and he knew it.

More than the impression, however, this was who George Darcy was: a man who would forever be Indian as much as possible for an Englishman to be. He was proud of that fact, proud of who he was and what he had accomplished. If his son and he were to have a relationship, whichever direction it evolved, it would be an honest one based on the man he was. Self-assurance was not a façade for George, which was why once the shock of the news wore off somewhere amid talking to William, George accepted this as simply another life event to face.

Thus, with a smile, he mounted the steps and rang the bell. Seconds later, the butler admitted him and escorted to the salon.

First his gaze alit on Ruby, Her Grace, the Duchess of Larent. She sat on a brocade settee looking every inch a duchess: bejeweled and dressed in a dark-purple gown of the latest fashion, her raven hair glossy and coiffed to perfection. She met his eyes, anxiety visible in the tight control she maintained with every feature to present a countenance of tranquility. George grinned and winked, the relaxing effect instantaneous, and then, as he started to lift his eyes away, he noted the oval locket lying on her creamy skin just above the dark crevice between her breasts. His eyes widened and snapped back to her face. Her smile had softened swiftly in the handful of heartbeats that had passed, George answering with a lift of his left brow before finally sweeping his gaze to the tall man standing in the middle of the room.

Alexis, His Grace, the Duke of Larent was exactly as George had envisioned. Tall and dark like his mother. Handsome and well built. He was nervous and obviously trying hard not to show it, the effect creating an illusion that was similar to George's hazy memory of the icy former Duke of Larent. Then he focused on the young man's eyes and knew instantly that this duke was not icy in the least.

So quickly the impressions and exchanges passed. George was barely over the threshold and still advancing into the room. The butler, surely ignorant of the situation, spoke into the palpable silence. "Your Grace, your guest, Dr. George Darcy."

George waited for the door to shut, leaving the three alone, and addressed Alexis first.

"I have always thought that was rather redundant, haven't you? After all, you do know who your guests are since you invited them, yes?"

"I agree." Alexis's baritone was firm, the power of a man born to a high station and the dignity of a peer of the realm imbued into those two words. George detected the faint tremor, though, as well as the shimmer of a warm smile playing about his mouth.

"I am not one for propriety, as I am sure your mother has told you. Under the circumstances, that is likely a good thing." George extended his hand to his son, who took it after a slight hesitation. "Unless I have been escorted into the wrong salon in the wrong townhouse, I do believe you are Alexis. I am George and very happy to meet you."

Then the duke smiled, a wide toothy smile identical to the one George had seen thousands of times in a mirror, and he clasped George's hand tightly within both his palms.

"And I you. Thank you for coming, George."

George's Memoirs
December 30, 1818

Georgiana and I are on solo baby watch, Jharna! The nasty cold besetting Elizabeth over Christmas responded well to my medicines, but you know how William worries over her. It is beautiful to observe them, it truly is, even though I delight in teasing him for being a clucking hen! He arranged a three-day romantic holiday at Matlock Bath. His purpose was to partake of the reputed restorative powers of the spas. I'm dubious of the wild claims of magical healing from dipping in or sipping from water with dissolved mineral salts and sulfur, but considering the strange treatments I have seen in my day, who knows? Fact is, William grabbed on to the mineral spring nonsense as an excuse for whisking Elizabeth away and having her to himself, hence my referring to it as a romantic holiday! Not that I blame him. Matlock is a lovely area, and if you were here, Jharna, I would be whisking you there and engaging in the very activities the loving Darcys are, I promise you that!

So while they cavort and gaze at the moonlight, we are in charge of an adorable one-year-old. Oh, what fun we are having with Alexander all to ourselves! Three days of nonstop play. Don't fret. I can be responsible when I must, my dear. He is taking his naps, being bathed, and eating proper foods, I promise. In between, we play. He is a busy one now that he has learned to walk, or toddle, which is apt since he falls as often as he moves forward, yet he is unusual in that he can focus on a task far longer than most infants his age. We spend hours with his new miniature castle, the tiny soldiers endlessly fascinating to him. I confess it is a delight to me. No secret how I adore children. I think of our wee ones in Junnar, missing them more than I can verbalize. Sasi and Nimesh write frequently, so I am kept informed, but it is not the same as being with them. If not for Alexander, I am not sure I could survive it. Ah well, I am here now and not unhappy about it. Less and less do I wake up with a vague confusion. The frigid cold drives that away almost instantly! God, I truly think I shall never get used to it. Forgive me, love, but as I shiver in my bed, I miss you for your warmth more than anything else. Not that the vision of loving you isn't one I long for as well, but if I am being honest, I wonder if that isn't pure lust as much as missing you. These two years are the longest I have ever gone without a woman. Honestly, I didn't notice the lack for a long while, my thoughts only of how I missed you, priya, in every way. I am only human—damn it all!—so the physical urges are taking over. What to do is the dilemma. Once upon a time, casual relations suited me just fine and the opportunities have been rife since I returned. Ruby has hinted that she is willing, and believe me I have been tempted! Why I resist is complicated, and I don't completely understand it myself. Casual sex does not interest me, Jharna. Well, it does in one sense, yet each time I begin to seriously contemplate an affair, I realize I do not want the emptiness. Does that mean I want to fall in love and marry? Yes, but I cannot fathom that happening at my age and after what we shared. This reasoning brings me to Ruby. I know very well that the loving would be stupendous. Or would it? Too much time has passed between us to be certain. Mostly, I refuse to do anything to jeopardize the relationship I have with Alexis. That is far more important than my lust. I suppose I shall remain open for whatever destiny has waiting for me. Or until I am near to exploding. Whichever comes first.

Speaking of Alexis, his Christmas gift was a new saddle and complete tack for Rathore. Can you believe it? I have my other saddles, of course. They were shipped along with my faithful old mount and the remainder of my belongings, those I wished to keep after the house sold. Honestly, I prefer my Indian saddles, as does Rathore. He is getting old and crotchety like me so hates change. The new saddle is exquisite and fits nicely on the thoroughbred William gifted me for my birthday last year, so whether on Rathore or Ghora, it will be used. Alexis is anxious to see my Marwari stallion, which will happen in February. As soon as William and Elizabeth return from steaming up the already steamy spas, we will be traveling to London for the occasion of Colonel Fitzwilliam's marriage to Lady Simone Fotherby. I am still stunned at that development and in shock that the colonel is leaving his bachelorhood behind! Who will I carouse with now? Yes, I know it is a charade, Jharna, but I do have a frivolous rogue reputation to maintain! Now I am on my own and will need to work even harder to convince of my devil-may-care ways. Ah, the tragedy of it all! Back to Alexis, he has invited me to the ducal estate in Dorset, where he is wintering with his new bride. She is a delightful young lady and I am ecstatic that my son has married a woman he loves. What a joy! I shall spend at least a month there, with Anoop and Rathore, and then probably jaunt over to Exeter to visit with Estella and family. She tells me there is a new hospital in the city with physicians from Philadelphia on staff. American medicine I know nothing of other than through journals and articles written by Dr. Benjamin Rush and others, so I must take time to introduce myself at least, as long as I am back to London by June when William plans for us to leave for Europe. So much for relaxing in my twilight years! Did you honestly think that would happen?

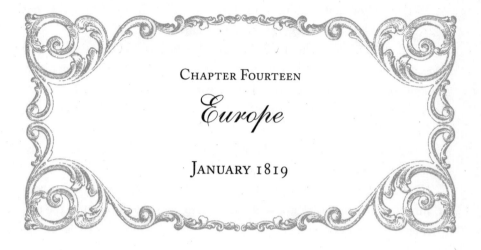

A RE YOU READY, COLONEL? The reverend will soon be at the altar with Bible in hand, so this is your last opportunity to sneak out the side door."

"No chance of that, Dr. Darcy." Colonel Richard Fitzwilliam stood at the mirror, adjusting the edges of his cravat with hands shaking from nervousness rather than fear. "I have been waiting for this day for longer than I realized and am anxious to claim my bride."

"Excellent! It warms my heart to see young men walking into the arms of matrimony with a smile on their face. Gives me hope for the future."

Richard looked at George's reflection, his brows lifting. "Public proclamations of a positive attitude toward marriage, Doctor? Are you sure you are well?"

"Don't perish from the shock. Despite my flippant attitude, I am not averse to the idea of marriage. In fact, felicity from every corner since returning to England has caused me to rethink my sworn bachelor ways. Yes, I know! The sun may stop shining if I speak too loudly, so forget I said anything! Instead, I'll offer one last chance for you to make a safe retreat. I can cover the exit while William explains to the guests that your sanity has suddenly been restored."

"Thanks, but I intend to go through with the ceremony, sane or not." He looked at Darcy. "How does my cravat look?"

"Perfect. Now quit fiddling with it or you will muss the loops. Fix your jacket, and by God, do something about that missing button."

"Lord! Have I lost a button?" Richard grabbed at his jacket, frantically fingering the edges lined with gold buttons before turning an evil eye upon his grinning cousin. "Darcy, I am wielding a sword and am nervous as hell, so be wise in how you choose to tease me."

The door opened, well timed to spare Darcy's life, and Mr. Charles Bingley stuck his head through the crack. "Colonel Fitzwilliam? Lady Simone is ready, so it is time for you to enter the chapel."

"Finally," George muttered, rising from the chair where he had been reclining and clapping Richard on the shoulder. "Stare her straight in the eye, my friend, and convey the depth of your love and devotion. Don't let nerves interfere. Cherish this day and remember every detail. Trust me, it is a memory you will want imprinted upon your mind for all eternity."

Richard stared into George's intent, blue eyes and nodded slowly. "Thank you, Dr. Darcy. I will heed your advice."

George squeezed the groom's arm, wished him luck, ignored Darcy's sympathetic gaze, and left the room to find his place at the family pews, clasping Georgiana's hand as he sat. The ceremony joining Colonel Richard Fitzwilliam in holy matrimony to Lady Simone Wrexham-Pomeroy, Marchioness of Fotherby, was lovely. The groom stood tall and handsome in his medal-emblazoned uniform with every button in place, a broad smile lighting his face as he gazed upon his bride, her visage equally radiant. Such depth of love was a joy to witness.

It was a dreary January day outside, but inside the church, the atmosphere was sunny. Congratulations spewed forth as frothily as the champagne served during the breakfast reception at the Fotherby mansion afterward. Guests were in high spirits and the celebration merry. George was in his element, meandering from group to group with a wineglass in his hand, his gay humor at the ready. One could always count on George Darcy to add life to a party!

He was still laughing at a bawdy joke by a trio of soldiers as he whirled around a corner and bumped roughly into a woman exiting the music room. She released a small yelp, George instinctively throwing his arm around her waist to prevent her tumbling backward into the empty doorway.

"Blast! Hold up there, madam! Steady on your feet!" An odd dance ensued as George righted his imbalance while struggling not to spill his wine on the startled woman in his embrace. The suddenness of the situation and his extreme embarrassment did not interfere with his awareness of her soft curves and pleasant perfume. "Please, forgive my clumsiness. I suppose this is a signal to end my wine drinking. Are you unharmed, madam?"

"I am fine, Dr. Darcy, so there is nothing to forgive. And please do not let this simple accident curtail your entertainment."

George frowned, mortification at his blunder replaced by confusion. She clearly knew him, or at least who he was. Reluctantly, he released the mystery woman from his embrace and stepped back a couple paces. He tried to peer into her face, but she was far shorter than he and kept her head bowed. For the life of him, he could not identify who she was, although the voice was familiar and faint recollection tugged at the corner of his brain. He swept his eyes over her figure, the dainty but voluptuous reality confirming what his senses registered while she was pressed against his chest.

"I am glad you are well, madam, and that my medical skills were not called upon. Normally, rescuing damsels in distress or attending to the wounds of a beautiful woman is a high point to my day, but not if I am the cause! I do appreciate your encouragement to continue my amusements, but I now believe my gaiety will be diminished if you do not accompany me, so I may express my contrition over a glass of punch."

She flinched visibly, the blond curls framing her face hiding all but the flushed curve of one cheek. George's lighthearted tease was clearly having the opposite effect than the one he intended, increasing his confusion but also heightening his curiosity. Unwilling to let the mystery go unsolved, he tried again.

"I see you shaking, and I think it is a code or law from the Crown for a gentleman to ease a lady's distress. I am certain I recall a specific article stating it is a chivalrous imperative when the distress is caused by a clumsy physician nearly knocking her senseless. Allow me to formally introduce myself—"

"We have been introduced, Dr. Darcy, and there is no need to trouble yourself. I am fine." She glanced up, then rapidly looked away with flaming cheeks and a nervous twist of the tresses falling across her neck.

"Mrs. Annesley?" George gasped in shock. "You look… different!" He bit his tongue before blurting what he wanted to say.

You look beautiful!

The woman before him was an utter contrast to Georgiana's drably dressed retiring companion briefly glimpsed in the shadows or corners of the rooms. Her golden blond hair was uncovered, the thick tresses twisted and curled into a becoming style. Her gown was pale blue, the color accenting her eyes, and designed in the latest fashion with feminine lace and colorful ribbons sewn strategically to draw one's attention to the finest attributes of her figure. A figure, George noted favorably, that was petite but surprisingly lush. A sheer fichu was draped over her slim shoulders and tucked into the low décolletage but did a poor job of hiding the alabaster skin underneath or concealing the fullness of her round breasts. Taken as a whole, she was wreaking havoc on his senses. George swallowed and dragged his gaze forcibly away from her bosom back to her averted face.

"I apologize for not recognizing you instantly, Mrs. Annesley. I had no idea you were here today."

"It was Miss Darcy's request. She insisted and would not relent no matter how I pleaded the inappropriateness."

"Why is it inappropriate for you to be at Colonel Fitzwilliam's wedding?"

"It is a family affair, Dr. Darcy, and thus not my place."

George snorted. "Nonsense! More than half the people here are not family. Probably walked in off the street for the food." He was encouraged to see a smile. "Georgie is fond of you, Mrs. Annesley, and speaks of you as a friend. As such, you should be here or anywhere else she invites you. I have often wondered why you do not join the family more often."

"Have you?"

She gazed up at him then, the question visible in the blue depths of her eyes, as was her obvious surprise at his statement. George discerned that his response was important to her but found it difficult to puzzle out why. At the moment, thick, golden lashes framing almond-shaped blue eyes captivated him.

"Mr. Darcy selected you as Miss Darcy's companion due to your capabilities and intelligence, Mrs. Annesley. He has spoken highly of you, and for William to do that says volumes! Additionally, an exceptional young lady like Georgiana chooses her friends wisely, so I must assume your contribution to any gathering would be beneficial."

"You are kind to say so, Dr. Darcy. However, I doubt my contributions would compete with your exciting stories and knowledge of the world."

"They have heard all my elaborated stories and are bored with my voice dominating conversations. Feminine gossip is always preferred, believe me. In my experience, those of the fairer sex liven up any conversation."

"Yes, I am sure you would have experience in that regard." She glanced away as she spoke, George catching a hint of pursed lips and an edge to her voice. Before he could conclude what she meant or why she was displeased, she went on in a more level tone, "Nevertheless, the fact remains that I am not a member of the family."

"Ah, yes, rules of propriety. How would we ever survive without them?" His dramatic nuance caused her to look up at him, George happy to see a glint of humor in her lovely eyes. "You are Georgie's companion, Mrs. Annesley, and a woman of breeding and excellence, so I am told. Not a farm laborer or stable worker shoveling manure all day. And if you were, the conversation would be even better! That I know from experience as well." He shrugged and grinned. "I disdain the bulk of English conventions, in case you haven't figured that out, Mrs. Annesley. Class divisions are just one of the rules I deem ridiculous. Servant or serf or king, they are much the same to me. The kings simply host better parties!"

Mrs. Annesley shook her head but kept her eyes on George's face, his pleasure increasing when she laughed. George felt his heart skip a beat and a shiver run up his spine.

"I shall have to accept your superior knowledge regarding a king's party, Dr. Darcy. And I appreciate your kindness, even if I tend to disagree with your opinions."

"Kindness has nothing to do with it, although it probably should, since I could have seriously wounded you with my hulking frame and sharp elbows, but now that you have the audacity to disagree with me, I am tempted to rescind the entire statement! I expect all to be dazzled by my superior intellect and wisdom. This is quite a blow, madam, and I may never recover."

"Yet did you not praise me for my intellect, Doctor? How beneficial could my contribution to a conversation be if I only nodded and agreed with all you said?"

"Ah ha! See how quickly you turned my words against me? Well done, madam. I detect a clever mind inside the beautiful exterior. Do you play chess, Mrs. Annesley?"

She blushed prettily at his praise and was clearly flattered at his reference to her beauty, yet there was a twinge of something that resembled disbelief or possibly disapproval. He could not decide, and in an instant, it was replaced by confusion and withdrawal at his question about chess. In truth, George was startled at the question too. It had slipped out and was accompanied by the vision of he and Mrs. Annesley sitting companionably across a chess table.

"I do play chess, yes," she replied hesitantly. "Miss Darcy and I play together from time to time and I have engaged… others in the past."

Instinctively, he knew she meant her husband. Inexplicably, George felt a pierce of jealousy, shocking him profoundly. "Perhaps you would condescend to challenge me sometime. I am always on the hunt for skilled competition." He could not look away from her eyes, the moment stretching as she peered intently up at him, assessing for what he did not know. Then, finally, she seemed to come to a decision and nodded slowly without breaking eye contact.

"I think I would like that, Dr. Darcy. Very much."

George wanted to say something witty, but he could not think over the rush of strange sensations coursing through him as they stared at each other. It defied logic, yet all George could grasp onto was a wild urge to kiss her! It didn't help that her eyes slipped to his mouth, her lips parting slightly. Thankfully, maybe, they were interrupted.

"Amanda! There you are! Oh, hello, Uncle. Sorry to interrupt."

"Amanda. Lovely name." George winced, for a second questioning his sanity, but when she smiled he no longer cared.

"You are not interrupting, Miss Darcy. Did you need me?"

Georgiana was examining both of their faces with interest. "I have great news to tell you, Amanda, but it can wait. I do not wish to intrude."

"You are never intruding, my dear. I would like a glass of punch anyway. Dr. Darcy, thank you for the conversation. I promise to dwell on your words seriously."

She curtsied and then linked arms with Georgiana, steering hastily away and leaving George standing frozen by the doorway. He could not tear his eyes away from the sensuous sway of her hips, watching until the crowds swallowed the duo from view. *Amanda.* Her name had never been spoken, at least not that he could recall, and while it was a lovely name, he knew his reaction to hearing it was more than the name being nice. Suddenly feeling the fool, George shrugged out of his trance and gulped the contents of the wineglass he still held in his hand.

First pretty woman in your arms after years and you act the ridiculous adolescent!

Grabbing a glass of champagne from a passing servant, George drained the bubbling liquid as he walked in the opposite direction from where the women had gone, chalking up his reaction to being too long without a lover and shoving the episode aside as best he could.

After a half hour of amusement, he had done a fair job of dampening the lingering sensations. He stood with Fitzwilliam on the terrace, the men retreating to a quiet location with cooler air. The drizzling rain had stopped and the clouds were attempting to part and allow the sun to shine through, but it was brisk. Still, better than the increased temperature from masses of people milling through the lower level of the house.

"Will you still be leaving on Monday?"

George nodded. "Anoop has everything packed, not that I intend to take all that much with me. I believe the gifts I have for everyone will take up more room than our personal belongings. I do appreciate the large carriage though. Thanks for that, William."

"I know how uncomfortable it is to squeeze a frame our size into a small carriage. I would rather travel on horseback. But Devon is a distance and the weather is unpredictable, so a carriage in this instance is best. I am having the team re-shod, but that will be done before Monday."

"Thank you again. You think of everything!"

"I try." Darcy grinned.

"Malcolm tells me you have the agenda set for Europe."

Darcy nodded at his uncle's question. "Mostly. He and Aunt Madeline are handling the connections in France, since they have friends in Paris and other towns. I have yet to write to Baroness Oeggl or plot the precise timeline, but we have months to prepare. I have to remain stealthy if I am going to keep it a surprise for Elizabeth on her birthday in May."

"So you still plan for us to depart in June?"

"Yes. Why? You weren't planning to stay in Devon longer, were you? Or in Dorset with your son?"

"I will be back in London by the end of March, as I said. You might want to rethink leaving in June, however. I could be wrong, but if we want to have time to reach Austria or Switzerland, wherever Mary is dwelling at the time, and do more than turn around after a quick kiss to your Aunt Mary's cheek, leaving in April might be better."

"What in the world are you talking about, Uncle?"

"As I said, I could be wrong, but I have a vague suspicion that your holiday at Matlock Bath accomplished more than ridding Elizabeth of a lingering cold. She may have picked up something else while there, and if you are still too obtuse to figure out what I mean, I am going to start using words and phrases that will make you blush. Do I have to resort to frank language of marital intimacy and the results of such activity?"

"Elizabeth pregnant? Do you think so?"

George chuckled at the delighted awe washing over Darcy's mien. "It is merely a suspicion at this point. Whether during your stay at Matlock Bath or before, if my guess is correct, Elizabeth is barely pregnant and probably only beginning to suspect herself. I would not have said anything except for our trip abroad."

"Maybe we should postpone until next year then." Awe and delight were still planted on Darcy's features, but he was also frowning with concern.

"By then you would have two babies to tote and the way you two are Elizabeth is likely to be pregnant again." George nudged Darcy's foot, chuckling again at the hint of rosiness brightening his cheeks. "Elizabeth is strong and will be fine. Pregnancy is no reason not to travel."

As he spoke, Georgiana and Mrs. Annesley came into view behind a nearby window. They were yards from the window and several people wandered in the space between, yet the older woman turned toward him, her eyes lifting almost as if she sensed him staring at her.

Fanciful nitwit! George chided himself. But he did not look away.

"Besides, Georgiana is of the perfect age," he said. "She will benefit greatly from touring the Continent. Will her companion Mrs. Annesley travel with her?"

"I imagine so. I haven't spoken of this to Georgiana, but Uncle Malcolm wants to take her to Italy. I thought we would all go, but if you are right about Elizabeth, that would be out of the question. I'll need to reconsider our agenda carefully."

"They are close, aren't they?" George watched the women fade into the crowd, his eyes scanning for a glimpse of a blue dress or coiled blond hair. "It seems logical that she would come along."

"Who?"

George glanced at Darcy's confused face and laughed. "We are off on different tangents, I see. I was talking about Mrs. Annesley." George told him about their earlier encounter, leaving the private feelings out of it. "It piqued my curiosity, and you know how dangerous that is! I have been living in the same house as the woman for over a year and think I have seen her all of a dozen times and spoken to her less than that. Has she always been so retiring?"

"No, now that you mention it. She is a bit reserved, true, but she used to join us in the evenings and the occasional meal. To be honest, Uncle, I have been immersed in my own affairs since Elizabeth and I married and haven't given Mrs. Annesley much thought. Horrible of me, I suppose. I know Georgiana cares for her and the two have grown close. As long as Georgiana is happy and I have no reason to distrust her, I haven't concerned myself. Elizabeth thinks well of her too."

"What do you know of her?"

Darcy was looking at his uncle with full attention now, George's casual demeanor not working. "Why the sudden interest? Is this pure idle curiosity or something more?"

"Considering today was the first time I have exchanged more than three words with the woman, I can't see it as more of anything. Just being a busybody."

Deciding it wasn't worth investigating, Darcy shrugged and answered vaguely. "She is a widow in her mid-thirties, I believe. Her husband was a book-keeper who worked for my mill partners and me. A good man. He died, oh, six years or so ago now. They never had children, and she was living with her sister in Kent and teaching in a girl's school when my partner Kinnison heard I was searching for a new governess for Georgiana. She was willing, her credentials were impeccable, and the situation has been agreeable. Now, if you will excuse me, I need to speak with Uncle Malcolm."

Darcy hastened away, leaving George leaning against the rail, absorbing the rattled information. After a minute, he shook his head, shoved the strangeness aside, and rejoined the party.

George's prediction proved true. By the middle of February, Elizabeth's pregnancy with their second child was obvious. Amid his ecstasy, Darcy proceeded with arrangements for a Continental excursion, revealing the surprise to his wife over a romantic dinner in March. Georgiana was told the following day, and by the end of that week, everyone was in a dither. George returned from visiting with his son in Dorset and then his sister in Exeter during the last week of March and quickly dove into his own preparations. Warmer clothes were definitely necessary to survive even the summer in Switzerland, George shocking everyone by purchasing English suits and fur-lined jackets for himself and Anoop. Replenishing his medical supplies also topped the list, George a firm believer in traveling with the mindset that anything could happen, needing just the right medicine for the job. After so many years of doing so, it was an established routine, and his trusty, old trunk was speedily reorganized to accommodate tools of his trade alongside personal belongings.

Hardly before anyone could breathe, it was April and they were at Dover walking the swaying docks toward the ferry that would transport them across the Channel to Calais in France.

"I can't believe I am willingly boarding a ship," George muttered to Darcy, who already looked as green as he did. "I thought when I decided to stay in England my sailing days were over."

"It is a short trip. Just a few hours, so we should survive. At least that is what I keep telling myself."

"Don't be such ninnies. Stand bravely at the rail, relish the fresh salt air, and ride the waves proudly! It is a fine adventure, and if we are lucky, we will encounter rough seas to enhance the fun."

They both turned to glare at the grinning Lord Matlock.

"Madeline, if we arrive in Calais and you can't find your husband anywhere, it is because William and I tossed him overboard." Lord Matlock laughed, as did everyone else, apparently mercy at the Darcy men's suffering in short supply.

Halfway into their voyage, Darcy disappeared below deck, preferring to succumb to his seasickness in private. George stayed on deck, tucked into an out-of-the-way nook with a view of the ocean and chewed on a hunk of ginger root. Years of seafaring had proven this to work best when the queasiness hit hard. So far, he hadn't emptied his stomach but he wasn't tempting fate by moving around or straying far from the railing.

"Dr. Darcy, I brought you some tea. It is a mixture of raspberry leaf, black horehound, and I am not sure what else. Anoop said it would help."

"Ah, thank you, Mrs. Annesley. I discovered this concoction on my first voyage home. It doesn't always work but has a better record than some I have tried." He drank the hot beverage in one long swallow and held out the cup for a refill from the pot she carried. "Pull up a barrel and keep me company. It will distract me, and I promise to warn you before my stomach rebels so you can scurry away. I'd rather not embarrass myself more than usual if I can avoid it." To his delight, she did sit, her face turned toward the rolling sea. "Seasickness does not affect you, I take it?"

"Not so far. This is my first time on a ship, so I was not sure what to expect."

"You never sailed anywhere? Not even a boat on a wide river? I do believe I envy you, Mrs. Annesley," he teased, toasting her with his teacup.

"Oh no! I envy you, Doctor, and the incredible sights you must have seen. Anoop says you have traveled all over India, and if half the natives are as delightful as he, I can imagine how marvelous it must be there."

"We have been to quite a number of places, yes."

In the few times he had encountered her since the wedding, George had not been able to exchange more than a few pleasantries. Today, she was wholly different, staring at him boldly with bright eyes and seeking him out directly. Additionally, she was wearing a figure-flattering new gown and pelisse in royal blue. Her bonnet was adorned with flowers, the brim shading from the harsh sun but not hiding her flawless features or spun-gold hair. All in all, she was captivating and once again George's thoughts were spiraling into strange areas. He was not sure what to think of his musings, including the faint bite of irritation at Anoop carrying on conversations with her. Whether that was due to a hint of jealousy or anxiety over what she had gleaned about him during chats with his Indian assistant, George was not sure.

"Do you miss India, Doctor? Do you think you will ever return?"

"I do miss it, yes, but I will not return. I have friends there I would love to visit, but it is a long way and this short trip reminds me of why I rarely came home during all those years and one reason why I decided to stay in England."

"If you had to pick one place that was the most amazing, what would it be?"

"Well"—he scratched at his chin—"I am not sure I could pick one to be honest." For a while, he spoke of India and the places he had gone. She asked some questions but listened mostly. George evaded references to Jharna or anyone else, keeping the focus on the sights and interesting events.

"It must be difficult to leave your intrepid life behind. England must seem dreary to you in comparison."

"On the contrary, Mrs. Annesley. I am not as awestruck by adventure as I once was. I suppose age has tempered my hunger, and now I am content to rest my ancient bones."

"You are far from old, Dr. Darcy." She spoke with force, almost as if angry at his jest, then flushed and ducked her head. "I only meant that an old man would not embark on this journey with your vigor and enthusiasm."

"Indeed, you have a point, madam," George chuckled. "I admit to being terrified of the snow I may fall into while in Switzerland, but aside from that, I am giddy as a child to see Paris again. I detect a fair amount of giddiness from you as well."

"I shan't deny the charge. France, Switzerland, and then Italy. It is more than I ever dreamed of and I would be lying to say I am not overjoyed at the opportunity."

"It shows. Your face is glowing and eyes sparkling." The pretty rosiness increased, but she did not look away from his face. "You have no trepidations over crossing the Alps?"

"I am sure it is my ignorance revealed, but no. I can't fathom mountains as high as the Alps reputedly are. Perhaps I will quake in my shoes once we are there, staring upward at the apex."

George cocked his head, his eyes intent on her animated visage. "I think not, Mrs. Annesley. I detect an intrepid streak within you that has waited patiently to be unleashed. Besides, William will ensure the crossing over St. Bernard's Pass is as safe as a stroll through Hyde Park before allowing Georgiana to take it." She laughed and nodded her head at that truth, George helpless but to laugh with her.

They talked the entire way to Calais, the crossing passing too swiftly for George's liking, which considering his initial misery was a remarkable admission! While tarrying in Calais for the ship to be unloaded and their carriages prepared, George brought a chess board to the table where Mrs. Annesley sat with the women, whose eyes were glued to the bustling docks outside the pub where they waited. She laughed at his grinning challenge, the game played with advice from the others making it more of a frivolous team effort than serious competition.

Traveling in a small caravan provided plenty of opportunities for George to observe and interact with Mrs. Annesley. Indeed, she was giddy, as were the other members of their company who had never been to France. Everything excited them, their questions and pointing fingers constant. George teased by pointing to idiotic objects like a blade of grass or small stone with overblown enthusiasm. They merely laughed and played along. It did not take George long to recognize that the carefree, friendly, witty Mrs. Annesley he conversed and jested with was her natural pose and not a new creation based on the unique circumstance. Why she suddenly relaxed with him after nearly two years of evasion was a mystery he was determined to solve.

By the time they reached Paris and entered the palatial mansion at number eighteen on the Rue Andre Dolet within the Marais arrondissement that was owned by the Marquis Dissandes de la Villatte, a friend of Lord and Lady Matlock, George had given in to the fact that Mrs. Annesley intrigued him. No longer was his attraction attributed to suppressed sexual desire and the fact that she was a lovely woman. Indeed, she was lovely, and indeed, his body was screaming for more than what he could manage himself. Nevertheless, George wasn't an innocent. It had been a long time since he had gazed upon any woman other than Jharna with fascination but not so long that he had forgotten what it felt like to connect with a particular lady.

He wanted her. No doubt there. She was beautiful and unconsciously sensual, arousing him by simply being near or when he thought of her. He could effortlessly imagine touching her, kissing her, tasting her, and all the myriad ways they could find pleasure together. However, George had never wasted his time with a woman, no matter how physically appealing she was, if he did not feel a strong affinity beyond desire. All the women he pursued relationships with were women he enjoyed being with in every way. Mrs. Annesley was such a lady, and with each passing day, George's esteem, infatuation, and yearning grew.

She fluctuated between gay animations bordering on coquettishness to shy withdrawal that hinged on being cold. The latter typically followed the first, as if she regretted being amiable or feared his response. What he could not deduce was if she wanted him to boldly seduce her and was miffed that he didn't or if she was sending a signal that her friendliness was not to be interpreted as an invitation. It didn't help clear his confusion that they were only alone long enough for his fondness and respect to increase but not for a serious, pointed conversation.

Then he wondered what action to take if he discovered without a doubt that she was seeking an affair. Did he want another casual interlude with no future? His body emphatically screamed yes, and loving her would be wonderful, he was certain of that much! Yet, would that be wise with a woman in his nephew's employ? Somehow, he doubted Mrs. Annesley was the type of lady to engage in wanton sex. It was one of many stellar attributes he appreciated, that she was proper and decent. And even if she was desirous of a purely physical dalliance, he feared emotions may entangle, thus hurting her when they parted in Switzerland.

So was he willing to offer her more? Was he in love with her?

That question brought him up short. George hadn't believed in instant love for decades. Attraction, yes. Lust, absolutely! Love as in the sort of love to propose marriage and plan a lifetime together? Honestly, no.

Aren't you a bit too old to want a lengthy courtship?

Well, there was that! Fifty-two wasn't *that* old. His health was superb and stamina as complete as when he was thirty. God knows his sexual appetite had not diminished! Nevertheless, after the years of joy with Jharna, George simply could not imagine binding himself to a woman for the rest of his life if she wasn't equally spectacular. Perhaps Amanda Annesley *was* spectacular, but a month of fleeting exchanges while in romantic Paris and clouded with physical cravings was not the wisest time to render logical decisions.

The dilemmas made his head ache.

The night before they were to depart Paris for the journey across France into Switzerland and the summer estate where his sister Mary, the Baroness Oeggl, was waiting for them with her family, George's circular musings and unresolved ardor drove him down to the kitchen for a midnight snack and cup of tea. Returning to his room with a slightly clearer head and satisfied stomach, George noted movement from the balcony at the end of the second level corridor. It only took him a minute to recognize the woman standing at the wall, gazing at the moonlit view of Paris, as Mrs. Annesley.

"Mind if I join you?" He spoke softly but she still jerked and whirled about. She was dressed in a nightgown and robe, the garments covering her more than her dresses did, yet she frantically drew her shawl tighter around her shoulders and self-consciously ran one hand over her loosely braided hair.

"The balcony is free for all, so of course you are welcome, Dr. Darcy."

George strolled to the railing three feet to her right, his gaze purposefully not on her but focused on the skyline. In part, that was to ease her embarrassment but largely it was due to the effect she had upon him. The robe and shawl did indeed cover her flesh, but the outline of her unsupported breasts left little to the imagination. The thick plait of golden hair falling to her curved bottom begged to be undone with fingers running through each silky tress. He leaned his elbows onto the ledge and clasped his hands in the air, bent slightly so that his head was level with hers.

"Paris in the moonlight is a wondrous sight to behold and one I never tire of. This is a marvelous view."

"That is why I came. The view from my room is over the garden, which is lovely, but I cannot see the skyline or the river. I waited until the house was asleep and did not expect to encounter anyone."

He looked at her flushed face, swallowing the lump of desire before able to smile. "If I am disturbing your solitude, say the word. I did not mean to intrude."

"No! That is… you are not intruding, Dr. Darcy. Not at all."

Her blush deepened and she turned her head back toward the vista—not before sweeping her gaze rapidly over the backside of his body, George noted with a surge of satisfaction. He was barefoot and wearing his typical sleeping attire of drawstring *paijamas* and a thin *kurta*, the ensemble designed for comfort and not modesty.

"How often have you been to Paris, Doctor?"

"This is my first visit since I was a medical student. My family traveled here three times in my youth, short stays like this one, but I lived here for six months, studying at the Pitié-Salpêtrière Hospital. I lived on the premises in the resident's barracks with nothing remotely nice as a view. I was in Paris, though, and did find some free time to explore the city. It has greatly changed in thirty years."

"I imagine so. There are many places in the world I would love to see, but

Paris has always been high on my list. We planned to travel here once but the war intervened."

George admired her profile in the faint illumination. "Tragic, but at least you are here now. Who is the 'we' you were to travel with?"

"My husband. Not too long after our marriage, we began arrangements. Then Bonaparte rose up and war was declared. That ended those plans." She shrugged.

George studied her for any signs of acute distress at the mention of her husband, but she was serene, the rosiness receding from her cheeks and her arms no longer crossed over her chest or clutching the shawl. The latter meant his view of her generous breasts was no longer obstructed, a fact he greatly appreciated. *Best not think upon it, George!* Dragging his gaze back to her face, he boldly pressed on.

"How long ago did your husband pass?"

"Over six years ago now," she answered without hesitation.

"Do you still miss him?"

"I do, yes. He was a good man and we were happy together. It does grow easier over time, but I do not think the sadness ever erases completely."

"Unless you were to love again."

"Perhaps then, yes. If the man loved me in return, that is. I would never want an unequal relationship."

"Nor should you settle for such. How long were you married?"

"Seven years. Not a great length, nor as long as we hoped of course, but they were wonderful years."

"You must have been very young when you married."

"Always the flatterer, Dr. Darcy." She laughed softly but kept her eyes trained on the quiet streets and rooftops. "I was three and twenty when we married. Not so young that I was innocent of what it meant to love someone and commit for what was intended to be many more years."

"I am sorry. I can imagine how painful and difficult it must be."

"Can you?" She finally lifted her eyes to his, George realizing in that instant that he had unintentionally scooted closer—or maybe she had to him—and they were now less than two feet apart. Even in the dim light, he could see the flecks of darker blue in her eyes and the tiny freckles dusting her nose. She was mesmerizing yet not so much that he missed the question underneath the question. She was sharing a personal portion of her life with him, and it was the perfect opening to share of himself. Staring into her eyes, the confession was tickling the tip of his tongue.

Tell her of Jharna. Share your awareness of love and loss. Tell her of your feelings for her, even if you are unsure what they are.

Instead, he said, "When my brother's wife died, Mr. Darcy's mother, James was lost in his grief. It was frightening to witness. Losing a dearly loved one is horrible. I have seen such grief far too many times."

"I am sure you have, Dr. Darcy."

"May I ask a favor of you? You may have noticed that I am not a stickler for formality?" She smiled and nodded. "Only patients or work colleagues call me Dr. Darcy. Friends call me George, and I like to think we are becoming friends. I would love to hear you address me as George."

She said nothing for minutes, all the while staring into his eyes as if trying to discern something he could not be sure of. It was extremely challenging to think clearly when she was so close that the perfumed warmth of her skin ignited his senses. His heart was pounding, anticipation for her response adding to the rush of emotions.

"When it is appropriate then yes, I will address you as George."

George flashed his most brilliant smile, the reaction genuinely inspired at the sound of her voice saying his name. "Thank you… Amanda."

She released a breathy huff when he whispered her name, George realizing their faces were inches apart when her exhaled breath brushed across his cheeks. He hadn't planned to kiss her, at least not consciously, yet there was no halting the urge. In the second before he met her lips, he knew she wanted the kiss as urgently.

"Amanda," he whispered as her eyes slid shut and lips parted. Then he was pressing his mouth against hers, and moments later, his world exploded. If asked even earlier that day, George would have declared emphatically that cataclysmic repercussions from a simple kiss were unlikely in a man his age and with his experience. He would have been a dead wrong and lost any bet placed. Only much, much later would he try to remember if the first kiss with Jharna had been as earth-shattering as this one with Amanda. He never would decide, not that he tried too hard to compare. Judging degrees of what was, in both instances, a profound impact was pointless anyway. And certainly at this moment, none of those considerations were flying through his mind. All he knew was that kissing Amanda was electrifying and rapturous. He also knew a kiss alone would never suffice.

How he ended up leaning onto the stone wall with Amanda drawn firmly between his spread legs remained a mystery. She did not seem to mind one bit if the pressure of her pliant flesh against him was any indication. That and her hands twisted in his hair, her passionate responses to his kiss, and her low-pitched moans revealed all. When he left her mouth to rain moist kisses along the slope of her neck, she arched further into him and clutched tighter. Cupping her breasts and stroking over her rigid nipples made her shudder and gasp aloud.

"You have enchanted me, Amanda." She shivered at each murmured word. "So alluring. Temptingly sweet. I desire you utterly and have for weeks." Again at her lips, George teased with his tongue, sweeping corner to corner with the tip before surrounding with his mouth and pushing deeply inside, meeting her seeking tongue again and again and again. Pulling away with a sucking grasp on her lower lip, he said, "I want you, lovely Amanda. Say the word and I'll take you to my room—"

"Uncle George! Are you in there? Wake up, please!"

The steady knocking and resonant timbre of Darcy from where he stood in the corridor in front of George's bedchamber door jolted him and Amanda. She yelped and spun away, her shock so intense George instinctively reached a stabilizing hand to prevent her falling. He missed because she retreated into the shadows by the wall. The mixture of arousal and shame visible on her face pierced his heart. George felt no shame; his concern was only to spare her further embarrassment. Fortunately, he had always been able to recover swiftly. Mentally that is. There was no way his physical state was going to resolve quickly! Hopefully, whatever William wanted would prevent him from looking downward.

He stepped away from the balcony wall, smiled at Amanda to reassure, and had no choice but to walk past her into the house and leave her alone. "I am here, William. Enjoying some fresh air. What is it?"

"Uncle! Thank goodness! Alexander woke up and vomited. Mrs. Hanford says he feels feverish. Can you come see him?"

Duty called. George snapped into doctor mode and, after retrieving his medical case, followed Darcy to their suite of rooms. Alexander, as it turned out, had probably eaten something that disagreed with him. A tonic settled his stomach, and within a half hour, he was asleep. By the time George returned to his bedchamber, Amanda had long since left the balcony, and he was faced with a sleepless night fretting over her and fighting the lust that was now multiplied after their shared kiss.

The next day dawned with a flurry of activity as they prepared to depart. George only caught glimpses of her as they loaded up the carriages. Attempts to sidle close or talk to her proved fruitless, not helped by the fact that she was clearly avoiding him. Why that was he could not be sure. God knows it wasn't easy for him to see her either. Not due to embarrassment but because even her presence in the same room heightened his senses and filled him with longing. It was a relief to enter the Matlocks' carriage, Amanda three carriages away with the nanny, Mrs. Hanford, and Samuel and Marguerite Oliver, Darcy and Elizabeth's personal servants. He could almost put her out of his mind as they bumped along the dirt road. Then at each stop to rest the horses and stretch, he only managed safe verbal exchanges. It didn't require his diagnostic skills to deduce that she was uncomfortable when he came close. Precisely why disturbed him, but since there was no way to arrange a private discussion, he retreated, giving her the space she was silently requesting.

Three days into their journey toward Switzerland, he encountered her by accident on the stairs of the *hôtel* where they were staying for the night. Private it wasn't but isolated enough for him to ask if she was well.

"I am fine, George. You have nothing to worry about."

He wanted to sing when she spoke his Christian name and reached across the narrow gap to clasp her hand. "Look at me, Amanda, so I know for sure." She did, a small nervous smile lighting her eyes. "Ah, better. I have been worried that you were angry or regretful, neither of which I would want you to be."

"I am not angry or regretful. It… was wonderful."

"Indeed, it was. I am relieved to hear you feel the same."

"I do." Her voice was barely audible and she had bowed her head.

"What is it that bothers you? Please, tell me honestly. I meant what I said before we were interrupted. I desire you, Amanda. Tremendously. But I have no wish to cause you pain so I will respect your decisions."

"I know you are experienced enough to deduce that my... desires are identical to yours, George. However, under the circumstances I think it best—"

Whatever she planned to say was left unfinished when Georgiana and Elizabeth rounded the corner to mount the stairs. Perfunctory well wishes for a restful night were given and they separated yet again.

As the subsequent days unfolded, George analyzed the "circumstances" from every angle. It was easy to presume what she had been about to say. "Under the circumstances, I think it best to remain friends only." As much as he wanted to argue, logically, he knew she was correct.

Unfortunately, their kiss ignited his fervor to possess her to a level that threatened to overcome his rational mind. Often, he felt downright disgusted with himself for letting libidinous urges rule him as if a weak adolescent. Then he would marvel at his fortune to experience powerful amorousness at fifty-two! Surely that was an indication of a strong connection between them. Or was he just so damned lonely and weary of missing what he and Jharna had shared that he was latching on to the first woman to interest and arouse him?

Buried far under the layers of emotion, he heard a faint Hindi female voice whispering, "You are afraid." George refused to listen to that voice.

Far from reaching any kind of a decision, George had little choice but to relinquish the unproductive examination. Never one to be depressed for long, and with beautiful scenery passing by and the excitement to see his sister, his funk was overcome well before reaching Geneva where they tarried for two days in a grand hostelry. He and Amanda reverted back to their casual banter, playing cards and chess in the evenings and strolling along the lakeside trails with the others. Neither said a word about their shared kiss and neither sought the other for a private interlude.

Two weeks after leaving Paris, their caravan pulled into the drive before the sprawling three-story farmhouse belonging to his sister Mary and her husband, Baron Oeggl. The vast estate sat on the easternmost bank of Lake Genève near Villeneuve at the foot of the Alps. George's last visit to see his sister was over thirty years ago after his time in Paris. Then the Darcy family's sojourn had been at the Oeggls Austrian home north of Vienna. Switzerland was another new adventure for the world-traveling man, so naturally his enthusiasm was high despite the patches of snow and frigid air that penetrated straight through the thick coats he wore.

Yet all of it—snow and icy cold, towering and breathtaking mountains, and even Amanda—were driven out of his mind the second he glanced at his older sister, Mary.

Baroness Oeggl was obviously unwell. She greeted them from her chair in the parlor, no one expecting her to rise from under the heaped blankets or move from the heat of the fire. George and Mary had never been close, even as youths. The eleven-year age gap as well as their differing personalities had prevented a deep love from forming. In the three-decade interval, George rarely thought of his sister and their sporadic letters were formal rather than intimate. Instantly, those facts disappeared and George's priorities changed. Naturally, he examined her and applied his considerable talent to improving her health, but nothing permanent could be done. So instead, they lounged before the fire and talked of Pemberley, their childhood, his adventures, and her life in Austria for hours while the rest of the household played and explored. Since frolicking in the snow held little appeal, he was content to watch Alexander and the dozen Oeggl children—all of whom flocked to the flamboyant "Uncle Goj"—and remain inside.

George's focus on his sister did not supplant his awareness of Amanda, however.

The farmhouse, as the Oeggls quaintly referred to the rustic mansion, was enormous, but with nearly the entire Oeggl clan summering along with the English company, every bedchamber was filled and finding a room empty was next to impossible. Amanda opted to accompany the women on their excursions each day, George usually not seeing her until the evenings, when the family dined as a group and then gathered in the lower-level salon or game room. If not playing billiards or darts or some other manly pastime with the gentlemen, George would join the ladies for cards or conversation. Humor was usually high, even with the frail baroness in the room, and once again George was forcibly struck by Amanda's wit and intelligence, as well as the fiery attraction. George refused to provoke the situation, however, blatant seduction against a lady's request not a tactic he had ever employed. He maintained a gentlemanly distance, sensing all the while that they were simply postponing the inevitable.

In that, he was one hundred percent correct.

It was a quiet evening in the farmhouse since all of the men with the exception of George had gone on an overnight trek into the mountains. Personally, he thought they were insane and no amount of taunting had convinced him that sleeping in tents pitched atop freezing ground would be entertaining. Mary had long since retired, as had all but the oldest of the children, and the lively game of whist played by the women was over. George sat in the chair closest to the fire, ostensibly reading a book. In truth, he was flipping through it randomly while sneaking sidelong glances at Amanda. She sat next to Georgiana, both of them with some sort of needlecraft in their hands. George ignored the project itself, his eyes following the rhythmic movements of her dainty hands and fingers while imagining the plethora of ways those hands could rouse him if moving over his skin. George knew next to nothing about sewing, or whatever she was doing, so was unaware of her distraction until Georgiana politely pointed out that an entire row of stitches was wrong.

"Oh my! I must be wearier than I thought. How foolish of me!" She released a shaky laugh and set the hoop aside with trembling hands. "My addled brains are not conducive to needlepoint. I believe I shall retire if you do not mind, my dear?"

"Of course not. Please, go sleep. I believe I shall enjoy the solitude of the music room while I can."

Amanda gathered her sewing basket, patted Georgiana on the knee, rose from the sofa, and walked to the staircase. George observed the entire exchange beneath lowered brows. Not once had she looked his way. Still he watched her lithe figure ascend the steps and noted the hesitation before she paused, gazed over her shoulder, and smiled at him. Instantly, his heart accelerated. It was only a smile, but he knew it was an invitation.

Seconds later, she was beyond his sight, and it took every ounce of his willpower to stay seated. Using Georgiana's exit to cover any obvious connection to Mrs. Annesley, George expressed his desire to retire. The effort to leisurely bid good night to Elizabeth, Lady Matlock, and the other women in the room before casually taking the stairs he wanted to dash up was monumental. He rounded the corner and spied Amanda leaning against the wall halfway down the corridor, saying nothing as he took her hand and led her to his bedchamber.

George slammed the door with a shove of his foot, not letting go of her hand or giving her time to turn around before drawing her backward against his chest. She melted pliantly into his embrace as he pressed his lips into the tender bend of her neck.

"Amanda, I am aching for you and beg you tell me immediately if you do not wish to go further. I cannot promise I will heed a later plea to stop!"

"I won't ask you to stop, George, and would be seriously vexed if you did!"

He chuckled at her cheeky answer, the rumbling sensation and fingers skimming the sensitive flesh above her bodice causing her to shiver. The fabric was thick, but George could see her nipples outlined underneath, and he easily crept under the lacy edge to palm each bare breast, proving they were as hard as he thought. A twist and slide of his hands was sufficient to peel the bodice away far enough to expose her generous bosom, the cool air and his stimulating fingers firming each pink nipple to stony points he hungered to taste.

All in good time. No need to rush.

It was a mantra difficult to adhere to, especially when she clutched his thighs and burrowed his rigid shaft between the crevice of her buttocks. He growled into her ear, the lazy travel up her neck ending as he savagely claimed her parted lips while grinding harshly against her. This led to several minutes of insane kissing, touching, and disrobing as their long-repressed yearnings soared free. George knew that for him it was primarily his lust for her but also three years of denied need raging to an overwhelming peak. He suspected that some of what she was expressing was the same, dimly hoping that the scale was tipped in his direction rather than simply want of a man. It was a sudden, strange line of thought, the accompanying stab of jealousy that perhaps he wasn't the first since her husband viciously shoved aside.

Their wild dance around the room had somehow taken them to a wooden bureau of drawers, Amanda clutching the knobs while George slipped each stocking down her legs, licking and nibbling the silky, white skin as he went. Licking his way gradually back up, he halted for a delirious handful of minutes at the juncture between her thighs. Opening her wide and drawing one leg over his shoulder, George coaxed and teased until she was gasping for air and spasming uncontrollably. Inhaling raggedly, he stood to his feet and stepped back a pace, his eyes thirstily drinking in the naked vision of perfection trembling against the wooden surface and staring at him with glazed awe.

Amanda was a petite woman, the top of her head barely reaching George's breastbone, and the shortest lover he had ever been with. Everything about her was delicate and small, except for her breasts, which were surprisingly large for her pixie frame. Her daintiness instilled an intense desire to protect and please, or at least, he told himself, it was only that and not a stronger emotion. Her diminutive stature and fine bones gave the initial impression of weakness or fragility, George abruptly worried that he may have hurt her by pressing into the hard wood.

He bent to plant a gentle kiss to her lips, his hands smoothing over her arms. "Did I hurt you?"

"Hurt me?" She laughed and shook her head. "Sweet George. If that is hurting me, then please, by all that is holy, do whatever you can to cause me more pain!"

His chuckle was lost when she snaked her arms around his waist and crushed her body into his with a well-placed squirm, her ravenous kiss muffling the sound.

George soon learned that there was nothing weak or fragile about Amanda Annesley. Nor did his worry that her petite frame might indicate insufficiency in accepting him inside her. Indeed, that proved to be easily accomplished and blissful beyond belief. She was tight and warm, the exquisite friction driving him absolutely mad. The feel of her breasts rubbing over his chest with each thrust, her hands and legs gripping and fondling as they undulated in unison, and her soft moans and sighs added to the intensity of their lovemaking. The long delay did not allow for an extended bout of loving, but at this point, neither cared. Haste to attain the glory of united ecstasy was perfectly fine.

For a long while, they held each other without saying a word. George stroked her hair and planted light kisses on her forehead. Happiness not felt in years blanketed his soul. For the present, he simply wished to bask in it and not analyze. It was Amanda who finally lifted from the safe cocoon within his arms, the smile on her face radiant as she swept fingers through his hair.

"I should return to my room before Miss Darcy tires of the pianoforte. She may come looking for me."

"No, do not leave yet. Please? You can give Georgie an excuse. Tell her you were in the library or walking the balcony." He gently squeezed one breast and circled his thumb around the nipple, thrilling at the instant response. "Give me some time to rest, and I am certain I can discover another way to cause you pain."

She laughed, bending to bestow a playful kiss that rapidly grew heated. "No jesting of pain, George. What you have shown me is pleasure unfathomable. Thank you for that."

He caressed her cheek, eyes serious in the muted light. "You do not have to thank me, Amanda. I should thank you for the gift you have given me. I hope this will not be our only time together, but as I said before, I respect your choice."

Something he could not decipher flickered through her eyes. It disturbed him but he could not comprehend why. Then it was gone and she was smiling and kissing him again. Her huskily whispered, "this will not be our only time," drove all concerns out of his mind. That and her stimulating hand which had him ready to love her sooner than he imagined possible.

In the three weeks that ticked away the time when he would depart with the Darcys while she stayed behind with Georgiana for their journey on to Italy, Amanda came to his room five times. It was not easy for her to slip away, George knew, but he also sensed that she restrained herself. Each time she tapped on the door, he was there in an instant, yanking it open and pulling her into his embrace before the door closed. Each time they loved, whether furious with need or tenderly building to a breathless climax, was stupendous. In those moments of loving and blissful aftermath, he forgot about the fact that they would be parted. When he did try to steer the conversation into weightier matters, she evaded by either a touch that drove him insane or by slipping away to her own room. It was frustrating, but he also knew that his own indecision and uncertainty allowed the topic to be avoided. During the light of day, they went on as usual. George spent most of his time with his sister. Amanda kept close to the women and enthusiastically planned for her trip to Italy. He thought of her constantly and caught her staring at him quite often, but nothing concrete was decided about their relationship.

Or was it a relationship? Were they simply two adults engaged in a mutually pleasing assignation and nothing more? Goodness knows he had executed enough of those in his day! Not for a second did he begrudge Amanda the freedom to do what all of his lovers had done. For some reason he could not quite place his finger on, George did not believe she was like those past lovers, yet there was also no clear indication that she wasn't. The logical option in light of their individual plans was to separate and then see what transpired when she returned to England next year. Nevertheless, he did not want to part without at least one serious talk.

Two days before the Darcys were to leave, George with them, he and Amanda made love slowly, drawing the pleasure out as long as possible and then collapsing in satiated bliss for a good fifteen minutes before either could speak. Then he rose, surprising her by wrapping her in a thick blanket and leading her to a pile of cushions before the fire. He poured from a wine bottle she had not noticed, handing her a glass and taking a long swallow himself before opening the conversation.

"Amanda, I am not the best at expressing my feelings or being overly sentimental—far too immersed in science and clinical rationality, I suppose. But I want you to know how special this time has been for me. I… well, I am going to miss you terribly."

She was silent, staring into the red liquid. He waited, frowning when she did not speak. "I suppose you will be busy and surrounded by innumerable dazzling sights so probably not missing me as much, but I confess my ego would like to think you might miss me a tiny bit."

"Oh, George. You have no concept of how profoundly I will miss you. Nothing in Italy, France, or anywhere else in the world could dazzle me enough to not think of you. Trust me in that and then let us leave the topic alone."

This time it was George who did not respond. The sadness in her tone pierced him, as did the slump to her shoulders. Finally, he reached out and tenderly lifted her chin. "Amanda, I never meant to hurt you. I swear I didn't! I sense that I have, and I wish I could say I was sorry for starting something we cannot continue but I can't say that. I am already counting the days until you are back in England. If only I had seen what was right in front of my eyes sooner. You are precious to me, Amanda, and whatever happens in the future, I want you to know that this time with you will live in my heart forever."

In the space of a minute her eyes changed from sad to angry. She jerked away from his hand. "George, please do not say such half truths. I know you care for me in your own way, but do not insult my intelligence by claiming something more. You have no reason to do so. I came to you with no illusions of a future or returned love. You hurt me more by pretending otherwise."

George's mouth had dropped open, his mind whirling. "I don't… I don't understand. Amanda, I would never lie to you. Never! Why would you think that?"

She face softened, the angry tone gone. "I am sorry. I should not have let my emotions rule me. I have no wish to hurt you either, George, and it is unfair to blame you for who you are. It is just… so difficult…" She closed her eyes and choked back a sob. "My common sense told me I was a fool to cross this line with a man who frequently dallies with women and loathes marriage or commitment. I thought if I kept those facts firm in my head, then my heart could not be touched. Even then I tried to resist, but I couldn't. I have loved you for too long." She clamped a trembling hand over her mouth, her body shaking with the silent sobs.

George sat stunned. He wanted to take her into his arms but was paralyzed. Grasping on to any one bit of what she had said was next to impossible.

Frequently dallies with women? Loathes marriage and commitment?

"You love me? How long have you loved me?"

"It does not matter."

"It does to me!"

"Why?" She looked up at him. "What difference does it make if I confess I have loved you since shortly after your arrival two years ago? Does it change where we are now?" She sighed and scooted until almost in his lap. Clasping his face between her hands, she leaned in and kissed him. "George, I do love you and think I forever will. But please do not fear I expect anything from you. I only wanted to be with you, to enjoy this time and feel your touch. I know you cannot offer me anything more, and I would not take it if you did. Not now. I am leaving and my heart cannot survive the next year with half-hearted maybes or false images of you pining for me. Please respect that and just love me one last time. That is the memory I want to hold on to. Please?"

She pushed him back onto the cushions, her mouth slanting over his with hungry insistence. George could not assimilate all she had said, especially with the instantaneous surge of flaming desire that her touch elicited. Hours later, after the deep, dreamless sleep of a man utterly spent from intense loving, George woke to find her gone. She did not come to him the next night and refused to meet his eye the handful of times he saw her during the day. As a tragic epiphany, the puzzling pieces of why she had faded into the background and shunned any contact with him until that day at the Fitzwilliam wedding made sense. The revelation was too late in coming and too shocking for him to comprehend. Before he had time to breathe past the agonizing turmoil of his emotions, he was saying his good-byes to the Oeggl family, including his sister

Mary who he knew would die before the year was over, his niece Georgiana, and Lord and Lady Matlock. Amanda Annesley was nowhere to be seen, but he would barely step foot on English soil before realizing his monumental mistake in not storming the house and telling her he loved her.

GEORGE'S MEMOIRS
FEBRUARY 5, 1820

Only one more month, Jharna. I wish I could count the exact days, but Georgiana's last letter only said they would arrive in time for Miss Kitty's wedding. I am doing my best to remain patient, but the effort to maintain my typical, flippant gaiety is growing tougher by the day. I weary of playing the carefree bachelor when my heart is bombarded with hope one second and intense fear the next. What if she met someone in Italy or France? What if she no longer loves me or her love has turned to hatred for abandoning her? Lord knows I hate myself for it and would not blame her one iota if she spit in my face. It is maddening that Georgie's letters contained only oblique mentions of her. I should have followed through on my plan to meet them in Paris after Christmas. Of course, if I had, my guilt over abandoning Elizabeth without realizing she was ill would have killed me. No, it was necessary for me to stay and tend to her. She is speedily on the road to full recovery, I am happy to say, and she and William are fine. Little Michael is a roly-poly baby now. Thank God for that. Those were some scary days, as you know with too many memories of our sweet Bhrithi. But Michael was born weeks later than she was, so while premature, the added time made a differ-ence. No point in leaving for Dover now. I may well pass them crossing the Channel and I definitely want to do more than wave at Amanda from the deck of a ship!

God, what a mess of things I have made! I have branded myself a hundred shades of a fool, and it is not enough. Why did I not tell her the truth? Even if I was not certain of my love for her, at least I should have told her of you, let her know that I am not the anticommitment cad she thinks. Yes, that hurt. Deeply. But whose fault is it for her assumptions? All mine. Yes, indeed, I am a fool. My pain over losing you kept me silent, all my stupid taunts and roguish claims working against me.

The misery of these eight months is what I deserve for being such an ass. It is Amanda my heart breaks for. She who was in love with me far longer and must be suffering more if she does not hate me, that is. Idiot was I not to notice her! How could I have possibly been so blind, Jharna? I replay those months over and over, trying to recall every time she passed me by or spoke a few words to me. Never did I take the time to get to know her. Oh if I had! We could be married now, living blissfully.

Then Anoop reminds me of what I know you would say as well: All of life is according to our destiny. Everything happens according to purpose. Etcetera. Maybe so. I guess I will find out when I see her.

I ache for her, Jharna. I can no longer distinguish the line between the constant sadness I bear inside at your death and the raw wound from Amanda. The hope I cling to is that she, unlike you, priya, *is still alive and might, I pray with all my heart, be willing to give me another chance. No further hesitation this time. Even if she slaps me or yells or runs away, I will grab her, kiss her, and then without a second's delay, ask her to marry me. I will confess all my sins even if I have to tie her to a post to listen to me. Surely her love cannot have faded. Can it? I told William not too long ago that great love does not die so easily with even years apart or death unable to sever the bond. Of course, I was thinking of you, as William assumed, but I was also referring to Amanda. I only hope those words were true for her. We will be leaving for Hertfordshire in a few weeks. William has obtained Netherfield Park for us, and with luck, I will be the next one married. Dare I pray for that dream to come true? I'll settle for her smiling at me to start.*

T HE MAN AT THE coaching inn directed George to "the fourth road on the left past the gray stone dovecote." The dovecote had been easy to spot, and if he didn't count the trail too narrow for a carriage, the gravel avenue stretching before him would be the one leading to the home of Amanda Annesley's sister.

He halted Ghora by the gate and took a moment to wipe his brow and run one hand through his hair. He had washed at the inn and quickly changed out of his dusty traveling clothes, but it didn't hurt to make sure he was presentable. It was doubtful tamed hair would be the deciding factor, but a few minutes to inhale and calm his pounding heart were worth spending.

When Georgiana and the Matlocks had arrived at Netherfield with Colonel Fitzwilliam and Major General Artois in tow but no Mrs. Annesley, George seriously thought his heart would cease beating. After days of extreme tension over facing her, the blow of disappointment was immense. The struggle to erect his usual façade of jocularity was nearly more than he could handle. The occasional strange glance from Darcy and Elizabeth alerted him to the fact that his acting skills were failing. Luckily, the house was filled to bursting with merry guests visiting for the nuptials of Miss Kitty Bennet to Major General Randall Artois, and with the strained addition of Mr. and Mrs. George Wickham, it was easy to fade into the background—as much as he was ever capable of. It was a joyous occasion and with the suspicions over Wickham's motives for attending, George was somewhat distracted.

Nevertheless, the day and a half before he could casually inquire of Georgiana as to where her companion was topped the list of the roughest patches of his life!

"She took a coach to Kent, where her sister lives."

"Oh, I am sure she must have missed her family. Kent is lovely, all but Rosings, that is. Whereabouts does her sister live?"

"A small town called Cranleigh just north of Maidstone. She plans to spend Easter there at least."

"At least? Is she not coming back?"

"I am not sure, Uncle. Maybe, but she seems uncertain of her future plans. I am twenty, after all, so not in desperate need of a companion." Then she walked away, George not sure if the sly glint in her eye was his imagination or not.

He asked no further questions and could do nothing until after Kitty's wedding when they were relocated to London. Easter was only a week away, but George was done with waiting. He threw the bare essentials into his saddlebag and set off one morning, swiftly covering the forty miles to Cranleigh. There was something vaguely chivalrous and romantic about it, or at least he hoped Amanda would see it that way.

The house was quiet, no one in immediate sight, which worried George, but a servant answered his knock quickly enough. She examined him strangely, that nothing George was unaccustomed to, and politely asked him to wait on the stoop while she fetched the mistress.

Mrs. Tadworth bore a striking resemblance to Amanda, even her warm smile the same, and thus pierced his heart. He glanced over her shoulder as she crossed the foyer toward him but no one was following.

"Dr. Darcy, what a pleasure. I am Amanda's sister, Abigail, and have heard so much about you."

"You have?"

"Indeed. Quite a great deal."

"I am not sure if that news is comforting or disconcerting."

"You can decide that after you speak with my sister. Please, come in. Shall I call for tea while we wait for her to return or would you rather go look for her yourself?"

"Based on what she has told you of me, would you suggest bolstering my fortitude with strong tea or not delaying the inevitable by seeking her out? To be honest, I have no idea what to expect."

"I suppose that depends on why you are here. But assuming you would not come all this way for a disagreeable purpose, then I will direct you to the path leading past the rear garden. Amanda went for a walk."

George set off down the indicated path with a somewhat lightened heart. He was afraid to presume anything, but Mrs. Tadworth's kind demeanor did not hint of a woman who hated him. It wasn't much to cling to, but it was something. She had no idea where Amanda might be, stating only that she preferred this path for her walks because it provided the best shade. He walked for a good half mile and then almost missed her entirely. If not for the clunk of something firm hitting the ground, he would not have peered into the rows of apple trees several yards to the right of the trail, and if not for a muttered curse, he would not have left the trail to investigate. Heading in the general direction of rustling branches and a voice he instantly recognized, George wove through the trees until he saw her. Immediately a broad smile split his face.

Amanda stood on the top bar of a tall, wooden fence, her back to him as she reached way above her head to pick the ripest apples on the higher branches, placing the ones she successfully grabbed into the woven basket perched atop the fence post. It was an absolutely endearing vision, and quite humorous with her running commentary, scolding the tree for being unyielding. As anxious as he was to see her face and declare his love, the delight in observing her secretly was irresistible.

One glance at her petite body, precisely the same as etched upon his mind, ignited the desire kept banked to a tiny flame these past months. His heartbeat and respirations accelerated, and for a solid minute, he was blinded by sheer animal lust. If she had turned then, all of his prettily rehearsed sentences would have been uttered while driving deeply and madly into her against one of the tree trunks! Inhaling, George regained control, and as the surge of ardor diminished, pure love swelled. As often as he had dwelt upon making love to her, he had dreamt of every other moment they spent together, even if a mere glance or smile from across the room.

Hesitating no longer, he left the shadows and crossed the distance between them. She still had not seen him, her focus on the fruit, and he waited until right behind her before speaking.

"You need someone taller to reach those branches. Think I can help?"

She yelped and spun about, George realizing belatedly that startling her while precariously balancing on a narrow pole was not a smart plan. Until, that is, she fell into his arms, at which point he decided it was a capital idea.

"Whoa there! I have you. Seems like you and I are always falling into each other's arms. Not that I am complaining in the slightest." He steadied her against the fence with her body firmly pressed into his torso and then cupped her stunned face within his hands. "Say something, Amanda. Anything. Or should I go first?" He bent until inches away from her parted lips. "What I should have said to you in Switzerland. I love you, Amanda Annesley. I love you with all my soul and never want to let you go. Please tell me I have not lost you."

"George? Have I fallen and hit my head? Am I dreaming?"

"No, silly," he laughed. "Let me prove it to you."

Then he kissed her, the spark jolting him as intensely as the last time they kissed months ago. But he pulled away after a light brush of his lips, wanting, needing to hear her thoughts before his ardor flared beyond his control. She was clutching his *kameez*, and her eyes opened when he pulled away, staring at him dazedly.

"I am here, Amanda, and would have come sooner, but I had to attend Miss Bennet's wedding. I was going to search for you in Paris, but other family obligations intervened. I'll tell you of that later, if we have a later. God, Amanda, please speak! It is killing me!"

"Sorry. I am just so shocked. I didn't expect you to come here. Not once. I thought you didn't want me—"

"I was a bloody fool, Amanda, an absolute imbecile to leave you, especially with so many erroneous conclusions. I want to explain everything, and I will, but the most important point, aside from that I love you and want you so badly it is agonizing, is that I am not in any way loathe to be married. In fact, for longer than I can begin to relate it has been my one greatest desire. Commitment does not scare me, Amanda. Not with a woman I love."

"You mean Jharna."

"What?" He was so stunned he released her face and moved back a step. She did not let go of him, though, and stepped with him.

"Georgiana told me. Recently. After she… well, you may not know of her news, so I won't say. But we are close and she sensed something wasn't right with me. I told her about you and me, that I loved you and most of what had transpired. That is when she told me of Jharna. George, I can't begin to convey my remorse for… everything. I was unbelievably unkind to accuse you as I did, leaping to judgments without giving you a chance to explain."

"No," he soothed, brushing the tears off her cheeks. "You did nothing wrong and were correct to make your assumptions based on how I acted. It isn't easy for me to talk about Jharna. Or at least it wasn't. Now it is different. She is a part of me as Mr. Annesley is you, but they are our past. None of that matters now, Amanda. We can talk it through later. Right now, all I need to hear is that you still love me because I love you and knew it before the ship docked in Dover. Can you put it all aside and tell me from your heart that you still love me?"

But she was already nodding her head emphatically, the smile lighting her face as brilliant as the sun. "I never stopped loving you, George. Never for a moment. Yes I love you! Immensely."

"Ah, music to my ears. I will never tire of hearing you say those three words and hope you do not either." He unraveled her hands from the sides of his *kameez* and enfolded them between his. "Before I kiss you and lose all control of my faculties, I need to know one other thing. Amanda, my beautiful, wonderful love, will you do me the tremendous honor of marrying me?"

"Yes!" She shouted it, George swearing later that the nearby branches swayed under the force of her positive declaration. Nonsensical as that was, his heart definitely skipped several beats before it started racing when she threw her arms about his neck and clamped her lips onto his.

It was hours before they returned to the house. Mrs. Tadworth was growing seriously concerned and about to send Mr. Tadworth out with a search party. Then she saw her sister stroll into view, her small body glued to the side of the towering gentleman who without any doubt was extremely happy with the position. In fact, happy was an inadequate word by a long mile to describe either one of them. Any number of adjectives could be used, especially if taking into consideration the leaves stuck in her sister's hair and the dirt smudges on their rumpled garments!

Mrs. Tadworth smiled. She waited until they mounted the back stairs before greeting them at the door, her only question of relevance being when the wedding would be so she could start planning.

❧

Not quite two months later, George stood before a tall mirror, adjusting the *sherwani*'s jeweled and richly embroidered collar. It didn't really need adjusting, but the activity occupied his hands. Unfortunately, the mirror also provided a clear reflection of the clock that he swore was ticking slower than normal.

"Nervous? It isn't too late to change your mind, you know. William and I will explain to the guests while you escape out the back and dash screaming for the forests of Pemberley."

George lowered his hands and turned from the mirror with a chuckle. "No chance, Richard. If you think you waited for your wedding day for a long time, imagine how I feel. I have faced copious challenges and terrifying situations in my life. Trust me, this does not enter even the bottom of the list. Now, how do I look? It isn't too much, is it?"

"Would Amanda want otherwise?" Darcy answered. "If you walked out there in an English suit or a plain Indian outfit, she wouldn't recognize you. She might pivot and head to a different church thinking she was in the wrong place."

"You have a point." George nodded seriously, turning back to the mirror.

He ran his palms down the gold and crimson designs spanning three-inches of the *sherwani*'s buttoned front, the intricate *zari* thread work extending from the ban collar, over George's broad shoulders, and down the entire length of the below-the-knee coat, and then around the bottom edge. The brilliant colors were a sharp, exquisite contrast to the shimmering ivory fabric of the thick coat lined in crimson satin. Underneath, George wore a *shalwar kameez* in the same ivory, the fabric lighter weight but as finely woven as the *sherwani*. The *mojari* covering his feet were beaded and embroidered to perfectly match the coat's design. Taken as a whole, George presented an elegant, exotic picture that would dazzle everyone in the room, especially his bride.

"This was my ensemble at Nimesh and Sasi's wedding. You should have seen what they wore. I paled in comparison. Alas, I did not have time to obtain a proper groom's suit, and God knows I wasn't about to wait any longer. These two months have been torture!"

Darcy shared a glance with Richard, both men grinning.

George's initial desire to dash up to Pemberley with Amanda on the back of his horse and be married before the week ended didn't pan out. Of course, while Amanda would probably have agreed to that if he pushed, George respected that a properly planned wedding was best. Plus, even though he had fun grousing about all the falderal, it was his first and only marriage ceremony, and he did want it to be special.

George wanted to be married in the Pemberley Chapel where generations of Darcys had stood and declared their commitment before God. To his delight, Amanda loved the idea, so it was decided to wait until after their long-planned trip to Rosings Park in Kent. George balked a bit, but the delay made sense not only to avoid irritating Lady Catherine by postponing a visit—not that George did not relish irritating Lady Catherine—but also, mainly, because he wanted to personally share his news and joy with Raul Penaflor.

Through all the traveling and changing decisions, Amanda was with him. George and Amanda were not blatant about their relationship, she with her bedchamber and he with his, but few were ignorant of the fact that they spent every night together and were blissfully happy as a result. Reserve was not a trait George Darcy possessed in vast quantities, so he made little effort to restrain his feelings for the woman who was, in just a few minutes, going to be his wife. Amanda was gradually becoming accustom to the tender touches and bold kisses from her lover that randomly occurred throughout the day no matter where they were or who was around. Marriage to a man of George Darcy's effervescence, eccentricity, spontaneity, and disregard for propriety promised to be a challenge at times, but then these were the exact qualities that she had fallen in love with from afar.

So naturally, she was fully expecting him to be wearing a flashy garment for their wedding and was actually rather surprised it wasn't a vivid green or purple! In any color or style, to her eyes, he was the handsomest man on the planet. This she had told him on numerous occasions, risking his arrogance swelling out of control, as she teased. George always thanked her for the compliment, following with the assurance that his arrogant pride had attained its maximum level the second she agreed to be his partner for life. As she glided down the aisle of the quaint church, George knew it was the truth. She wore blue, to his delight, her gown a mixture of pale shades and darker hues, layers of fine muslin and silk accented with ribbons and lace to fashion a stunning dress. Seeing it on her lush body, and imagining peeling it off later, nearly made him collapse. As soon as she reached him, he clasped her hands, bending to kiss her lightly on the lips and whisper, "You are sublime and I love you forever."

"Well now, if it isn't a bother, may I conduct the ceremony first, Dr. Darcy?"

George winked at the aged rector. "Carry on, Reverend Bertram. You have the floor!"

The Greatest Adventure of All

JANUARY 2, 1821

G EORGE CLOSED THE DOOR behind him and spared a precious minute to lean into the jamb. He was exhausted but knew that his smile was wider than it had ever been in his life. Seven months ago, he had not thought it possible to be any happier. How wrong he was! The grin grew even wider and suddenly the weariness fled from his body. With an exuberant launch from the door and jaunty gait, he hastened down the hallway to the parlor where his friends and family were waiting in anticipation.

Rounding the corner, he halted three feet inside the door.

Darcy launched up from his chair and strode toward him, eyes worried and expectant. Elizabeth's expression was much the same, although she did not rise from her seat due to the newborn infant nestled at her breast and the thirteen-month-old asleep on her lap. Searc McIntyre did not rise either but did scoot to the edge of his chair, Raul Penaflor doing the same and clutching tightly to the hand of his wife, Anne. Malcolm and Madeline, the Vernors, Richard and Simone Fitzwilliam, Mr. and Mrs. Bennet, Charles and Jane Bingley, Anoop and his wife Hortense, and several others who had traveled to Pemberley for Christmas and then decided to tarry specifically for the news he was about to impart. Before he could, his gaze settled on the man standing across the room by the window. His son, Alexis the Duke of Larent, was staring as expectantly as the others, although as a supposed "new friend of the family," he kept his excitement leashed.

Only ten seconds had passed but apparently that was an eternity to a child.

"Uncle Goj, is Auntie Manda a mama now?"

George threw his head back and laughed. Whooped, actually. Then he bent down and snatched Alexander off the floor, blocks tumbling, and tossed him in the air. "Yes, Alexander, your Auntie Manda is a mama!" He hugged the boy close and addressed the grinning and clapping audience. "And I am a papa! Can you believe that? All went well and my wife performed brilliantly. As did her delivering physician, I must add. I had to wait until I was sure everything and everyone was fine. Amanda is resting now."

He stopped talking and administered a series of tickles to Alexander, the boy shrieking in delight, until Elizabeth interrupted.

"And?"

George lifted his brow. "And what?"

"The baby! Tell us about the baby before I lay my daughter down and come over there and punch you!"

"I can tend to the task sooner, lassie," McIntyre grumbled. "Several of us can if ye don tell us, Darcy."

"Oh, the baby. Yes, well, that might be more difficult than you all think."

"George, I am warning you."

"All right, Elizabeth. No need to get testy. William, your wife does have a temper, doesn't she?"

"You have no idea," Darcy muttered, flashing a grin toward his wife, who tossed her head and kept her glare on George.

"I thought it best to save the introductions for a bit later, all things considered, but I am pleased to announce the newest additions to our family. My son James Ullas Darcy and daughter Emily Priyala Darcy."

"Twins?!" The shouted question came from several quarters, George's booming laugh ringing and rising to the ceiling.

"Did you suspect?"

"Of course! I am an excellent diagnostician, after all."

Darcy whistled. "Well done, Uncle. So much for your quiet days as a country physician."

George clapped Darcy on the shoulder, joy alighting his face and bestowing a youthful glow to the man who, at days away from fifty-four barely looked a year older than his nephew. "Bother that! Quiet days are not my style. Give me new adventures anytime."

"This might well be your greatest adventure yet."

"I certainly hope so, William. And I am more than ready for it. This adventure I have prepared for all of my life."

THE END

Historical Notes and Acknowledgments

THE HISTORY OF INDIA is vast, ancient, and complex. As a Westerner, I soon realized there was no way I could completely grasp all of it, or even part of it, with complete understanding. I purchased many resource books and have literally over two hundred web pages bookmarked (and many more I read but did not save) in order to present the world, culture, and medicine of India from 1789 to 1818 as comprehensively and accurately as possible. I had some help along the way and want to extend my thanks to three people who helped me immeasurably. Dr. Krishna Rajani, Associate Professor at UCSF Fresno and Director of Newborn Programs at Community Regional Medical Center in Fresno: Dr. Rajani has been a friend and colleague for years, his gracious offer to answer questions and direct me to the proper Indian resources proving invaluable. Dr. Girish Patel, pediatrician and practitioner of Ayurvedic medicine: Dr. Patel has been pediatrician to my children for over twenty years and also a colleague at the local hospital NICU where I worked for eight years. His personal knowledge of Ayurvedic practice and loaned texts of the history were studied until dog-eared! Gita Patel, wife to Dr. Patel: Gita is in every way amazing! Her knowledge of India's history, Hindi and other dialects, yoga, art, Hinduism, cooking, and just about every other topic Indian breathed life into George's story, but best of all, Gita has enhanced my life by her friendship.

Note on languages: The bulk of Indian languages and dialects are based on ancient Sanskrit, both the Classical and Vedic forms. Standard, or Modern, Hindi has been the recognized official language of India since 1950. Prior to that, there wasn't a "standard" language throughout India, although Hindi was the most common. However, the Hindi spoken two hundred years ago would have varied from the Hindi of today. Additionally, the regions and empires within India spoke their own dialects, heavily influenced by Sanskrit and by extension Hindi, but in some cases completely different. Another point to consider is that Sanskrit was a spoken language for centuries before it became a written language. In 1 BCE, the first Sanskrit inscriptions were in a Brahmi script, and over the centuries, the types of script changed as often as the dialects. In the late nineteenth century, *devanāgari* became the standard writing system for Sanskrit with attempts to transliterate the script phonetically into English based on the Latin alphabet. What this meant for me is that tracking down precise words in particular dialects wasn't easy! Thanks to the assistance of Gita Patel, a friend of hers fluent in Marathi, and several books, I chose words that are as close to correct as possible and which were pleasant to the ear or possible to pronounce. Pronunciation is another huge factor, many of the script alphabets not clearly transliterating into English. "Kshitij" is a prime example: The "ksh" is one letter in Hindi, spoken in a way that sort of sounds like K-S-H blended together but not exactly! Suffice to say, I never could say it as well as Gita, and she had to write it in Hindi script to say it right.

Note on place and people names: Partially because of the language issues mentioned above, but also because of the constant upheavals during the centuries in India, the names of places have radically changed. For the sake of historical accuracy, I chose names proper at the time of my story. Hence it is Bombay and never Mumbai. I have included a map to help, but if you search on a present day map for just about all of the regions or towns Dr. Darcy visited, you will not find them. It was also interesting that many of the names were spelled differently by contemporary mapmakers and writers of the period. For instance, Poona is in some places written as Puna. Tipu Sultan is also noted as Tipoo Sultan. Primarily, these differences in spelling are due to the transliteration issue mentioned above. Tipu when spoken sounds like Tipoo! For my story, I chose the most common spelling I found on various documents and written in historical essays. Once I established a name, I did not change it, even if historically within the twenty-eight years Dr. Darcy was in India it might have changed.

Note on the British East India Company: Founded in 1591, the history of the EIC is so complex that there is no possible way for me to sum up what I learned, and I only learned the essentials for the time period Dr. Darcy was there. One book that was instrumental for me was *Raj: The Making and Unmaking of British India* by Lawrence James. The BBC online also has a fabulous summation: www.bbc.co.uk/history/british/empire_seapower/east_india_01.shtml

There are numerous points I could make, but one that stood out for me in writing the years of Dr. Darcy is that the EIC at this point in history was primarily a trading vehicle, stable transactions for profit the main goal. Internal conflicts threatened that stability, and gradually as the latter half of the 1700s progressed, the EIC became more involved in Indian politics and wars. Sometimes that was because they had no choice, and other times it was due to expansionist tendencies that were never sanctioned by the British monarchy and parliament. Rivalry with the French over trade, and other issues closer to home, added to the increasing conflicts. Nevertheless, the EIC was not largely on a quest for power—yet—and the close supervision by the Crown kept matters from getting too out of hand. Another vital fact of these decades is that Indian ideals, culture, etc., were supported and not seen as needing to be "fixed" or "improved" by firm, benevolent rule. After the turn of the century, a shift in thinking took stronger root, the changes building one upon another until 1858–1947, the era of the "British Raj" that we now tend to immediately think of when hearing about India or the EIC.

Note on medicine: My two favorite books on the history of medicine were *The Greatest Benefit to Mankind: A Medical History of Humanity* by Roy Porter and *Patient's Progress: Doctors and Doctoring in Eighteenth-century England* by Dorothy and Roy Porter. And, of course, the books on Ayurvedic medicine lent to me by Dr. Patel, which included detailed treatments for various diseases. This topic is even more complex than the history of the EIC, so all I will say here is that every reference I made in the course of this novel is factual. The physicians, researchers, and scientists named are real figures prominent in their fields and critical to the advancements we now enjoy in Western medicine. The treatments used by Drs. Darcy and Ullas, among others, are period true. Ayurvedic and *Yūnānī* medicine systems are ancient and in both cases astoundingly advanced. They also still exist to this day. It was a joy to highlight the realities of lost medical art forms and to show that, while seemingly barbaric to our modern minds, practitioners of medicine on down through the ages have performed incredible feats. Their dedication to healing and discovering the answers is to be applauded. Without their failures and successes, we would not know what we now do.

Lastly, a special thanks to Frank E. Smitha, who created the base for the map I altered to show India as relevant to Dr. Darcy's story. He graciously granted permission for me to include this map in the novel, so you, my readers, can better visualize.

Glossary

apothecary: a druggist licensed to prescribe medicine. In Georgian times, apothecaries could be educated or hold degrees, or they could be apprenticed. In the country, an apothecary may be all that is available and, if well trained, could be as skilled as a surgeon or physician.

Avatarana: descent of the Ganges; Hindu celebration to honor the sacred river's descent from heaven to earth; a soak in the Ganges, or any body of water since all spring from the Ganges in Hindu tradition, on this day is said to rid the bather of ten sins or ten lifetimes of sin.

Ayurveda: an intricate system of healing that originated in India around 600 BCE and can be traced to the **Vedas**. Considered a "science of life and longevity" with balance between the physical and spiritual the foundation. The *Suśruta Saṃhitā* and the *Charaka Saṃhitā* are encyclopedias of medicine and the foundation of Ayurveda medicine.

Bombay: the seven original islands under British rule by 1668 were Bombay, Colaba, Mahim, Mazagaon, Parel, Worli, and Little Colaba. Bombay Governor Hornby's venture to combine the seven into one large island named Bombay (present day Mumbai) began in 1782 and was complete by 1838.

Eventually, additional small islands were connected, including the much larger Salcette Island.

chacha: Hindi for uncle; *chacha-jee* used to add a respectful nuance.

choli: a short or below the waist, tight-fitting shirt worn by women under a sari; often sewn of the same fabric as the sari but not always.

churidar pyjama: a garment similar to a **salwar** but tightly fitted so that the contours of the leg are revealed; the fabric is longer than the wearer's legs, worn to fall into gathered folds over the legs.

daaktar: Hindi for doctor; used to address non-Ayurvedic doctors (they are *vaidya*)

deshmukh: title given to a person who was granted a territory of land to rule over in the Maratha Empire. Loosely translated as "patriot" and roughly equivalent to an English duke.

Dhamdhere: a Maratha clan. A high-ranking, powerful military clan in the empire with many serving as peshwas and sardars. Clan capitol is Talegaon.

dhoti: a long, rectangular piece of unstitched cloth wrapped around the waist and legs and knotted at the waist; the methods of wrapping and knotting vary in style; worn by men only; can be long or short.

Hatha yoga: a system of yoga dating to fifteenth-century India, derived from ancient Sanskrit texts, focusing on posture, breathing, and meditation to improve physical health.

haveli: a private mansion, usually with historic or architectural significance; most influenced by Persian and Asian styles with a central courtyard and fountain common.

inoculation: also "variolation"; process of infecting a person with an infectious disease in a controlled manner to minimize disease severity and induce immunity; originated in India as early as 1500 BCE for smallpox; forerunner of vaccination.

jutti: a shoe of leather similar to a **mojari** but typically with a closed back and straight toe.

kameez: a loose tunic, usually with long sleeves and a collar; can be simple in style and fabric or highly decorated; always worn with additional garments; wide variety of styles for men and women.

kurta: also *kurti* if short; a loose shirt falling to the knee and without a collar.

licentiate: a person who has received a formal attestation of professional competence to practice a certain profession or teach a certain skill or subject

lungi: a type of men's loincloth similar to a sarong; a stitched tube tied at the waist; can be short or long; worn by women in some parts of India.

Maharashtra: an Indian state that once covered the bulk of western India; ruled by the Marathas until 1818, when it came under British rule as part of the Bombay Confederacy.

Maratha Empire: an Indian superpower that existed from 1674 to 1818; founded by Maharaja Shivaji Bhosle, it took twenty-seven years of war against the Mughals before firmly in control; the Maratha Empire once covered much of South Asia and established Hindu rule in India; called the Maratha Confederacy from 1761 to 1818; governed by a Peshwa after 1749, during which time the empire reached its zenith in power.

Marathi: the name of the people of Maratha; also the language spoken by the people, a dialect of Hindi.

mata: Hindi for mother; intimate, personal term; *mata-jee* to add a respectful nuance.

memsahib: feminine form of **sahib** used to address women.

mojari: a leather shoe with a closed, curled toe and open back; created by artisans and highly embellished.

musnud: a throne of cushions used by Indian princes.

namaste: most popular form of greeting and bidding farewell; both palms are placed together and raised to just below the face as the person bows; universal to all Indians.

paduka: oldest Indian footwear; essentially a sandal comprised only of a sole and a knob fitting between the big and second toe; multitudes of varieties and forms using every type of material; can be plain or elaborate.

paijama: also *pyjama*; loose, lightweight trousers fitted with drawstring waistbands; worn by both sexes.

peshwa: "Prime Minister" of the Maratha Empire and head of the army; supervised and governed under the king's orders and in his absence; de facto rulers after the death of Emperor Shahuji in 1749. Capitol: Poona.

physician: a person who is legally qualified to practice medicine; doctor of medicine with a degree from a university; a person engaged in general medical practice, as distinguished from one specializing in surgery; a person who is skilled in the art of healing. In Georgian times, a physician was an educated gentleman who rarely touched a patient, obtaining information via observation and verbal report to diagnose and treat.

pita: Hindi for father; intimate, personal term; *pita-jee* to add a respectful nuance.

sahib: meaning varies throughout Indian cultures and history; literal translation is "owner" or "proprietor" with the essence of "friend, associate, and companion" present; traditionally an Indian term for princely rulers and other leaders, usually in conjunction with another term (i.e., *Maharaja Sahib*); later became common as a courtesy title for any Indian or non-Indian person in authority, similar to "Mister."

sadhu: a Hindu holy man similar to a monk.

sagarmatha: Nepali name for Mount Everest in the Himalayas; Qomolangma in Tibetan; "Peak XV" to British until mapped in 1856 and named after Colonel Sir George Everest, Surveyor General of India, who opposed the name.

sari: also *saree*; an unstitched length of cloth up to nine yards worn draped around a woman's body; can be plain or highly decorated; hundreds of ways to drape; often worn over a **choli** and petticoat but not always, especially in the past.

sati: religious practice of a widow voluntarily burning alive on her husband's funeral pyre; steeped in ancient history and tradition, the practice was never widely popular, and numerous attempts have been made to ban it entirely, although it does still occur.

shalwar: loose, pajama-like trousers cut wide at the top and narrow at the ankle; can be baggy or form-fitting; worn with a **kameez**; traditionally, a man's garment but today can be worn by women.

sherwani: a long coat-like garment worn over a **shalwar kameez**; very formal; originally worn only by court nobles of India and Pakistan.

stillroom: a working room where medicines, cosmetics, perfumes, and household cleaners are prepared, alcoholic beverages are distilled, and herbs are dried; maintained by a female kitchen staff member called the "stillroom maid" or simply "stillmaid."

surgeon: a medical practitioner who specializes in surgery; sawbones. In Georgian times, a surgeon may be educated and licensed, but it was not required. Not considered a "gentleman" because they touched the patient and performed "work."

vaidya: a doctor of Ayurveda medicine.

Vedas: translates as "wisdom" or "knowledge"; precise dating of origins is unknown, but appeared over five thousand years ago, making the Vedas the oldest known Indian literature and Hindu scriptures. They are considered divinely inspired.

Yūnānī medicine: translates as "Greek Medicine"; a system of healing influenced by Greek, Islamic, and Indian medicine developed by Avicenna in 1025, documented in his *The Canon of Medicine*; flourished under Mughal rule.

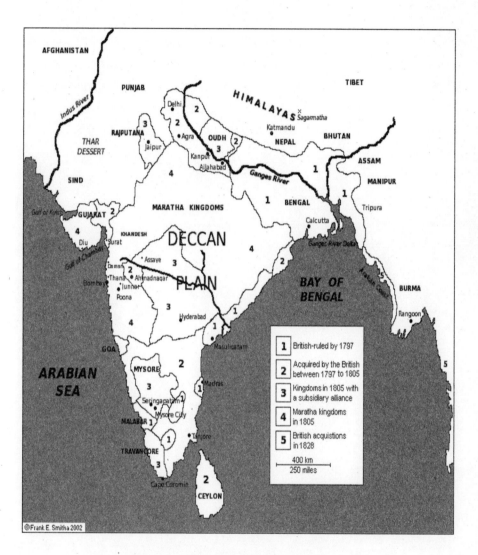

MAP OF INDIA AS TRAVELED BY
DR. GEORGE DARCY FROM 1789 TO 1817

About the Author

Sharon Lathan is the bestselling author of the Darcy Saga sequel series to Jane Austen's *Pride & Prejudice*. Her previously published novels are: *Mr. and Mrs. Fitzwilliam Darcy: Two Shall Become One*, *Loving Mr. Darcy*, *My Dearest Mr. Darcy*, *In the Arms of Mr. Darcy*, *A Darcy Christmas*, *The Trouble With Mr. Darcy*, and *Miss Darcy Falls in Love*. Sharon is a native Californian currently residing amid the orchards, corn, cotton, and cows in the sunny San Joaquin Valley with her husband of twenty-seven years. When not hard at work on her faithful MacBookPro laptop or iMac desktop, Sharon is at the hospital where she works as a registered nurse in a neonatal ICU. For more information about Sharon, the Regency Era, and her novels, visit her website/blog at: www. sharonlathan.net or search for her on Facebook and Twitter. She also invites everyone to join her and other Austen literary fiction writers on her group blog at www.austenauthors.com.

Mr. and Mrs. Fitzwilliam Darcy: Two Shall Become One

by Sharon Lathan

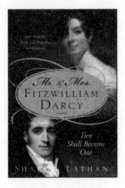

A fascinating portrait of a timeless, consuming love

It's Darcy and Elizabeth's wedding day, and the journey is just beginning as Jane Austen's beloved *Pride and Prejudice* characters embark on the greatest adventure of all: marriage and a life together filled with surprising passion, tender self-discovery, and the simple joys of every day.

As their love story unfolds in this most romantic of Jane Austen sequels, Darcy and Elizabeth each reveal to the other how their relationship blossomed from misunderstanding to perfect understanding and harmony, and a marriage filled with romance, sensuality, and the beauty of a deep, abiding love.

"Highly entertaining... I felt fully immersed in the time period. Well done!"—*Romance Reader at Heart*

For more Sharon Lathan, visit:

www.sourcebooks.com

For a celebration of all things Jane Austen, visit:

www.austenfans.com

Loving Mr. Darcy:
Journeys Beyond Pemberley

by Sharon Lathan

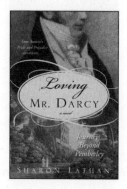

Darcy and Elizabeth embark on the journey of a lifetime

Six months into his marriage to Elizabeth Bennet, Darcy is still head over heels in love, and each day offers more opportunities to surprise and delight his beloved bride. Elizabeth has adapted to being the Mistress of Pemberley, charming everyone she meets and handling her duties with grace and poise. Just when it seems life can't get any better, Elizabeth gets the most wonderful news. The lovers leave the serenity of Pemberley, traveling through the sumptuous landscape of Regency England, experiencing the lavish sights, sounds, and tastes around them. With each day come new discoveries as they become further entwined, body and soul.

"A romance that transcends time."—*The Romance Studio*

For more Sharon Lathan, visit:

www.sourcebooks.com

For a celebration of all things Jane Austen, visit:

www.austenfans.com

My Dearest Mr. Darcy

by Sharon Lathan

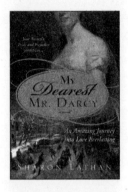

Darcy is more deeply in love with his wife than ever

As the golden summer draws to a close and the Darcys look ahead to the end of their first year of marriage, Mr. Darcy could never have imagined his love could grow even deeper with the passage of time. Elizabeth is unpredictable and lively, pulling Darcy out of his stern and serious demeanor with her teasing and temptation.

But surprising events force the Darcys to weather absence and illness, and to discover whether they can find a way to build a bond of everlasting love and desire…

"An intimately romantic sequel to Jane Austen's *Pride and Prejudice*… wonderfully colorful and fun."—*Wendy's Book Corner*

"If you want to fall in love with Mr. Darcy all over again…order yourself a copy."—*Royal Reviews*

For more Sharon Lathan, visit:

www.sourcebooks.com

For a celebration of all things Jane Austen, visit:

www.austenfans.com

In the Arms of Mr. Darcy

by Sharon Lathan

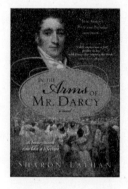

If only everyone could be as happy as they are…

Darcy and Elizabeth are as much in love as ever—even more so as their relationship matures. Their passion inspires everyone around them, and as winter turns to spring, romance blossoms around them.

Confirmed bachelor Richard Fitzwilliam sets his sights on a seemingly unattainable, beautiful widow; Georgiana Darcy learns to flirt outrageously; the very flighty Kitty Bennet develops her first crush; and Caroline Bingley meets her match.

But the path of true love never does run smooth, and Elizabeth and Darcy are kept busy navigating their friends and loved ones through the inevitable separations, misunderstandings, misgivings, and lovers' quarrels to reach their own happily ever afters…

"If you love *Pride and Prejudice* sequels then this series
should be on the top of your list!"—*Royal Reviews*

For more Sharon Lathan, visit:

www.sourcebooks.com

For a celebration of all things Jane Austen, visit:

www.austenfans.com

MISS DARCY FALLS IN LOVE

by Sharon Lathan

The choice of a lifetime...

One young lady following her passion for music.

Two strong men locked in a bitter rivalry for her heart.

A journey of self-discovery, and a trap of her own making.

Georgiana Darcy is going to have to carve out her own destiny, however ill-equipped she may feel...

"The love, passion, and excellence of style, as well as the writer's superior talent with words is sure to win her new fans or satisfy old fans with this one."—*Long and Short Reviews*

"Lathan proves she is indeed a master at writing both Regency romance and Austen continuations. *Miss Darcy Falls in Love* positively oozes with yearning and sweet romance."—*Read All Over Reviews*

For more Sharon Lathan, visit:

www.sourcebooks.com

For a celebration of all things Jane Austen, visit:

www.austenfans.com

MR. DARCY'S UNDOING

by Abigail Reynolds

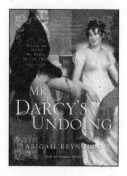

What could possibly make a proper gentleman come completely undone?

What if Elizabeth Bennet accepted the proposal of another before she met Mr. Darcy again? In Abigail Reynolds's bold and playful retelling of the Austen classic, a devastated Mr. Darcy must decide how far he is willing to go to win the woman he loves. Consumed by jealousy, he knows that winning her will throw them both into scandal and disgrace, but losing her is unbearable. Mr. Darcy is going to have to fight for his love, and his life…

"Abigail Reynolds offers a fanciful story, replete with
anguish and raw emotion, exploring another possible road
not taken by Jane Austen herself… an inventive,
fiery, Regency romance."—*Austen Prose*

"Abigail Reynolds, one of my favorite Austenesque authors,
is a skilled storyteller, an ardent admirer of Jane Austen,
and quite proficient at infusing a lot of emotion, tension,
and passion into her stories!"—*Austenesque Reviews*

For more Abigail Reynolds, visit:

www.sourcebooks.com

For a celebration of all things Jane Austen, visit:

www.austenfans.com

WICKHAM'S DIARY

by Amanda Grange

Enter the clandestine world of the cold-hearted Wickham...

...in the pages of his private diary. Always aware of the inferiority of his social status compared to his friend Fitzwilliam Darcy, Wickham chases wealth and women in an attempt to attain the power he lusts for. But as Wickham gambles and cavorts his way through his funds, Darcy still comes out on top.

But now Wickham has found his chance to seduce the young Georgiana Darcy, which will finally secure the fortune—and the revenge—he's always dreamed of...

"Grange, an obvious Jane Austen fan, has given an amusing and totally believable account of a wastrel's life. *Wickham's Diary* takes its place among her previous diaries of Jane Austen heroes."—*Historical Novels Review*

"A short, fast read that is just plain enjoyable, double if you are an Austen fan to begin with!"—*Fresh Fiction*

For more Amanda Grange, visit:

www.sourcebooks.com

For a celebration of all things Jane Austen, visit:

www.austenfans.com